WHEN
THE
NIGHTINGALE
SINGS

BOOKS BY SUZANNE KELMAN

A View Across the Rooftops
When We Were Brave
Under a Sky on Fire

SUZANNE KELMAN

WHEN
THE
NIGHTINGALE
SINGS

Bookouture

Published by Bookouture in 2021

An imprint of Storyfire Ltd.
Carmelite House
50 Victoria Embankment
London EC4Y 0DZ

www.bookouture.com

ISBN: 978-1-83888-794-0
eBook ISBN: 978-1-83888-793-3

This book is a work of fiction. Whilst some characters and
circumstances portrayed by the author are based on real people
and historical fact, references to real people, events, establishments,
organizations or locales are intended only to provide a sense of
authenticity and are used fictitiously. All other characters and all
incidents and dialogue are drawn from the author's imagination
and are not to be construed as real.

Dedicated to the remarkable Hedy Lamarr. Also, to Joan Curran, whose life inspired the character of Judy Jenkins. And to every invisible woman of the past who contributed, strived and endeavored to make a difference, but were never recognized during their lifetime.

May the silence of their collective voices not be forgotten and their daughters be heard.

Faith is the nightingale that sings in the darkest hour.
Theodore L. Cuyler

Prologue

If she'd learned anything in her eighty-five years, it was that friendships forged in the fire were the hardest to extinguish. They were the ones seared into your being, melded to your heart, a forever charred part of your soul. And Judy had experienced that during the Second World War, the most significant furnace of her life. She wished it was something she could have taught her students, as easily as she had taught them the physics of gravity: the richness of that kind of friendship.

But at her age she now understood, the only way to truly know it was to experience it with another human being, to walk the narrow path through the flames together. Hold their hand to stop them from being consumed, as they did the same for you. It was for that very reason she had never given up hope through all these years, because her once-dearest friend was a part of her very being, and she knew even in the many years of silence between them that she, was part of Hedy's too.

Drawn abruptly back from her reverie by a scattering of raindrops that splattered across the glass, Judy stared at the steady stream of rain distorting the view of a sycamore tree. The mild snap of weather that had encouraged the first spring flowers from the ground had been replaced this morning by ominous, gray, rumbling clouds and a vicious east wind that tossed the tree's branches around as if it was juggling the leaves. Its violent blasts rattled the sycamore, wrenching tender new growth from its limbs, turning them into dancing spirals that cavorted across the campus in wind-whipped cartwheels. Accompanying the dramatic tumble of leaves, tremendous gusts whistled through cracks in the sealed university windows, high-pitched and urgent, finding their way to Judy and chilling the back of her neck.

Rubbing gnarled, arthritic fingers across her sagging skin and attempting to draw in the collar of her blouse, Judy wished she could be back in her room in front of her little electric fire in her comfortable beige cardigan. Above her she could hear the excited jostle of an audience filling the room, everybody here to see her. Somehow it seemed so ridiculous. She closed her eyes, reminding herself who she was doing this for. There had been so much excitement at the announcement in the home and on the part of her caregiver, Karen, as if it were a perfect bow to decorate the winter of her life. She hadn't the heart to tell them all the awards and accolades meant little to the dying.

The dying.

She let the words wash over her again. She was dying. That reality was biting. It still felt raw and unreal to her, even three months after the diagnosis. Being terminally ill was so final; she'd hoped to just die quietly in her sleep but now there would be doctors and hospitals and pain. At least it brought her some clarity. Measuring her life in days and weeks, maybe months if she was lucky, was an interesting experience. With that kind of finality, everything became crystal clear, no more so than when she'd thrown out her most important exam results while doing her death cleaning the week before. Things that seemed so vital in her earlier years were of no consequence now. All that remained were memories of love. The love she had shared throughout her life with Tom. The love she felt for her best friend, Hedy, too. Even after all this time.

A bedraggled sparrow landed in the branches of the tree in front of her and stared at Judy in desperation, its brown mottled feathers splayed like a fan, buffeted by the wind and rain.

As she watched it tuck itself under its wing for shelter, the rhythm of the rain lulled her, and Judy's eyes became heavy. This new medication seemed to make her drowsy all the time. She would rest them just for a few seconds.

All at once the presence of the sparrow brought something back to her and her eyes blinked open with the reminiscence. The nightingale. The sound of a nightingale had woken her in the middle of the night, from a dream about the war. She closed her eyes again, scavenging through the corners of her hazy memory to retrieve the scraps of recollection. She had been dreaming about the first time they had met. No, that wasn't the first time they'd met, Judy reminded herself, but that second meeting had stood out. Because it had been the first time she'd met a real Hollywood movie star.

She swallowed down the sadness that recollection brought with it.

Waking from the dream the night before, she'd lain in her bed listening to the nightingale, its sound a comforting presence as she'd attempted to drag herself back from the 1940s. Hedy was like a nightingale, she had told Judy once in jest. Because they sing at night.

Had the nightingale been a sign? Wanting to hear it more clearly, Judy had fumbled with her side lamp, then, stumbling out of bed, had shuffled across to the window, her creaking bones slowly straightening her body into an upright position. At her sill, she'd lifted the window to listen. Taking in a deep breath of the cool spring air with just the edge of the rain to come, Judy had allowed it to blow through her white candyfloss of hair. She hoped it was a sign. She had wanted more than anything to put their friendship right, and now that she was coming to the end of her life, she just wanted to see her friend one more time.

Sitting at her dressing table beneath the window to listen, she opened the side drawer and, running her fingers across the crystal turtledoves inside, she took out the letter beneath them that had been in that spot for years, wondering how a friendship that had been the most important part of her life was no longer part of it any more. She wasn't sure why, but something had stopped her from throwing it out with all her other papers. Holding the letter carefully in her hand, Judy rubbed two fingers reverently across the flap. It was as thin as crepe paper with age, yellowing and worn with the re-reading. The very last letter she'd received. She imagined Hedy putting this in the post. What had been her thoughts when she'd done that? Had she known they would never see each other again? At least not for all these years? She opened the letter one more time, noting the date at the top, January 1942, and then re-read the words she knew by heart. Finishing it, she'd folded it and placed it in her handbag on her bedside table. If Hedy couldn't be with her in person tomorrow, at least a little piece of her would be.

All at once, the rattle of a doorknob wrenched her back to the present. Her caregiver stood there in the frame. "Just a few more minutes now, Mrs. Jenkins. Are you ready?"

Judy took a moment to remind herself where she was. She was in the basement of a university campus building, waiting to go upstairs and get her honorary degree. The degree they should have given her many years before, back when she had earned it. She forced a smile onto her face.

"Yes. Yes, I'm ready."

"Do you need anything? Have you got your speech?" Karen enquired, coming over and straightening Judy's clothes.

"Yes, I have my speech."

This was an odd phenomenon, Judy thought. One she'd had to become accustomed to. It felt like yesterday, the hair she'd smoothed down and the clothes she'd buttoned. Now, in front of her, a woman not much older than the refugees she'd taken care of was doing the same for her.

As she reached the door, she called out after Karen. "Is everybody we invited here? Are there any guests out there for me who aren't from the home? Maybe a friend I invited?"

Karen looked perplexed. "A friend? I didn't see any friends to invite on your guest list. Apart from us, of course," she said quickly, apparently not wanting to draw attention to the sadness of her statement. Karen looked panic-stricken. "I would have contacted any friends if I'd known you had any. I'm so sorry, Mrs. Jenkins. Was it someone special?"

Judy shook her head. "I wrote to her myself. But I guess not," she whispered.

Karen nodded and exited the room to check if they were ready for Judy.

Judy sighed. Sitting down at the table, she pulled out a handbag and took out a compact mirror to check her hair. There were her green eyes, now misted with age. The crinkles in the corners were becoming crepe-like. Her face had a waxy hue to it, and there were red spots on her cheeks and age spots on her forehead. She'd never thought about wearing makeup when she was younger. Now she wished she'd learned how to do that.

She closed the compact and put it back into her bag, and there again was the letter, the letter Hedy had sent her after the bombing raid on Oahu.

"This honor is for you as well, Hedy," she whispered. "I'm sorry you came to hate me. I'm sorry about everything. You should have received recognition for what you did too."

Judy swallowed down a tear and rolled back her shoulders. She would not wallow in all the unfairness of the past. She was only going to think good thoughts. Judy drew in a deep breath.

"It's time," Karen announced as she walked back through the door, wringing her hands. "Are you sure you're going to be okay?"

Judy nodded. "I'll be fine. Just show me the way."

Taking the time to straighten up her body, Judy ambled toward the door out into the hall then climbed haltingly up the stairs to the side of the stage, balanced by her stick. In the auditorium, she could feel the energy, hear the excitement—lots of people she didn't know commemorating her for a degree that was of no consequence any more. But she could bring a bit of joy to the home, make Karen feel like her job was validated, so it was worth it. She wished Tom was here. He would have loved this. He would have got a real kick out of it. Patting her on the arm, Karen made her way out to sit in the audience.

And as Judy waited, someone she didn't know or had never met introduced her. He spoke enthusiastically about her work on the proximity fuse, the invention of chaff, and then lastly the... she couldn't even think about that last awful project right now. She felt the usual stinging guilt for what she had done, even after all these years.

All at once, she heard clapping again and realized that she had not heard his last words. But she must have been introduced. Slowly she made her way out onto the stage. The room was bright and filled with light. Students young and old were on their feet, applauding her, and she nodded and waved graciously. If only they knew what she was really thinking. She would give up all of this for one more day with her beloved Tom or to see her dear friend Hedy again. But it was kind of them to recognize her work.

The man dressed in university finery walked over to her and handed her the honorary degree. She looked down at it. Her father would have loved to have held this in his hands. Sixty years ago, it would have meant something. Now, it was a piece of paper. She graciously thanked him and then went to the microphone. Carefully scanning the crowd as the entire room enthusiastically clapped their encouragement, Judy didn't see the striking features she was looking for and swallowed down her disappointment. Pulling her speech out of her handbag, her fingers grazed the frayed envelope as the audience calmed to a murmur.

Even after all these years, she still felt shy about public speaking and was aware that her voice was tight and elderly, her body swaying slightly with the imbalance, a light sweat prickling across her forehead from the medication.

She cleared her throat.

"Back in 1937 I started a job right here in Cambridge as one of only four women scientists in the whole of the Cavendish Laboratories organization. It was a very different time, when women were heralded more for cooking in their kitchens and staying home to raise their children than for inventing strips of aluminum foil to confuse our enemy, but nevertheless, that was my passion. More than anything I wanted to change the world using my scientific skills and soon after I joined the lab, doing my utmost to halt an encroaching enemy that was already marching across Europe…"

All at once a noise at the back of the auditorium distracted her from her notes. Someone had opened the large wooden doors into the building and they creaked their displeasure. Bright white sunlight streamed into the room accompanied by a light breeze and the faintest smell of warm, wet pavements after the rain. Judy squinted her eyes and caught her breath with tentative hope, because framed in the doorway was the silhouette of a woman.

Chapter One

Schwarzenau, Austria, summer 1937

Hedwig knew she only had about a thirty-minute window to escape her husband. She hurried down the back stairs of Schloss Schwarzenau, clinging on to the highly polished mahogany banister with one hand, and yanking up her heavy, midnight-blue, jeweled dress with the other as she attempted a fast tiptoe down the creaking stairs, though it was hard to be quiet in her high-heeled shoes. Finally reaching the bottom step, she sped across the service hallway, moving swiftly to a second staircase that would take her up to the servants' bedrooms. She held her breath past the kitchen, where inside she could hear echoing voices mingled with the clatter of dishes and the scrubbing of the vast pine table. Climbing the steps, she cursed them as they creaked as well. On the gloomy landing, she rushed along the dimly lit corridor, and on reaching a scuffed brown door, knocked the code that she and Anna had decided on. Before she had even finished the rhythm, the door was yanked open and the ashen face of her maid greeted her. Hedwig rushed inside and closed the door behind her, panting.

Turning her back toward Anna, she felt her maid hastily start to unhook her dress.

"I thought something had gone wrong," hissed Anna as her trembling fingers made their way with speed down the back of the gown. "How long have they been in the smoking room?"

"About ten minutes," Hedwig managed to get out as she attempted to recover her breath. "I kept hoping that General

Müller, the one Fritz complained about the last time he was here, would tell one of his long-winded stories about the Great War. Sometimes it can work in my favor that my husband is so friendly with the Third Reich. I would have escaped sooner if it hadn't been for Major Fischer. He just wouldn't leave me alone, kept pawing at me, breathing his whiskey breath all over me. He is disgusting."

Anna released the final hook and the gown slid to the floor. Wearing just a silk slip, Hedwig tugged off the diamond necklace and stuffed it into the pocket of her folded coat on the bed next to her open overnight bag.

She turned to face Anna. "Did everything else go well?"

The maid handed her a tissue as Hedwig hastened to the mirror and, staring in its mottled reflection, attempted to rub off as much makeup as she could.

"Yes, Fräulein Sylvie is sleeping soundly with whatever you gave her."

Hedwig's lip curled in amusement as she wiped off her eye shadow. She had crushed up some of Fritz's sleeping tablets into the other maid's cocoa powder that she knew she drank every night, because Sylvie was always prowling around, and if she'd caught wind of her planned escape she would have gone straight to Fritz. Besides, the only way safely out of the castle was for Hedy to be mistaken for Sylvie herself.

"Also," Anna continued, "your trunk went out this morning, and it will arrive in London at your friend's in the next few days. I paid the driver extra to make sure that he took good care of it, as you told me to."

Taking Sylvie's maid's uniform down from a hanger, Anna pulled the dress over Hedwig's head and started to do up the buttons. It fitted her perfectly. Even in the dark, plain outfit, Hedwig's trim figure looked stunning. Hedwig had hired Sylvie just the month before, after making her decision to leave her husband, making sure she was the same coloring and build as her mistress.

Anna placed the starched white apron over her head. Sitting down on the bed, Hedwig hastily pulled on the thick black stockings and slipped on unflattering work shoes as Anna affixed a lace cap in her hair.

"As long as you keep your head down, I think you could easily be mistaken for Sylvie."

Hedwig nodded as Anna continued.

"I will take your bag to the edge of the walled garden. No one will pay attention to me carrying something out through the servants' exit. I will disguise it as something to be thrown out. That way, it won't look like you're leaving with the silver."

Both drawing in breath, they dashed out into the corridor and back down the servants' stairs, Anna heading toward the garden and Hedwig to the rear stairs in the main house. It was her best hope of not being seen by the other servants, who would be sure to tell Fritz. She turned in the service hallway to wave, and Anna looked panicked and called out to her in a desperate, high-pitched whisper, "Your earrings!"

Hedwig put her hands to her ears. The diamonds that her husband had given her for their first anniversary were nestled there. Tugging them from her lobes hurriedly, she ran back toward Anna and placed them in her maid's hands.

"For you, Anna, for all your trouble."

"Madam, I couldn't possibly…" she started to say.

Hedwig stopped her with a raised hand. "I don't know what's going to happen after this. Once I'm gone, you may lose your position. If any of this comes back on you, I want to know that you've been taken care of."

Anna thanked her, tears in her eyes, and they parted again.

Hedwig rushed back up the staircase, moving swiftly toward the front door. She knew it was risky leaving through the main entrance but the only other way out that was not overrun with the staff cleaning up after the party was the servants' exit and from there she could be seen clearly from the room her husband was in. As she crept along, she could hear muffled laughter coming from the smoking room, and from the dining room the sound of the butler and some of the castle footmen clearing the last of the dishes. She had to be careful. Anna was the only one she could really count on. Many of her husband's staff were on his side, and she knew they even listened in to her telephone calls. Hedwig's heart began to thud in her chest as she strode toward the main door. She couldn't believe she had finally found a way to escape. She'd been planning it for so long. Now, tonight, finally the opportunity she'd been waiting for.

When Fritz had told her they were to have this large gathering of his clients, she'd alerted Anna to the fact that tonight she was going to leave, and they had quickly put into action the plan she'd had in place for over a month. All of her most expensive gowns and some of her treasures, photographs, and childhood mementos had already been placed in a chest to go ahead to family friends in London. And at his dinner party, she had been the perfect hostess, making sure that her husband had plenty to drink, keeping him merry but also keeping him from sensing any tension in his wife.

Their beautiful dining room with the view of the lake had been laid with all the best china and crystal, decorated to perfection with long cream candles and a profusion of pink roses from the garden. It'd all gone so perfectly. In a way, she would miss this beautiful life, though she would not miss the prison it had become to her in this loveless marriage. She wouldn't miss some of the guests, either, particularly the members of the Third Reich, whom she found arrogant. And the Italian leader, Mussolini, hadn't been able to keep his hands off her when her husband wasn't looking.

She tiptoed past the smoking room, hoping not to draw attention. The main front door was just in front of her. Any minute now, and she would be free.

All at once, somebody strode out from the dining room. It was one of the footmen. Holding her breath, Hedwig put her head down and tried not to catch his eye as she pretended to be fussing with a plant in the hallway. He was juggling a rather large platter that took up all his concentration, and, distracted, he just nodded in her direction as she responded the same. Waiting for him to pass, she opened the front door, and, closing it silently behind her, Hedwig walked out into the fresh night air.

Once outside, she raced to the walled garden to meet Anna.

Her maid quickly handed the bicycle to her with her bag placed in the basket.

Hedwig climbed onto it and took in a deep breath. "Thank you, Anna, for everything."

"Please take care of yourself," said Anna. And forgetting her place for a moment, she threw her arms around her mistress and hugged her.

Hedwig tried not to cry. It was not going to be easy leaving her life when she wasn't sure of what was waiting for her. But she knew she couldn't stay in Austria, not with the way the Reich was influencing it, especially because she was Jewish, and Hitler openly abhorred her race.

She cycled down the driveway, passing the beautiful flower garden she had only just planted. She would never see the tulips come up next year, and that saddened her a little. Somebody else would get to enjoy them. Her freedom was worth it. She had everything she needed for a few weeks now, plus the dress that Anna had painstakingly sewn all of her other jewelry into. This was what she was going to live on in the next few months.

Hedwig pedaled down the large driveway, heading toward the road. It was a beautiful night. A radiant moon illuminated the stone driveway as she crunched along it. Outside of the gates, she drew in a deep breath for the first time in the last hour, every minute taking her farther away from the marriage that had stifled her, from the man who had kept her captive, and from the life she no longer belonged to.

As she cycled through the brisk night air, all around her, it was silent, just the sound of her own breath being drawn in and out of her lungs gradually calming with the rhythmic motion of the bicycle. She would not stop at the Schwarzenau train station but pedal on to the one over ten miles away, Göpfritz an der Wild. Fritz had been sleeping in his study for over a month since their argument and she didn't expect he would know she was gone until she was far away. But, still, the further she got away from the castle, the safer she would be.

As she traveled she turned her thoughts back to what had happened a month before, the conversation that had cemented the end of her marriage, and still she felt the deep-rooted pain.

It had been yet another night of entertaining his clients and she'd tried to be engaging and interactive for a while, but, becoming bored with the conversations about munitions and arms deals, she'd excused herself and gone to bed early.

When Fritz had arrived in their bedroom two hours later, she could tell he was drunk. Throwing open the door, he fell into their room, yanking at his tie as he stumbled and swore. Slamming the door shut, he staggered to his dresser, and Hedwig placed the book she'd been reading down on her nightstand and prepared herself for what she knew was to come. Her husband had become harder to live with over the last year, and his outbursts and jealous tantrums had become more and more frequent. Normally their battles ended with them yelling at one another. But she was tired of it.

Before they were married, she'd thought his character was engaging, his fiery tendencies, his passion, his envy as being protective. But as time had gone on, his all-consuming personality had slowly stifled her, strangling her until she could barely breathe.

Not wanting a row, Hedwig decided to keep the conversation light as her husband flung his jacket on the chair and started aggressively to unbutton his shirt.

"Did you have a good time?" she asked gently.

He fixed his gaze on her in his dresser mirror, his eyes swimming with the alcohol as he pierced her with his fury.

"You don't have a good time," he mocked her, pulling his shirt out of the top of his trousers, "when you have a wife who is so disobedient!"

She swallowed down the acidic fire in her throat and the anger brimming in her chest. She really didn't want to fight tonight. He had never hit her but sometimes his anger was so ferocious that it felt as if he'd slapped her across the face. Tonight, she was tired, worn out, and sick of this.

"I had a headache. I had to come to bed."

"Don't lie to me, Hedwig," he said, ripping off his shirt in frustration, a button going flying and skittering across the floor. He marched into the bathroom as he continued to shout his grievances and filled a bowl of water.

"Everybody else's wife was there, listening and being attentive, but where was mine? Well, her majesty just wandered off to bed. It makes me look so foolish."

She slipped on her satin robe and stood in the doorway of the bathroom, knowing if she didn't respond, he would be even more volatile.

"Darling, I'm sorry," she purred at him, looking up through feathery lashes, trying a new tack. Maybe if she were desirable enough, he would stop yelling at her: she was actually starting to get that headache she had lied about.

Fritz began to splash his face. In between scooping up water, he continued to berate her. "The trouble with you, Hedwig, is you have been spoiled. Spoiled by your father. By everyone you've met. You think the world revolves around you. The fact of the matter is, you're nothing more than that face, and one day you won't have that. You will be old and ugly and you'll die with no one to love you."

She bit back a scalding reply instead kept her tone even. "Surely *you* will still love me, even when I'm old?" she responded, toying with him, placing a hand on his arm.

He yanked his arm away from her, drying his face with a towel. Looking into the bathroom mirror again, he found her eyes. "You make it impossible for me. First, you embarrass me in front of all of my friends, and secondly, I thought you could rise above your past and be the obedient wife I needed you to be. But you are still that whore who flaunted her body on camera for everyone to see when you completed that despicable act."

Hedwig felt a tightening in her stomach and held back her desire to slap him as he had started throwing her past in her face every time she upset him now. A few years before, she'd been involved in a film called *Ecstasy*. Young and naive, she had just been following the director's instructions but she had become infamous for appearing on screen nude and simulating having sex. All over Europe it had been scandalous. Though he'd married her knowing her past, even seeming a little tantalized by it, as time had gone on, Fritz had become more and more obsessed with the film, trying to buy up every copy he could get his hands on.

Hedwig flounced back into the bedroom, trying to sound airy. "Well, if you won't love me, then I will have to go back to acting." She felt satisfied, knowing how much that would needle him. At her own mirror she ran her hands through her soft brown curls. All at once he was behind her.

Wrenching her around to face him, he grabbed her shoulders, crushing her, his eyes wild, his breath reeking of brandy.

"Listen to me, Hedwig Kiesler. No one in the movie industry is ever going to see you as anything other than the little whore you were in that film. You are nothing more than a body and a pretty face. And for every man, you're only good for one thing.

Mark my words, no one in this world is ever going to want you for anything else."

She sucked in breath, her anger deflated as she felt paralyzed by fear and deeply wounded by his words. He had said worse things to her when he had been drunk, but something about this exchange jarred her to the core. And the truth was, on some level, she feared his words were true.

"Take your hands off me," she snarled, tugging her arms out of his grip as she marched over to the bed to get some distance between them.

Swearing at her, he strode to his dresser, and, wrenching open the drawer, he pulled out pajamas and from his side of the bed grabbed a pillow.

"I'm going to sleep in my study. You disgust me."

"Good!" she shouted after him and meant it.

Once he'd slammed out of the room, she pulled out her gold cigarette case from her bedroom drawer, and with her hands shaking violently more with anger now than fear, she lit a cigarette and took in a deep breath, his words still ringing in her ears: "You're only good for one thing, and no one in this world is ever going to want you for anything else." And as she tossed and turned, unable to sleep that night, she had made her decision. She would wait for the right time, but she would leave him, find a man to love her just for who she was, her mind and personality as well as her looks.

The next morning, she had sat at her dressing table, her face pale. Her eyes showed the despair she was feeling. And somehow, she was unable to shake the sting of his words. Was it true? Would she never be wanted for anything else? She looked at her face. Was it her fault that her features were arranged in such a way that people found her attractive? She knew for certain their marriage was over, and now she had to prove that his words were wrong. Taking up her comb, she brushed her hair vigorously, becoming determined and making a plan. Hedwig would go out into the world; she'd be taken seriously for who she was. Yes, she'd use what nature had given her. Didn't everybody? But one day, people would respect her for who she was, not just what she looked like. From that morning on, she had put her plan in place, waiting for just the right opportunity. Now, she was going to fulfill her destiny and prove Fritz Mandl wrong.

*

As the train pulled out of the station from Vienna toward Paris, she breathed a sigh of relief. She'd done it; she'd left him as she'd promised she would. But as she relaxed to observe the beauty of Austria rushing by outside her window, there was also sadness. Her marriage was over, and she had gone into it thinking it was going to be forever. Tears sprang to her eyes.

Her mother would be furious, so the last place she planned to go was home. Mama had always seen Fritz as a good match for her headstrong daughter. Though she didn't feel very strong right now. On the outside she would continue to show the world a brave face, to hide that inside she felt like an impoverished child, alone and not worthy of love from anyone or anything. One thing Fritz had said that was true: beauty faded. One day, she would be old, and before then she wanted to do something worthwhile with her life. But until then she would go back to acting. It would serve her for a short time. And then she would find a wonderful man and have a family and finally do something that made her happy. Something that fulfilled her on a much deeper level. And she couldn't wait for that day.

Chapter Two

Cambridge, England, summer 1937

Racing along the banks of the River Cam, Judy Morgan retrieved her bicycle, and, mounting it, she threw her textbooks into the front basket, along with her blanket. Blinking her eyes, she tried to clear her vision from the mistiness of sleep and wake up fully. She couldn't believe she'd dropped off. Having finished rowing for the fun of it with her teammates in the late afternoon, Judy had been tired and had some reading she wanted to catch up on, hoping to go on to study for her doctorate at some point. But she'd barely opened the pages of her book when she'd fallen asleep in the warm sun, on the banks of the beautiful river that ran behind the colleges in Cambridge.

Judy pumped the pedals as hard as she could toward her room at Newnham College. She didn't dare even glance at her watch, knowing without looking that, with the dip of the sun descending in an amber glow beneath the edge of the river, it was late. As she raced along the ancient streets, Judy barely noticed the huddles of little red rooftops, collections of spired churches, or any of the university's grandest buildings, because tonight she couldn't be late.

As she swerved onto the main road, her pace abruptly dwindled to a crawl with the sudden buildup of traffic and she remembered, with frustration, Saturday was market day. Even though the stalls were packing up, the roads were heaving with life. Buses, motor cars, horse-and-carts, and, of course, the many bicycles Cambridge was infamous for, thronged the whole street. As she wove her bike dangerously in between the traffic, Judy finally turned toward her destination. Panting heavily, she rushed up the driveway of Newnham College. Dispensing her bike into a bike rack, she raced across the court, her wiry body leaping up the stairs of the sunken garden and in through the red Victorian building's front doors.

A couple of the girls already descending the college's main staircase en masse tutted at her timekeeping.

Judy pushed past them, running in the opposite direction to the stream of undergraduates coming down the stairs.

Colleges at Cambridge had regimented schedules, steeped in the tradition of its six-hundred-year history, and she knew they weren't going to wait for her. She flew into her room. Quickly throwing off her rowing attire, she pulled on her dress robes and raked her hands through her curly, brown hair. Still out of breath and now sweating with the exertion, she bounded out the room and down the stairs two at a time and just managed to join the end of the crowd as they all filed quietly into hall. Eating in "hall" was an evening ritual, and tonight was important because they were graduating. She moved to her place and stood catching her breath as the girls around her looked at her with disdain.

Judy offered a weak smile. At twenty-four, she had never felt so lonely as she had here at Cambridge. Coming from a small village outside Cardiff, she had felt the odd one out at home because she was a girl interested in science. It was because of that she had hoped to find friendship here with people who had the same interests as herself. But the women at Newnham had taken an instant dislike to Judy on meeting her. Many from influential families, they had appeared to resent the fact that Judy was from a lower class, on a full scholarship and yet always seemed to score the highest in her classes.

Judy stared at the white tablecloth in front of her as they all waited by their chairs for the fellows to be seated. The dinner gong chimed and the fellows paraded in, also in their robes, and made their way in procession down the middle of the room to take their places at the top table.

Prayers were boomed out in Latin, and they were all allowed to sit. It wasn't long before they were eating elegantly prepared French cuisine. The girls around her talked in hushed whispers, ignoring her completely as they discussed their excitement at graduating. There was also an air of disappointment, as earlier their male counterparts had made their way to Senate House to kneel before the vice chancellor and receive their degrees. There wouldn't be any such honors for the girls. Though women were allowed to study, they weren't permitted to receive an official degree, nor any honors: instead they would receive what was known as a Tripos certificate to confirm that they had completed their studies. But still, they were all grateful to have the time at Cambridge that they'd had. As the girls talked amongst themselves, Judy reminisced.

Cambridge life had been difficult at times, and she had worked hard to pass all her exams, but it had also been incredibly rewarding. She remembered with fondness the freshness of the mornings as she'd walked across the courts in her robes at breakfast time on the way to the laboratory to attend her first lecture at 9 a.m. She had especially liked that time of the day, with the shafts of morning sunlight creating haphazard patterns as it stretched, blinking, through the spiky Gothic towers, the whole experience accentuated by the sweet smell of dewy grass on the lawns and the university abuzz with anticipation of all they would learn that day. It was a world unto itself, with its own customs and rituals. A place where the pupil and the teacher mingled in an ongoing debate and it wasn't uncommon to see two solitary figures walking the grounds at one college or another, one fellow, one undergraduate, discussing and putting the world to rights. She wondered, now she was leaving, would there ever be another time for that kind of reflection in the future? She doubted it.

She'd been fortunate to have studied under the Cavendish professor of physics, Ernest Rutherford, and she would miss his lively banter and passion for his subject.

One of the other girls appeared to read her thoughts. "It's going to be hard to leave, isn't it?" Judy and the other girls agreed.

They continued discussing which buildings they found the most fascinating. Judy listened, realizing she would miss the libraries and the museums, the lecture rooms, and the laboratory where she'd spent so much of her time.

"I've always loved St. John's," said one girl, gushing about the beautiful college with the plum-colored bricks and vast courtyard.

"But Trinity is famous for Sir Isaac Newton and Lord Byron," added another.

"Walking through the King's lawn with its chapel is so delightful," offered another.

Forgetting herself, Judy chimed in without thinking, "I like the Pepys Library at Magdalene."

The girls around her stopped eating and stared at her as though they were amazed she had an opinion. The silence was painful and once again Judy felt the sting of rejection that had marked her time at Cambridge.

As they started on their extravagant chocolate dessert, the other girls discussed how they would stay in touch and plans to get together during the summer. No one included Judy in their conversation. It was as if she wasn't even there.

"Have any of you started applying for work?" asked one of the girls.

They all nodded.

Judy stayed quiet, not wanting to mention that she'd applied to the Cavendish Laboratory here in Cambridge in the hope that she could continue to pursue her studies in physics. Professor Rutherford had encouraged her to apply, and she loved the idea of doing something to contribute to the world. Create something that saved lives, or make some other important breakthrough. Madame Curie, whose work on radiation was legendary, had inspired Judy's interest in science. Curie had been one of only a few women to win a Nobel Prize so far, and the only female scientist ever to win twice. Judy decided she didn't need fame, but she wanted to do something that would make the world a better place.

After the official dinner and a speech from the principal, the young women made their way out into the hall. One of them invited a large group, which didn't include Judy, to her room to gather. Judy went back to her own to finish her packing.

As she moved downstairs later to empty her rubbish, she passed by one of the girls' doors, the one that had offered the invitation, which was slightly ajar. Laughter drifted out into the corridor, and she caught sight of the group sitting in front of the fireplace, talking and joking, listening to music, and all drinking wine someone must have brought in. Moving along the corridor, she pushed the rejection from her thoughts. She would not let herself dwell on the sadness. Cambridge had given her a remarkable education and that was all that mattered.

Chapter Three

Hedwig found Stefan at his usual table at his favorite Parisian street café, and his eyes lit up when he saw her. And all at once, all the heaviness in her body, the stiffness of her shoulders, and the tension she'd been holding on to, flowed away. Her heart was home. She was with her beloved oldest friend, a man who was like a brother to her.

He leapt to his feet and ran to greet her.

"Earwig, what are you doing here?" he asked, using her childhood nickname as he enfolded her in his arms. The smell of fresh air, coffee, and cigarette smoke lingered on his blue cotton shirt as he pulled away from her and held her at arm's length to study her. "You left him at last, didn't you?" he surmised confidently.

Hedwig clenched her teeth to stop her chin from quivering. She wasn't going to get emotional. Not again. She just nodded her head.

"Good for you," Stefan responded enthusiastically, guiding her back to the table and pulling out a chair for her. "François," he shouted to a tired-looking waiter whose face was darkened by day-old stubble. "A strong cup of coffee for my oldest, dearest friend from Austria."

"This is your friend?" said François, feasting his eyes upon her.

"Yes, a very good friend. And don't forget that," Stefan said, warning him. Then he beamed at Hedwig. "So, you finally took the plunge. What sent you over the edge?"

She didn't have the heart to tell him the words that had stung— the things that Fritz had said about her being no more than a body that men would desire. It felt too raw and embarrassing. So, she stated brazenly, "It was easier and less messy than killing him."

"He didn't deserve you." Stefan chuckled, sitting back on his chair, pulling his cigarettes out of his shirt pocket and shaking two out of the packet onto the table in front of him. He automatically lit one for Hedwig and handed it to her. She took it with a trembling hand as he lit his own.

"I told you that before you married him, Hedwig. It has to be someone special for you."

She gave him a broad smile. "I wish other men saw me as you do."

"Well, I do know men and the truth is they don't see past their basic desires," stated Stefan. "They never give themselves time to see the beautiful woman you are inside."

"I wonder if that is really true," she mused to herself in a whisper.

In response he grabbed her hand, looking intently at her. "Don't let him destroy your confidence. You are the smartest, funniest, most audacious woman I've ever known. And God help anyone who gets on the wrong end of your temper. But with all that passion and fire comes great conviction. You have all it takes to be successful and be anything you want."

She sighed. "Thank you, Stefan. I knew this was the right place to come."

"Well," he said, balancing his cigarette on the edge of the ashtray and locking his hands behind his head. "What shall we do with you? When was the last time you were in Paris?"

She shrugged her shoulders. She didn't even remember; maybe with Fritz, a year ago.

"I am going to show you the town in a way that you've never seen it before. Drink your coffee, and we'll get going."

"Aren't you supposed to be working?" she enquired, knotting her eyebrows.

"The article can wait. The nice thing about working in France is people aren't so uptight about the deadlines as they were in Vienna. I want to take my best friend out for the day."

She swallowed down her coffee and they finished their cigarettes as Stefan threw some money on the table and took her hand.

"First, I think we need to go to the Louvre. Paintings always cheer you up." She suddenly felt a glow of happiness. "But we'll go via my apartment and drop off your things first."

"How is the work coming on?" she asked.

"I love being a journalist. You know that. And with this Hitler business there are plenty of stories. I've got to do something since—if there is a war, as some are saying there may be—they won't let me fight."

He took her to his little attic apartment in Montmartre, and she dropped off her things in the bedroom, enjoying the eclectic, cluttered environment that so reflected her friend's personality. On a shelf she noticed a gift she had given him. A music box she had taken apart and re-created as a child. Ever since she'd been young she had loved inventing and understanding how mechanical things worked. Thrown across the bed was an expensive jacket that looked far too big for Stefan's slender frame.

She picked it up and hooked it on the end of one of her fingers as she stood in the bedroom doorway.

"Someone special?"

Her friend responded with a faint blush. "Let's just say someone who is special *right now*... we will just have to wait and see."

They perused the Louvre together, and she suddenly felt calm. "Are you still painting, Hedwig?" he asked, one hand shoved in his pocket as they both stared at the *Mona Lisa*.

She nodded.

"I think you have amazing talent. Maybe you should stay here and become an artist; there are plenty of people who do that."

She shook her head. "I want to go back to acting. I'm going to go to London, to Mama's friends."

They'd been conversing the whole time in German, and now he spoke to her in English. "What about learning a new language? I don't remember you doing so well at school with that."

She answered the best she could in her own English. "I'm going to have to learn, then, aren't I? Because one day I'd love to go to Hollywood."

He spun her around to face him. "And if anyone can do it, you can. You could be anything you want to be. You have to let the real you out so people can see it."

She smiled, but now she felt afraid after leaving Fritz. She didn't ever want to be that vulnerable again. Stefan was the only person who got to see her as she really was. She could feel a much-needed protective shell gathering around her since leaving Vienna, particularly around her heart.

They spent the day enjoying the town, taking a rainy boat trip down the Seine, lunching at Maxim's, where Stefan blew a week of his wages, and in the evening, he took her to the Moulin Rouge. They laughed and drank, watched women kicking up their legs in a blur of lace and feathers, and by the end of the night, she felt better. And when her oldest friend saw her off at the train station the next morning, she almost begged to stay. But remembering the clothes on his bed, and that he had a life of his own, and knowing she must live her own life, she stopped herself.

As they parted, Stefan kissed her on the cheek. "You know I am not a good letter writer, so while I'm not with you to remind you, don't forget who you are, Hedwig. Only make friends with people as smart as you. And remember to hold your temper so people see the real you. You wait and see: the whole world will bow down in awe of your genius."

She nodded at his wise words and, waving from the train window, she felt content; it had been right to come to see her closest friend. Since her father's death, there was no man in the world apart from Stefan who could make her feel so completely loved.

Chapter Four

A couple of days after graduation, Judy's rowing team had decided to have an early morning picnic with some of the male graduates on the banks of the River Cam to say goodbye. Though the girls in her team were a little friendlier to her, she didn't feel really close to any of them, perhaps because she was so shy she tended to blend into the background whenever she was in a large group. The girls sat on the bank sunning themselves in the early morning heat as the boys surrounded them in their boaters and blazers, discussing the world that they were going out into. One of the boys was reading the newspaper and read out an article with great indignation to the group.

"I can't believe Austria is so friendly toward Hitler."

One of the chaps who was lying on his back, his hands locked behind his head, chewing on a piece of grass, grunted. "You need to know your history. Austria has wanted this for a long time. They think that they will be stronger with Germany on their side."

"But what will it mean to Europe?" the other lad persisted with great passion, throwing down the newspaper with disgust.

"What will it mean for us?" exclaimed one of the girls. "If what they're saying does happen, could there be another war?"

People around the blanket shook their heads and voiced their disagreement. "Surely not. Nobody wants another war, not even Hitler."

"Well, my friends," said another boy, sitting up on his haunches and squinting because of the bright sunshine, "that's because you haven't read *Mein Kampf*, Hitler's book where he outlines that's exactly what he wants to do."

They continued in this lively debate between themselves. Nobody wanted to see another war. Though, somehow, Judy felt it might be inevitable.

After the group said their goodbyes, Judy decided to take herself on a trip to London, a place she'd always wanted to go and see. She would spend the afternoon there before changing trains on her way home to Wales, but she had wanted to visit the Science Museum for a long time.

Arriving late morning, she made her way to the large building in South Kensington. It was a beautiful day, and the city was alive with tourists and its usual energy. Reaching the impressive gray stone building, more suited to a Roman temple than scientific exhibitions, she made her way inside. In the marble hallway, the building was cool and hushed like a library and from the entrance she could see the many levels of displays above her on their floors. Light streamed in from the round-windowed ceiling and long pendant lamps illuminated glass and metal fixtures with every type of scientific discovery and invention.

She looked at what was being offered that day, and there was a tour to do with radiation, something she'd been fascinated by most of her life, not least because of her love of Marie Curie.

She arrived at the exhibition hall at the stated time and started to follow the crowd as a young tour guide walked them through the rooms.

He was a rather arrogant man and, at one point, suggested that though Madame Curie was cited for so much of the work, it was likely her male scientific partners and her husband that were the brains behind her discoveries. Judy frowned as she listened. It didn't seem fair to her what he was suggesting, but it didn't surprise her either. She'd learned that, as a woman, often people didn't think it was possible for her to outshine the male students.

All of a sudden, it was as though she heard her own thoughts. Behind her, a woman in heavy-accented English said, "Ridiculous!

You make her sound as if it wasn't possible for her to be as intelligent as a man."

Judy searched the crowd to see who had spoken, but she couldn't see another woman, just men and a party of schoolchildren listening intently to the tour guide. As they moved away and the crowd cleared, she saw where the voice had come from. Sitting on a stone bench, one leg folded under herself, and eating an apple, was a lovely young woman. Judy turned and nodded to her, and the woman smiled back.

Judy moved across to her. "I was just thinking the same thing."

The woman beamed and, finishing her apple, held out her hand.

"It makes me furious. Well, as we're the only two women here, maybe we should introduce ourselves. My English isn't very good, so I'm practicing whenever I can. Nice to meet you. My name is Hedwig."

Judy laughed. She asked her in what she assumed might be her own language, "Are you German?"

Hedwig looked grateful to have someone speak in her native tongue.

She shook her head. "No, actually, I'm Austrian. It's hard to speak English all the time, but I have to learn it."

"Are you interested in science?" asked Judy, continuing in German, glad she had studied it during her degree.

"Always," stated Hedwig.

As she sat down next to her, Judy was drawn in by the young woman. She was mesmerizing, with the most beautiful face she'd ever seen. It was a fresh face without makeup, but there was a sparkle to her eyes, and her dark hair parted down the center was long and curly.

"Are *you* interested in science?" asked Hedwig.

"I've just finished studying for my degree in physics at Cambridge."

Hedwig's eyes lit up. "I would love to do something like that. But the life that I've come from in Austria, that kind of thing was impossible and even harder now for someone Jewish. I was only allowed to take care of our home."

Judy nodded her understanding.

The two of them got up and started to walk around the room together, talking easily. It wasn't until they were at the second exhibition that Judy realized she didn't feel remotely shy with this woman. She usually became nervous around people she had just met, but she was instantly drawn to Hedwig. She came across as so confident, even though she was a woman abroad, alone in a strange country. Though Judy didn't pry, she was sure that it was probably something to do with the upheaval in Europe as Hitler rose to power.

"Do you know what you're going to do after university?" continued Hedwig.

"I'm hoping to join the Cavendish Laboratory," said Judy with a smile. "It's a very notable institution. I want to continue my education, researching things such as radio signals and radio waves."

"How wonderful. If there is another war, as it is rumored there could be, I imagine these are the sort of technologies that will be needed," mused Hedwig. "I wish I could do something like that." She sighed and folded her arms.

"Are you studying yourself?" asked Judy.

"If only I could," responded Hedwig. "Right now, I am acting, doing what I can to make money until I figure out who I want to be."

"That doesn't seem such a terrible career," said Judy. "I'm sure you're marvelous at it."

Hedwig shook her head. "I'm struggling to find work, particularly with my accent." They finished walking around the exhibition together, and as they came to leave the building, Hedwig turned to her. "Would you like to get a drink or something? It is so nice to talk in my own language and I haven't really made any friends here in London."

Judy felt a twinge of sympathy, hearing the young woman's loneliness and knowing all too well how that felt. She knew there was a late train for Cardiff that evening, so impulsively she agreed. She had time to have a drink with her new acquaintance.

They made their way to a tiny tea shop nearby and even though Judy's shyness stopped her from really initiating conversation, Hedwig didn't seem to notice or care. She was enthralled by Judy's studies and asked her so many questions about her time at university. Also, she had a great sense of humor that kept Judy laughing, as she talked about her ambitions as an actress.

They conversed the whole time in German, and as they talked, two older women on a table close by kept scowling at them.

"Do you see that?" whispered Hedwig, the anger obvious in her tone. "There is so much prejudice here already. People automatically think, when they hear my accent, that maybe I'm some sort of spy for Hitler."

Judy felt compassion. She was in a difficult situation.

The time passed quickly and Judy knew she couldn't put it off any longer; the last train to Cardiff was leaving in an hour and she still needed to get to Paddington station.

They paid for their tea and on the way to the door, one of the women who had been scowling at them said something under her breath about them being Nazis.

Hedwig stormed over. "Not everyone who speaks German is from Germany or a goose-stepping Nazi. Some of us are actually escaping that regime. How dare you look down at me because of the language I speak!"

Judy swallowed down a laugh. How she wished she could be that bold.

Hedwig marched back to her side and turned to her without a hair out of place. "It's been lovely to meet you, Judy, and I wish you great luck at Cavendish Laboratory. Did you say that's back in Cambridge?"

Judy nodded, her lip curling in amusement at her friend's brazen show. "Yes, I'm hoping to be going back to Cambridge soon. If I get the job," she said, crossing her fingers.

"You'll get it," assured Hedwig with confidence." I just know it."

Judy smiled. "And good luck with your career as an actress. I hope you find work that makes you happy."

"I will stay in London for now. There is nowhere else in Europe for me to go right now," said Hedwig with great sorrow. "And who knows, maybe I could go to America or somewhere? There may be work for me there."

Judy offered her hand. "Goodbye, Hedwig. It's been lovely meeting you."

"You too. Enjoy your dazzling scientific career. I admire you. There are not many women who could do that. It's a brave course of action. Goodbye, Judy…?"

"Morgan," added Judy.

They shook hands and turned away but as she started to leave, Hedwig caught up with her again. "Look I know we have only just met, but would you mind awfully if I wrote to you occasionally? It's been so nice to connect and I'm a great believer in fate."

Judy felt her cheeks redden as she agreed. It was the first time she had ever really made a friend and she'd warmed to Hedwig instantly, enjoying her spunky openness. She seemed to be a woman who really knew her own mind in a way Judy envied.

They swapped addresses and Judy gave out her Welsh address, informing Hedwig that her mother would pass on any letters after she had a place to stay in Cambridge.

As Judy made her way to the train, she clutched the torn Science Museum brochure Hedwig had scrawled her address on and felt a glow of happiness. But soon her thoughts were on other things:

her journey home to Wales and the letter she hoped she would get from the Cavendish Laboratory offering her a position.

Arriving home in Cardiff, a letter was already waiting for her. She had been accepted to start her post the following month.

"*Da iawn,* darling," Judy's mother congratulated her in Welsh, gathering her daughter in her arms.

Her mother was short and stocky with black hair and ruddy cheeks. Judy's father was the same height and build as his wife. "Bookends," her father always used to joke.

"Who'd have thought we'd have raised such a distinguished scholar?" he added, reading the letter Judy had handed to him.

"You'll be going back to Cambridge, then?" her mother enquired. "Are you sure you want to do that? You could get a good job right here in Cardiff. I'm sure we need scientists here too," she persisted.

"I know, Ma," Judy assured her. "But I want to do something of real value and to do that, I will need to work at a prestigious laboratory."

Her mother looked disappointed but nodded her head with resolution.

"Well, as long as you're happy," she responded with a sigh.

She nodded. "I am, Ma, and this is my dream, to do something worthwhile, something for good, and I can't wait to get started."

After her mother had gone to bed, Judy and her father curled up in their cozy front room around the black Welsh slate fireplace, as their very elderly tabby cat stretched out on her father's lap. Judy sighed in contentment, inhaling the familiar scent of coal dust and books, and just the edge of the damp, Welsh cold that whipped down through the hills and valleys and always found its way through locked doors and around her ankles no matter how bright the fire blazed.

In the light of the golden flames, her father's eyes glistened with anticipation. "Tell me everything, Judy," he crooned in his rich deep tone that would not have been out of place on the radio instead of here by this humble fireside.

Judy was amused by her father's enthusiasm. For as long as she could remember, he had started every intimate conversation with her with those very words. As an only child, she'd been fortunate to have her parents' undivided attention. Still, with her father, there was a special connection, something more than she often saw in other people's parents, as if the two of them were peers, allies on an adventure all of their own.

"I've just completed four years at Cambridge. Where would you like me to start?"

He chuckled. "Just the things that make you come alive."

Judy drew her feet underneath her, and, pulling her mother's knitted blanket across her lap, she began to tell him all the discoveries she had made lately through her studies. And even though a lot of what she was talking about she knew was way over her father's head, he barely breathed as he listened intently to everything she had to share.

Once she was finished, he punctuated the end of their conversation as he always did with the same words: "I'm so proud of you, Judy." And though she had heard them so many times before, it still filled her with joy to know the pleasure it gave her father to be a part of her world. "I just know you're going to be a fantastic scientist," he continued, as he got up to pour himself a nightcap. "You're going to change the world, Judy Morgan. I can just feel it. I was talking to that Bobby Jones the other day. His daughter was at school with you. Remember her?" Judy had a vague recollection of a tall willowy girl with white-blonde pigtails as he continued, "She's already on her second baby, you know? She hasn't even given herself a chance to try something different. Now don't get me wrong, I'm all for people marrying and having children. I hope you will one day. But you have to do something first, don't you, Judy?" he said, handing her the brandy that she would just sip out of politeness. "I wish more people would do what you are doing."

"It's not as easy as you think, Da. It's a little like swimming upstream, being a female scientist. You should see the men's faces whenever I offer my opinion."

"Then you are going to prove them all wrong," he pronounced as he got to his feet and slammed his hand down on the mantelpiece. "You're going to be the first woman to show those men what you're capable of. Improve the world with a scientific breakthrough. That'll put them all in their place, Judy. That's what you will do. You mark my words."

She looked at her dad's face, now alive with his passion. And she so desperately wanted to achieve something in her life that would justify his belief in her. As he continued to encourage her, she turned and looked back toward the flames and hoped more than anything that she would do this for him. He had often told her how he had never been allowed to pursue his own passion of being an actor and had been forced to follow in the dreary family business as an accountant. And though now he was philosophical about it, she knew that that was why he was adamant about seeing her fulfill her own destiny. As if her doing that would somehow make his sacrifice worthwhile.

Chapter Five

September 1937

Hedwig sat gazing at herself in the dressing-room mirror in her second-class cabin. Knowing the importance of what she was preparing for, she hadn't left the cabin since she'd boarded the *Normandie* at midday. Everything depended on the first impression she was going to make this evening. If her plan didn't work, she had no other option, so she just had to look the most beautiful she could.

As she applied the last of her makeup, she put the finishing touches to her letter for her new friend as she reflected on her decision.

September 10, 1937

Dear Judy,

You will never guess where I am, so I am just going to have to tell you.

Right this minute I'm sitting in a tiny cabin on the SS Normandie on my way to America! Can you believe it? I have been hiding down here for hours preparing for what might be the performance of my life so far.

The cabin I'm sitting in is small but snug with a tiny bunk in one corner, which is overwhelmed right now with all of my best dresses which I have been trying on. Every stick of makeup I own is out on the dressing table, along with the silver brush and comb set my mother gave me for my eighteenth birthday. These second-class cabins are far too dark. Apart from the light at the dressing table, it is only lit by little wall lights in the shape of seashells on the dark paneled walls. But in its defense, it smells divine in here, a real sea smell, as it creaks and groans all around me, the salty scent of the sea air drifting in through my open porthole accompanied by the restful sound of the waves as they lap along the base of the ship. I have been down here for hours getting ready, and trying to apply mascara and draw a straight line under my eyes is not easy with the constant movement, I can tell you.

As I sit here writing this, I wonder what you think of my decision. So, there is something I should let you know, now we are friends. I can be impulsive and irrational but I always follow my heart. This time it told me to get on a ship to the USA. I am still pinching myself for doing it but sometimes you just need to take a leap of faith, don't you think?

Let me tell you the story of how this happened.

Since we met at the museum, I stayed busy in London, trying to get work as an actress. It was hard, though, especially with the influx of refugees from across Europe, so much competition.

But then, the other day, I heard a Hollywood executive was coming to London to look for talent, so I decided I would put myself forward. However, I was disappointed to hear that he wasn't offering actresses a lot of money. Then I started to have second thoughts (I think that is the right English term?). What if I was perfect for that job? What if he would have offered me more? I could be the next Greta Garbo! So, taking my heart in my hands and with some of the money I got from some jewelry I sold, I booked myself passage on the Normandie, a ship I knew he was traveling home on.

I'm so nervous. Somewhere on the ship, my destiny could be waiting. Mr. Mayer of MGM—watch out!

Anyway, enough about this. You know, I am still marveling at the fact that we met the way we did in London and was so thrilled to get your letter telling me you have got your job at Cavendish. Maybe both of us will get to live our dreams, you as a great scientist and me as a Hollywood actress.

Well, I must go. I can hear the band starting up for the evening and I don't want to miss an opportunity to see Mr. Mayer during dinner.

Much love,
Hedwig xxx

Hedwig slipped the letter into an envelope and went over her plan for the evening. On boarding, she had already befriended some of the stewards who had greeted her, hoping that a little persuasion and a generous tip might help her find her the way into the first-class dining room that evening.

As she finished getting ready in her cabin, she placed the diamond necklace that she had stuffed into her pocket the day she'd left Austria around her neck. That and the pair of emerald earrings she was wearing were the only jewelry she had left now. It all glinted in the mirror, setting off her cream-colored skin wonderfully, the perfect accompaniment to her most flattering gown. The black and white sequin dress with the plunging neckline fit her like a lizard skin. She felt a little overdressed for the first night out, but she wasn't interested in ship etiquette tonight, only in winning the movie studio executive's heart and attention.

She finished applying her crimson lipstick, blotted her lips with a tissue, and stood up to view herself in the full-length mirror. The dress's midnight-black sequins shimmered like coal dust under the light and the white orchid design sewn into the bodice had an iridescent quality that rainbowed with a lilac hue. She looked pretty impressive, even if she had to say so herself. She turned to check her reflection from the back. The plunging V exposed her creamy white shoulders and the high split highlighted her legs as she straightened the line of her stockings.

If this didn't work, then nothing would. After dusting a powder puff across her chest to reduce its glow and feathering fingers through her curls to soften them a little, she was ready. Hedwig placed a hand on her chest, feeling her fluttering heart below it, and took a deep breath, remembering Stefan's words.

"Hedwig Kiesler, you can do this. You can be anyone you want to be. No one gets to decide who you are but you," she reminded herself in the mirror.

For a second her ex-husband's face flashed through her mind and her stomach tightened as she remembered his cruel words, too, but she shook him from her thoughts. She would take great pleasure in proving him wrong. Reassured by her own words, she opened the cabin door and started to perform.

She was an expert at playing a role. Hedwig had studied all the great actresses on the screen and had practiced the look and feel she wanted to project to the world. She knew how to create a scintillating performance. Gone was the little Jewish girl who'd grown up in Austria and who'd feared that she would never be taken seriously or loved for who she was, and emerging from her cabin was the movie star she wanted to be.

Hedwig sauntered up the corridor, taking her time. As she went, she pretended not to notice the open-mouthed adoration she saw from the men around her and the looks of hostility from their wives. Treading catlike upstairs, she swaggered toward the dining room. Her plan was to make an entrance, passing through the dining room on her way to the ballroom. She hoped Mayer would have enjoyed a good meal, even as her own stomach reminded her she hadn't even left her cabin to eat all day. As she approached the corridor, the sound of the thirty-piece band wafted up the deck to greet her from the ballroom, where they were playing a lively rendition of "Pennies from Heaven." She hoped that was a good omen. Arriving at the dining room, she bobbed her hair with her hand and a faint scent of the expensive perfume that Fritz had bought her last Christmas permeated the air around her.

Greeting people at the door was one of the stewards she'd already befriended that day, and as she noted him run his eyes down her body, she knew her dress had the effect she'd wanted. Wishing her a good evening, he didn't even ask her about where she was situated on the ship and, assuming she was a first-class passenger, opened the door for her. She nodded and tipped him anyway and prepared to make her entrance.

The *Normandie*'s dining room was spectacular and expansive. A cream-colored carpet stretched down the staircase into the room. On either side, the walls were decorated with gold wallpaper and floor-to-ceiling panels of warm amber lights. On either side of the stairs, a profusion of fresh, white lilies perfumed her descent. Placing her hand on the gold-tasseled banister, she glided down the steps, trying to nonchalantly find her target. As she reached the bottom stair, the smell of roast chicken, rosemary, steak, and mashed potatoes wafted across to greet her, making her stomach cramp with hunger. But she knew she wouldn't be eating tonight. There wasn't room in this dress for even a potato chip.

Hedwig took a minute to study her route, deciding her best course to be seen. The room was filled with elegant round tables draped with white linen tablecloths, and the best crystal glimmered under candlelight. Huge chandeliers lit the room with white-gold light, and lively conversation was taking place all around her. She decided to move slowly between the tables and make her way to the door into the ballroom at the far end.

Hedwig prowled the room, surreptitiously looking for the table she was hoping to impress. She'd seen pictures of Mayer in the fan magazines and had a good idea what he looked like. As she passed table after table, a hush fell on the room. All at once she spotted Mayer, sitting with his wife and a party of Hollywood actors. She flipped back her hair, straightened her back, and extended her neck, slowing to a dawdle and adding just a little more swagger to her step as she passed their table. Catching their eye, she flashed Douglas Fairbanks Jr. a brilliant smile. She continued walking past them, through the dining room and out the main door at the end of the room, where she hoped tables wouldn't be numbered.

As she entered the ballroom, the band had just finished playing a set, and people politely clapped all around her. In the dramatic silence, Hedwig strode across the room, enjoying the effect she was having, accompanied by the whispered speculation on who she was. Reaching a table, she seated herself down and pretended to be oblivious to the stir that she'd already caused.

A waiter approached her table. "Can I get you a drink, madam?" he asked, blushing nervously. He was trying to be professional but also finding it hard to keep his eyes from her cleavage. Hedwig ordered a drink. Before he left the table, she asked him if he could send over the bandleader to speak to her before his next set. The steward nodded, his face growing red as he made his way to the bar. She desperately wanted a cigarette, but didn't want to spoil the illusion she was creating. It was the power she had, the power of allure. As she finished her drink, the bandleader came over. She asked him for her favor and also slipped him money across the table. He seemed enchanted and more than happy to oblige her.

Once she saw Mayer and his party enter the ballroom and take up a table at the back, she signaled to the bandleader that she was ready. After he finished the next set, he introduced her.

"Ladies and gentlemen, I want to welcome a very talented and beautiful European actress who would like to sing for you. Please welcome to the stage Miss Hedwig Kiesler." There was polite applause around as people strained to see the new act. Hedwig paused for a couple of seconds to create drama, then, draining her drink, got to her feet and glided onto the stage. She was a little nervous but swallowed it down behind a brilliant smile.

She nodded to the bandleader, whom she'd already informed she was planning to sing a sultry version of "Stormy Weather," made famous by Ethel Waters.

As the band started to play, Hedwig crooned the melody with great emotion. She wasn't the best singer in the world, but she knew she could hold the audience's attention and she wanted Mayer to watch her for at least three minutes. When she sang the last line, the applause was genuine, and she was relieved.

It was as she was leaving the stage that she noticed Mayer and his wife clapping and whispering amongst themselves. Douglas Fairbanks Jr. was on his feet, applauding loudly. So, instead of returning to her table, she made her way to the back of the room, where there was a sign for the powder room. She didn't need to use it, but its course would take her straight past Mayer's table.

As she sashayed past them, Fairbanks was still standing.

"Miss Kiesler!" he cried out with gusto and an outstretched hand. "Will you join us for a drink? We're all in the movie business here."

She flashed her eyes around the table, pretending to feign disinterest. But then she returned her best smile.

"I'd be delighted," she said.

Fairbanks pulled out a chair and introduced the rest of the party around the table. And when he got to Mr. Mayer, the studio executive, shook her hand, saying, "You have quite the talent there, young lady."

She answered him smoothly, "I'm hoping to take full advantage of that, sir."

He nodded.

Fairbanks was clearly smitten by her and monopolized her time as he tried to dazzle her with scintillating conversation.

As the evening wore on and with the help of the alcohol, everyone started to loosen up, and finally she found her way to the side of Mayer's wife, Barbara, when she asked to see Hedwig's emerald earrings.

By his wife's side, Mr. Mayer observed her in a detached manner, but seemed to approve of the connection she was making with his wife. "Who did you work for in Europe? What films have you done?" he enquired, still apparently a little wary of her as though wondering if it was an act. He had probably seen many young women try to garner his attention in the past.

In response, Hedwig was vague. She wanted a fresh start and didn't want him to judge her on *Ecstasy*. But even with his wariness, by the end of the evening it was evident to everyone that he wanted her for MGM.

His wife seemed to be particularly interested in helping her. "You'll have to change your name," she offered as she sipped on her cocktail. "Hedwig is too long and Kiesler sounds so very Jewish, and the problem is that's not very popular these days. Take it from me, I know," she said with a half-smile. "But for the movie business, you should have a more attractive name. Something that has more appeal, more... *amore*."

"What about Amore?" suggested Fairbanks, trying to be helpful.

"Hedy instead of Hedwig, Hedy Amore? Hedy Lamour? That's better but not quite right," Barbara said, shaking her head. "How about Lamarr? Hedy Lamarr. Now that is lovely. I have always loved the actress Barbara Lamarr."

"Hedwig, would you be willing to change your name to Hedy Lamarr?" enquired Mr. Mayer, lighting a large cigar and blowing out blue smoke across the table at her.

"Of course," she agreed with a grin. "I want to be successful."

"Oh, and you will be," reassured Fairbanks, taking her hand and kissing it with dramatic flourish. "Now dance with me so I can tell you all about your new life in America."

She whirled around the floor a couple of times with Douglas, who chatted with her all about Hollywood. What it would be like. And though she continued to play her part of nonchalance, inside, she was cheering. She had done what she'd set out to do. To draw Mayer into a contract with her, for MGM.

For the rest of the trip across the Atlantic, she continued to meet with the group of Hollywood stars, ensuring she took full advantage of showing off her figure when she swam in the pool and sunbathed on the recliners. It was on the last day, when she was alone, that Mayer approached her.

He looked serious as he sat next to her on one of the deck chairs. She was sprawled out on a lounger, getting a little sun.

"I'm happy to sign you, Hedy. But when I saw you for the first time, there was something familiar about you. So, I wired the studio to do a little investigation work. I have to do that occasionally."

He pulled out a note and her stomach tightened. Not showing her the contents, he scanned it again, folded it, and placed it back in his pocket. A tight, all-knowing smile crossed his face and he lowered his voice. "I didn't want to mention this at dinner in front of my wife, but I now know all about your film in Europe, *Ecstasy*, and want to warn you, Miss Kiesler—you will be expected to keep your clothes on while you are working for me."

Hedy's face flushed and it was as if she'd been stabbed in the stomach. She had hoped no one would find out about her past. His words and the way he warned her made her feel dirty, though she fought to keep her expression neutral. She didn't want him to see how much his words had stung her. Mayer scrutinized her for assurance, and as he did so, she could see that he had pigeonholed her. Would he ever take her seriously as an actress? Could he still respect her?

She lay back on her lounger and put her sunglasses back on to hide the tears brimming in the corners of her eyes. Instead she allowed a smile to play on her lips.

"Whatever you want, Mr. Mayer," she purred.

He nodded and walked away then, and she sat with her disappointment. *You got your contract*, she reminded herself. *What does it matter what this one man thinks of you?*

On the last night, she was invited to sing again. And she enjoyed putting her heart and soul into it. She sang "Someone to Watch Over Me," composed by George Gershwin.

When she rejoined the table, Fairbanks commented, "You only seem to know how to sing sad songs, Hedy. Do you know any happy songs?"

She shrugged. "No, sad songs like sad stories are much more interesting to me," she responded, pouting her lips.

As Hedy left the ship the next day, she was overjoyed. Monday morning, she was due at Mayer's office to sign her contract and couldn't believe she'd managed to do it. Hedwig Kiesler had boarded the ship as a Jewish soon-to-be divorcee and had disembarked as Hedy Lamarr, up-and-coming Hollywood film star. She had everything in front of her now and nothing was going to hold her back.

Chapter Six

September 1937

On her first day at work, Judy was apprehensive, though she was glad to have settled in to the room she had rented in Cambridge the week before. It was a modest bedsit, situated on the first floor of a large converted Victorian house with a small kitchenette and a view of the alley. The landlady had promised her that if another room came up with a view of the garden, she would put Judy's name on the list. But Judy had assured her the room would be fine for what she needed. Judy didn't plan to spend a lot of time staring out of the window, envisioning instead that she'd be visiting the great libraries in the city, and continuing her studies. Her landlady seemed kind, but of the no-nonsense variety. When Judy had arrived, she had showed her to her room but had been clear about the rules. "No gentlemen callers after six and no overnight visitors of either sex." Judy had assured her with reddening cheeks that she didn't intend to entertain either.

Cycling to work on her first day, she tried to calm her churning stomach. She hadn't even been able to have any breakfast, she'd been so nervous. Her letter confirming her appointment at the Cavendish Laboratory was tucked in her pocket with the message from the institute's director about how she was exactly the graduate they had been looking for.

Arriving at the address she had been given, Judy dismounted and parked her bicycle. It was a crisp day in early autumn, golden and scarlet leaves had already started to fall and, right above the bike rack, a magnificent horse chestnut tree was laden with an abundance of its green spiky husks. The ride in had frozen her cheeks and ears, and she took a minute to recover her breath. In front of her was an impressive entrance with late Victorian Gothic grandeur that had the words "Cavendish Laboratory" carved into an arch of cream stone over the front door.

As she stood working up the courage to go inside, a group of young men came out the front door, sidestepping her, deep in a conversation about radio frequency detection. As they passed her one of them winked at her, and she felt her cheeks glow as she looked down at her shoes, suddenly feeling awfully conscious of herself.

She was wearing a tweed skirt and a businesslike blouse, hoping that would be acceptable attire and also that it made her look a little older. She didn't want to be winked at; she wanted her peers to take her seriously.

Inside, the secretary at the front desk pointed her toward the office of the man who would be her manager. The name "Dr. Finnegan" was printed on a brass nameplate that was missing a screw on one side. After knocking gently on the door, she waited outside patiently. No one answered, so she knocked again a little harder.

"Come in," said a gruff voice.

She moved into the office and closed the door quietly behind her.

The large room was dark and oppressive, even with the bank of thin, elegant windows on one side. It smelled of stale tobacco and burned coffee and had the appearance of an overstuffed junk room. Every available space was filled with piles of files, books, and broken equipment. Three large bookcases were crammed to bursting, with their contents thrown haphazardly onto the shelves with little care. One book was even bent back on itself, straining at the spine. On the wall opposite the windows, a grubby chart hung with a brown stain and missing one of its drawing pins. Next to it, a degree sat crookedly in its frame. As her eyes adjusted to the dim light, she realized at the back of the office, behind another pile of files, a man was writing at a desk made level by yet another thin book thrust under a table leg. Judy hovered by the door and waited for him to finish. He was a large man with silver-rimmed glasses. With his head down over his desk, she could see his hair was starting to thin on top. His suit was slightly crumpled, the elbows looking thin and shining from wear. It felt like she waited forever before he finally looked up. Putting down his pen and seeing Judy, he instantly looked annoyed.

"Yes?" he said, with a tone that implied she was wasting his time.

"Dr. Finnegan," she managed to squeeze out in a tiny breathy voice.

He sat back in his seat, locking his hands together across his chest, looking her up and down, but didn't say anything in response.

She pulled the letter out of her pocket, feeling that she may need it to clarify who she was. Judy attempted to tone down her Welsh accent as she spoke. "Miss Morgan." He just peered at her, and she felt incredibly self-conscious as she tried again. "I'm Miss Morgan. Judy Morgan."

No response.

She continued, now unable to keep the tremble from her voice. "I believe you were expecting me today… I'm meant to start… here at the laboratory."

In response to her declaration, he grunted his obvious disapproval. Then opened his hand so that she could put the letter that she was fingering into it. Flicking it open with a twist of his wrist, he looked her over one more time and then started to read the words in front of him, all the time shaking his head and tutting.

Was she in the wrong place? Why was he making her feel so uncomfortable? He didn't even invite her to sit down.

Finishing the letter, he threw it carelessly into an overflowing in-tray. Taking off his glasses, he rubbed his forehead then dragged his hands down his face, stretching and circling his open jaw. Then, replacing his glasses, he addressed her directly for the first time.

"I'm going to be honest with you, Miss... Miss...?" He shook his head as though he had already forgotten or didn't care about her name.

"Morgan," she reminded him.

"I'm not a big fan of women taking men's jobs. I think a woman should be at home with her children, or at best working as a secretary. It wasn't me that assigned you to this lab. For whatever reason, the people higher up feel the need to bring in anyone that is qualified, even if they are female."

She swallowed down a huge lump in her throat. Throughout the years she'd been at Cambridge, there had sometimes been an underlying distrust of women working, as though they weren't clever enough to be able to understand all the scientific facts. But this was the very first time she'd seen such prejudice in another person, particularly as he didn't feel any need to hide it.

Finnegan stood up from his desk and paced to the window, looking out. With a deep sigh, he spoke to her as he stared out at the street. "I expect you to be on time. I expect you to work hard, harder than the men, to show me you're worth keeping. And I'll tell you, Miss Morgan," he continued, turning on his heels, "if for any reason you don't show me what I'm looking for, I won't have any problem replacing you with a man. No matter what people above me say."

She sucked in breath and her brimming feelings, totally mortified. She didn't know how to respond to any of this.

Shaking his head at her silence, he strode past her, grabbing his lab coat. He pulled open the door, thrust his hands into his pockets, and snapped at her to follow him as he marched off down the hall.

Hurriedly, Judy followed behind as she glanced over at his secretary, who gave her a sympathetic look, apparently already aware of her boss's feelings on employing women.

He marched her down a long corridor until they arrived at a door that said "Office 10" on it.

He strode inside. Meekly, she followed behind him.

"This is the office you will be assigned to. You'll have a partner, of course. Everyone has their own desks and working area."

She looked around the room; she knew there would be times when she would be doing calculations and reports in this office and times when she'd be building and testing equipment in the laboratory.

Large tables were already set out with blueprints of technical equipment and calculating charts. On the individual desks were pencils, slide rules, drawing equipment and graph paper to help the scientists document ongoing experiments. Groups of men were huddled around in lab coats and stopped to watch the unusual phenomenon as she entered. She automatically felt conspicuous. On one side there was a huge blackboard. Two men were in front of it working out a calculation.

She nodded in their direction as she followed Dr. Finnegan to the end of the room. "You'll be working here, with Mr. Jenkins."

The man he referred to, Mr. Jenkins, was sitting at a drawing board, huddled over some diagrams, pencil in hand. On the mention of his name, he swiveled on his stool and, seeing Judy, beamed.

Inwardly she breathed a sigh of relief. He had a friendly face, and, jumping to his feet, he put his hand out to greet her.

"Thomas Jenkins, but everyone calls me Tom," he stated.

Dr. Finnegan didn't seem fond of this familiarity.

"Mr. Jenkins," he said, correcting him sternly, as he cleared his throat. "You'll be working with Miss Morgan."

"I'm looking forward to it," said the man with another warm smile as he shook her hand.

"Well," said Finnegan, "I'll leave you to get acquainted. And if you have any problems, you talk to my secretary. Do you understand?"

Judy nodded and waited, holding her breath until she heard his footsteps altogether leave the room and the door shut behind him. It was as if the whole room exhaled and a friendly murmur came back around the office.

The man in front of her hovered nervously. He was large and awkward and though he was being friendly, he also appeared to come across a little shy, too.

"Don't call me Mr. Jenkins," he finally said. "I'm not too fond of that kind of formality. My name's Tom. And you are?"

She had no idea. She couldn't remember her name for a second, she was so shaken up by everything that had just happened.

He grinned. "I take it you do have a first name?" he enquired gently.

"Yes," she spluttered out, eventually. "Judy, I'm Judy Morgan."

"I can't wait to work with you, Judy. I, er… saw some of your work when you were studying with Rutherford."

She furrowed her eyebrows. "You studied at Cambridge too? Under Rutherford?"

"Yes, yes," he stated coyly, changing the subject. "Don't let Finnegan get under your skin. Apparently, he is a brilliant scientist, but no one thinks much of his management skills."

She was relieved it wasn't just her. She had so wanted to give a good first impression.

"Let me show you around, officially. Here's a place for you to hang your things," he said, pointing into the corner overflowing with men's coats and hats. Judy just stared at it. He shuffled from foot to foot and swallowed hard, apparently trying to work out what else to say. "I'll take you into the other room," he said at last, relieved to have filled in the awkward silence between them.

He ushered her into another room. "Here's the lab that we'll probably be doing a lot of work in. It's all new now, isn't it?" he commented, nodding toward the brand-new technology. She looked around her. Lining the walls were large steel-framed cabinets filled with the latest electrical equipment. Inside, valves glowed and relays hummed and bundles of wires connected panels of dials, meters and switches. In another area, there was a microscope protected behind a barrier. Two scientists were running an electrical test as they entered. And Tom continued to point out the types of measuring equipment in a whisper, with the hum of the test being done in the background.

He then walked her through to the lecture theatre.

"We come here for lectures and once a week for any updated information we need to take into account."

Judy nodded, looking around. It was similar to the lecture halls they'd been in at the university.

He escorted her back out, holding the door open for her.

Then they wound their way back through the corridor until they were back in the office where they'd begun.

"Are you ready to get started?" Tom asked.

Judy nodded. She was already feeling exhausted. Exhausted with the stress and tired with the feeling of unease.

The only saving grace was that Tom was so friendly. Sitting next to her at the desk, he started to familiarize her with everything they were working on at the moment. Now she felt comfortable. With blueprints and charts, she started to feel at home.

It was a couple of hours later when she was leaning over her desk, using her slide rule to double check some calculations, that her stomach emitted a large, low rumble and she was horrified. Judy hoped Tom hadn't heard it.

He didn't look up from his drawing board or pay any attention. But a little while later he appeared and offered her an apple.

"Would you like this? I've overpacked my lunch again and I thought, with all the busyness of it being your first day, you may not have had time for breakfast."

She took it from his hand and nodded her thanks as he walked off to finish his experiment. She hadn't even thought to pack a sandwich for lunch.

Judy managed to make it through her first day, grateful for Tom's apple, which kept her going. But as she cycled home, she was thoughtful. She was so grateful to be working for the Cavendish Lab, but she was also really concerned about Finnegan. Was he going to hold her back? He didn't seem like a man who would be happy to have her make any kind of strides in the scientific community. Her thoughts of changing the world for the good, and naive dream of becoming the next Marie Curie seemed ridiculous all of a sudden, and now she just hoped she could do well enough not to get sacked. The only bright spot in her day had been Tom. At least he would make her days a little more pleasant. But as far as her job went, she would have to work hard to prove herself. Still, that was exactly what she was going to do.

September 30, 1937

Dear Hedwig,

Well, I just finished my first full week of work, and I'm exhausted. Not quite as adventurous as sailing on the Normandie *and meeting movie studio executives. I'm amazed at your audacity. I so wish I could be braver like you.*

I like the lab I'm working in. However, my boss, Dr. Finnegan, is very difficult to work with. He didn't want a woman in this role, which he makes evident at every opportunity he can. I need to find some of your courage to be able to defend myself. I know I am lucky to get this position, but I also want to be able to stand up for myself when confronted with his prejudice.

What I'm working on is quite exciting, though I can't go into much detail. But I have a very pleasant lab partner. His name is Tom. He's helpful and tells jokes all day. Lately,

I have noticed he has started following me outside into the courtyard to have lunch with me even though it is starting to get chilly. I'm not sure if he's married. He doesn't talk much about his family. But he's a brilliant scientist, and I look forward to working with him over the next few years.

I love your new name. Hedy Lamarr! It sounds so glamorous. Not that you aren't glamorous, of course. And I know you're going to be an incredible actress. I can't wait to hear more about the films you will be working on. How exciting that you get to work in Los Angeles. Your description made me want to visit America—it sounds so different to here.

Well, don't forget to keep in touch. I've added my new address here in Cambridge. Keep me posted.

All my love,
Judy

Chapter Seven

March 1938

The driver swung the silver-blue Cadillac onto North Beverly Drive and slowly eased on the gas as it glided toward the studios. On the horizon, the sun had risen into a wedge of neat blue sky over the Hollywood hills, its golden glow still trailed by a ribbon of rising fog whose presence contradicted the already high morning temperature. Guarded by sentinels of towering palm trees, the car slipped by pastel-colored mansions wrapped in the same warm glow that encompassed everything in Los Angeles.

Hedy inhaled deeply, reveling in the intoxicating scent of gardenia flowers on the breeze, their fragrance a pleasant contrast to the tangy smell of lemon trees and wet grass still bathed in morning dew.

Running her fingers through her coif of soft brown hair, she tugged her sunglasses up onto her head, attempting to use them to corral the wisps of flyaway hair that whipped around her face, threatening to stick to her ruby-red lipstick. The studio would be doing her makeup for the shoot, but she hated to head out without something on her face.

The fresh-faced driver glanced back over his shoulder, flashing perfect white teeth and questioning eyes.

"Is this your first picture for MGM, Miss Lamarr?" he asked, raising his voice a little to be heard over the hum of the engine, his white-blonde hair rippling across his forehead.

Is it that obvious? she thought but wasn't about to admit it.

"I have made movies before," she responded, flashing a smile and averting her gaze, not wanting to elaborate. She hoped she was exuding the calm and sophistication she wanted to portray. She would be doing as much acting off camera as on, she presumed. She couldn't let anyone see who she really was. She had to make this work.

As he waited at a four-way stop, she turned her head from him, pretending to be engrossed in watching an older woman in a purple muumuu, full makeup, and sparkly earrings walking a tiny, fluffy, white dog.

She sensed his gaze as he fixed her in his rearview mirror.

"You're not American, are you?" he surmised, nodding his head, pleased with his assessment.

Hedy felt her stomach cramp; was her accent still so obvious? She had been studying like mad to learn English and practicing the American accent that she heard from announcers on the wireless to blend in since she had arrived.

Turning away, she answered him with another curt smile but said nothing, hoping that would end their conversation.

"I had that Miss Crawford in my car last week," he continued with pride, his arm muscle straining under his white shirt as he steered nonchalantly with one hand toward the lot. "Her usual driver wasn't available, so they asked me. She was a very nice lady. Gave me a huge tip."

I'm sure she did, on her salary, thought Hedy to herself. Her passage on the *Normandie* had cost most of her money and now she was living carefully on what she'd got from a pawn shop for her emerald earrings, until the studio check cleared. At least Mayer had been good to his word and he had signed her a seven-year contract, but she had been under a trial period and he hadn't put her to work straight away.

They arrived at the studio's cream-stoned entrance with the words "Metro-Goldwyn-Mayer Studios" emblazoned across the top, and, ducking out of his gatehouse, the guard nodded at her driver and waved them in. Inside the studio gates, it was like entering a different world.

Swarms of people in motion thronged their way ahead, many in costume, all bustling about the lot in the earnest business of making movies. The Cadillac driver shifted down to a crawl to avoid the heaving masses, once slamming on the brakes to allow two stagehands wearing the same style brown fedora hats, shirtsleeves rolled to the elbows, to guide a large flat painted with a depiction of the Rockies across their path. Hedy watched with amusement as they lumbered along, one with an unlit cigarette dangling from his lips, the other in mid-yawn, neither acknowledging the car that had nearly mowed them down—reaffirming that the making of movies had the right of way on the MGM lot.

As they idled in the hot sunshine, the smell of gasoline fumes mingled with the rising heat. A gaggle of chorus girls, dressed identically in black and white polka-dot dresses with starched ruffled petticoats and red bows in their lacquered curls, clipped past them in their tap shoes. As they rattled along, they chatted animatedly with each other, and Hedy caught conversations about sore feet and the unbearable heat on one of the soundstages even though it was barely 10 a.m. Hedy swiped perspiration from her own forehead and felt frustrated. She needed to get out of this heat too, before the makeup melted off her face, and would have got out and walked if she'd had any idea of where she was heading. She had just been given a soundstage number and had no idea where in this swirling world of constant activity it could be.

The car inched forward again as a man, followed by a bustling entourage, turned a corner and strode in front of them. He had thick dark hair and wore an open-collared shirt and cream linen pants. In one hand, he held a lit cigarette and, folded under the other arm, a script. Hedy could tell by the stir created in his wake that he was "somebody." But it wasn't until they inched closer that

she realized it was her co-star in the film she was making, Charles
Boyer. He had been the instigator of getting Mayer to star her in
this picture after they had met at a party. As they crawled past him,
he noticed her straight away and beamed.

"Well, if it isn't the lovely Hedy Lamarr, my beautiful leading
lady," he exclaimed in his sexy French accent, its lilt comforting
her, and she enjoyed the connection of another European. He had
promised to hold her hand through her first Hollywood movie.

Hedy returned his smile. "Need a ride?" she drawled.

He shook his head. "I like the exercise. Besides, it's just the
next stage over."

Hedy placed her hand on her driver's shoulder. "I'll get out here,"
she said, "if you wouldn't mind some company?" she enquired of
her co-star.

"I would be delighted," he responded, opening the door and
helping her out.

"Here, kid," she said, leaning into the Cadillac and tipping him
well. His eyes lit up; he would never know that was the only money
she had for lunch. But who needed to eat anyway? She wouldn't
have Joan Crawford hearing how that new up-and-coming Hedy
Lamarr was tight with her money.

Placing her sunglasses back down to cover her eyes, she swished
alongside Charles in her periwinkle wide-leg pants and a figure-
hugging sleeveless cerise blouse she knew showed off her figure to
the best of its advantage. As they walked, she enjoyed the excited
hum all around them as extras caught sight of him, making his
way to work.

"Have you learned your lines?" he joked with her as he took
a drag of his cigarette and, shifting his script, plunged his other
hand into his pocket.

Hedy nodded. "Every last one of them," she sang back. "Have
you?" she enquired, throwing back her head and shaking out her
now-dampened curls.

Charles laughed. "I'm sure I will have plenty of time while you are in makeup."

They turned in to the crowded soundstage that had the number emblazoned on the outside. And once her eyes acclimated to the dark inside, Hedy was transported to the Hollywood version of North Africa for the film *Algiers*. With the way the temperature was already climbing, inside would reach Algerian temperatures for realism before long. Extras were already milling about, napkins tucked around their necks to protect costumes from their dark makeup. Men in multicolored kaftans and red felt fezzes, women in belted pants and colored yasmaks. Set dressers were busy rolling out yards of sheer red fabric on a fixed bed and patting dust out of round velvet cushions. Above their heads, stagehands shouted to one another as they swung in a North African backdrop that would have felt like the real thing if it had been accompanied by the smell of North African spices instead of the engine grease from the hoist and fresh, wet paint.

Hedy tried not to show how in awe she was. In the movies she had featured in in Austria, they had always been on a tight budget and she had never seen anything like this before. An elegant woman strode up to greet her; by her side, her assistant wore a crisp white apron carried a bolt of fabric over one arm and there were two dress pins attached to her collar.

Hedy acknowledged her curtly and extended her hand in a businesslike manner.

"Miss Lamarr, I'm Irene Lentz. I'm taking care of costuming this picture. We got your measurements ahead of time, but I need you to try on a couple of the outfits we have set aside as I'm not sure your size is right."

Charles Boyer stamped out his cigarette with a mischievous grin. "It looks all right to me."

Hedy flashed him a cheeky smile as she followed the dresser into the wardrobe department. She was busy trying on different black and white hats to match the black dress she would be wearing for a scene toward the end of the movie when her director found her.

John Cromwell was a tall, thin man with hawk-like features, a wiry mustache, and a perpetually disappointed expression. He had come up through the theater, which had influenced his "*we're all pulling together to make the best movie we can*" spirit. Wearing a neat bow-tie and tweed jacket, he entered the room as one of Irene's assistants was switching out a black hat for a white one with a black polka-dot veil.

"Miss Lamarr." He smiled, removing a hand from his pocket and shaking hers. "I'm really looking forward to working with you."

Hedy just nodded. As her English wasn't that great yet, she didn't want him to fire her because he thought her accent too strong.

He started to set up the scene they would shoot that afternoon with her in it, only half of which Hedy understood. He must have mistaken her quietness for fear, because as he left he reassured her, "I have been talking to my cinematographer and we are planning to film you in a way that will give Garbo a run for her money. So, nothing to worry about, you're in safe hands."

She smiled, feeling the pressure again. He was talking about her and Greta Garbo in the same sentence and all she could think about was she had seen Garbo the year before in her latest film, back when she'd still been married to Fritz. And now she was here.

He stepped outside and then poked his head back in the door as if he had a final thought. "Not that I'm telling you how to do your job, but if you're looking for an opinion, Irene, I like the one with the polka dots," he remarked to the costume designer.

Once she had been through makeup, Hedy walked onto the set that afternoon. There was a hush on the soundstage as she took her place in the scene. She began reciting her lines to herself over and over again as she waited for her co-star. Even though this was her first day on set, they would be filming a scene close to the end, when she and Boyer would have to kiss, and she wished it had been something with less pressure.

As cameras rolled into place and lights were adjusted to illuminate her beauty to its full advantage, Boyer strode onto the set and took his position, draping across the bed where the scene would take place. Sensing her nervousness, he squeezed her hand. Just as they were about to roll, a commotion on the set distracted the crew, and with a sinking heart, she saw Mayer had come down to watch her first day of shooting. She was already feeling so much pressure; this was not helping.

They started to film and she forgot her first line. Shaking his head, Cromwell made a joke about first-day jitters and they started rolling again. But each time she struggled to make her words have any expression. After about thirty minutes, Cromwell came over to give her further direction and she could see he was concerned.

"It's her first day," reminded Boyer protectively. "I'll work with her, don't worry."

He smiled over at Hedy, but she just felt sick. While they took a break to change the reels, she strode outside for some fresh air. She desperately wanted a cigarette, but she was in costume and she knew she may need to kiss Boyer if she ever made it through the scene's opening lines. When she came back on set, she noticed Mayer and Cromwell deep in conversation. God, she couldn't get sacked her first day.

She panicked as she made her way back to the prop bed.

Boyer gave her an encouraging smile as the director called action and he delivered his line again. "You're beautiful, that's easy to say…"

The director called a hold, again. There was a problem with the sound. As he did, Mayer took his chance to walk over and address her. "Have a good shoot. And, Hedy, don't worry about anything else but looking beautiful. I have been speaking to John and we realize that you are new to this, so he's going to do lots of lingering close-ups. I've decided to work with the ad department and we will work up a big campaign, promoting you as the most beautiful woman in the world. People will just flock to the cinema to look at you, so you don't have to be worried about a great performance. Your face did that for you already."

He nodded, looking very pleased with himself as he left the soundstage, but Hedy was humiliated and angry. Yes, she planned to use her beauty to help her win parts, but she wanted to be taken seriously for what she could do as well. Biting her tongue—as she remembered Stefan's advice to control her anger when all she wanted to do was tell Mayer where to stick his contract—instead she offered Boyer a placating smile and fought back the frustration that threatened to turn into tears.

"I think I will go to the bathroom while they are repairing the sound," she whispered.

Boyer nodded, swinging his legs off the bed and lighting a cigarette. He thrust his free hand into his pocket as he wandered away, preoccupied. She could tell that even though he was being kind to her, he was concerned too. After all, this was his reputation as well, if the film bombed.

Sweeping into the bathroom, she strode into a stall, slammed and locked the door, carefully swiping away the tears that were brimming. Blinking her eyes to dry her lashes, she swallowed down her hot emotions. She didn't have time to go back to makeup, and the last thing she needed was for her eyes to be red and swollen on the screen.

Hedy sat on the seat and felt all her frustration. What had made her think she could do this? As she sat deep breathing to contain her boiling temper, her late father's encouragement interrupted her gloom. He had always instilled a sense of resilience in her. Her thoughts drifted to a time when she had been a young child and they had been walking through the streets of Vienna at twilight, and he had stopped her to watch an electric street lamp burst into life, a fairly new and exciting event. He had crouched down beside her to teach her about the miracle of electricity as she'd stood wide-eyed and in awe.

"Did you see that, Hedwig?" he had enthused. "No gas, no lamplighter or flame. Just invisible current."

"It's like magic," she had murmured as her father had explained how it worked, then added, "Mr. Edison never gave up until he had perfected that light bulb you see there." He pointed his finger toward the glowing bulb. "It took him a long time and many failures. When someone asked him about that he said, 'I have not failed. I've just found ten thousand ways that won't work.' Our greatest weakness lies in giving up. The most certain way to succeed is always to try just one more time."

Her father had pulled her close then, whispering into her ear, "Remember that, Hedwig. Not everything will come easy; you just have to figure out what is wrong and do something about it. Then, my darling, you will make your own magic."

Hedy was bolstered by her late father's words. That's what she was going to do. Let them bill her as nothing more than a beautiful face if they wanted to. She would make her own magic. She'd work hard, harder than anyone else, and become the best actress in the world, so one day they would have to take her seriously. With that, she stood up and opened the door, and, shaking off all the insecurities of Hedwig Kiesler, she strode out onto the set as Hedy Lamarr.

March 14, 1938

Dear Judy,

Tom? And who is this "very pleasant lab partner"? You skirted over him quite quickly in your letter, without any juicy facts.

How tall is he? Is he handsome? Does he hold your test tubes for you? (Ha ha!) I know I'm playing with you, but I want to know all the details of this mysterious man in your life. I had a silly little fling myself when I first got here, with a very handsome British actor. It was wonderful but brief, and all over before it even began. I wasn't upset; I am too busy working and concentrating on my career to worry too much about love at this stage.

And yes, Judy, you do need to stand up for yourself, know your worth. You have worked hard at university to get that job. Don't let some man put you down and make you feel less about yourself.

Since I arrived in California a few months ago, I have finally started working on a film. I was thrilled to get the opportunity to star opposite Charles Boyer, who is very popular over here.

Though I won't lie to you, it is so much more complicated than I thought, and all the audacity in the world doesn't stand a hope if I can't do the job. It's not the acting, though I had terrible stage fright on my first day of shooting. Just with my accent and the fact I am still learning English, I feel I am missing something. I only really understand about half of what the director is asking me to do, and the other day, I heard someone whisper the word "wooden" when describing me to another actor. I guessed it meant the same in English as it does in German. I did give that man a piece of my mind, but I was also crushed. I want to do well and get good parts. I see other English-speaking actresses getting parts I could do standing on my head, and I worry that I will never get a chance to prove myself.

Anyway, this is just a quick note. I'm waiting outside Mr. Mayer's office. There may be a part coming up for me, and he wants to talk to me about it.

By the way, I now also have an agent, which is very exciting. Who knows, Judy? Maybe this will all go somewhere after all.

Much love to you and your new mysterious man…

Kiss, kiss,

Hedy

Chapter Eight

Early spring 1938

Judy settled into her work at the Cavendish. There was plenty to keep her busy with the ongoing concern of a possible war with Germany. The whole country was on tenterhooks, and the entire scientific community was geared toward working on military equipment to aid the potential troops, if required.

It wasn't long after she started her job that she began to work on radio waves, looking into their potential use against enemy forces. One morning, she and Tom were summoned to the lecture hall for a special secret presentation by two scientists working for the Telecommunications Research Establishment on behalf of the Royal Air Force, Edward Shire and Amherst Thomson.

Judy was familiar with their work, as were the rest of her colleagues. They filed into the large lecture room and sat down. On the blackboard was a chalk drawing of a missile being fired, with a trajectory line sketched to the intended target. It didn't take long for the two scientists to communicate the research they wanted to share.

"If we eventually go to war," Shire stated, "one of the most important things we need to be effective at is destroying military targets." He stepped toward the desk, where a huge box was placed. "We have invented a technology we call the proximity fuse. It is a type of radio-wave-activated explosive that would mean a shell could be detonated close to its target and we wouldn't have to hit it head on. This can be used in several ways and create a lot of damage. The problem is the size." He lifted it up for the audience to see.

Next to the box, there was a much smaller metallic silver bullet-shaped cylinder, which the other scientist held up in his hand so they could compare the dimensions.

"This is about the size of an artillery shell. We need to make this large box fit into this explosive. What you'll be doing here at Cavendish is working on reducing down this electrical technology so it can fit into the cap of this warhead."

Judy took extensive notes and felt a rising excitement in her stomach. As a physicist, she had a singular passion for reducing electronics and had always hoped that she could work on that specific team. But ever since Judy had started the year before, she had only been assisting on other projects. She'd not yet gotten to work on something so firmly in her wheelhouse.

Tom murmured something similar to her while they were taking a break. "I think they're going to ask you to be on this team, Judy. This is absolutely your expertise."

Judy smiled but also felt nervous. At the end of the presentation, the two renowned scientists passed out documentation. She and Tom studied the specifics. Already, her mind was whirring with all the different ways that she could make the technology smaller. She could take the usual wireless valve and shrink it down, using various new components.

At the end of the lecture, Finnegan came over specifically to introduce the visiting scientists to Tom and Judy.

"This is Mr. Jenkins," said Finnegan, ignoring Judy completely. "We're thinking he will be working on this."

Tom looked a little bit annoyed at the fact Judy hadn't been introduced, so he remedied the situation. "This is Miss Judy Morgan. To be fair, this is *her* expertise," he said, and he started to outline all that she'd been working on, which was the exact technology that was going to be needed.

Finnegan interrupted Tom, seeming to grow impatient with being required to recognize Judy's talents, and didn't even give her a chance to add to the discourse. As he dominated the conversation, she felt herself reddening and once again cursed her shyness. She had so much to say on the subject but was never given a moment to add her opinion.

Later, when she and Tom were back in the office, he confessed his surprise that he had been asked, and not her, to head up the team.

Judy shrugged her shoulders.

"At least I will be working on something for the greater good," she insisted, trying not to let her own discouragement show. "And you will do a fine job, Tom. There is plenty of time for me to head up a team in the future."

Even with that day's disappointment, that night, she could barely sleep. Judy couldn't wait to get back to the lab the next day and get started. This was precisely the kind of project that she'd wanted to work on since she had started at the Cavendish. It was an ingenious idea that radio waves could activate and trigger explosives. That could be used in so many ways to protect their troops, not just on land, but at sea and in the air.

The next day, she and Tom started work. And she worked so hard that day she was barely aware of lunchtime, until Tom told her they must stop and eat. So passionate was she about her subject, that was how most days went from then on.

It took them about six months to develop the proximity fuse prototype, and they couldn't wait to present their development to the rest of their scientific community.

On the day before their presentation, Judy and Tom were working through quite a complicated final hypothesis on the blackboard when Dr. Finnegan walked into the office. He paced up and down impatiently as he listened to Judy talking Tom through the calculation she had been doing. Finnegan peered over Tom's shoulder, but they continued in their work, neither of them wishing to look away from the in-depth place they were in. Eventually, their boss coughed unceremoniously.

Judy flicked her eyes to him and turned. "Can we help you with something, Dr. Finnegan? Is this about the presentation tomorrow?"

"Not exactly," he said in his authoritative tone, which Judy knew meant that he would ask something of them they weren't going to like. "My secretary, Miss Stenner, is out again today, and they fear it might be her tonsils, which could mean a couple of weeks of her being home."

Judy tried not to let the anger ball up inside her, as she had a feeling she knew where this conversation was going.

Tom swiveled on his heels. "Do you have a replacement for her in mind? We have some important documentation coming through from London today for the presentation tomorrow."

Finnegan's eyes settled on Judy's forehead, and he cleared his throat before he spoke. "That's why I'm here. Miss Morgan, we need someone to stand in for a few days, and I know you have some skills in this area."

Tom looked questioningly to Judy. The confusion evident on his face, but Judy knew exactly what Dr. Finnegan meant. "If you're talking about typing," she responded in a flat and even tone, "then I took no more than any other university undergraduate. I did the same as Tom and the other gentlemen in this lab."

"Ah, yes," he said, starting to pace up and down as he continued, "of course, but I think this kind of work is much more suited to you." Judy knew that all he was missing at the end of the sentence was "because you're a woman."

Tom's face was flushed scarlet; clearly, he was as frustrated with what was being asked as she was. "We are in the midst of something significant right now. We have to prepare for tomorrow," he stated, attempting to keep his tone even, but Judy could sense his panic.

Dr. Finnegan started to lose his patience. "But you already told me you have important documentation coming in, Mr. Jenkins. I surely need someone at that post for when that arrives. Without

Miss Stenner, everything we are doing would grind to a halt. Miss Morgan, just be a good girl and fill in for a couple of days, will you? I'm sure I can get one of the other men to help you out with these calculations, Mr. Jenkins, and I'm sure Miss Morgan doesn't mind stepping in when she is needed. We've all got to pull our weight, haven't we?"

Judy looked across at Tom, her expression resolute.

"I'll open the post," she informed Tom, "and then I'll check in with you at lunchtime. We can cover anything else important later."

Tom stood back, a stream of frustrated air leaving his body. The tension in the room was palpable, but Finnegan didn't seem to notice.

As she headed to the door, her boss spoke to her again. "Any chance of getting a cup of tea as well, my dear? There's a good girl."

Judy looked back over her shoulder toward Tom, and though she didn't say anything, she hoped her face betrayed her disgust.

Ten minutes later, she made her way quickly into Miss Stenner's office. This wasn't the first time she'd been asked to do something like this, and it was beginning to get old. Apart from Tom, so many of them just thought of her as a secretary in a lab coat. Why did she have to do this just because she was a woman? She wasn't even that good at it. She looked at the pile of letters waiting in the in-tray and, sighing, pulled off her lab coat, hung it on the back of the door, and, sitting down, took a deep breath. The sooner she got through it, the sooner she could get back to Tom. She thought about the cup of tea she'd just delivered to her boss's desk. Waitress and secretary—was there no end to her required talents?

She beavered through as much of the correspondence as she could, cursing her fingers that were so adept at handling circuitry but were all thumbs on a typewriter. She tried not to panic as she thought of Tom trying to finish everything alone.

At lunchtime she rushed back to the office, and the pair of them worked through their lunch hour and late into the evening to make all the final preparations for their presentation. Neither of them said it; they both seemed to feel the discouragement of their boss's complete inability to see her for the scientist she was.

April 10, 1938

Dear Hedy,

Mysterious man??? You made me blush! As far as looks go, Tom is actually very pleasant looking, not movie-star handsome as you are seeing every day, but he has a lovely smile and is very kind and courteous. And we are JUST lab partners.

Well, spring has finally arrived here in England after a very drizzly and cold winter. It is lovely to see the daffodils flowering and the beginning of new growth on the trees. I'm glad you are feeling settled in California. I imagine the weather there is vastly different to here. I picture you sitting by the pool as you learn your lines before going out for something called brunch.

I am also starting to find my feet in my job at the Cavendish. The nice thing about being in Cambridge is that it's all familiar to me. The only thing that continues to mar my working day is Finnegan. He continues to see me as some sort of glorified secretary. And it's so frustrating that, coupled with my shyness, it means I spend most of my time feeling exasperated around him. There's so much I want to add when we are discussing specific experiments, but I just become tongue-tied. I am going to try and be braver, as you encourage me to be. It's just not natural for me and I can always think of many wonderful and clever things to say back to him... but only as I lie in bed at night, hours later.

The news in Europe continues to be of a great concern here, as I'm sure you are following in your American newspapers.

You will have seen about the Austrian Anschluss, of course. I hope all your loved ones are safe. Hitler seems to be gaining power all the time. And everybody here is quietly concerned that things will continue to get worse, though our Prime Minister still believes there is a place for diplomacy to stop things escalating.

This situation, however, has brought a heightened excitement within the lab that we can do something to help, and right now, the government is ploughing money into research and anything we can do to prepare the country just in case.

So glad to hear the movie you are working in is going well; Charles Boyer sounds very jolly. Don't let the man who runs the studio get you down either. In some ways, though our jobs are very different, we're both in very similar situations, me with Dr. Finnegan and you with Mr. Mayer. I'm going to try and find a way to stand up to Finnegan's bullying and you should too. One day he will see past your looks and give you the parts that you want, just as one day I hope to prove myself to the point that I'll be able to lead a team.

Well, I must go. I'm writing to you during my lunch break, and that MM (mysterious man) just came outside with his sandwiches and I don't want him to see I am writing about him. Also, even though it has been wet today, the sun just decided to make an appearance. Though I love the warmth on my face, I'm finding it hard to see what I'm writing as I sit here. But I'm not complaining. I can't wait for summer.

Keep me posted about everything and thank you for your letters.

I'll write again soon,

Much love,
Judy

Chapter Nine

Early 1939

It was during a party at MGM to celebrate the announcement of her next movie, *Lady of the Tropics* starring opposite Robert Taylor, that Hedy saw her old friend Douglas Fairbanks Jr. "Well, if it isn't the songbird," he said, pulling a French cigarette from his lips as a twirl of smoke circled her face, his English accent clipped with its usual hint of mirth. "How are you doing, Miss Kiesler? Found any happy songs to sing lately?"

"Didn't you hear? I'm back on the market now my divorce from my crazy first husband is finalizing, so I will keep singing more sad songs till I find that love of my life."

"If only I was single," he flirted, kissing her hand. "One day, we need to work together," he added with a smile.

"I'd love that. Maybe you should talk to Mr. Mayer about it. He seems to only want me to do movies about exotic women with mystique. That's the way he keeps casting me, anyway."

"I have an idea," he said, grabbing a glass of champagne from a waiter passing with a tray. "Mary and I are having a few friends over this weekend. Maybe you could make some more contacts, have some director fall in love with you and cast you in his next musical. You could learn to sing some happy songs."

Hedy smiled at the thought.

Fairbanks continued. "Do you think you could join us at our place on Catalina Island? It will be very low-key, just swimming, drinking, and fishing. Just me and some other Hollywood types—

John Wayne, Ward Bond—and there will be some other people that you might like. It would give you some relaxation time before you had to start work."

"I've really got to learn my lines," she responded with a deep sigh.

Fairbanks shook his head defiantly, apparently not taking no for an answer as he took a sip of his champagne. "It's the perfect place. You can lie on the beach or sit all day and watch the men fish and learn your lines. Come on. It will be fun."

Hedy was tempted, not only as a career move—sometimes she found that socializing like this was actually the best way to get offers of work. But also, it'd be nice to let her hair down and have some fun with new friends before they got into the painstaking, daily, grueling schedule of making movies. As glamorous as it looked on the outside, it was a lot of hard work. Often up early in the morning for makeup and staying up late into the evening learning lines.

"Okay," she said.

"You can bring someone if you want, if there is someone special?"

"No, it's just me right now."

"Well, allow me to escort you to Catalina. I'll come and pick you up."

She smiled. "That would be delightful."

The following weekend, she found herself racing down the 99 in Fairbanks's open-top silver-blue sports car.

"If I knew you were going to pick me up in an open-top," she screamed to him through the bluster of the wind rushing between them, all the while trying to cling on to the brim of her hat, "I wouldn't have bothered having my hair done."

He roared with laughter.

They soon arrived at the most beautiful beach house, a sprawling pink villa with Grecian-style pillars and a well-kept lawn that descended right onto the beach. People were already milling around, and before she met anyone she dashed upstairs to tidy herself up. As much as this was a party, she, like many of the other women in

Hollywood, always felt she was on display and even off the screen needed to give a flawless performance. On arriving downstairs, someone handed her a cocktail, and Fairbanks introduced her to the other guests. There were many she didn't know.

"Now, here's someone you might find interesting," he said, "Mr. Gene Markey. He's a screenwriter, so be nice to him because he can make you sound fantastic, or the opposite."

"I wouldn't dream of doing that to such an enchanting lady," Markey mused back with a twinkle in his eyes, and there was something she instantly liked about him. Most men she talked to would look her up and down as they met her. This guy didn't take his eyes from hers, kindly talking to her. He was absorbing, though plain-looking, in his late thirties she guessed. Dark, with a square chin and a thick neck.

But the fact that he wasn't that good-looking seemed to fade into the background as they got into a lively conversation. He was fascinating to talk to. He also treated her with such respect, making sure that they found somewhere comfortable for her to sit, being attentive to her needs, listening to everything she had to say with great interest.

They talked late into the afternoon, and when the rest of the men went off to fish the next day, he stayed behind to keep her company. She explained to him about her lines, and he was happy to run them with her. They sat out together on the veranda, sipping pink lemonade, reading through her script, stretched out on Fairbanks's comfortable gray and white striped loungers. He wore a mushroom-colored suit, a silk paisley patterned cravat in the same hue tucked into the neck of an ivory shirt. She wore her salmon-colored pedal pushers, buckled with a thick black patent belt, a black-and-white striped tank top and a white crepe blouse. At her ears were her now-favorite clip-on saltwater pearls with the silky, white luster and a single strand of the same was around her neck. As she read her lines, he encouraged her in her delivery and gave her feedback when she wanted it. And Hedy found she really enjoyed his company. She hadn't felt this comfortable around another man since the last time she'd been with Stefan, her best friend. She had recently had a letter from him informing her that, with the ongoing unrest in Europe created by both Hitler and Mussolini, he had been moved to London by his editor to continue his work.

Markey was a man who was completely different to Fritz, she realized. Her ex-husband had been so controlling, possessive, and obsessed with his own happiness. Gene seemed only obsessed with hers and what she needed. By the end of the weekend, they were more than just friends, and she knew they would start dating. She'd heard he'd been married to another Hollywood star, and they talked about it. But he was honest about his feelings regarding the unrealistic world of Hollywood, honest about his life. He was genuinely a breath of fresh air.

What followed was a whirlwind romance. And before she'd even finished her next picture, they were wildly in love. It was nothing like her first marriage. They had deep and meaningful conversations about everything. He was kind and articulate, and very funny and for once, she was starting to feel really loved. She often revisited Fritz's words. "You're only good for one thing, and no one in this world is ever going to want you for anything else." The words still kicked her in the gut whenever she thought about them and she hoped that Fritz would choke on his breakfast when he read about the man who was now so besotted with her, and treated her like a queen.

He proposed to her the month after the picture closed, on a beach at sunset in Malibu, where they had been taking a vacation, and she knew she had to say yes.

A number of weeks later, on the day she was leaving for Mexico to get married, there was a knock at the door, and she couldn't believe it when she opened it. There on the doorstep stood Stefan.

She burst into tears. "What are you doing here?" she asked, as he came in and hugged her deeply.

"I couldn't let my best friend get married without me to give her away, now could I?" he said, breaking into a broad smile.

"How did you even know to come?"

"I got your letter announcing your engagement and decided to reply in person. I couldn't miss your wedding. I want to know all about this man who thinks he is worthy of you."

"Oh, you'll love Gene," she said, glowing. "He's the most wonderful person in the world."

"He'd better be, for you, Hedwig."

All at once she felt calm and whole. Here was her dear oldest friend, who loved her more than anything in the world, who would give her away to a man who appeared to do the same.

They both traveled to Mexico together with Gene, and Stefan stood smiling proudly at her side as she married the man of her dreams.

April 14, 1939

Judy, darling,

I've got the most amazing news to tell you. I got married!!!!
Can you believe it? I am so in love, I can barely sleep and I'm so glad I went to that party I was invited to where I met Gene. He's everything that Fritz wasn't. He's kind and attentive and so funny. I just can't believe that I finally have someone who really loves me for who I am, and I know Gene does. It's been a total whirlwind romance and he adores wining and dining me. He drops by my set every day to bring me little gifts or flowers. We have even decided to adopt a baby together. We ran away to Mexico for the ceremony and I'm so deliriously happy. My darling childhood friend Stefan

turned up to surprise me too—have I told you about him? He's like the brother I never had. I'm not his type if you catch my drift, but he's the most fun, with the kindest heart in the world. Though Gene and I only had one weekend away on our honeymoon before I had to come back to work.

Right now, I'm sitting outside the soundstage, waiting for them to call me back on the set in a minute. It is so hot inside I'm attempting to get some fresh air while I'm waiting for the final scenes on the movie I'm working on, *Lady of the Tropics*. We are having to film extra scenes, as our lovely director, Jack Conway, has been taken ill and Mayer has sent over another director, Leslie Fenton, to take over shooting some of the scenes that have been missed. It's created a little bit of drama here because the film is already set to open in August. It is an enjoyable film and cast, though I'm unfortunately playing another pouting foreigner. I do hope that once my accent gets better, they'll start casting me in other things. I don't mind them trading on my looks for now, but like I told you before, it would be nice to get my teeth into something meatier.

It is frightening to hear what's happening in Europe. My heart breaks for Austria and all the people I left behind who are still there. I hope that a miracle will happen and put a stop to Hitler's expansion across Europe. We all sit here, reading the newspapers, and we're shocked at everything that is going on. Though I was glad to read yesterday that both France and Britain pledged their support to Rumania and Greece if they are attacked. Though it does leave your little island in a vulnerable position in standing up to the Reich like that.

Please stay safe, Judy. I've been trying to get my mother out of Austria for a while, and at last she's in England. I am hoping in the next few months after this film is finished to be able to get over there to London and bring her back with me. Of course, if I come, we have to find time to see each other. Though I will know more about the timing once we can figure out a visa for her. It is still very hard to get one for America but we're hoping to get her into Canada and then eventually to the U.S.

It is difficult to imagine the unrest in Europe when life here is so very different in California. I have to admit, though, Los Angeles suits me. I love the world of Hollywood. And most of my leading men are delightful, though I did have an unpleasant experience last week...

I had a table read for another movie I'm in that's coming up next year with an actor called Spencer Tracy. I don't know if you know him. He's quite popular over here but we did NOT hit it off. I nearly lost my temper with him so many times. He came across as quite sullen and stand-offish to me, and I could just tell he didn't like me very much. Keep your fingers crossed that the movie goes well regardless.

Anyway, I have to go. The makeup artist needs to put more dark makeup on my face. I am wearing so much in this movie.

Take care and keep up the excellent work.

Much love, Hedy xxx

TELEGRAM

CONGRATULATIONS (STOP) I AM SO VERY HAPPY FOR YOU (STOP)
POSTING OFF A GIFT TOMORROW (STOP)
MUCH LOVE JUDY (STOP)

MISS JUDY MORGAN
10:10 AM

*

September 4, 1939

My dearest Hedy,

I'm sure by now you have heard our terrible news. War was declared here yesterday. I know we'd all talked about it, and in many ways, we'd prepared for it, but nothing can make you ready for such a shock. As it was a Sunday, my landlady, Mrs. Greenwood, invited me into her little kitchen so we could hear the Prime Minister's speech on her tiny wireless after the 11 a.m. deadline for Hitler to respond. I remember sitting there in her dimly lit kitchen, gripping a cup of tea that turned cold in my hand with a tap dripping in the background, and neither of us was able to speak or move to turn it off as we attempted to let the words sink in.

At work the next day, the fear was palpable in our office as we were instructed to prepare. We went through several drills of how to evacuate to the shelter quickly if, or when, bombs are to rain down on our country. I hope more than anything that that doesn't happen as it has happened in Poland. We were all also trained on how to put on our gas masks quickly. We were issued them a few months ago with the ongoing concern. I have to take it everywhere with me now, as there is talk of us being fined if you are seen without it. It is a constant, sad reminder that doesn't let me forget what is going on. Then because we are a laboratory and there are many combustible materials, we spent all today securing things safely in case of an attack.

I wish I could say I was putting on a brave face, but honestly, Hedy, between you and me, I'm terrified. I feel so far away from my parents in Wales and so alone here in

Cambridge. I wish you were here to make me laugh or to tell me a joke or one of your funny stories about your work in the movies. I could do with a good friend's shoulder to cry on right now. Instead, I'm doing what everybody else in Britain is doing, trying to put it out of my mind, get on with my work, and follow our Prime Minister's advice, to play our part with calmness and courage.

Please take care of yourself, dear Hedy, and please keep us all in your thoughts and prayers.

Much love, always,
Judy

September 25, 1939

Oh, my darling.

I am sending reinforcements to bolster your spirits and embolden your courage. Look out for a large package of chocolate, and I'll try to find a way to sneak some alcohol your way through my contacts in England. Also, I'm going shopping in Beverley Hills to see if there's somewhere I can find a stylish tin helmet for you. The ones I see in the newspapers are awfully dull.

All joking aside, I am thinking of you and praying for you all back there and look forward to better days. Let's hope this will all be over very soon.

Much love always,
Hedy. Kiss, kiss.

Chapter Ten

October 1939

Judy paced up and down the office, waiting for Tom to return. He had gone to use the telephone in the main office to call the test site and find out if they were ready. She had not even taken her coat off since she had arrived for work that morning. When she finally saw his face appear at the door, he was beaming.

"All set, Judy," he said cheerfully as he opened the door. "Let's get going." She felt the butterflies in her stomach as she tightened the belt on her coat and walked to join him.

After their presentation the year before, which had been received with great enthusiasm, they were now at the next step. Today was the day they'd be testing the prototype of the proximity fuse warhead they'd been working on. Since war had been declared the month before, it added even more pressure to their work as they raced to keep the Allies a step ahead of the German technology. They had taken the first prototype that had been given to them by Shire and Thomson, and they'd managed to get it down smaller so they could fit it to a rocket and test it. It would need to be redesigned to become even smaller to fit in regular ammunition shells, but this at least would test it at this size and make sure that it was working correctly.

That morning, she and Tom traveled out to the test site together. Judy could barely speak, she was so nervous. Tom, on the other hand, seemed unable to stop talking.

"The technicians said it would be all set up by the time we get there. I don't know if Finnegan's going to be there, but he might be. At least we've got a nice day for it," he continued to babble on as they drove toward the area that was set up for military testing. They arrived at the restricted area and drove up to the gate where military police waited for them.

Tom rolled down his window and showed their papers. "Judy Morgan and Tom Jenkins. We're the scientists involved in the test today." The military guard looked over their paperwork and nodded.

"At the back of the field, sir. Past the hangars on the left here. Everything's been set up for you."

Tom nodded and smiled. He rolled up the window and looked at his lab partner. "Well, here we go, Judy Morgan. Time to see if this works."

They drove across the grounds. Military personnel were everywhere, and the munitions experts were finishing setting up the site. They were greeted by Chief Armourer Hellard, a tall, lean man with a prominent nose and red wavy hair, who escorted them to the area they would be observing from, as Judy looked up at the sky. It had been rainy and misty that morning, but now, at least, it was clear with overcast gray clouds. It would make it easier to see the rockets, which she was grateful for. As she approached the test site, she noticed that Finnegan was already there waiting, and her stomach clenched. He had told them the day before he wasn't sure if he would be able to make it to the test, and inwardly she'd hoped that he was busy. She would have much rather just given him a report the day afterward. Now she would feel the pressure. If something went wrong, she knew once again she would be blamed for it.

Tom reassured her. "It's going to be fine, Judy. Don't let him intimidate you," he whispered, nodding in their boss's direction. Far off across the firing range, three gunmetal-gray balloons were suspended hundreds of feet in the air, bobbing and weaving in the gentle breeze, trying to escape their cables. Hanging from each of the balloons was a half-sized mockup of an airplane. Each was constructed in different materials to check the radar systems and see if they could sense them to trigger an explosion.

At the field table, a radar unit had been set up to monitor how close the rockets got to the balloons. Ammunitions people were still finishing up and fixing the scaffolding that would fire the rockets.

Finnegan turned to greet them.

"Here we go then," he said in a very businesslike way. "I hope this works."

Tom looked down, but it was Judy that spoke. "We have full confidence in it," she said, wondering where she'd suddenly got her courage from. But she started to feel angry toward Finnegan and his constant need to put her down and make her feel inadequate. Something was beginning to rise up inside of her, and she'd wanted to voice it.

Tom looked across at her and smiled his admiration. Finnegan turned away awkwardly and fixed his gaze on the radar screen.

Chief Armourer Hellard explained how the test would work that day. They would fire off each rocket one at a time and give the scientists time to take notes before they fired the next one. As directed by the scientists, the mock planes contained all the different materials known to be used by the enemy aircraft.

Judy centered on the radar screen as they got started. Hellard fired the first rocket, which streaked into the air with a whoosh, the trail glowing white as it tore toward the first balloon. It was only a few seconds, but it felt like an eternity as Judy waited for the detonation. It exploded close to the airplane, shattering it into pieces and shredding the balloon. Judy's stomach relaxed as she made notes of the trajectory and materials used, while Tom breathed a sigh of relief next to her.

They fired off the second rocket with the same result. Now she was starting to feel more confident. Hellard fired the third rocket, but this time it shot past the target and out into the gray, gloomy sky, detonating just before hitting the ground. Her heart sank a little as she tried to read the materials that had been used in this third experiment. They would have to do some more investigation to determine why the shell wasn't sensing those.

She was deep in scientific thought when Finnegan turned to them as Tom spoke. "Well, two out of three isn't bad."

"Tell that to the people that are being bombed by the third plane," stated Finnegan harshly. "Let's get that one right, shall we."

Judy's stomach clenched again as he looked directly at her. She couldn't help but take it personally.

Finnegan strode off to his car, and Tom and Judy stayed a little longer to talk with the explosive experts to understand some of the trajectories that had been used and the alignment with the balloons.

When they got back to the lab, she got to work, looking at all the information she had prepared for the testing. She wasn't going to let Finnegan bother her. As much as she wished she didn't, she needed to find a way just to get past it.

It was about four months later, and they were still in the midst of developing the new shell, believing they'd fixed the third materials problem, when one day they were called to a special presentation.

Filing into the lecture hall, she noticed that another man accompanied Finnegan. And knowing him from other interactions, she recognized him as Sir Henry Tizard, the head of the Aeronautical Research Committee and one of the most important advisors in the country. Her heart sank as she knew what this might mean.

Finnegan started by recapping the work they'd been doing on the proximity fuse, then Tizard took over. "As much as we'd like to make this proximity fuse a British invention, we have to face facts. And the reality is we don't have the money to develop this any longer, to get it from the medium-size warhead that you have all developed, and reduce it further to fit in artillery shells. However, England is very proud of its inventors and scientists and all the work you have done. And you will all be recognized for that. But we will be moving this particular piece of technology research over to our American friends, who have more money to develop it, so that we can finish the task that you have so ably started for us. His Majesty thanks you, as does the British government, but unfortunately, we have to face facts and what's most important is that we win this war. The other projects that we had previously put on hold will now take your full attention."

Judy's heart sank, but she was also grateful to have been a part of the project. Tom gave her a reluctant smile as they left the lecture theater and made their way back to the office.

It was a few months later, when she'd been looking over some paperwork about the fuse that she noted that though her lab had been recognized for the work that they had done on it, her name had been left off the list of scientists. Tom's name was there, of course, but no mention of her own contribution, and once again she felt the now familiar sting of frustration and rejection.

Chapter Eleven

November 1939

Hedy saw the flicker of the headlights from the car that turned onto her driveway, and she crushed out her cigarette into the overflowing ashtray and marched to the front door to do battle. For the first few months of their marriage, Hedy had been so in love and so happy. She didn't know it was possible to experience that much bliss. Her new bridegroom had meant the world to her. They had even adopted a baby together, little James, who was now sleeping in his cot in the nursery, his nanny in the room next to him. But then her and Gene's schedules had started to clash. He was working on a new screenplay for a different studio, and she was on set at MGM filming, in between her other movies, what she hoped would be the final shots of *I Take This Woman*. This film had been a grueling experience of never-ending production woes, having been stopped and started more than once since early 1938. It had got through two directors and created long stressful days of Hedy having to work with a very begrudging Spencer Tracy, who felt she was getting all the billing and he was just along to prop her up. It had taken so long to produce that the cast had sarcastically renamed it *I Retake This Woman*. So, when she and Gene did see each other in the evenings, they were both exhausted. And now she felt as if she was raising their son alone, and it had put a real strain between them. After just six months of marriage, she began to wonder if she'd done the right thing. Yes, she had been madly in love. But not enough for both of them. When the fan magazines reported that he was secretly seeing another actress, she had felt bitterly disappointed and had confronted him, and he had denied it. But tonight she had proof.

She heard the key turn in the lock, and she paced the hallway, arms folded, waiting for him.

When he saw her there, his shoulders visibly slumped forward. "Do not yell at me tonight, Hedy, I'm exhausted, and I have a huge rewrite to do for the film."

Hedy was not dissuaded; he had been avoiding her for a week now, and she didn't know when she would have an opportunity again when James was in bed, and she and Gene were both home.

"I'm not surprised you're exhausted," she snapped, her chin set resolutely as she confronted him in an angry whisper, not wanting her words to drift up the stairs, "when you've been out all day having long lunches with—what's her name—that young actress on your film!"

His eyes flicked to meet hers, and for a moment, she thought she saw guilt, then it was gone as he swept by her and, removing his hat and coat, threw them on a chair, then strode into the front room to pour himself a drink.

She followed him, closing the door behind them.

"Do you deny it?" Hedy demanded, her tone furious.

He just peered back at her as he took a swig of his whiskey and, loosening his tie, strode out onto the patio.

Hedy was adamant; he had been avoiding her like this for weeks, but tonight he wouldn't get away with it.

"Just answer me, Gene, are you screwing someone else?"

Gene chuckled. "The last I heard, lunch is just about eating, and no, I don't deny eating with a cast member; I was going over her new lines with her."

"Oh really," stated Hedy, now pacing again, "Then how come you were heard saying, 'I can't come over tonight, but I can come tomorrow night. Hedy won't know, she's busy on her picture.'"

Gene visibly swallowed down his whiskey hard and for once seemed lost for words.

When he eventually spoke, he was angry. "What, are you spying on me now, Hedy? Not enough that you have to shout at me anytime I'm home. Now you have people tracking my every move?"

"I wouldn't waste my time," she shouted, now unable to prevent herself raising her voice. "Someone from MGM was at the table right by you, and they called me. Someone whose husband has also slept with other women behind her back. All I want to know is why, Gene? Why would you do it? You have everything here, a lovely home, a new baby, and me waiting for you."

She saw him cringe at that, and she felt her deep-down insecurities all at once raising their ugly heads. Surely, he would deny it was anything to do with her?

He turned away and looked out toward their pool, becoming almost philosophical. "Things change, Hedy."

"What things?" she demanded.

"Feelings. We got married so quickly. I think we were both swept up in the physical attraction for one another, and the reality of marriage is… well, it's different."

Hedy almost laughed in his face; with his receding hairline, paunchy belly and plain looks, that was not why *she'd* married him. "What do you mean, swept up in the attraction? Are you saying that all I was for you was a pretty girl on your arm?"

She saw it then; she had hit on the truth. He shook his head, but the expression on his face confirmed it. And she felt her heart sink. How had she done this? How had she thrown herself into a marriage with a man who had only cared about the outside of her? The very thing she had been terrified of doing. The grief and weight of her realization crippled her, and she collapsed into a patio chair, feeling sick.

Gene turned to her again. "Look, Hedy, we screwed up. This isn't working for either of us. We don't need to keep banging our heads against a brick wall to know that."

"What about James?" she spluttered out, gulping down air to stop herself from throwing up. "What do I tell him as he grows up?"

"Tell him the truth. That things didn't work out. And that we both love him even if we are not together anymore."

As if on cue, from the house, James's little cry drifted out the open window. All at once, she needed to be with him. Hold him, feel the unconditional love of her child. Heaving herself up, she started toward the patio door.

"The nanny can get him," Gene insisted. "Now this is out in the open, I think we should stay and discuss the next steps."

"Next steps?" Hedy shot back as she strode toward the house. "I already know my next step, Mr. Markey. I shall be divorcing you for cruelty. You have never taken this marriage seriously; you have hardly even been home. It is as if you had your fun, then moved on to the next warm body. And I'm not going to be the kind of wife who sits here waiting for a man until he's finished in another woman's bed. I'm worth more than that." She said the words but wasn't even sure she believed them herself.

Was she worth more than that? Why did she never feel worthy?

She didn't look back as she made her way upstairs, fighting the mixture of burning anger and rejection that rose in her chest. James was already being soothed by their nanny, who was surprised when Hedy burst into the nursery.

"I'll take him." Hedy insisted, practically tearing the baby from her arms, and she held James close. Burrowing her head into his tiny chubby shoulder, she inhaled his sweet baby scent. James responded by locking his little arms around her neck.

At least James loved her for who she was, she thought as she jiggled him up and down to calm him. She looked out the nursery window. Gene was still standing there, gazing out across the pool, and she knew at that moment it was over.

It took longer than it had with Fritz for her to come to grips with this new reality. She had failed and was getting divorced again.

The second loss was harder than the first. In her first marriage, because she had been focusing on escaping she didn't consider it failing; she could chalk it up to being young, to being vulnerable. But she was older now; she was a Hollywood actress making her own money. She didn't need anybody. How did she manage to get it wrong once again?

The day Gene moved out into his own place, she felt a deep sadness. Would she ever find someone who truly loved her? Would there ever be honesty in her life? *No one will ever want you for you, Hedy Kiesler*, she mused to herself.

That evening, after Gene left, Hedy had got drunk, downing shots of tequila till late into the night. She had a day off from shooting the next day and had decided she had the right to be drunk if she wanted to be.

As she went to bed in the early hours of the morning, she sobbed in silence, feeling all of her loneliness. To the world, she was seen as a success, on the arms of her good-looking co-stars. But in her own personal world, she was once again desolate and needy. And the only people she could count on were Stefan and Judy, who both lived a world away. Even her mother appeared to put conditions on her love.

Hedy slept all the next day and when she finally got up it was already evening and her mouth was dry and her head pounding. She had not wanted to get out of bed, not even for James. She knew he was in good hands as the nanny adored him. She just lay there crying and feeling sorry for herself. When she finally got up to make herself a drink, Hedy remembered her first marriage and reminded herself she would heal. Until then she would throw herself into her work and being the best mother she could be for James. She hoped that she would meet somebody again at some point in the future. But the next time, she would be careful. She wouldn't make the same mistake again.

November 15, 1939

Dear Judy,

I don't quite know how to write this letter because I feel so sad and my heart is breaking.

My marriage is already over and I can't believe I've been so foolish again. Gene turned out not to be the man that I thought he was.

Almost as soon as we were off the honeymoon, he changed, becoming withdrawn and aloof. Spending more time on the set didn't help, nor that he was away working with Paramount on his new movie, but still, I thought we could make it work. We even adopted the baby I told you about, an adorable little boy we called James because… well, a few reasons, but I so wanted us to be a family right away.

Judy, it feels as if my life is falling apart, not unlike the whole world right now. I have been so sad following all the news since war was declared in Europe. It feels so difficult being so far away. As much as I live here in America, in such a different situation, my heart is still European. I think about you all there.

Your work at least sounds wonderful. I envy you being able to be in a lab every day doing important war work. Right now, my life is a mess, and because of my public persona, I have to have it all together in front of the movie cameras and in the spotlight of the press.

The sad thing is, I found out Gene had an affair with an actress from the movie that he was working on and I was crushed and devastated by that. What is wrong with me? Why wasn't I enough for him? Sorry to wallow, it just hurts so much, Judy.

On top of that, working with Spencer Tracy has been a total nightmare. I suppose it hasn't helped that my life's been in so much turmoil, but we did not get on at all. He's civil with me, but I can tell he doesn't like me. It's amazing when I'm working on movies with people I like, how much fun they are. When I'm working with people like him, though, they feel like they go on forever.

Anyway, darling, this was just a quick scribbled note to update you and I have to go, because darling little James is crying and I want to feed him and get him into bed. It may surprise you, but I rather love doing all the motherly things. It makes me feel wonderful and normal.

Well, take care of yourself. Remember to keep your head down. Hopefully, if I can get to England soon, we'll get to see each other again.

Much love and kiss, kiss.
Hedy

November 30, 1939

Dear Hedy,

I am so sorry to hear about you and Gene, you know I am here for you if you need me. I'm sure you're right about work keeping you apart but still I can't understand how he could have done this to you. Please don't let one man's mistakes affect your self-confidence. You are an amazing, loving, kind woman and I'm sorry he just couldn't see that.

You are also right about the world feeling as if it's falling apart. Nothing and no one feels safe any more. We just have to find happiness wherever we can. And for you I am so glad you have your lovely little boy. I can only imagine what a comfort that must be for you. I can't wait to have children and feel that special bond I see between mothers and their children. I think it is wonderful that you adopted and very courageous, I'm not sure I could do that. But I know James will be very loved in your home.

Much love
Judy xxx

P.S. Here is a little scientific question to keep your mind off things: Why is it that we use really low radio frequencies to communicate instead of other frequencies of light such as infrared, ultraviolet, and X-rays, etc.?

Chapter Twelve

June 1940

Tom handed Judy a drink across the crowded pub. "One gin and tonic," he shouted to be heard above the din.

Judy reached up over the cluster of heads and took the glass from him and mouthed the words "Thank you," as she knew he couldn't possibly hear her.

Collecting his pint from the bar, he pressed his way through the crowd to get closer to her, and she watched him approach her, as she had so many times before, in all of his awkwardness. She took in his features once again. He was about six foot, with a large square frame, brown hair cut short, and a pleasant face with a heavy chin and chestnut brown eyes that were gentle and attentive and right then set on her own, intent on his pursuit of getting to her. She couldn't help but smile as he stumbled through the throng. He wasn't cavalier or charming; he was Tom, her friend, lab partner, and what he lacked in charisma, he made up for in kindness. He was also a brilliant scientist, one of the best she had ever worked with, and she loved the way he viewed everything around him with a childlike fascination. She was also pretty sure he had remembered everything she had ever told him about herself. Which wasn't a lot, because she was perpetually shy about her personal life, but even in the little she had shared with him, he would often bring it up in a conversation months after she'd told him, and she liked that about him.

Finally, after numerous "excuse me's," he made it through the crowd and, hoisting his pint over the top of another lady's head,

made it to her side. Just then, someone knocked into him from
behind, and he almost toppled over her, some of his pint sloshing
onto the floor in front of them. She blushed a little with the closeness of his body as it brushed up against her own.

He seemed even more mortified than she was. "Judy, I'm so
sorry," he apologized.

She nodded her understanding as she brushed a few drops of
beer from her skirt. He pointed to the far end of the pub, where
it was a little quieter.

They made their way into the corner. All around them everyone
was in high spirits as, on the bar, the landlord had placed a pho-
nograph and big band tunes filled the air. Their lab had just won
another two-year war contract and, as much as nobody wanted
this war, this meant there would be plenty of work for them for the
next few years. The only available table was tiny, and to sit down,
they had to both squeeze behind it as they blushed at one another
with the proximity. To deflect their mutual embarrassment, Tom
held his pint up toward her.

"Cheers," he proclaimed.

She gently clinked her glass with his and took a sip. Peering
around the blue smoky room, she was entertained by the antics of
the rowdy group around them. It had been a warm June day and
the evening hadn't dropped in temperature at all.

Tom looked uncomfortable and very hot beside her.

"If you want to take off your jacket, feel free," she shouted into
his ear, knowing he was just respectfully keeping his jacket on as
it wasn't polite to sit there in his shirtsleeves. He nodded, looking
relieved, and, taking it off, he placed it on his lap. With a sideward
glance, she noticed how broad his shoulders were, pulling the
fabric of his white shirt taut across his barrel chest, and there was
a slight fragrance of Brylcreem as he adjusted his clothing. He also
loosened his tie, and his Adam's apple was pronounced beneath
his collar button as he took in a relieving breath and swallowed

down a sip of his pint. Through the thin cotton fabric, she could feel the heat from his body next to her arm, causing the hair on her skin to stand up. And, she was surprised to note, it sent a little thrill through her body.

"I can't believe so many people came out tonight," he shouted back toward her again.

"I know," she answered.

"I didn't know that this many men worked at the Cavendish," he continued.

She thought again how Tom was a great lab partner, treating her with such respect when so many of the men didn't. But Tom saw her for the scientist she was. Even though Finnegan continued to show his disdain, Tom always talked about all the work she'd contributed, speaking very highly of her.

Over the last two years, they'd both been working closely together, now more intently since war had been declared the year before. They'd worked side by side each day in the lab, but this was the first time they'd ever been out socially. So, as they sipped on their drinks they just smiled awkwardly at each other, as it was almost impossible to be heard. They'd arrived late, with the party in the pub in full swing, as they'd had a delicate experiment that had needed careful supervision and they hadn't finished in the lab until 10 p.m.

The Dew Drop Inn was located on Gwydir Street, less than a mile from the lab. It was a favorite of many of the technicians, and the landlord had been willing to keep his bar open for this private party so they could all celebrate their new contract. Though Judy, and she was pretty sure Tom too, had never been here before this evening.

The two of them sat and talked as best they could, mainly about their work, and finally, Judy couldn't stifle a yawn.

"I should go," she said reluctantly. "I have that research paper to write up tomorrow, and I need to get some sleep."

As she stood, he stood too, respectfully, and seemed to be struggling to say something.

She waited patiently, as gulping down the last of his pint seemed to give him the courage for something he wanted to say. All at once he blurted out, "May I walk you home, Judy?"

Judy swallowed and wanted to say, "Yes, of course," with the confident assurance she saw other women say those words. But instead, she became tongue-tied and just stared at him blankly, feeling her cheeks growing warm again.

He continued as though he felt it was important to explain.

"It's just so late, and I wouldn't be much of a gentleman if I let you go home alone."

Judy stared at her shoes and nodded, then they pushed their way back through the crowded pub and out through the front door. After the stifling heat inside, the outside was pleasantly chilly. Tom put on his jacket.

"I think I'm deaf from being in there," he stated, shaking his head and smiling at her, his brown eyes crinkling at the corners. "I'm not really a sociable person. I prefer a circuit board."

She nodded her understanding as they made their way awkwardly down the road, their feet echoing on the quiet street, lined either side with a row of cream and gray stone terrace houses packed tightly together. All the homes were blacked out because of the war, making their experience eerie and removed. Judy tried desperately to think of something to say, and by Tom's anxious expression and awkward smiles, he was doing the same.

"I think the new fuse the Americans are developing is going to work, you know," he finally blurted out.

"Yes, I agree," she replied, now back on familiar ground.

Because of the lack of street lights, it was easy to see the evening sky, full of stars with a full moon beaming down the road toward them. They crept along, as it was late and most people were asleep.

"Isn't the peace lovely?" Tom whispered to her.

She nodded. "Much better out here."

They both laughed.

About halfway down the street, something caught their attention because the night was so quiet. A deep rumbling buzz that seemed to be coming from far off filled the air.

"It sounds like a plane," whispered Tom. They both stopped and peered into the sky but couldn't see anything. The rumble grew louder and more ominous. Judy suddenly felt nervous. Why would a plane be traveling at night so close to the ground? They hadn't been bombed in Cambridge before now, but she'd read about other places that had. Any sound like this was bound to be disturbing.

She afforded a side glance at Tom and could just make out his tense expression in the moonlight.

"Think it's friendly?" asked Judy.

"I hope so," said Tom, continuing to peer out toward the darkness to where the sound was coming from.

All at once, they both spied the same thing at the same time. A flash of moonlight glistened across what appeared to be glass. Judy shuddered, trying to believe what she was seeing. She had done extensive work on the enemy planes at the lab, and there was only one plane with that type of a glass cockpit. That was a Heinkel He 111, a German bomber. But surely a German bomber wouldn't be flying over Cambridge?

Instinctively, Tom reached out and placed his hand on her arm. Judy was grateful for his reassurance. "I think we should go back to the pub," stated Tom, the apprehension evident in his tone. "I'm not sure we're very safe here on the street."

Judy nodded.

Just then, they saw the whole thing, as a full shaft of moonlight glinted across the wings, illuminating the blue underside. They could just make out the silhouette of a pilot in the glass-fronted cockpit.

"German," said Tom, squeezing her arm and leading her back toward the pub.

They started to trot back down the road at a hurried pace. Judy glanced over her shoulder, partly in awe, partly petrified. It was so low, she was afraid that it would scrape the roofs of the houses on the street. All at once, the sound of an air raid siren ripped through the air, encouraging them into a run as they rushed back toward the pub.

As they quickly ducked back into the building, the plane roared overhead, the sound deafening as it reverberated all around them and utterly terrifying. Judy and Tom fought their way back in through the hordes of people pouring out onto the street, looking up toward the sky.

Inside, people were shouting to one another, alerting each other to what they were seeing.

"Bloody hell, it's the Jerries!" someone shouted from the doorway. "They're going to bomb us, right here in the pub!"

As the sirens continued to screech over and over again, people started to make their way down into the cellar, directed by the pub's landlord. "This way, everybody, this way!" he shouted.

The clatter of shoes on the stone stairs and people panicking heightened the tension as they all hurried to make their way down into the dark, dank cellar. Some found coordinating their descent hard, still inebriated after a night of celebration. Judy clung on to Tom's arm as they raced down the stairs. Above them, the sound of the bombers grew louder and more ominous, vibrating the building with their low, menacing hum. It was disorientating in the semi-darkness and it smelled strongly of malt and hops. They all crowded in, taking up every available space.

All at once she was aware of Tom right behind her. Gently holding her shoulders, he pulled her close to his chest and whispered in her ear. "We are going to be all right, Judy, don't worry. I'm right here if you need me." She was so grateful for his assurance and didn't realize how much she'd needed to feel the touch of another friendly human being until that moment.

As her eyes acclimated to the darkness, she saw at the far end there were some chairs and tables. A man was pulling them out, placing them on the stone cellar floor. It was cold down here, though it was actually refreshing after the heat upstairs. Tom commandeered two chairs and offered one to Judy. There was an eerie silence around the room as they all sat waiting for what this meant—the sound of the siren reaching its barreling roll over and over.

All at once, the first bombs dropped and the sound was terrifying, bouncing around the stone walls and shaking the floor. People screamed around her. As chunks of masonry and cement crumbled down from the walls and to the side of her, a stack of empty beer barrels collapsed and rolled around the floor. She could hear somebody sobbing as another bomb, just as loud as the first, shook the walls again.

At some point Judy had taken Tom's hand. She hadn't realized she had done it until she felt the warmth as he gently squeezed it. "Don't worry," he reassured again, "this is a pretty safe building."

She nodded, calculating wall tolerances in her head to distract herself, and squeezed Tom's hand in return. His face was so close to hers now and for some reason, under these circumstances, she didn't feel shy with him. Even holding his hand felt natural and he just made her feel safe.

The evening continued with the bombs rocking the building as they all sat there staring at the ceiling, willing it not to come down on their heads. By the time the all-clear sounded two hours later, Judy's head and stomach ached with the tension.

Slowly they started to emerge back up into the pub. The whole of Judy's body was still trembling and she felt disconnected from reality somehow. Upstairs, the pub was a mess. Behind the bar, glasses had fallen from the shelves and smashed all across the floor. Pictures had been knocked from the walls, and chairs and tables were upturned.

As they shuffled outside, they automatically looked to where the bomber had been heading. The sky was ablaze with fire. The sound of fire engines and ambulance bells filled the air, along with the smell of smoke, the sound of cracking wood and shattering glass, and ongoing small explosions all across the Vicarage Terrace area.

"That was so close," Tom stated, the shock evident in his tone. Placing his hand gently on her shoulder, he continued, "Let's get you home."

"I wonder what they were after?" Judy whispered as they both headed off in the direction of Judy's lodgings. Tom, not knowing, shook his head.

Gwydir Street was now alive with people as they moved back down it. Some stood in huddled groups in the middle of the road, clinging to one another, arms wrapped protectively around their children as they all stared toward the inferno that had been their city. It was then that Judy realized something: she had believed, not unlike the shocked faces around her, that maybe because Cambridge wasn't a large industrial city with an ammunition factory or ongoing war work, they would be spared the bombs that were expected to fall on so many of the bigger cities. That somehow, they would be safer. But now she knew, nowhere was safe from Hitler's fury.

She arrived home, and Tom wanted to make sure she was all right and saw her inside. Her landlady, Florence, was still awake, wearing a dressing gown and curlers.

"Thank God, Judy," she said. "I've been worried sick about you. I knew you were down in the Vicarage area. Did you hear? They've bombed it badly. A neighbor came and told me all about it."

Judy nodded. "We were there. This is Mr. Thomas Jenkins," she said, introducing her escort. Respectfully, he shook Florence's hand.

It was then that Florence must have realized she was in her curlers.

"Dear Lord, I didn't expect company," she said, tightening the collar of her dressing gown and bobbing her curlers back into place. "Oh well, you had better come into my flat. Judy isn't allowed late male callers, but I can put the kettle on. We can have a cup of tea to strengthen our nerves."

They filed into Florence's tiny kitchen and huddled around the little table as Florence started to boil water. "Unbelievable, isn't it?" she said. They all looked suddenly toward the window, as if somehow that was going to explain what was going on. "It doesn't feel real until it happens to you, does it?"

They sat and drank tea, and then Tom excused himself. Judy walked him to the front door.

"Thank you," she said, "for everything."

He smiled and offered her his hand. She took it and shook it.

"I'll see you tomorrow, Judy. Try and get some sleep. We'll know more then. Brings it home, doesn't it, how important our work is?"

She nodded. He nodded back in response, then, placing his hat on his head, he made his way down the street as Judy watched him go, his journey illuminated by the fiery orange glow above the city.

She retreated back into the house, noticing Florence standing in her doorway.

"He seems nice," she mused as she pursed her lips. "Do you work with him?"

Judy nodded.

"Nice and polite," said Florence. "A good sort, you can tell. Nice clean fingernails."

Judy wished Florence a good night and made her way up to bed, but didn't sleep very much, after the trauma. The only thing that gave her a little joy was the memory of Tom's hand holding hers during the bombing raid. Did it mean something? She realized, with a start, that she wasn't opposed to that if it did.

June 18, 1940

Dear Hedy,

I wanted to write you a quick note to let you know that I am okay. You may hear about this or read about it in the newspapers, but tonight we were bombed here in Cambridge. I was actually out at a pub, not far from where the bombs were dropped. Cavendish Lab was celebrating a new contract. I won't lie to you; my hand is shaking as I write this note. It was the scariest thing I've ever been through in my life.

Fortunately, Tom and I were able to shelter in the cellar of the pub we were in, but I never want to go through anything like this ever again. I'm up pacing the kitchen now. Tom just left. He walked me home. He was worried about me, but now I can't sleep. Just know that I'm all right and safe and I'll write you a longer letter when I'm feeling calm again.

Much love,
Judy

June 26, 1940

Dearest Judy,

I just got your letter. I didn't hear about the bombing in Cambridge, but I'm so glad you wrote to let me know that you are okay. How frightening for you. I can't imagine what it'd be like to be in a raid, though it sounded like you had some company?? The mysterious Tom again. How come you were both downstairs in the cellar together? Did any romance blossom in the dark as the bombs dropped all around you?

I suppose you were too frightened to think about it, but please let me know if anything developed in that direction, especially as he also walked you home.

Write again soon.
Much love.
Kiss, kiss.

Hedy

P.S. The answer to the brain teaser you sent me in your earlier letter is that higher frequency light such as ultraviolet and X-rays, etc., get scattered in the atmosphere for the same reason that the sky is blue—which is why we've evolved to see in the visible spectrum and developed electronics to communicate using radio frequencies. Thank you for the distraction xxx

Chapter Thirteen

June 1940

Hedy, already bored with the party, swanned out through open French doors onto the balcony. Leaning against the railing, she stared out toward the sea. The sultry evening air was thick with heat, its piquant stagnancy mixing with the intoxicating scent of camellias and night jasmine that wafted up from the garden below. Far off, shaggy palm trees swayed in the bay, illuminated by shafts of silvery light from a ripened moon. A breeze rippled the water's surface, disappearing into a shimmery puddle that skimmed the top of the beach. As the water breathed out frothy waves, it nudged at the sand so gently it appeared to be trying not to wake it.

From behind her, laughter floated out into the air. Accompanying it, the strain of the piano's crescendo of "Moonlight Sonata" and the clink of crystal glasses clashing in friendly toasts. Even after nearly three years, Hedwig Eva Maria Kiesler still couldn't believe she was here in Hollywood. She had been worked like a racehorse after the success of her first picture, *Algiers,* completing as many as three films each year since then, just finishing one with Clark Gable that also starred Spencer Tracy again and as much as she adored the work, it was challenging. Mastering a new language was hard enough, but this was like a whole new world. She wondered how long she could continue this charade before someone unmasked her and found out who she really was.

All at once she became aware of another presence, as measured footsteps echoed out from the French doors at the far end of the balcony. Retreating into the shadows, Hedy turned to watch. The man paused in the doorway. His silhouette extinguished all the light leaking out from the room, conveying that he was tall, well over six feet. His starched white sports coat and crisp shirt reflecting brightly in the moonlight contrasted with his sharply creased black trousers. Everything about him suggested money and the kind of quiet assurance that comes with it. As he stepped forward, a shaft of light illuminated his face. He had chiseled features, heavy eyebrows, and a dark mustache, his dark hair trimmed to a stylish length. He was not movie-star handsome, but pleasing, with a strong chin, nose, and high cheekbones, the sort of face that did well commanding a board room. He paused and lifted a cigarette to his mouth, and its golden glow reflected his eyes that shone like polished onyx as he stared out to sea. His face was familiar to her, but she couldn't place him as an actor and wondered if he was a producer or a studio executive. He had that aura about him.

As he blew out circles of blue smoke in the stagnant air, the scent of burning tobacco rolled toward her. Hedy stood motionless, tightening her grip on the railing. Maybe he wouldn't see her. She just wanted five minutes to catch her breath without being stared at, grabbed, squeezed, or having to make polite conversation with influential financial backers whose eyes never seemed to get higher than her cleavage.

He ground out the cigarette beneath his heel and the lingering smoke caught in the back of her throat. Even though she coughed quietly, he was alerted to her presence.

Advancing toward her with a smile, he closed the distance between them in a few long strides. He seemed even taller by her side, and she had to tip her head up to meet his gaze as the smell of brandy, smoke, and a lemony shaving soap wafted between them. He leaned on the balcony, one wrist crossed over the other, and Hedy noticed a rather expensive-looking watch—probably Cartier—just visible beneath his cuff.

"Miss Lamarr, isn't it?" His tone was deep, warm, assertive, and it was not a question so much as a declaration.

She smiled.

He offered her a cigarette, flipping open an engraved gold cigarette case. Hedy shook her head, not because she didn't want one—God did she ever want one—but she just didn't want the smell of smoke lingering in her hair or on her breath. He helped himself to another. He must be a producer, she decided. They were all chain-smokers. Flicking open the lighter, he ignited the end of the paper, which erupted into a copper glow. Filling his lungs with the tobacco, he blew out a line of gray smoke across the balcony, and without the wind to carry it, the haze curled back around her, stifling the scent of jasmine in the air.

Then he turned and took in every detail of her face as he spoke to her. "I hear the picture went well. I was just talking to your director, who seems pleased. He was saying you and Mr. Gable are magical on screen and it will be a big hit."

"I hope so." Hedy nodded, turning her head back toward the water. She felt awkward, wondering why he had not introduced himself. "I had a marvelous time on the film," she drawled, hoping that it would win her some points if this was a producer.

"What about the party? Are you having fun?" he enquired, taking another deep drag of his cigarette.

Should she tell him the truth? She'd become bored with it an hour ago. She loved acting, but being with so many vapid people who cared more about their looks and egos was wearing. She plumbed for something in the middle.

"I think it's fine, though I haven't even met our host yet."

An amused smile crinkled the corners of his lips.

"Well, we should do something about that," he responded softly, offering her his hand. "Howard Hughes, a pleasure to meet you."

She shook his hand gently, which was warm and smooth, and hoped that the dim lighting would hide her reddening cheeks at not knowing her host. The air became stiff between them, not only from the awkwardness, but also because of the sultry heat.

He leaned in to whisper into her ear. "Want to know a secret?" He continued without giving her a chance to respond. "I'm actually not a big fan of parties. I'm doing Mayer a favor. I'm hoping to do more in the film industry myself, and well, I have this big house. Honestly, I would rather be out working on one of my airplanes."

Hedy turned back to meet his gaze. This was something of interest to her. Something that she wished she could talk more about. "Do you design them yourself? I am fascinated by air travel. It's going to be the future, you know. I know one day people will hop on planes just to go from one big city to another. Like you would take a train."

He seemed amused by her comment. "I'm surprised you take such an interest."

"In my spare time I love to think up inventions. When I was a girl in Vienna, I would walk around the city with my father and he would point out all the mechanical marvels and explain to me exactly how they worked. Now, I find just talking about such things makes me nostalgic." She went on to describe some of her favorite inventions as Hughes became enthralled. Before long, they were in an in-depth conversation about the combustion engine's inner workings and flight dynamics of his H1 racer. Hedy was just relieved to talk about something other than movies.

All at once, a couple of the guests burst out onto the balcony. One, an elegant woman in a gold lamé dress, eyed the two of them quizzically. As she stepped into the light, Hedy saw it was one of her co-stars, Claudette Colbert.

"Well, there you are, Mr. Hughes," she purred. "We have been looking everywhere for our host. Somebody wants to make a toast and thank you for your party."

Colbert strode out onto the balcony and hooked her arm into Howard's. He stopped and turned toward Hedy. "I do hope you'll join us, Miss Lamarr."

She nodded and followed him inside.

Mayer had just arrived and gave a relatively dry speech about the upcoming opening of *Boom Town*, which was set for early August. He seemed to give the same one for every movie, Hedy noted, just changed the name of the film, and they all toasted their host with champagne. With the deed being done, Hedy felt it was time for her to leave. An entourage of other women was now surrounding Howard. She walked toward the door and asked the butler to call her a taxi and fetch her coat. As she waited in the hallway, she was suddenly aware of somebody behind her. It was Howard, his face showing concerned.

"Ah, you're slinking off into the night."

"I have to be up early tomorrow for a photo shoot for a fan magazine," she offered with a reluctant sigh, "so I really should get going. But Mr. Hughes, thank you so much for a lovely party." She offered her hand, and he took it and kissed it. She dropped her chin and looked up at him through veiled lashes. "Very gallant," she purred.

"It's Howard. And I was hoping that we could see each other again, maybe go out for a drink this week?" he said, beaming.

She tried not to show her excitement. Not only had she enjoyed their conversation, but she knew he could probably help her in the business. He knew a lot of people in the film industry.

"Also," he continued, "I'm pulling together a small party for my friend Janet and her husband Adrian. A trip on my yacht at the end of the month. Do you think you could come?"

"Will I need my bathing suit?" she said with a smile.

"Not necessarily, but that doesn't mean you won't be swimming," he flirted with her.

"I can't think what you mean, Mr. Hughes," she said, feigning confusion.

"It's an early evening cruise. We're leaving at about seven. We'll eat dinner and stay overnight, and then come back later the next day. I know a lovely little place that we can anchor up for the day. We can swim, lie on the beach, drink champagne. You know, enjoy ourselves, as rich people do."

She arched an eyebrow. "Some of us are born rich, but some of us have to work for our living. I really should go. But yes, I'd be delighted to come."

"I will have my driver pick you up if you like."

"That would be wonderful," she agreed.

The butler arrived back with her coat. Slipping it around her shoulders, she made her way outside to wait for the taxi, pondering once again the lifestyle she was becoming a part of. The film industry had its ups and downs and could be hard work. But it presented marvelous opportunities she could only have dreamed of in Vienna. Though she had to admit there was still a side of her that wanted to do something bigger, something longer-lasting, as if making movies wasn't her destiny, only the path leading her to what was her real legacy. Her hope was that she wouldn't miss that opportunity when it presented itself, while being swept up in this world of make-believe.

Chapter Fourteen

A couple of days after the bombing of Cambridge, Judy was engrossed in her work when Tom just blurted it out. She had been sitting down, working on a complicated hypothesis, when she felt him moving nervously behind her. At first, she thought he disagreed with her calculations, as he was being so quiet and, instead of commenting in the affirmative, as he usually did, Tom was shifting from foot to foot. Judy turned to look up at him and noticed that he seemed very uncomfortable. His face was flushed and a bead of sweat was forming along his hairline. She wondered if maybe he was ill.

Noticing her concern, he puffed out his cheeks and then spoke.

"Judy, I was wondering if you'd like to come on a boat with me?" he asked in one long stream of words, a slight quiver in his tone. She blinked a couple of times, trying to comprehend what he was asking. He must have realized that it sounded odd, so he tried to rephrase it. "What I meant to say was, I was thinking of going out on Sunday, maybe take a trip on the river, and I wondered if you'd like to come along with me."

At first, she didn't really understand what this had to do with the experiment they were studying. Then, slowly, it started to sink in. Tom appeared to be asking her to step out with him, on a date.

This, of course, made her blush crimson. To play for time, she peered down at her calculations again, hoping that somehow the group of numbers on the paper, now blurring in front of her eyes, was going to give her the right words to say.

He carried on awkwardly: "I know it's very short notice. And of course, if you don't want to go, it's not a problem at all. But as we're not working on Sunday... and I know you are off... and might enjoy having some time with... somebody. It doesn't have to be me, of course, but I was thinking..."

She put him out of his misery with a raised hand and, not looking up, nodded her head and then carried on working on the equations. She heard him blow out air behind her.

"I will meet you at the central boat pontoon at one p.m., if that's all right."

"Uh huh," she managed to squeeze out as she nibbled on the end of her pencil, staring obliviously at her work.

She wished she could just say something. Why was she always so tongue-tied whenever he spoke to her like this?

Hardly sleeping on Saturday night, she was up with the lark, getting ready when Florence stopped by to pick up her rent.

Judy invited her in as she went to get the money.

"You look nice," Florence commented with a sniff. "Going out?" Judy blushed crimson and Florence guessed, "You've got a date, haven't you? I bet it's with that Mr. Clean and Wholesome."

Judy walked to the window and looked outside. "I don't know what I was thinking in saying yes," she mused, shaking her head. "I don't know what he wants."

"What he wants?" Florence sniffed, again. "I imagine he wants what all men want." She folded her arms across her ample bosom. "Just remember, it can't happen here." Even though she was being stern, Judy had learned her landlady had a heart of gold.

"Florence!" she shrieked. "I would never..."

Her landlady started to chuckle in a low rumble. "As long as he stays on our doorstep, I'm sure you'll have a marvelous time."

"I don't even know what to wear," Judy flustered as she described the date.

Florence quirked an eyebrow and smirked. "Why don't you wear your rowing gear from when you were at the university? That should get him hot and bothered!"

Judy shook her head as she handed her the money. "Mrs. Greenwood, you are incorrigible."

Her landlady pushed the rent money into her pocket and left with a wry smile.

Judy started trying on different outfits. She never thought much about clothes. All she really had was for work, as she didn't go out socially. Tweed skirts, boring jumpers, a couple of plain blouses and a few lighter skirts for summer. She decided on the most comfortable skirt of the three she had, that was also thankfully the least matronly looking.

Staring at her hair in the mirror, she sighed in resignation at the mass of tight brown curls that sat there like a hat on her head. She had never been able to do much with it and always kept it pretty short. Otherwise, it just became unruly waves. Taking the comb, she started to work it through, smoothing it down the best she could. Adding the prettiest of her blouses, she put on a pink cardigan that her mother had bought her for her last birthday.

She was on her way down the stairs to the front door when Florence appeared in the hallway. "You look nice. Clean and tidy," she added flatly.

"I don't have going-out clothes," she informed her, defensively.

Before she said anything more, Florence had sprayed a rather sweet-smelling perfume around her in a halo of scent. Judy was mortified.

"Won't do any harm," said Florence, shaking her head. "Maybe it will distract him from those shoes you're wearing."

Judy looked down at her feet and sighed. She decided to walk into town and on her way tried to think of one or two things she could talk about with him that wasn't about work, but it all sounded so dry and boring. It was a warm day, though the clouds were heavy and gray with the ominous promise of rain. She had decided to arrive early to plan her conversation, but was mortified when she turned the corner to see that Tom was already there, pacing up and down, apparently deciding to be early himself. As her stomach coiled around itself, she sucked in a deep breath. She could do this. It was just Tom. They talked at work together every day. She was going to pretend they were at work, and if the conversation dried up, she would talk about the last experiment they had been doing. They would just be sitting on a boat while they did it, she encouraged herself. As she walked toward him, her heart thudded in her chest. She swallowed down the dryness in her throat.

By the time she reached his side, she knew she was blushing again. She was a little comforted when she looked up to see that he was reddening as well. "Judy," he acknowledged stiffly, shuffling his feet; he always did that, she noticed, when he was unsure of what to do. In this instant he seemed to be weighing up how to greet her, whether to shake her hand or not.

He settled on a compliment.

"You look lovely," he said in a genuine way, handing her a small bouquet of flowers he had in his hand.

She smiled and thanked him. They were a lovely bunch of pink carnations.

"I thought we might like to go for a picnic, so I brought some food," he informed her, lifting up and showing her a wicker basket he had by his side. "I thought we could maybe take one of the boats, find a nice spot on the side of the river, and just enjoy the afternoon. If you want to, of course."

She nodded as they made their way to one of the boats. He steadied it and helped her in, and, folding her skirt tightly around her knees, she tucked her hands under her legs as they sat awkwardly opposite one another, both avoiding eye contact.

The boat keeper pushed them off and once they were adrift on the water, she started to relax a little. This was familiar territory for her. And it brought back all the good memories of being at university, when she was racing. As Tom methodically rowed, Judy looked out, watching a family of swans gliding down the river. They talked pleasantly, if haltingly, about the weather and the sights they passed along the way. They also talked about their years as undergraduates.

After about twenty minutes Tom eyed a nice spot on the bank beside a weeping willow tree. He guided the boat to the edge and helped Judy out. Then, carefully, he pulled out a picnic blanket and placed it on the ground. Judy sat down and locked her arms around her knees, taking her time to look around her to avoid having to say something. Tom opened his basket, which had been meticulously packed. Handing her a plate and a serviette, he offered her an egg sandwich.

As she nibbled at the end of it, not feeling hungry at all, she desperately tried to think of something to say. They both gave each other awkward glances and stiff smiles.

"I wonder if you know much about how bees hibernate?" Tom asked finally, trying to break the deadlock. Grateful for any conversation, Judy shook her head as Tom started to go into a very long explanation of a study he had completed while at Cambridge.

She followed up with remarks about the ingenious shape of swan beaks. Which even to her sounded ludicrous.

It wasn't long before their conversation returned to their work, and, both on safe ground, they talked about the preceding week's experiments.

After they finished eating, the silence became unbearable again. Finally, Tom reminded her they had to get the boat back within the hour. As she stood and brushed crumbs from her skirt, Judy felt such a sense of discouragement. She had hoped that on her first-ever date, somehow, she would have become a different person. Someone with stimulating conversation and some self-assurance. Instead she felt incredibly plain and insignificant. She imagined that Tom was probably very disappointed and didn't think he would ask her to walk out with him again.

As they climbed into the boat and stroked down the river, all of a sudden the weather began to change quite rapidly. The dark clouds that had been looming all day began to rumble with thunder and she felt a light pattering of rain. Tom, who had the oars, was rowing clumsily though she didn't want to embarrass him. He started to look a little panic-stricken. All at once, with his attention being diverted by the weather, he steered the boat into a group of weeds, dragging them through an overhanging tree. Judy ducked her head to stop herself from becoming entangled as she fought off stray branches and started to laugh.

Tom seemed mortified. "I'm sorry, Judy. I'm awfully sorry."

"Please don't worry, it could happen to anyone," she said as she tugged leaves from her hair. "Tom, would you mind if I rowed?" He looked at her, surprised. "I used to row for Newnham. I can get us there a lot faster, I think."

He seemed more than happy to hand over the oars. They continued to laugh as they swapped places, trying not to tip the boat up.

"This is a fine kettle of fish," he joked as she started moving in brisk strokes down the river. "I was hoping to be all manly and show you how good I was at this."

In the midst of their dilemma, they started to relax, and the conversation grew easier. Particularly after the heavens opened up and they got soaked. She stroked as fast as she could, speeding them down the river until they got to the boat ramp, and, after dropping off the boat, raced for cover under a nearby tree, both laughing hysterically.

"Wonderful picnic," she said.

"Absolutely," he said. "I've probably given you a cold."

"It's exactly the date I was hoping for," she joked back.

They huddled together under the tree as a clap of thunder rang out overhead, the rain dripping down their faces. He stood next to her, a wet blanket under his arm. His shoulders and shirt were soaked, her cardigan sodden. But she finally felt relaxed with him.

"Thank you, Tom. This was a lovely idea," she shouted out over the sound of the rumbling sky.

"Not exactly what I had planned. I was hoping it would be special." He paused, then become coy. "I have to be honest with you, Judy. I haven't really asked a girl to do anything like this before. But I just felt as if…" He swallowed then, as if he was trying to find the right words. "That you would be the right kind of girl to enjoy this."

She smiled. "I did enjoy it, Tom, even with the rain, and I do enjoy your company," she managed, even though she lost steam and her voice petered out with her confession.

He beamed then. "So maybe you might want to do this again sometime?"

"No, thank you," she joked, shaking her head, looking out at the rain. "You can keep *this* kind of experience."

He laughed. "I meant to walk out with me."

She smiled. "I knew what you meant, Tom. And that would be lovely."

Once the downpour stopped, they made their way into town to a tea shop. Shaking off their wet things, they went inside and sat down. Now the awkwardness was broken between them, they seemed to talk easily the damp evaporating off their clothes as they made their way through two pots of tea. He told her about his life and his family. And she talked about her mum, her dad, and how hard it was to be a working woman. "People just don't take me seriously, Tom, and it's frustrating. I love what I do."

"And you're brilliant at it," he added encouragingly. "I couldn't want for a better scientific partner."

Soon they got talking about other things and their dreams for the future, including their desire to have children. He was talking about how much fun it was to be around the young.

"What about you, Judy?" he said without thinking. "Do you want children?" He suddenly seemed to regret asking such a personal question and started to get flustered. "I beg your pardon, that was probably a little too forward of me. I quite understand if you don't want to share that."

She touched his hand to reassure him without even thinking about it and then, realizing, pulled it back quickly. "I can't wait, Tom. Honestly, I can't wait to get married and have children. It's been my deepest wish for my whole life. Ever since I can remember. I love being a scientist. I love everything about it, but I can't imagine there'd be anything more fulfilling than being a mother."

He smiled. "I know what you mean," he added wistfully. "I think about that… being a dad. Frightening time we are living in, though, isn't it, when you think about it? What kind of world are they going to grow up in?"

"Well, first we need to win this war. And then hopefully the world will be a better place for everyone."

After their cups of tea, they made their way home, and he walked her back all the way up to the flat. He stood at the door as she opened it.

"You'd better get home, Tom," she said as she stood in the doorway. "I don't want you to catch a chill."

He nodded his head, and for a long moment they stood there awkwardly looking at one another. Finally, he reached his hand forward to shake hers, and she took hold of it gently and shook it quickly before pulling back. "See you tomorrow, Tom."

He started to walk down the stairs as she leaned over the banisters to add, "And thank you. I had a really good time."

"Apart from being soaked and having to row yourself back home, I suppose," he called back up to her with a laugh.

"Especially because of that," she confirmed.

With the commotion in the hallway, Florence ducked out of her room just in time to see Tom disappearing out the front door. Looking up at Judy, who was still standing peering over the banisters, she screwed up her eyes.

"Good grief, looks like it was a disaster. You look like a drowned rat."

"No, it was just perfect," said Judy, running her hand through her tight damp curls, "and I think we'll be walking out again."

Florence looked incredulous as Judy went to run herself a bath.

Sitting on the edge of the tub, she felt all warm inside. It felt good to be around Tom. He was a nice man and was very kind. And with a tightening of her stomach, she hoped he would indeed ask her out again. And she would definitely learn how to say yes without blushing.

July 16, 1940

Dearest Hedy,

I hope you're sitting down because I have some news. Guess who asked me out on a date? I can hear you shouting, "I knew it!" from here. Yes, you were right. I think something did blossom in the cellar of that pub during the air raid. It seemed to give him the confidence to finally ask me.

I know you're going to want to know all sorts of details, but let me just frame it for you this way. It started very awkwardly. I'm not sure it's a good thing for two scientists to step out together. We had nothing personally to talk about, and you know how I've told you I'm so shy, but we did get a break. There was a downpour, and Tom was trying to row me down the river when we got caught in it. You'll never guess, though! I ended up taking the oars off him and I got us back quickly and safely, and that seemed to break the ice. We came away soaked to the skin but in good spirits.

He is such a nice man. I've never felt like this before. I think about him all the time. Is that normal? I find myself imagining being in his arms at the most inappropriate times. He leaned across the desk to point out an equation to me today, and in a moment of sheer craziness, I wanted to throw my arms around him and kiss him.

Please tell me I'm not suffering from some strange delusion or disease. Is this what it's like to be attracted to another person? Is it always so unpractical? Having never been in love before, I have no reference point, and I'm too embarrassed to take out a book from the library. My landlady just thinks we should hurry up and get married. But how do I know he's the right one for me, Hedy?

I can't think of a better person to ask about love than a film star, with all those stories you work on. I am also registering many unusual physical symptoms. For example, my heart beats faster whenever he's around, and my mouth dries up more than usual. And when he brushed his hand against mine the other day, it felt as if an electrical charge shot through my body. Please tell me this is normal, and I'm hoping it passes quickly because I'm finding it awfully hard to concentrate on my work.

Write back soon and tell me everything. I am woefully inadequate and need your help!

Love,
Judy

TELEGRAM

DEAR JUDY – (STOP) –
VIVE L'AMOUR – (STOP) – EVERYTHING IS NORMAL – (STOP) –
GOD BLESS YOUR FAST-BEATING HEART – (STOP) –

TAKE TWO ASPIRINS AND GO TO BED – (STOP) –
KISS KISS – (STOP) –
HEDY

HEDY LAMARR
4:04 PM

Chapter Fifteen

July 1940

The sleek white yacht cut through the dark still water with such precision, it barely created a ripple as it pressed forward into the open waters. Seated on a spacious cream leather sofa, one leg tucked beneath her, Hedy placed her chin on her hands, resting on the smooth, warm veneer of the yacht's stern as she looked back toward the beach feeling a little morose. In the dusky evening twilight, and with distance, the harbor lamps became mere sparkles suspended in mid-air. The crashing waves on the black rocks, just silent flashes of spray. Both Fritz and Gene's faces flashed into her mind. The mistakes she had made in love always seemed to weigh her down. Why couldn't she see her past like this view? From this distance, the shore was a silent echo of what it had been like up close. Why was it that her past had so much power over her? Once again, she thought about Fritz's cruel words and Gene's expression when she had insinuated having her as his wife should be enough. She wished more than anything she wasn't so affected by her ex-husbands' opinions of her, but somehow the way they'd seen her had distorted her own view of herself. No matter how many pictures she did, or how much people seemed to love her, she still felt empty inside and unloved, a fraud, just waiting to be uncovered.

Howard Hughes tottered toward her in his white yacht pants and a blue and white polo shirt. In his hand, two glasses of champagne. He handed one to Hedy, who gathered her pink cashmere sweater around her shoulders for warmth and, slipping into her public persona, flashed him with her emerald-green eyes.

"Cocktails and champagne? I do believe you're trying to get me drunk, Mr. Hughes," she purred.

He cocked her a half-smile. "I was hoping it wouldn't show," he responded. Sitting down next to her, he slipped his arm behind her on the sofa and drew himself close to her.

"Tell me about your engine," she asked, turning to look at him directly, a curl of her lip with the insinuated innuendo.

Howard chuckled as she continued.

"I've been watching the way this yacht glides through the water. It gives you a very comfortable ride."

Howard pulled his arm away, and, hunching forward, shook his head. "Of all the people I've invited onto my yacht, not one of them has ever asked me that question."

"If by people you mean women," she responded with a smirk, "why does that surprise you? I thought you'd be used to me by now. You should know I'm more interested in your toys than anything else."

"Anything?" he teased her.

She took a sip of her champagne and paused for dramatic effect. "Well, almost anything," she drawled.

Janet Gaynor and Adrian Greenburg, for whom Howard was throwing the party, were in a lively conversation in the stateroom when two other guests of the yacht party came out onto the deck from inside the cabin, where they'd all been enjoying cocktails. Howard had invited an eclectic group of people aboard, which was no surprise with him being so eccentric himself. Hedy was enjoying the variety. For months she'd been only with movie people and it was nice to talk about anything other than the latest director, or the problems they'd all been having with co-stars. The man who wobbled down the deck toward her was short and square. He had blonde hair, blue eyes, and a brooding expression. On his arm was a dark-haired woman with short, cropped hair and plain features and a timidity that caused her to look nervously over at her husband, constantly.

Howard stood up to introduce them. "George Antheil, have you met Hedy Lamarr yet?"

The brooding expression broke into a smile. "Not officially, but I'm acquainted with her movies."

"You'll find I'm less pouting in real life," she joked as she leaned forward to shake his hand.

"This is Boski," he said, introducing the woman next to him, "my wife." Avoiding her gaze, she shook Hedy's hand limply, barely taking hold of her fingers, and her smile appeared disingenuous.

"As well as being a movie star," Howard continued, "did you know that Hedy is an inventor?"

George's face lit up.

"I think you two would get on very well," Hughes encouraged. "George is a composer, but also likes to dabble in inventing."

He nodded his head and sat down, while Boski just looked uncomfortable.

"How fascinating," Hedy answered. "I'd love to know more."

In response, Boski pulled up a deck chair very close to George's, apparently wanting to mark her territory. This wasn't unusual behavior around Hedy. It was sad for her, but women often felt insecure around her, and it meant that she had no female friends in California she felt she could trust.

Howard offered them both a glass of champagne as George lit a cigarette and offered his open case around to everybody else. Hedy decided to risk it. She drew out a slim white cigarette and he lit the tip with his silver lighter. Slowly, she drew the smoke into her lungs and let it curl gently out of her nostrils.

It didn't take long for Hedy and George to get into a deep conversation. Just long enough for Boski to become bored. Not even touching her drink, she placed a small, white hand on his arm.

"George, I'm getting a little bit hungry. I would like to go inside for some more hors d'oeuvres."

George patted her hand as if he were appeasing a child. "Why don't you go ahead, dear? I'm not hungry right now."

Boski looked put out. Obviously, she had planned to separate him from this group but it hadn't worked.

"Would you like me to bring you anything else?" she enquired flatly.

"No, I'm good, honey. Thank you."

Boski stood up and tottered back toward the door as the three of them became immersed in the world of invention.

As the evening wore on, their conversation, as always, strayed to the war and what was being done to counteract the Germans' onslaught on Europe.

"I was reading," stated Hedy, "only yesterday about how the British Navy is suffering catastrophic damage from enemy torpedoes. Somebody needs to invent something that will help them."

Howard shook his head and laughed. "I'm sure you could do it, too, Hedy," he joked.

George's face lit up. "In all seriousness, I would be up for trying to do something like that, too. Maybe you should come by sometime to my studio, and we could have a go? Work together on something?"

"Now, now, old boy," said Howard, leaning forward and crushing out his cigarette into a solid, crystal-cut ashtray. "It may have slipped your observation, but Miss Lamarr is supposed to be seeing me," he teased.

"I am?" enquired Hedy, with raised eyebrows.

"It's in all the fan magazines, didn't you know?" stated Howard with a smirk, topping up their drinks.

"I guess we must be madly in love, then, if it's in all the magazines," she responded sarcastically, fluttering her eyelashes comically, playing the coquette.

In reality, as far as she was concerned, nothing was agreed between them, even though they had been out on the town a few times together since his party, and this invitation onto his yacht.

"This would be purely business," said George. "I'm only interested in Hedy's mind."

"Well, *that* makes a change," said Hedy as she held up her glass to toast his confession with her champagne. They all laughed.

"Do you want to get together sometime and talk a little bit more? Who knows, maybe we could help these Brits win the war?"

"You mean you don't think just making movies is going to do that for us?" she said in an ironic tone. "I know there's more that we can do," she continued with conviction. "Howard wants me to work on something in his factory too. The way I'm going, maybe I'll be able to give up the movie business altogether and become a full-time inventor."

"Well, that would sure be a waste," said George, shaking his head. "That face isn't meant to be hidden behind a chemistry table."

All at once, Boski appeared in the cabin's doorway, her hand on her hip, her expression thunderous, and Hedy could tell that this conversation was over. They needed to put the poor girl out of her misery.

George knew it too.

"Well, it's been lovely chatting to you, Hedy, and Howard. I'm starting to get a little drowsy with this sea air. I might take a nap before I change for dinner and see you later."

Boski looked relieved as he joined her and she clung on to his arm, claiming her mate.

Later, with an excellent dinner of fresh sea bass and an exotic salad served in the wood-paneled state room, all of Howard's guests had a marvelous time. After a decadent chocolate cheesecake for dessert, Hedy slipped back out onto the deck in her bare feet to be alone, her white, strappy sandals in her hand. She stood looking up at the stars and the moon, enjoying the rocking motion of the boat and feeling the warmth of the polished wood deck beneath her feet. Out at sea, it was so still and so quiet. She felt safe away from the cameras and constant show of Hollywood, and for a quiet moment she could actually hear her own thoughts.

As she closed her eyes to enjoy a cool breeze on her face, she thought about her work. In a way, she loved the attention. But George's words had struck a chord in her: "That face is not meant to be just hidden behind a chemistry table."

When she had come to Hollywood, she had wanted of course to be successful and make money. But in every movie, she was still being cast as the mysterious exotic. Something lofty and unobtainable. It was so far from her real personality, and the longer she was here, the less she felt like herself.

Howard joined her on the deck. "I love it out here in the evening," he whispered. "It's so peaceful, isn't it?"

She smiled. "I was thinking the same thing."

Howard placed his hand on her arm. Hedy turned and looked up at him. In the moonlight, she could see his eyes taking in every inch of her face. He seemed to be emboldened for a minute and, placing his arms around her, he drew her in for a kiss.

She surrendered to it, not because she felt an incredible attraction for Howard, but because it felt nice. A perfect end to a perfect day. A way of saying thank you to her host. It was a warm, friendly kiss, but it didn't stir her. She wasn't sure if she was still smarting from her last very public separation just ten months before and wanted to protect her heart, or if it was just that she didn't feel that way about Howard. But there was the sound of lapping water as their backdrop, the moonlight streaming across the deck, illuminating his strong features and dark eyes. Surely if she felt more for him, it would have been the perfect romantic moment? But she didn't feel anything yet. Maybe if she spent more time with him...

As he pulled away, he stared down at her. "I did mean what I said earlier," he murmured, "even if I didn't say it in quite the right way. I would like to see you, Hedy, on a more permanent basis."

"I gathered," she responded.

He smiled. "May I escort you to your room?"

She nodded.

Slipping his arm around her shoulder, he walked her back to her bedroom. As she stepped into her cabin, he stood framed in the door, and his six-foot four-inch build barely fit within the tiny space.

"I guess I'll see you tomorrow, Mr. Hughes," she said, turning and placing her hand on the doorframe.

"It's Howard, Miss Lamarr," he responded with a nod, and he left her.

The tiny cabin was small but luxurious, a far cry from the cabin on the *Normandie*. Honey-colored paneled walls were polished to a high veneer as they creaked and rolled with the swaying of the water. A cozy bunk was dressed in white silk sheets and topped with a goose-down comforter and pillows, reminding Hedy so much of Austria it made her heart hurt for her homeland. In front of the porthole was a well-stocked writing desk and chair with the name of the yacht embroidered in gold lettering on the rich royal-blue seat pad. A stack of matching blue and white towels, and a divine-smelling soap, were placed next to a sparkling white porcelain sink.

Hedy put on her satin nightgown and slipped into her tiny bunk. She had been working so hard, she hadn't realized how much she had needed this break. Just to enjoy the peace and quiet. As the rocking of the boat lulled her to sleep, full moonlight streamed through the porthole, illuminating the paneled wall, and that night Hedy slept like a baby without even stirring once. She couldn't remember the last time she'd slept through like that, and she felt like a child on holiday.

The next morning, she was woken by the call of the seagulls. They were up early, diving, swooping, and gliding through the morning sunlight. Looking out of the porthole, she noticed

Howard's captain had parked them next to a sandy cove, with a beautiful, white, pristine beach. She couldn't wait to go and try it, and for some strange uncontrollable reason, she wanted to swim. Throwing on her bathing suit, she made her way out of the cabin, a blue-striped towel draped over her shoulder.

Janet and Adrian were already up, helping themselves to coffee, fresh fruit and croissants that were now all centered buffet-style on the table.

As she approached, Adrian looked up from his newspaper.

"Good morning, Miss Lamarr. I say, are you going for a swim? I love your suit," he mused, drawing his finger up and down in the air and admiring what she was wearing in a way that only a fashion designer could.

"I thought I might try it," she answered as she sashayed through the room, grabbing a slice of pineapple on her way by.

Out on the deck, the morning was perfect, a picture blue sky, hot and sun-soaked. The tide was in on the beach and looked so inviting.

Throwing her towel onto a deck chair, Hedy got up onto the top rung of the boat's ladder and dived in before anyone could stop her. The water was glorious. She swam a couple of strokes and then rolled over onto her back, allowing her body to drift on the rise and fall of the gathering waves. With her ears below the water, she observed the birds flying above and her world became still, quiet, and echoey. All she could hear were her arms and feet circling under the water. She turned and kicked her legs and stroked her arms toward the shore, enjoying the feeling of spaciousness and being alive. Her head was warm with the heat, her body cool with the water. Soon the shore loomed closer into view, and, reaching the beach, she shook her hair and padded up onto the soft, hot sand that stuck to her toes. Finding a smooth black rock, she lowered herself down and let out a deep, contented breath. Soaking up the sun's warmth in the stone, she shivered a little as the water dried slowly on her wet limbs.

Closing her eyes, she licked her salty lips and inhaled the water's limey scent mingled with the drying seaweed that lined the beach. As she listened to the waves breaking on the shore, she must have dozed off, because the rhythmic splashing of oars in the water awakened her. Leaning up on her elbows, she saw Howard coming toward her in a tiny boat, cigarette drooped out of the corner of his mouth, his white sleeves rolled to the elbow, exposing his strong brown forearms. Dragging the little boat up onto the sand, he held up her towel and a toweling robe to explain his presence in one hand and a bottle of champagne in the other.

She shook her head and called out to him to be heard over the rolling tide. "Champagne at ten in the morning? I think I've had enough to drink, Mr. Hughes."

Reaching back into the boat, he produced a carafe of orange juice, like a magician taking a rabbit out of a hat.

"Champagne mimosas are an American tradition," he shouted back. "You want to fit in, don't you?"

She shook her head in dismay as he trotted up the beach to join her.

Throwing down his own towel on the rock, he passed her the robe. She wrapped herself in it, enjoying the warmth of the fabric against her shuddering limbs, which were still drying off. He went back to the boat and fished out a champagne bucket and two glasses. Returning, he sat next to her, and, sinking the bottle into the gritty sand, he braced it between his knees and carefully worked on the cork until it slid out with a pop. He swished champagne into the glass and a dash of orange juice and handed it to her.

She took a sip. "I do believe you're trying to take advantage of me, Mr. Hughes," she said with a curl of her lip.

He lay back on his elbows and smiled. "Would that be such a dreadful thing?" he enquired.

"It depends," answered Hedy. "I don't want to get a bad reputation."

"And you think dating me would create a bad reputation for you?"

"Well, what about you and Katharine Hepburn? I heard you and she were an item."

The pain was evident in his eyes, and he attempted to disguise it by sitting up and fumbling with the champagne bottle, pouring himself a drink.

"That's over," he said in a quiet, flat voice. "It's been over for a while. Besides, I heard she wants to leave Hollywood."

"Hepburn? Well, that would be a sad thing."

"She prefers the stage," said Howard, taking a sip of his mimosa. "Besides, Hedy, you and I have so much more in common. We're both inventors."

Hedy smiled. "Maybe so. Which reminds me, when am I going to get to see what you're inventing?"

"How about Saturday?" he said. "Are you shooting next weekend?"

"The movie is, but I'm not in the scenes, so I might be able to swing it."

"Why don't you come over at one o'clock and I'll take you on a factory tour."

"Sounds thrilling," she said, finishing her mimosa and lying back on the rock again, her head spinning with the early morning alcohol. All at once, Howard was hovering over her, his silhouette blotting out the sun.

"I can see why Mayer wants to bill you as the most beautiful woman in the world."

Hedy felt her stomach cramp. As much as selling her that way worked for the studios, there was still something about it that she hated.

"I guess 'Austrian inventor' wouldn't have worked quite the same way," she stated. *Let alone "Jewish,"* she thought quietly to herself, closing her eyes.

He drew very close to her. She could feel his breath on her cheek, smell the salt on his skin. She opened her eyes again; he was inches from her, staring down at her lips.

"Well, Mr. Hughes, are you going to kiss me or just stare at me?"

He broke into a broad grin, lowering his head, and his lips found hers. They were warm and sweet with the orange juice. As the wind whipped her hair across both their faces, he slipped his hand beneath her head, pulling her closer, deepening the kiss. As he did so, his other hand started to rove over her body. Caressing her hips, running the flat of his hand down across her stomach, causing goosebumps on any exposed skin. He was hungrier for her than he had been the night before. He slipped his hand lower, and as his hand caressed her inner thighs, the sand, now dry on her legs, stung her skin.

Before it became too heated, she pushed him gently away and sat up. Hedy realized with a jolt she wasn't ready for this. Apparently, she *was* still smarting from the failure of her recent marriage. She hated the fact that after leaving Fritz, she had fallen so deeply in love with Gene that she'd jumped into a second marriage blindly. It had been a big mistake. Hedy hadn't been prepared for the ongoing pain she would feel when she had found out he had slept with someone else. His betrayal of her had only reinforced what Fritz had told her. That she would never be wanted for herself, only for her body.

Now she didn't want to take anything too fast at this time in her life. She was building an image, and though being around a billionaire wasn't such a bad way to go, she didn't want to be pinned down to anybody right now after two failed marriages.

Catching her breath, she stared out to sea and ran her hands through her damp curls.

"So, next Saturday, then," he said breathlessly.

"Saturday," she answered evenly, standing up and brushing off the sand. "Though I wouldn't mind a lift back in your boat," she added, pointing at it as it rolled back and forward on the edge of the sand, rocking in the ebb and flow of the tide.

"It would be my honor," he said, gathering up their glasses.

Back in the boat, he rowed out toward the yacht as Hedy trailed a hand in the water. It was a strange life. The rest of the world was at war, including her beloved Austria, and here she was living in a little slice of paradise. Something about all that didn't feel right to her.

Once the ship docked, Howard had some work to do on the boat, so George offered Hedy a lift home. First, he dropped off his wife, who needed to get to work, much to her chagrin. On dropping off Hedy, George realized he didn't have her phone number in case they wanted to get together as Howard had suggested. He called out to her before she entered her house. Swishing back to the car, she took out her lipstick and wrote her number on his windscreen, with a smile.

"You'll never forget it now," she joked.

"Neither will Boski if she ever sees it." He laughed, shaking his head as he waved and drove off.

Hedy felt optimistic as she bounded back into the house. She was finally meeting people more like her, people interested in science and inventing. Maybe she would finally find a way to incorporate it into her life, to do something she found much more worthwhile.

Chapter Sixteen

Late summer 1940

After their first date on the river, Judy and Tom started to meet regularly and go on outings together. They began to relax in one another's company, and she really enjoyed being around him. He was such a kind man and very thoughtful with her, always bringing flowers, always escorting her home, and making sure she felt safe and cared for in between. As the months went on, she started to feel a great deal of love for him. And she sensed that Tom felt the same way, though he never said as much. It was in the little gestures that she saw his care. And though he was more physical with her, holding her hand or touching her arm, he still hadn't kissed her. And there was always a certain awkwardness when he said good night to her at the end of the evening when they'd been together.

They'd also got closer in the lab, so engrossed in their work, trying to find essential solutions to aid the British in the war.

It was a warm summer day when Tom invited her to go out for the afternoon to the Sedgwick Museum of Earth Science. Even though Judy had lived in Cambridge for a while, she hadn't had time to visit this well-known museum since she'd been a student, and she was excited to see several of the new exhibitions.

Tom picked her up after lunch, and, taking the bus into town, they arrived at the enormous Victorian building with red and brown brick walls, imposing and grand. The two of them walked up the steep steps flanked by the proud stone lions at the bottom of the stairs.

They wound their way through the exhibition. And Judy could tell there was something on Tom's mind. She had made comments about a couple of the different displays, and he seemed vague and removed. She was concerned; this wasn't like Tom, who was always so attentive and engaged.

At one point Judy pointed out a particular mollusk, and he just nodded his head, then added almost excitedly, "Of course, they work better as a group. I don't know if you knew that." And he went into quite a broad explanation of why mollusks, as a collective, had a stronger chance of survival than they did alone. She listened to his fervorous explanation, surprised he was so enamored by the life of shellfish.

After they'd walked the museum, they strolled to a local tea shop for a cup of tea. The tea had just arrived at the table when he seemed to be looking awkward again. As he took off his jacket, she could see he was sweating.

"Is everything all right, Tom?" she enquired, starting to become concerned about his wellbeing. They had been under a lot of pressure at the lab.

Tom coughed and cleared his throat. "Yes, Judy, everything is fine. I was just thinking about the mollusks."

Judy took a sip of tea and frowned. "Mollusks?"

"At the museum," he continued, "and… how they survive better together."

Judy nodded, and she was about to talk about something else they'd seen there when Tom stopped her by placing his hand on her own.

"Some things work better together. Don't you think, Judy?"

She nodded again. There was a scientific theory for that, and she started to expand upon it: "Oh yes, as you were saying earlier, clumping is a wonderful way of creating group protection…"

And then he stopped her again. "I was thinking, as in people. Some things work better when people are together and not apart."

Judy really didn't understand what he was trying to say. Then all of a sudden, something dawned on her.

"Judy, how would you feel about something like that, for you and me?"

She blushed red. Was he proposing to her? She started to smile, but couldn't say anything. Once again, she was tongue-tied.

Tom took a quick drink of his tea before he continued. "I've been thinking of this for a long time, Judy. And I think I would very much like to be like the mollusks with you."

She wanted to say jokingly, "What, clinging to a rock somewhere under the sea?" But she knew what he was trying to say and how difficult this was for him. She swallowed down her embarrassment and took his hand in hers and held it.

"I think… that would be… wonderful, Tom," she managed to splutter out. "If I think you're asking me to marry you?"

He nodded. "Oh yes, yes, of course, did I not say that?"

"Yes," she said, "I guess you did in your own unique way."

And they both beamed at each other.

They decided to get married three weeks later, since there was no need for them to wait. They had known each other for three years and time felt of the essence during this war. Unfortunately, there would be no church wedding, as churches were hard to book at that time, with lots of people getting married, so they decided on a registry office. Secretly, Judy was glad. She couldn't imagine having a great fuss around it, with everyone staring at them.

He walked her home that evening, and at the stairs, she turned on the landing as she usually did to say goodbye, and suddenly he put both hands on her shoulders. She looked up into his eyes.

He was so full of love for her. And he also looked a little embarrassed.

"Judy, would you mind awfully if I kissed you?"

She shook her head and smiled. "You are my fiancé, Tom. I think that's fine now."

He drew close to her very slowly, holding her shoulders gently as his lips met hers. The kiss was soft and warm and so unexpected. It was the first time Judy had ever been kissed, and she wondered if it was the first time Tom had ever kissed anyone. As a scientist she couldn't help but analyze the experience; she was amazed that a kiss felt so different to touching a hand or an arm. The closeness with another human being, this safe vulnerability she felt with Tom: it was a connection between them that she'd never felt before. As he held her, Judy felt so alive to everything she was experiencing. The heat of his body next to hers. The softness of his lips. The smell of shaving soap on his skin. Instinctively, Judy found herself moving in a way she hadn't expected. She put her arms around his neck and pulled him in closer, and he slid his arms down to her waist and pulled her closer too. And she could feel his heart pounding in his chest, his breath quickening. When he eventually pulled away from her, she struggled to let him go. She wanted to stay there in his arms kissing him for the rest of the evening. She'd had no idea how complete and heady it could feel to be that close to the man she loved.

Tom caught his breath and then smiled awkwardly.

"Thank you, Judy," he whispered. "Thank you for saying yes. I promise I'll try to be the best husband I possibly can for you."

She felt so much love for him.

"Thank you, Tom, and good night."

He nodded, adjusted his hat and headed for the stairs.

Touching her fingers to her lips, where Tom's had just been, Judy watched him heading down the stairs and felt the tears well up inside. She was so happy.

*

At the service three weeks later, her parents had made it all the way on the train from Wales. Her mother brought a little spray of lily of the valley with her, especially for her daughter's wedding. Judy had no idea where her mother had got it so late in the season, but it was a lovely memory of home. Her ruddy-cheeked mother whispered and cried through most of the service, and her dad seemed to need to shake everybody's hands, proclaiming in a booming Welsh voice, "Jonathan Morgan, my daughter's the one getting married." He said it with a great sense of pride, as if he was in awe of that very fact.

Unfortunately, Tom's parents had died a few years before, but several of the scientists from the Cavendish came, along with a distant uncle of Tom's. As soon as the service was over, the bride and bridegroom went for something to eat with the guests but then left straight away on their honeymoon, as Judy's mother sobbed into her handkerchief.

Tom and Judy would be honeymooning in Clacton-on-Sea, which was just a short trip from Cambridge, and Tom had booked them in a very grand hotel there. On arrival, they put their bags in their lovely room and went for a walk, enjoying the sunset from Clacton Pier. She loved being with Tom. Holding his hand, and walking comfortably by his side. As they strolled they talked about their work and their dreams for the future after the war. There was an ease between them now.

"I can't wait to have a family," said Judy. "I can't wait for my children to look just like you."

Tom flushed with embarrassment. "I was hoping they'd look like you."

"What, with tight curly hair? And squirrel-like eyes," she responded with a smile.

"I don't think your eyes are squirrel-like. I think they're beautiful," he said.

She was surprised. It was the first compliment he'd ever given her about her looks. But he seemed so sincere and almost offended at her view of herself.

They walked back to the hotel that evening and had a lovely dinner, but as the evening wore on, she started to feel apprehensive.

She wasn't quite sure what to expect from their wedding night together. She had bought herself a comfortable cotton nightdress, and after they went back to the room, she stood looking at herself in it at the bathroom mirror. Why'd she bought something so matronly? At the time, she'd thought maybe she would get lots more use out of it. But was this the right thing to be wearing on her wedding night? She wasn't sure. She brushed her hair and made her way nervously into the room.

Tom nodded and passed her on his way into the bathroom, his leather wash bag tucked under his arm. He seemed to take forever as she sat nervously on the edge of the bed, waiting for him to arrive. When he did, he looked as awkward as she felt in his green striped pajamas. She stood up quickly to greet him as he walked over to the bed.

"May I touch your hair, Judy?"

"You don't have to ask," she said. "You're my husband now. Of course you can touch my hair."

He nodded and ran his fingers through her curls. "I've been wanting to run my hands through these curls since the day I met you," he said with a smile. "Judy, you should probably know I've never really done anything like this before."

She chuckled. "And what makes you think I have?"

He continued, "Obviously, I know the logistics of, you know, what happens, but I really want to make you happy."

"And, Tom, you will. Do you know how I know that? Because we care deeply about each other and we'll find our way. Even if it takes a little time to figure all that out, so I'm not worried."

He looked reassured as she pulled his head down toward her then and kissed him tenderly. His arms slid around her waist again as they started to succumb to the emotions flooding their bodies. And then as if it was the most natural thing in the world, he lifted her gently onto their bed to make love for the first time.

Dear Hedy,

I just wanted to drop you a line on this postcard to thank you for your amazing wedding gift. The crystal turtledoves arrived miraculously in one piece and how clever of you to order them from Harrods so they would get here in time. Hedy, I'm so in love, I had no idea I could be so happy. We are having the most marvelous time on our honeymoon. I had no idea that intimacy could be so thrilling and Tom seems to be getting younger by the day with the chance to relax. We are both fat as pigs because the hotel's allowed to have extra rations, and as red as tomatoes from the hot sunny days. It will be hard to go back to work.

Sending you much love,
Judy and Tom (the Jenkinses) xxx

Chapter Seventeen

Late summer 1940

Hedy arrived at Howard Hughes's factory the following weekend. Both she and George had been invited over for a tour and to see his H-1 racer. As George opened the door and she stepped out of his car, the heat of the California summer bore down and also rose to meet her in the smell of hot tarmac mixed with the engine oil that drifted out from the open hangar door. As she closed it behind her, the metal of the car door was hot in her hand and she was glad she had opted for her favorite shell-pink silk calf-length dress that accentuated her tiny waist, her white lace gloves and pink silk scarf in her hair and not something darker and more formal. Folding her soft leather handbag under her arm, she checked her pearls at her neck and swaggered toward the open hangar with George by her side.

Inside the factory it was cooler; the brick walls were painted a pale duck-egg blue, and the airplane that took center stage was being worked on by a handful of mechanics. As she clipped across the concrete, the group of men inside became alerted by the visitors and stopped to watch her enter. Taking off her sunglasses, Hedy slid them onto the top of her head as it took a minute for her eyes to adjust from the bright sunlight and be able to focus on the impressive plane in front of her. She recognized it straight away as the H-1 racer, the plane in which Hughes had broken the world speed record, and it was magnificent. Standing about twenty-five feet long, with a wingspan of around thirty-two feet, its sleek silver body glinted in the shafts of sunshine that streamed in from high windows. All the way down the silver-colored fuselage, a line of flush rivets shone to perfection in long neat rows.

Howard's foreman came out to meet them and, shaking their hands, led them into the back office where Howard was poring over plans at his desk. "Mr. Hughes, your guests are here," he announced, and at once, Howard's face changed from frustration into delight.

"Welcome," he said, unrolling his shirtsleeves, which were hitched up below his elbows. Buttoning his cuffs, he put on his jacket and strode toward them. "George," he said, pumping his visitor's hand enthusiastically. "Hedy," he added, his tone warm as he kissed her on the cheek. "I'm glad you could both make it."

"That's some fine bird you've got down there," said George with a whistle. "Do you think she'll fly?" he said jokingly.

Howard laughed as he opened up the door and ushered them through. "I don't know, George. Do you want to go up with me as a navigator and see?"

George threw his hands in the air. "I prefer to stay on the ground. I'll leave the sky for the birds."

Making their way back into the vast building, Hedy listened as Howard talked them through the logistics of the airplane. Hedy's mind was already at work as she looked it over.

After they'd finished the factory tour itself, they went upstairs, and Hedy asked if she could look at the plans. Hughes took them to the drawing office, where blueprints were standing on a vast easel, and she started to look over them with interest.

"Get any wind drag with these wings?" she queried, resting the corner of her sunglasses in her mouth as she pondered the diagrams.

Howard went into a long-involved explanation about wind speed and the basic design.

"How fast does she go?" she asked. He gave her a value, and she slowly nodded her head. "I bet I could make it go faster," she added with a wry smile.

Later, as they were back at Howard's house, relaxing, she went into more detail. They were sitting out by the pool, drinking old-fashioneds over ice when he brought it up again. "You were saying," he said, "earlier at the factory about the plane's speed. What makes you think you could make it go faster?"

"The wings. They seem a little solid and boxy to me. You need something more aerodynamic."

Howard smiled and shook his head with disbelief, and so did George, who was picking his way through a bowl of nuts and flicking them up into the air, catching them on his tongue as she chatted.

"What do you mean?" said Howard.

"Okay, do you have any books here by any chance?"

He smiled. "Of course."

"Encyclopedias?"

"Yeah, I should think so," he said. "Follow me."

She followed behind him, George tagging along with interest. In his vast library, the atmosphere was of cool reverence with the smell of wood and money. From floor to ceiling, numerous bookshelves were stocked with every kind of book, many gilded and leather-bound.

"Does the Library of Congress know you have all these books?" Hedy asked with a smile. "They should be bringing people for a tour here."

Howard chuckled as he studied the shelf until he found the section where the encyclopedias were.

He pulled out a couple of books he thought would be of interest, and she started to look through them. As she was deep in her research, George and Howard soon gave up and returned to the pool to continue their drinks.

Hedy's mind was whirring with a million ideas as she pored over the books at the table. Eventually, she found what she had wanted to.

She came back to the pool and placed the two books she had on the table. "Here," she said, "look, this is the fastest bird in the world."

Howard cocked an eyebrow. "Fascinating, Hedy. What has that got to do with planes?"

"Look at the way the wings are; they're created for speed. And here," she added, pulling out another book and pointing to another section. "This is the fastest fish, and look at the fins on it. Do you see what they have in common? They are streamlined, not square like your planes are."

He nodded, humoring her. "So, what do you suggest?"

"Do you have some graph paper?"

"Of course," he responded. And going back to his study, he came back and produced some for her. She spent the rest of the afternoon sketching out ideas until she eventually presented them to her companions. "Something like this. I bet you'd get another ten, fifteen miles an hour just changing the shape of the wings."

Howard was impressed. "You might have something here, Miss Lamarr. I should employ you."

She beamed.

A few hours later, Hedy was still poring over the design when George excused himself.

"Unlike you millionaires and movie stars, some of us have to earn a living," he said, kissing Hedy on both cheeks and making his way to the door. "Think you can get a lift home?"

"I might know someone who has a car," she joked, flashing a smile over at Howard.

"Howard," George said, placing a firm hand in his host's own, "it's been a pleasure. Thanks for inviting me over. If ever I feel like dying, I'll take a trip in one of your airplanes with you."

Howard laughed. "You wait and see," he shouted as George started to make his way across the gravel driveway. "You'll be doing it one day. Everybody will."

"Not me. I'm going to leave those kinds of heroics to daredevils like you," responded George as he jumped into his car and, with a wave of his hand, he tore off down the drive.

They went back to the pool, where Hedy started sketching yet another design.

"Would you like a drink, Hedy?"

"Huh?" she answered, not even looking up, completely engrossed in what she was doing.

"Come on in. Inventing time is over," he said, taking her hand. "It's time for us to relax a little and eat."

Hedy gave in with a sigh. When she was inventing, she couldn't think about anything else. She looked at her smiling host and realized, actually, she was getting hungry.

"I had my cook prepare a little snack earlier and leave it in the refrigerator. I thought you might like something to eat." Taking her hand, he led her into his dining room. It was already set for dinner with the best crystal and silverware, and she smiled.

"Just a little snack? Who else are we inviting? Royalty?"

"Just you and me," he said, going into the kitchen and bringing in a platter of sliced cold meats expertly and beautifully presented and a very colorful salad. "It might look impressive, but it's really just sandwiches," he said, bringing her a loaf of Italian bread.

She cut herself a tiny slice and, plucking at an olive with a cocktail stick, sat back in her chair to survey her companion. "You're very fortunate, Mr. Hughes."

"That, I know," responded Howard with a smile. "But in what instance are you talking about here?"

"Well, you get to do this all day. You get to play."

"You're not playing when you're on set?"

"Well, yes, but it's different. I have to look like this all the time. It takes a lot of work. You can roll up your shirtsleeves and be in grease and engine oil all day."

"I can assure you, Miss Lamarr, I am never going to be in grease and oil all day. I have a little aversion to that. I prefer to stay very clean."

"Ah, good to know," she responded, plucking another olive and rolling it up in a thin sliver of prosciutto as they continued conversing with ease until they finished eating. The sun was setting and they walked out onto the balcony where she had first met him and Hedy looked out again toward the sea.

She shivered a little with the evening's coolness, and Howard, standing at her side, offered her a cigarette. This time she took one. She had no one to impress at the moment. Howard seemed to be a sure thing, if she was so inclined. She lit it and took a deep drag as they stared out toward the crimson sky and blue water.

"It's lovely here, Howard. I'd never get tired of this view."

"It looks a lot better with you alongside it," he added, looking over at her.

"Well, that's a corny line," she joked. "Where did you pick that one up? At the movies?"

"It would probably sound more gallant if Mr. Errol Flynn were saying it," he responded with a laugh. He slipped his arm around her shoulders, and she got close to him. She liked him. He was amicable. But he didn't make her stomach flip-flop or her skin shiver as she'd had with other men. She was beginning to feel a bit discouraged that she would ever find real love. Was she ever going to find a man who was faithful but could also make her heart pound wildly again?

Finishing their cigarettes, they crushed them out in the ashtray and looked out again toward the water. Taking her hand, he drew her close and brushed her lips with a gentle kiss. As he pulled away to judge her reaction, she moved in closer and slid her hand to the nape of his neck, pulling him toward her for something more meaningful. His lips were warm, soft, and full. As they gave themselves fully to the kiss, his hand drifted down her cheek, and his fingers grazed the side of her neck and traced her collarbone. As he deepened the kiss, a breeze stirred the scent of jasmine from the garden below, mingling with his lemon aftershave and her own expensive perfume and the effect was intoxicating. Hedy slid her hand down his chest, feeling his heart beat wildly beneath her palm, his breath starting to quicken. He pulled her closer and slid his hands down to her hips, and she could tell by the tension in his own body that he wanted more.

Finally pulling away from her, he was breathless, and in a husky voice she hardly recognized, he asked her if she wanted to come inside. Catching her own breath, she nodded. Taking her by the hand, he led her toward the bedroom.

"I take it as you're not putting up a fight this time, you've reconsidered dating me," he whispered to her.

"Oh, is that what this is? I thought this might just be sex."

He laughed, then lifted her in his arms and carried her onto the bed. "Would that make a difference?" he asked as he slid onto the bed next to her.

"Uh-huh," she said. "I'm not averse to making love. I'm averse to being shackled to somebody."

Taking his time, he feathered her face and neck with kisses as he unzipped her dress, and she unbuttoned his shirt; then, gently, he started to make love to her.

After that night, they started seeing each other more regularly, but as much as she enjoyed his company, she only really enjoyed it when they were deep in conversation about inventing.

As a gift, he bought her an inventing kit and table that she could put in her trailer during shoots. It was stacked with test tubes and scientific equipment. Finally, she could immerse herself in whatever her current idea was and when they were together the two of them would often sit poring over ideas that she had until early in the morning. It wasn't uncommon for Hedy to lie naked across his bed as he smoked, listening to her theories. But no matter how much time they spent together, she still didn't feel any more for him than she had initially.

He would always be a lovely friend, but she simply couldn't see this going anywhere. When, a few months later, she heard that he had been seen with Katharine Hepburn again, she received the news with mixed feelings. She didn't like being deceived, especially after what had happened before, but it wasn't so terrible that she wouldn't be seeing him romantically any more. Besides, she had moved on. *Boom Town*, her movie with Clark Gable, was by all accounts a box office hit and she had bigger fish to fry with her career.

Chapter Eighteen

Judy was just finishing for the day when one of the other scientists called to her through the door.

"Someone is waiting for you in reception, Judy." She furrowed her brows, trying to think who it could be. Tom was away working at the other lab and wouldn't be back till late that evening. And she didn't have many friends here in Cambridge, just the people she worked with at the Cavendish. She made her way out of the door and into the hallway.

But as she approached the desk, her heart jumped into her throat. There, standing rocking on his heels, was the unmistakable figure of her father. He must have sensed her and turned and beamed when he saw her approach. "Now there's my girl," he said in his distinct Welsh accent, and the secretary smiled. He was obviously very proud of Judy.

"Da!" she exclaimed, as he folded her in his arms, almost crushing her with his exuberance. "What are you doing here?" she asked, catching her breath as she managed to pull away from him. He had only been at her wedding a few weeks before and he so rarely left Wales and was so busy with his job, she was surprised to see him on a weekday.

"Can't I come and see my girl now and again? See what she's up to? Now this is a grand place, isn't it, Judy," he continued, surveying the building with a complimentary air. "Any chance I can get a tour of your lab?"

Judy chuckled and shook her head. "Unfortunately, Da, no. Everything here is top secret."

He beamed again. "Of course it is. It's right that my girl would be working on top-secret things. Very proud of you, we are."

Judy smiled and linked arms with him. "To what do I owe the pleasure? Don't tell me you've just come here to see me?"

"Yes, I have," he said, not sounding very convincing. "And I want to take you out to dinner."

"Take me out to dinner?" she echoed. Judy was shocked. She'd never been out for dinner with her father. When she was growing up, they'd always been watching their pennies, especially with Judy at university. And going out for dinner was something that rich people did.

"Take me somewhere you like, love. Don't worry about the price," he said.

"Oh, you don't have to worry about it. I can pay for myself."

"Let me treat you, Judy. I've come here specially to do that."

She could see there was no arguing with him, so she took him to a place down the road that wasn't too expensive but had a lovely ambiance. She had only ever been in it once at a work party.

After they settled down with their food in front of them, he stretched across the table and took her hand. "I'm so proud of you, Judy."

"Ah," she said, battling her embarrassment, trying to fend him off.

"I always knew you were going to do something special. Your mother always thought I shouldn't encourage you, but I just knew there was something in your eyes, my girl. Something that said that you had somewhere to go in your life and nothing was going to stop you. Now, look at you, doing top-secret business, putting Hitler in his place with your inventions."

Judy shook her head and chuckled. "I wish it were the case, Da, but not everybody sees me as you do. The man I work with never wants me to get on. He's constantly putting me down. Not giving me any recognition for my work."

Her father shook his head as he finished his dinner. "Don't you worry, Judy, one day everybody's going to know what you're doing and who you are. Don't let one man hold you back. Just keep doing the right thing, and it'll all come out in the end. Life has a way of doing that."

"But there is only you and Tom who believe in me."

"Tom's a good man," her dad reiterated. "I'm glad you found him. But one day they'll be saying that Judy Morgan put the world to rights. I've been following it all in the newspaper, you know." He pulled a small leather book out of his pocket, and there folded neatly inside were several newspaper clippings. Everything to do with science, everything to do with Cambridge. Anything that was allowed to be in the press. She couldn't believe it. "I show this to everyone back at home. They're all sick of me talking about you." He chuckled.

As they were finishing their dessert, she saw something in her father's eyes.

"What is it, Da? Something's wrong, isn't it?"

He'd never been able to lie to her.

"Is it Ma? There's something wrong with her. Is she ill?"

He shook his head. "It's nothing like that, love."

"Then tell me, Da."

He swallowed hard before he spoke and she could see tears in the corners of his eyes.

He met her gaze directly, his voice low and serious. "I've been called up, Judy."

She just stared at him. "What do you mean called up? Aren't you too old?"

He let out a low rumbling chuckle. "Apparently not, as I have been recalled back to my old regiment and I'm prepared to do my duty, Judy, just as you are doing yours. And you know why I'm not worried? Because I know my daughter is back here making it safe for everybody. I came to see you because I wanted to tell you myself. I didn't want you to hear it over the telephone or in a letter. I wanted to make sure you were all right."

She mirrored the tears in his eyes, reached across the table, and squeezed his hand. "Oh, Da!"

"Now, none of that, Judy. We've all just got to do what we've got to do. And I'll take care of myself, and you take care of Tom and continue your work to put an end to this war."

She nodded, fighting back the tears.

After they finished their meal, she tried to convince him to stay the night. But he just shook his head. "I need to get home to your mother. There's the last train out, and she'll be worried if I don't get home. You young people have your own life to live without your old father coming and causing trouble," he said with a twinkle in his eye.

She hugged him so tightly at the station, not wanting to let him go. Burying her head into his jacket, she breathed in his scent, the woody tobacco mingled with the leathery smell of his shaving soap. She hated this war. Hadn't it already taken so much from them all? Why her dad? He climbed onto the train and, turning in the window, he waved enthusiastically. As the train pulled away, he shouted to her: "Think of all those new soldiers I am going to meet and bore to death talking about you." The last thing she heard was his deep barreling laugh as he made his way inside.

She waved vigorously, watching the train go and feeling that her heart was going with it.

*

September 1, 1940

Dear Hedy,

Thank you for your letter, and I can't wait to see you in London. I'm so glad you made it safely here from America. Everyone here is on tenterhooks since the controversial bombing of Berlin at the end of last month. Some people are grateful we are teaching Hitler a lesson; others are concerned we are provoking a madman. So, I think it is a good idea that you will be escorting your mother back with you to the U.S., via Canada.

Tom and I will arrive on the train tomorrow and make our way to the hotel.

Thank you once again for paying for our room. You didn't have to do that. In response, Tom and I would love to treat you to lunch when we get there.

I'm so excited to see you again. I can't believe it's been over three years since we first met. Reading your letters makes me feel so close to you, but it'll be wonderful to catch up in person without waiting for a letter to arrive. See you soon.

With all my love,
Judy, and of course, Tom xxx

Chapter Nineteen

September 4, 1940

Judy and Tom arrived early at the Savoy, feeling a little bewildered by all the beauty and opulence of the hotel in the contrast to a London preparing for war. On the way down from Cambridge, all the station signs had been removed to confuse the Germans if they made it onto British soil, the platforms along the route filled with people in uniform.

As they'd arrived at London's King's Cross station there had been so much activity. Buildings were protected by towering sandbags, while the newspaper vendors continued to shout about the aftermath of the bombing of Berlin that had taken place in August, the first time Britain had gone on the offensive.

The porter took them up in the lift as Hedy had insisted on paying for a room for them to stay there that night. But nothing had prepared them for the sheer size and beauty of the room. They unpacked and Tom had worn his best suit, and Judy had changed three times before she'd even made it out of their room. They both felt much more comfortable in a lab than in a swanky hotel in London.

"I must say," remarked Tom, whistling as they sauntered toward the lift, "she's obviously doing all right in the movies if she's staying somewhere like this."

They found the restaurant, and the maître d' greeted them.

"We are waiting for a guest," Tom told him, "a Mrs. Markey. Could you show her to our table when she arrives?"

"Of course, sir," the waiter said humbly with a slight bow.

Judy started to giggle by Tom's side as the maître d' escorted them to a very lavish table and pulled out a chair for Judy to seat her.

Tom circled around, trying to figure out where in the other three chairs he wanted to sit.

Judy shook her head. "Are you feeling a little out of sorts, Tom?"

"I most certainly am," he said under his breath.

Hedy made her entrance ten minutes later, bringing the restaurant to a reverent hush with her beauty. Apparently unaware, or just used of the affect she had, she breezed over to their table in the shadow of the maître d'. As she moved toward them, Judy couldn't help remembering the young woman she had met three years before, so lost and lonely: this was a very different person.

Tom, already out of his depth, jumped to his feet a long time before she'd reached the table and stood there awkwardly as she approached. He seemed completely beguiled by her and Judy was afraid he was going to bow as he reached forward to shake her hand.

Hedy gushed her hellos, giving Judy an extra-long hug before she slipped into the chair the maître d' offered her. Reaching across the table, she grabbed Judy's hand again.

Judy looked down with horror at her own bitten-down nails and flaking skin as she slipped her hand into the smooth white manicured fingers of their guest. Turning their hands over quickly so Hedy's was on top, she felt all of her shyness return as even the word "hello" stuck in her throat. This was so different than opening her heart in her letters to her dearest friend.

Hedy, on the other hand, was charming and unaware. She was saying how sorry she was to have kept them waiting. Taking everything in her stride, she ordered a glass of wine and removed her sunglasses. The maître d' left to do her bidding.

"Things have changed a little since the Science Museum, don't you think?" joked Hedy. And as Judy grinned, Hedy went into a long retelling of their first meeting for Tom's benefit. He listened politely, making all the right noises at the right time, without once letting on he had heard Judy's version of this event many times in the last few years.

As they relaxed together, Hedy quickly slipped from her public persona, becoming like an excited adolescent. The smooth sophisticated woman was gone and, in her place, a charming girl eager to connect with this old memory. Judy couldn't believe the physical change in her since they had met before, though; she was so much more glamorous now.

It didn't take them long to get onto the subject of physics and they talked warmly and with such ease. Judy realized as long as you didn't get drawn in by her beauty, Hedy was still so much fun and, as before, very intelligent. Tom seemed to struggle with the spell she had cast, however, dropping knives and forks, glowing red and stumbling over his words, which Judy found fascinating. Tom was always a little tongue-tied with new people, but she'd never seen him like this until now.

As they started lunch, Hedy shared some of her latest inventions, one being a cube that could be placed in water to create cola for the troops.

"But the problem I have," she said, pausing to take a sip of her wine, "is that there are different pH balances in the water in different states and I can't be assured of the outcome."

"Most important," commented Tom, tucking into his steak, "to have a stable and reliable subject to test it on."

"Of course," said Hedy, "but that doesn't stop me still trying to make it possible."

At the end of the meal they got their first insight into Hedy's fame, when a young woman leaving the restaurant passed their table and as she did so, her eyes grew wide.

"Excuse me," she said, her voice high and expectant as they all looked up at her, lost in the world of science, "but aren't you that Miss Hedy Lamarr?"

Tom and Judy stared at the young woman and then both turned to Hedy. How did this young woman know their friend?

Hedy didn't seem perturbed about it at all and merely smiled. "Why, yes," she said, "would you like an autograph or something?"

"Yes, please," said the woman, "I just saw you in that new picture *Boom Town*. You were brilliant! What's it like to kiss Clark Gable?"

"I would never kiss and tell," responded Hedy, with a smirk and what seemed a well-rehearsed response.

With a shaking hand, the woman brought her a piece of paper to sign her name and couldn't hide her excitement.

After she'd left their table, Judy began to get an insight into her friend's life. Of course she mentioned her films in her letters, but it was alongside all the other events in her life and even though Judy and Tom didn't know much about Hollywood, even they knew who Clark Gable was. Judy felt ridiculous; of course, Hedy was a big movie star now, she thought to herself. *Look at her.* She was so beautiful. But she could tell by Tom's face that he was as bewildered by this as she was. Hedy seemed oblivious to all the excitement, though, and picked up the conversation where they had left off.

When another woman came over for the second autograph, Tom clearly found he couldn't hold back.

"I'm sorry," he said, "we didn't realize how intrusive this would be for you; we could have met somewhere less public. We don't really go to the pictures often," he said, nodding toward Judy.

"I thought as much; it's the most charming thing I love about the two of you," responded Hedy, taking another sip of her wine. "I am grateful for my work. Don't get me wrong. And this face has been helpful. But honestly, between the three of us, I so wish I could be taken more seriously for my mind. Beauty does open doors, but not always the right ones. I would give anything to have your life. Every day working in a lab, inventing things, with all that freedom. Being noticed for my work instead of my new haircut. That, to me, would be a dream come true."

Judy thought about Hedy's words: was she being noticed? It still felt like an uphill battle every day to be taken seriously because she was a woman. Finnegan had still not warmed to her, even after all this time, and always spoke over her head to Tom when he came into the laboratory to talk to them both.

The next evening, when they were back in their own beds, Judy paused from the thank-you letter she was penning to Hedy and looked thoughtfully across toward her husband. "Tom, what did you think of Hedy?"

Tom, who was deeply engrossed in his Sherlock Holmes novel, took a moment to react.

"Huh?"

"Hedy Lamarr, my friend. What do you think of her?"

Pulling himself from the page, he furrowed his brows and stared up at the wall as if he was contemplating her question. "What did I think of her?"

"Yes. What did you think of her?"

"I thought she was very nice, her theory on radiation therapy was interesting," he said and moved back to his page.

Judy had wanted more. "Is that all? She was very nice?"

Tom seemed to sense this would be a longer conversation, and he picked up his bookmark, placed it between the pages of *The Hound of the Baskervilles*, and dropped his book onto his lap. He was sitting up in his twin bed, propped up by two pillows in his usual green and white pajamas. Judy was by his side in her own bed. "I thought she was very knowledgeable about what she had to say. She obviously has a fine scientific mind, and I think her premise is very plausible."

Judy interrupted him before he continued. "I mean, do you think she was beautiful?"

Tom flushed at her question and stared at his wife, beginning to realize where this conversation was going. If she'd needed to know the answer, her husband had just conveyed it. She felt her heart sink. It was hard being in love with somebody. She felt vulnerable around other women, particularly someone as beautiful and as smart as Hedy.

"Do I think she is beautiful?" He repeated the words, appearing to play for time. "Yes, Judy, I think she's beautiful, like in a Hollywood kind of American kind of a way. I think she's beautiful like I would say a grand house is beautiful or a wonderful-looking motor car."

"Does it make you regret marrying me?"

Tom looked over and shock crossed his face. "Never for a minute have I ever regretted marrying you. Oh, Judy," he said, shaking his head. "I still can't believe you said yes. Sometimes I lie here in bed and look over at you in the morning and think, Tom Jenkins, how did you get to be this lucky? I think Miss Lamarr is lovely, but I've also learned something essential in my life: beauty doesn't always go all the way. Sometimes it's only skin deep. And then there are some people whose beauty just streams out of their face."

He picked up his book again, and, licking his thumb and fingers, started to find his page. "I am fortunate that I married the latter, someone who's beautiful inside and out."

Judy sat up in bed. "Tom, I'm not stupid. I know I'm not attractive."

He looked puzzled. "What do you mean, you're not attractive?"

"I have tight curly hair and a face like a chipmunk."

"You have a very odd view of yourself; I've never thought your face was like a chipmunk, or a squirrel," he said, starting to chuckle. "In fact, no woodland creatures have ever entered my thoughts." He paused, then continued. "I love your eyes and your features.

And your wavy hair; I spend most of my time at the lab trying not to run my fingers through it. I want you to know something, Judy Jenkins. I love you very much, and no one or anything is ever going to convince me of anything but that. Not only are you the most beautiful woman I have ever known, but I am also fortunate that I have somebody who I can talk to about things that are really important to me. You have such an incredible scientific mind, and I work in awe by your side every day. Judy, your Miss Lamarr is lovely, but I have the best. So, I don't want the rest."

"Oh, you corny old charmer." She chuckled in turn.

He went back to his book and looked down at his page. "I'm afraid corny is all I can do."

"I'll take it," she said. "Thank you. And if it's any consolation, I feel the same way about you, Mr. Jenkins."

September 5, 1940

Dear Hedy,

Just a little card to say thank you for the lovely time we had in London with you. Tom and I enjoyed ourselves immensely. I do wish we could see more of each other like that. Maybe once the war is over and we are not all so busy, but until then know I am so grateful for your friendship and look forward to brighter days.

Much love,
Judy

Chapter Twenty

September 6, 1940

Hedy slipped out the Savoy hotel lift and toward the American Bar, where she was meeting Stefan and her mother, who had adored him ever since he and Hedy had been childhood friends. She was so excited. She couldn't wait to see them both. It'd been so long since they'd last all been together, with it taking a while to organize the paperwork to allow her mother to leave Austria, and not a moment too soon. Hitler was definitely on the move now, conquering Europe as he went, invading Belgium, the Netherlands, Luxembourg and France in just six weeks, beginning in May of that year. With Austria already annexed since 1938 and with her family's Jewish heritage, she'd been starting to hear things that were very concerning about some of Hitler's laws and ideas about obliterating the Jewish people.

Hedy swanned into the bar, wearing her cream suit and black satin blouse, polka-dot shoes, hat and clutch bag. Inside was an elegant room with a fresco of London on the main wall and a tall bank of windows on one side. The center of the room was dominated by a white grand piano, which was often played by the famous American composer and pianist Carroll Gibbons, who now lived in Britain and was a regular visitor to the Savoy. All at once she spotted them, as Stefan jumped up from the table they were sitting at and came up to swing her in his arms. "Earwig!" he exclaimed, spinning her in a circle. She cringed once again at the pet name he'd had for her ever since they'd been children. He had never got out of the habit of referring to her as a British insect.

Her mother looked gorgeous as always and got up to greet her. The smell of Chanel wafted on the air between them as she air-kissed her daughter, and slipped her soft, well-manicured hands into Hedy's own.

"Darling, we're so glad to see you at last. It feels like an eternity, doesn't it?" she said as they settled down at the table to enjoy a drink and got into a lively conversation. "Stefan and I just saw your last picture here in London. You were wonderful, darling."

They chatted and caught up with everything in their lives. But their conversation quickly moved to the ongoing war.

"I'm so glad you booked my passage, Hedwig. It seems like we'll be getting out of London at just the right time. Did you hear about the bombing of Berlin last month?" Her mother took a sip of her sherry. "Ever since that happened, everyone's been on high alert here. They feel that London will be a target."

Hedy nodded. "That's one reason I wanted to come and get you. I have booked our passage on a ship out of Liverpool in two days. If they do decide to start attacking London, at least we'll be on the other side of the country." She took her best friend's hand. "I do wish you were coming with us, Stefan, now France is occupied and things here in England are so tense."

He rocked back in his chair. "Well, you need not worry, I am leaving England."

Hedy and her mother stared at him.

"I've got a new posting. They need correspondents in the Far East, and as I won't be able to fight because of being deaf in this one ear, I thought this could be another way to support the fight. It's the one I really wanted."

"Far East?" her mother repeated, pursing her lips together in a tight, thoughtful, crimson circle. "I remember as a child how you always were interested in those Oriental languages, but really I think that's a frightful plan."

"Well, you have to do what you feel is right," Hedy encouraged.

"Now I have a way. I'm being sent by the paper to Peking to follow a group of fighters called the Flying Tigers."

"Flying Tigers?" asked Hedy, arching an eyebrow.

"I came to interview the guy in America. It's rumored that he has organized a group of flyers going from the U.S. They have volunteered to fight for the Chinese against the Japanese to defend the Burma Road."

Stefan took a drag of a cigarette he was smoking and nodded his head, getting quite animated.

"There is a guy called Claire Chennault who has organized a hundred P40s and pilots to help support the Chinese air force." His expression darkened and his voice dropped as he continued. "I have never got over those pictures of women and children being slaughtered in the Marco Polo Bridge Incident during the Japanese invasion of Manchuria. That is why I feel so compelled to take this assignment."

"Don't forget to stay safe," her mother added.

Stefan gave her hand a reassuring squeeze. "Don't worry, I always do."

Hedy looked concerned. "How will we stay in touch with you so far away?"

"You'll be able to read my articles," he said, taking hold of her chin playfully, "and I promise to write."

"Well," said her mother, "I should go and start packing if we're leaving tomorrow. What about you two?"

"I am going to take Hedwig shopping," Stefan said, going over and kissing her mother on the cheek. "Lovely to see you again, Gertrude. Come on, Earwig, let's go and explore. If the Germans are coming, we should enjoy everything we can about London while it's still here."

"Are you sure it's safe?" asked Hedy.

"Nowhere is safe right now. We may as well live a little bit dangerously." Getting to his feet, he pulled his best friend up and, taking her hand, he started to lead her out of the hotel. "When was the last time you were in London?"

"When I was poor," joked Hedy.

"Good, I sold everything ready for this move. There was no point in going back to Austria after Hitler decided to visit Paris. I am bored with all those red and black flags and people goose-stepping all over the place."

"What about your friend? The one in Paris," she enquired.

She saw the pain cross his face before he looked away regretfully. "Well, let's just say it was wonderful while it lasted."

She squeezed his arm. "I'm so sorry, Stefan."

He shrugged it off with a forced bravado and pulled her in for a warm side hug. "I will always have my girl, though, won't I?"

She brushed his lips with a kiss. "Always," she whispered, tapping his cheek fondly. "Let's start by doing some shopping, shall we?"

The weather outside was glorious. The sun was shining. It was so beautiful for an early September day.

"Where would you like to start? Should we get you a new hat?"

Hedy shook her head in disbelief. "You're going to come to the hat shop with me?"

"Sure," he said. "It sounds like fun."

They jumped on a bus to Regent Street and she led him in and out of all different shops, Stefan causing mayhem wherever he went by making the shop girls laugh by trying hats on himself and finding the oddest combinations to put together for Hedy to try on.

After a couple of hours, he announced, "We have to go to Harrods."

But by now, Hedy had a lot of parcels and she was exhausted.

"First, I need a cup of tea," she declared, as she dragged him in the opposite direction. Hedy mused about how London looked so strange compared to when she had left on the *Normandie*. All the windows were taped up, with piles of sandbags around many of the significant government buildings. And there were signs already out for the Underground stations and pointing the way to shelters. But somehow, it didn't feel real, almost like a movie set, Hedy thought to herself as they moved past it all. Everything prepared, but nothing going on.

Finding a tea shop, they ordered some sandwiches and tea. They were halfway through their conversation when a buzz outside alerted them to the fact something was happening. Getting up and walking to the window, they looked out and were startled to see people standing and staring, looking up into the air. As they followed the gaze of the crowd, Hedy could see, miles away and getting closer, hundreds of planes like tiny insects buzzing across the sky. She felt her heartbeat quicken and her throat tighten. What if they were German?

Two young girls who had just arrived in the tea shop, one tall and dark, the other with red hair, both wearing Royal Air Force uniforms, sat talking in a hushed tone. As she walked past their table, Hedy overheard the one with the dark hair saying she was going to go straight to her barracks as she would probably be needed that evening. Her words alerted Hedy to the fact that this was something serious.

As the girls left, Stefan shouted over to them, "Go get 'em, girls!"

They both turned and smiled hesitantly, looking rather apprehensive.

"I think we should find somewhere to be safe," said Hedy, worrying.

"It will probably be much more exciting in here," said Stefan, looking out the window again and lighting himself a cigarette. "We'll get a front-row view."

"I don't want a front-row view," she said. "I want to be safe. Do you think my mother will be okay?"

"They have a shelter in the hotel. I'm sure she'll be fine. Come on then, if you're anxious."

It was as they went back out onto the street that the sirens started their eardrum-piercing screech all across London.

Hedy looked nervously over at Stefan. "What do we do?" she shouted. She'd never been in anything like it before.

All at once, people on the street became very active, scattering in many directions. Stefan grabbed her hand and started to race with her toward one of the shelters. People weren't panicking, but you could see they were concerned. The two of them hurried down into the nearest Underground station, and as they hit the bottom step, the first bombs started to drop on London.

It was terrifying. Hedy had never felt anything like it. Not just the sound, but the feeling of everything around her shaking and crumbling. The concrete creaking under the weight of the explosions. People screamed and children sobbed. Suddenly, she felt her best friend's arm around her.

"Don't worry, Earwig," he whispered into her ear. "It's going to be fine. We're safe down here."

Taking off his coat, he placed it on the ground, and she sat down on it. Her whole body shook as the bombs continued to drop one after another. How could anything be this loud? How could anything be this terrifying?

With one incredibly loud bomb, she screamed and buried her head in her best friend's shoulder.

He whispered to her, "Do you remember when we were children, and you'd be scared of the thunder?"

She was listening but not saying anything.

"Do you remember the story I would tell you?"

She tried to rack her brains, but it was hard to concentrate with the intensity of what was happening above her.

Stefan pulled Hedy in close and started the story.

"Once upon a time, there was a beautiful young princess named Princess Hedyrina who lived in a magnificent crystal castle atop a high hill in a distant land.

"Surrounding the castle, there was a thick, dark, haunted forest. People from a nearby village beyond the wood came to the castle each day to work, but no one ever dared to venture through the wood at night. Because once it was quiet and dark, the strange noises that emanated from deep in the center of the forest became louder. A haunting, creaking, groaning, and roaring sound..."

As she listened to his words she started to grow calmer, glad for the distraction.

"Many stories were told about what was living deep in the woods, but most believed that a fearful dragon came out at night to protect his forest. Now, the king and queen of this castle, Princess Hedyrina's parents, were always very nervous about the safety of their only daughter, who they believed was far too delicate and fragile to be alone. So they commanded a brave young warrior to watch over her. Sir Stefan was strong, bold, handsome, and one hell of a stylish dresser."

Hedy started to chuckle. "Okay. Okay. I get the general idea; get to the good bits."

He gave her his mock look of disgust as he continued.

"Sir Stefan went everywhere with Princess Hedyrina. Protected her from unruly thornbushes, sheltered her from rainstorms, and pulled her out of the path of wayward horses.

"But as Princess Hedyrina grew older, she became tired of being taken care of, and she also got very willful and headstrong."

"I don't remember that part of the story," interjected Hedy, pulling away from him. He pulled her close again and whispered into her ear.

"Well, she's grown up a lot since I first told this story."

Stefan paused as, above them, another bomb detonated, rocking the whole platform and shaking masonry and clouds of dust from the walls. Stefan pulled off his waistcoat and sheltered Hedy under it as he continued speaking louder to be heard as Hedy gripped his arm.

"One day, Princess Hedyrina made up her mind to prove everyone wrong and show them she wasn't as fragile and delicate as they all thought but could be as brave and strong as Sir Stefan. So one night, while he was sleeping, she stole his sword and made her way on trembling legs into the middle of the forest to confront the dragon. It was very dark as she crept through the woods, and the further in she got, the darker it became until she couldn't even see her hand in front of her face.

"As she stumbled forward, the dragon's roar grew louder. The sound of his bones creaking and the whoosh, whoosh, whoosh of his fiery breath. Trembling from head to foot, she held the sword up in front of her, ready to take on her enemy as soon as it showed its face.

"All at once, a flash lit up the sky, and a crack of thunder struck a tree beside her, setting it ablaze in a streak of golden-white light. Terrified, Hedyrina screamed and began to run, but she became disorientated, and instead of running back to the castle, she ran straight toward the center of the forest and the dragon's lair. As the rain started to pelt her, the mud slowed her step, and the unruly undergrowth snagged at her clothes.

"Stumbling over a protruding tree root, she tripped and fell, the sword clattering away from her right at the foot of the roaring dragon. Trembling, she cowered and waited for her foe to devour her. Another streak of lightning lit up the sky, and she prepared to meet the eye of her infamous enemy. But instead of a dragon as she had expected, in front of her was a beautiful waterfall roaring its way through a rocky ravine. Below it, on a bank of the waterfall's edge, a large oak tree creaked whenever the weight of water bounced off the rocks and pelted its branches. All at once, she realized that it wasn't a dragon after all, and what she had discovered would set her kingdom free from their fears. Feeling emboldened by her new discovery, she got to her feet, but she was still a long way from the castle, and it was very, very dark; how would she make it home without the sword for protection or light to guide her? In desperation, she clutched her hands to her chest, and below them, she heard the thumping of her own heart that was almost beating out of her chest with fear. As she listened to its rhythm, it started to calm her and reminded her of the drums she would hear when the soldiers from her kingdom marched. *Thumpity, thump, thumpity thump, thumpity thump…* as she listened, she could hear it speaking to her: it was saying, 'You are brave; you are safe; you are loved.' Hedyrina felt reassured and fearless. She didn't need the sword; she didn't need a light; her heart could guide her all the way home. Crossing her hands across her chest as the rain continued to pour, she walked to the rhythm of its words. Repeating them to herself over and over again. 'You are brave; you are safe; you are loved.'

"After that night and hearing Hedyrina's story, the whole of the kingdom was set free from the fear of the forest. The people would swim in the water of the falls, climb the oak tree, and camp under the stars on the banks of the ravine, lulled to sleep by the falling water.

"And whenever Princess Hedyrina was afraid, she would cross her hands across her heart and listen to its song."

Stefan kissed Hedy gently on her cheek as she let out a breath she had been holding.

"Just remember that, Hedy darling, you only have to look no further than your heart to know you are brave, you are safe, you are loved. Especially by me."

It did remind her that she was brave. But right now, more than anything, she wanted to be back in America, at home with little James, who had stayed there with his nanny.

The raid persisted for a long time—hours upon hours into the night. And when the all-clear sounded, and they came above ground, the devastation was incredible. Fire lit the sky and she heard people murmuring about the East End by the docks. And the whole air was muggy and clammy with dust and smoke. Sirens rang out from every direction. People hobbled along, some injured, caught by flying masonry, or from falling in the rush.

Stefan put his arm around her and offered her a handkerchief, which she put around her mouth to stifle the smoke. And quickly, they made their way back to the hotel, though it took them a long time through the mayhem that was now London.

When they got there, they were fortunate to see that the bombs hadn't hit the Savoy. A first aid station had been set up in the lobby for people who had sustained injuries, and the hotel doctor was treating them. Alarmed, they saw Mrs. Kiesler sitting out on one of the couches. They rushed over to her.

"It's nothing," she said, batting them away with a hand. "A glass smashed in the room, and I got some in my leg. I'll be all right in a moment. I'm so glad to see both of you." She held her arms out toward them. "Do you think we'll still be able to get to Liverpool for the sailing the day after tomorrow?"

"I don't know," said Hedy as she hugged her mother. "We will just have to do the best we can."

The next day they checked out. It took them a long time to get to Liverpool. Many of the train services were down, but eventually, they made it across the country. Stefan came to see them off. "Are you sure you don't want to come with us?" said Hedy, sobbing on his shoulder as they parted. "It'll be safer in America."

He shook his head. "I have work to do, Hedy, and I can't hide in another country. These stories must be told. Sometimes I can't even sleep at night when I consider all the injustice in the world, and my hope is by reporting about it, maybe, just maybe in my small way I will expose all this wrongdoing. Then incidents like the Marco Polo Bridge will never disappear into history without the world knowing what really happened. Knowledge is power,

Hedy, and it's why I am a journalist. I couldn't stay, sitting around, watching it all from abroad without doing something."

"When do you leave?"

"I'll be going in the next couple of days. I pray this war will be over soon and we'll all be together again."

They held one another tightly on the dock.

Then, pulling away from her, he presented her with a tiny package from his pocket.

"What's this?" asked Hedy.

"Just a little something I picked up yesterday before we left London. Let's call it an early birthday present."

"But my birthday isn't till November."

But I won't be around for that, so…"

She opened up the paper and inside was a midnight-blue velvet box. She lifted the cover; nestled in white satin was an exquisite silver heart necklace. She slipped it out of the box and held it up in awe, letting it dangle from her fingers, catching the light. Engraved on the front were the words, *To my girl. Always remember: you are brave, you are safe, you are loved. Especially loved. With all my heart, Stefan.*

Tears brimmed in her eyes as he placed it around her neck, saying, "I thought you might need a little reminder when I am not here to tell you stories."

She gripped it between her fingers. "I will never take it off, Stefan, thank you so much."

Hedy noticed her mother was waiting for them and looked fragile, as though she'd aged ten years in the last day. Hedy knew she should get her on the ship. Stefan, on the other hand, looked the opposite. He looked resilient and buoyant, as though he was ready to tackle anything.

As she waved to him from the deck of the ship, clutching her birthday present at her neck, she had this terrible foreboding that she would never see him again, and the power of that thought took the breath from her. She dismissed it quickly. Of course she would.

Once the ship set sail, she followed the news from on board. London was bombed the next day again. And the day after that. It seemed like the war they'd all been dreading had started at last in London and she prayed Stefan was safe. It felt like only a matter of time before the Germans arrived onto British soil.

As they sailed across the Atlantic, she thought about Judy and Tom. She hoped they'd made it safely home, back to Cambridge. She couldn't remember a time when she had been so relaxed in someone's company. The fact they didn't follow her movie career was so refreshing and novel. It had felt good just to be Hedwig Kiesler again for a few hours, and she found herself continuing to be drawn to Judy. So many of the women in her life wanted something from her, or despised her, but she had not sensed any of that. They just had an easy friendship, built on their shared love of science. She craved the simplicity of that kind of relationship in her life.

On board she took care of her mother in their cabin, sent a message to her agent to tell him she was safe, and walked daily in the fresh sea air. The air raid had had a huge impact on her and more than anything she decided she must find a way to help in the war effort. This had given her a glimpse into what it felt like here in Europe. Stefan's words rang in her mind. "I can't hide in another country." She acknowledged they were so removed from it in America. She was determined to help as much as she could, and she had an idea of how she could do that.

September 15, 1940

Dear Judy,

I'm so glad you missed the raid on London—it was terrifying. Fortunately, we all managed to get to shelters in time and only my mother had a slight injury. How do you live under this constant fear? The only joy for me this trip was your visit. It was so wonderful to see you and to meet your new husband, the mysterious Tom (haha). He seems so lovely, and so obviously adores you; the two of you look wonderful together. You have a glow all about you. I admit I'm a little jealous but also so happy for you, my dear friend.

Mother and I arrived in Canada safely, where she'll be ensconced until we can get her into the U.S. and I've come back home.

I have concerning news, though; my dear friend Stefan is on his way out to the Far East. I am so scared for him, Judy. To leave Europe and go to China feels like "out of the frying pan and into the fire" as they say, is it not? We have always been close. He is like a brother to me, and I worry about his safety. I worry about all of our safety.

I desperately want to do something. I love my job; I love being in movies. Honestly, though, I wish I could do more. I wish I could be doing what you're doing, working for the war effort, inventing things in the scientific field to help the Allies.

The good news is it seems my career has really started to take off since the success of Boom Town. Apparently, it's not such a bad thing to be paired with Clark Gable. Now the studio is taking me more seriously. I'm hoping this will mean better parts. Comrade X is set to start soon, that's another one with Clark. All being well, it will do well too. I'll be glad to see the back of working with Spencer Tracy again, though. Mayer is thinking of casting me in another film with him. Keeping my fingers crossed that doesn't happen!

On family news, James is starting to sing nonsense songs. He looks so cute with this goofy grin. I adore him and everything that motherhood is.

Sending you much love and watch out for the next parcel. I'm going to be sending you some chocolate. I couldn't bear to see the rationing when I was over there, and I hope my packages help, at least to brighten your day.

Take care, darling, and we will be together again soon.

Much love,
Hedy

TELEGRAM

DEAR HEDY (STOP)
CHOCOLATE ARRIVED YOU ARE SUCH A DEAR (STOP)
NOW TOM AND I WILL HAVE TO LET OUT ALL OUR CLOTHES! (STOP)
SAVING SOME FOR CHRISTMAS WE WILL RAISE A TOAST TO YOU (STOP)
LOVE JUDY AND TOM (STOP)

MRS. JUDY JENKINS
9:32 AM

Chapter Twenty-One

It was in October that Judy knew there was something wrong with her one morning at work. She'd felt waves of nausea earlier when Tom had given her a cup of coffee in the morning, and somehow it had tasted off. But now, as she listened to her husband presenting their latest findings in the lecture hall at the Cavendish, she knew she was going to be sick. Her stomach was churning, and she was swallowing down bitter-tasting bile and gulping the air, trying to slow down her breathing. What would Tom think if she left in the middle of the presentation? But it was no good; she couldn't stay.

While he turned toward the board to show an equation, she quickly moved along the row, excusing herself as she went, and bolted for the door. Racing through the corridor, she just made it to the lavatory as her stomach wrenched, and into a cubicle just as everything from her stomach came up. There was a feeling of relief and wretchedness all in the same moment.

As she continued to heave over the toilet bowl, one of the Cavendish secretaries came out of one of the other cubicles. She tapped on the door.

"Are you all right in there?"

Judy wiped her mouth with her cotton hankie. "Yes," she said in a tiny, dry voice.

"It sounds like you've had something that didn't agree with you."

Judy finished retching and, flushing the chain, sat down on the toilet seat to think. What could have upset her stomach? Being the scientist, she was, she needed to understand.

They'd wanted fish pie the night before. But Judy had been unable to get fish, so she'd had to improvise and it'd just been a vegetable pie. So, it couldn't be that. She'd had no breakfast this morning, only half of the cup of coffee that Tom had given her.

All at once something dawned on her. They'd been so busy on this project; she'd completely lost count. Wasn't she supposed to have had her monthly two weeks before? Or maybe it was three. Surely it couldn't be a month? She may have just missed it altogether. Was that possible? She tried to fight the excitement rising in her chest. They so desperately wanted a child. But she didn't want to speculate until she was sure.

At the sink, she rinsed her face and hands under the tap. In the mirror, she noticed she looked gray, but she couldn't help but smile at herself. If this was what she thought it was, it was what she'd wanted her whole life.

"Don't jump ahead of yourself, Judy Jenkins," she said out loud to herself. She would go to the doctor's after work and book an appointment. She wouldn't say anything to Tom until she was sure.

Once she left the bathroom, she rushed back toward the lecture hall and tiptoed inside. It had apparently just finished and people were surrounding Tom, asking questions.

Slipping a peppermint, which she always kept in her pocket, into her mouth, Judy went to join him by his side.

"Ah, and here's Judy," Tom said, announcing her arrival. "As you know, Dr. Finnegan, she was a great help on this. And I couldn't have done any of this work without my—"

Dr. Finnegan cut him off. "I'm sure she was of help," he said. "But, Tom, I do feel that acknowledgment should go to you."

Tom looked deflated. Little pink spots surfaced on his cheeks, which Judy had come to realize meant he was seething.

"I really think that Judy should also be recognized on this paper," stated Tom in one long, slow tone.

Dr. Finnegan appeared not to hear him, turning away and talking to a colleague.

After the group cleared, she beamed at her husband. "You did a wonderful job, Tom."

"Finnegan is never going to recognize you for your work. You know that, don't you?" he said, shaking his head. "The man is an absolute... I'm not going to say the word. Not in female company," said Tom, in his staunch sensibleness.

"He is," stated Judy, responding to what Tom was not saying. Tom appeared not to notice the fact that she'd been missing during the lecture, for which she breathed a sigh of relief.

She returned to the lab, but Judy's stomach did not settle all day. She knew that there were certain herbs she could take, and she'd heard about ginger and peppermint. They grew peppermint in their garden and she had dried some this summer. She would make a tea with some when she got home, just in case this happened again.

Informing Tom she had to pick up a few groceries on the way home, she insisted he walk back alone without her, and she rushed to the doctor's surgery, where she booked an appointment for three days later, when she knew Tom had a trip planned to one of the other laboratories.

She could barely control her excitement as she planned the appointment, and when she was sitting there three days later, it was hard for her not to hope for the best. When the doctor examined her and confirmed that she was probably pregnant, though it would be a while before they would know for sure, she knew she would have to tell Tom. She was still feeling queasy in the morning, but she didn't care now that she knew exactly what was going on.

On her way home, she walked past a baby shop, and in the window was the most beautiful blue matinee jacket. Dare she go and buy it? She couldn't resist it. She paid for it and carried it home in a brown paper bag, feeling so much excitement. The beginning of their life together as a family. Judy had always wanted a big family, as she'd been an only child, and now she was going to make up for it.

She dreamed about her life surrounded by children. Tom playing with them, teaching them to fly kites and repairing their bicycles. Judy taking care of them and taking them to school. She wondered what her baby would look like. She hoped it would look like Tom. She tried to imagine a short, smaller version of her husband, and it made her smile as she made her way home.

She managed to get some sausages from the butcher's, which were Tom's favorite, and she decided she was going to tell him right after dinner. But when he arrived back from the lab, he was not in a good mood. The officials he'd gone to see at the other lab had questioned all of the calculations that Tom and Judy had come up with. "I wish you could have been with me, Judy, but you know how Finnegan is. You can explain things so much better than I can. It's horribly frustrating," he said, as he took off his jacket and rolled up his sleeves to go and have a wash in the bathroom.

"I have some good news," she said, shouting up the stairs, wondering if it would cheer him up. Tom poked his head out of the little bathroom. He was still scowling and she just couldn't bring herself to tell him. "We have sausages for tea," she said meekly.

Tom smiled and nodded. "Lovely," he said, his tone lightening a little.

When she brought his dinner to the table, Judy just stood there in front of him, wringing her hands. She just couldn't sit down; she was so nervous. Eventually she started to pace the room.

"Are you not going to join me?" he asked with a quizzical look.

"In a minute," she sputtered out, "but first, there's something I've got to tell you."

She must have seemed distraught because he looked up with great concern.

"What is it, Judy? Bad news? Is it something to do with the war? Has someone we know got hurt or killed?"

Judy shook her head. "It's nothing like that. I have, erm…" She tried to find the right words. "I have missed something." She always found it difficult to talk about personal matters, even with her husband. She was still shy about such things. "And that means that we're going to get a little something." Tom peered at her, his expression blank. He was not picking up at all on any of her insinuations. "A little person."

"A little person?" Tom repeated, still not understanding.

"I'm…" She took a big deep breath. "I'm pregnant, Tom."

She wished she could have bottled his expression. It went from confusion, to shock, to being astounded. He repeated the words, word for word, "I'm pregnant, Tom?" as though he was trying to come to terms with it himself. "Judy, are you telling me the truth?"

"No, Tom, I'm lying," she joked with a smile. "This seems like a good thing to joke about."

He stood up straight away, pulling out the serviette he'd tucked in the top of his shirt. "You're going to have my baby?"

"Well, nobody else's, yes. I hope it's yours."

"Oh, Judy," he cried. "Oh, Judy! *Oh, Judy!*" He walked toward her then and hugged her tightly. And then, thinking better of it, he released her quickly.

"You need to sit down. What do we need to do?"

"Stop flapping, Tom. It's going to be fine."

He didn't seem to hear her, as he automatically pulled out her chair and sat her in it, whether she wanted to sit down or not.

"I will do everything we need to do. I will take care of everything. Oh, Judy!" Then he picked her up again, hugged her, and then sat her back in the chair. He really did not know what to do with himself. She started to giggle at her husband.

"Please calm down and sit down."

He did as he was told, and stared at her. And then she saw, there were tears in the corners of his eyes. In the whole time she'd known her husband, she'd never seen him cry. He always felt he needed to have this stiff upper lip. When he was feeling emotional, she would see his chin quiver, or his voice would become tightened, but she'd never seen tears till now.

"I can't tell you what this means to me," he said. "I can't tell you what it'll be like to have a baby with you, Judy."

She smiled, tears now in her own eyes. "I know, Tom." She went over to her husband and put her arms around his neck and held him. She knew he'd be embarrassed about the tears, and she didn't want him to see that she'd seen. When she pulled away, he coughed, excused himself to get a drink of water, and he was gone a while. She knew he was probably having a little bit of a cry, but she wasn't going to draw attention to it.

When he arrived back, he sat down at the table, and they spent the rest of the evening talking about everything that they were going to do. How they were going to change the spare room into a nursery and some baby names they liked the sound of. She'd never been so happy or more complete than she was right now. She had everything she wanted. She had a job she loved. A husband who loved her. And now she was going to have the much-wanted baby. If there hadn't have been a war on, life would have been perfect.

November 6, 1940.

Dear Hedy,

I have the most amazing news. I didn't know in London, but… I'm pregnant! I can't tell you how excited I am. Tom is over the moon and has already started painting the spare room. It's what we've always wanted. I love my work, but the idea of having my own child, as you have, fills me with so much bliss. Tom has become very doting since I told him. Continually pushing me down into chairs and opening doors for me. I tell him I feel fine. In fact, I feel wonderful.

I don't know when I felt better, but he is insistent. I am so distracted by all this. I can't get over the fact that a little person is growing inside me. I spend my days wondering what color eyes it'll have. Will they be brown like Tom's, or green like mine? Will it have my curly hair or Tom's straight brown hair?

I'm secretly hoping for a boy. I don't know why. I think I want that for Tom. He gets such a kick out of the whole thing. The nursery is full of little gifts he keeps bringing home. With all this indulgence, our ration card is looking rather sad. I have nothing left for curtains I need in the house, as he is spending it all on gifts for the baby. But it's lovely to see the nursery coming together, with a little cot in the corner that will soon be a bed for our little one. I stand in front of it sometimes just staring at it, imagining a baby sleeping there.

What exciting news about your movies! Do keep up the good work, and I promise that Tom and I will try to get to see one at the cinema when we get some time. In the meantime, I hope you have a lovely Thanksgiving, I believe they celebrate that over there this month and let's hope that next year is going to be better. These Nazis seem bent on taking over the world, but I know on this small isle we're going to fight every day, and hopefully, with the work that Tom and I are doing right now, we can help with that pursuit.

Well, take care. I have to go. I'm writing this in my lunch hour, and Tom just called me back in; we are in the middle of something important. I feel the luckiest person in the world.

Lots of love,
Judy

TELEGRAM

DEAR JUDY AND TOM – (STOP) –
I AM BESIDE MYSELF WITH HAPPINESS FOR YOU
BOTH – (STOP) –
BIG CONGRATULATIONS – (STOP) –
MUCH LOVE AUNTY HEDY – (STOP) –

HEDY LAMARR
8:17 PM

Chapter Twenty-Two

October 1940

One morning Hedy woke up and felt the exhaustion of her filming schedule and the continuing concern of a world at war. The onslaught of bombing in England, now being called the Blitz, the first night of which she and Stefan had experienced in London, had continued relentlessly, with Hitler spewing out all his anger on the British people night after night. And the sheer worry of what was coming next robbed her of sleep.

Throwing on her silk wrap, she sat down to eat her breakfast and was met with more shocking headlines, reminding her of the one that had broken her heart the month before, when the ship SS *City of Benares* had been sunk on September 18th with 260 of the 407 people on board being killed. Eighty children had perished when the ship had been torpedoed. She had read the news in between takes and had been so heartbroken that she had rushed straight to her dressing room just to hold James close to her, as he had been on set that day with his nanny.

The air caught in her throat again this morning as she read about the growing unrest in Japan, and she thought of her Stefan so far away in the Far East. She had not heard from him since she left him in England the month before. Unable to eat any food because of the knot now growing in her stomach, she poured herself a strong cup of coffee, walked to her window and looked out toward her garden.

She felt so fortunate here in Los Angeles. She had bought a lovely home she had called Hedgerow Farm and it was so idyllic where she lived. It was hard to believe that Europe, her Europe, was fighting for its very soul. The day before, she'd read about how the German U-boats were on the verge of winning the war at sea. They were more advanced and faster, outmaneuvering the British and their older weaponry. As she sipped her coffee and looked out at the sunrise, she decided there had to be a way that she could even the chances for the British. She revisited her idea of inventing something that would help them: surely there was something she could do?

*

The inspiration she'd been looking for came to her in the most unusual way when she had been at Howard's a few days later. He had guests over, and they'd had a wonderful dinner. Afterwards, they all sat out around the fire pit that he'd placed on the beach near the water, until it became too chilly.

As the other guests left to go home, Hedy lingered with Howard. He had reunited with his girlfriend, Katharine Hepburn, but she was away working and Hedy sensed he was feeling lonely. Hedy and Howard's relationship had moved from the awkwardness of past lovers to being good friends, where it probably should have stayed in the first place, she often reflected.

Making their way back to the house, Howard prepared brandies for them both to warm them as they continued their conversation.

"Why don't you put some music on?" Howard suggested from the bar, signaling to a rather splendid-looking Philco radio in the center of the room.

Hedy walked over to look for the switch.

"It's on the table," Howard informed her, pointing to a box across the room.

Hedy furrowed her eyebrows and walked to where he had indicated. "What do you mean, it's on the table?"

"The box in front of you. It sends a signal to the radio. You don't have to get up and change the channel."

Hedy was amazed. She picked up the box, a little square item with a circular dial on it that looked very similar to a telephone without a receiver.

"Go ahead," encouraged Howard, "press the on button."

She pressed the black button marked "on" and turned the dial to a number.

"Point it toward the radio," continued Howard.

She followed his instructions, and the radio burst into life.

Hedy lifted the box with surprise.

"Where's the wire?" she asked. "I can't even see them."

"There are no wires." Howard chuckled, walking toward her and handing her a glass of warming amber liquid. "It's called a mystery control. A radio signal changes the channel."

Hedy was amazed. She turned the dial again; another channel crackled onto the wireless. She sat down, scrutinizing the box, and continued to change the channel.

"You're giving me a headache," said Howard. "Just pick one."

"This is amazing," she mused, her brain buzzing with all the ways this could be used.

When she got home that night, she made notes in her inventing book. Why couldn't this somehow be used against the Germans?

She went to bed that evening thinking about it, and when she woke up in the morning, she suddenly had an idea. What if she could use this same technology to help control the torpedoes that were being sent by the British? She started to recall everything she had read in the newspaper about torpedoes.

The Germans had become very adept at being able to block the signals. So, when the British would launch their torpedo, the Germans would block the signal and the torpedo would go off in a different direction, no longer on target to hit the German U-boats. What if she could use this way of moving the signal like she'd been able to move the channels to give the British more of a fighting chance so that the Germans couldn't track it? When the enemy attempted to block the signal, it would already be moved to a different transmission.

She continued to chew on these ideas as she went to the studio that day. When she was done with the morning shoot of the film they were finishing up, *Comrade X*, she walked off the sound studio and bumped into George Antheil, who was on his way to the commissary, and they decided to go for a cup of coffee together.

Hedy couldn't wait to tell George about her idea.

"I don't know, George," she said, shaking her head and sitting down at one of the tables. "I'm not sure I want to keep doing this. I'm thinking of quitting MGM and going to work for the Inventors Council in Washington instead. Because what are we really doing for this war?"

George lit a cigarette and sat back in his chair. "I think entertaining people is good. It's a distraction. We're a distraction for people."

"I want to be more than a distraction," stated Hedy, with great frustration. "I want to do something. I want to achieve something."

"Like what?" he enquired as a waitress filled their coffee cups and placed the pot on the table.

"I have ideas all the time, ideas that could help this war."

She pulled out her little inventing book and showed him her latest idea. On every page she had made notes, drawn pictures, and added calculations. She'd even cut out an advertisement for the Philco radio from her morning newspaper and had pasted it to one of the pages.

"If I could find a way to use this signal"—she pointed to the radio signal changer—"just like this box was able to change the channels, I think I could change the frequency of a torpedo, make the signal hop from one to another. Making it impossible for the enemy to track. Then we may give the Allies a chance."

George nodded, deep in thought. "Look, I understand the need to do something," he stated, suddenly becoming serious. "I don't tell a lot of people this but…" He took in a deep breath and fixed his gaze on a spot on the table, pausing only momentarily to rally himself before he spoke, almost in a whisper. "My younger brother was killed in a plane that was shot down. He's famous in all the ways you don't want to be known. He was the first American to be killed as a result of the declaration of World War Two. Even though as Americans we are not even at war."

Hedy sucked in her breath. She'd had no idea.

"So, I understand, Hedy," he continued. "I wish I could help, too."

He flipped through her notebook in awe. "All these ideas are yours?"

Before she could answer, there was a buzz around the room as Clark Gable walked in with Spencer Tracy. Passing their table, the former leaned in to kiss her dutifully on the cheek as Tracy looked away, avoiding eye contact.

"Hedy, darling, are you learning lines for our scene this afternoon?" Gable enquired, noticing her inventing book as she slammed it shut to hide the contents. He looked curious.

"I don't need to," she purred, placing her hands with her beautifully manicured fingernails on his arm. "I know them all by heart, so I don't get too dazzled by your charm when King calls 'Action'."

Gable laughed in a low, deep rumble. "I feel the same way about myself," he joked, very tongue-in-cheek. She knew that Clark was always a little amazed at his screen appeal and they often joked about his adoring fans. "George," he added, acknowledging Antheil with a nod, and he and Tracy made their way to a table at the back of the room.

"How's it going?" asked George in a hushed tone.

"Same as always," Hedy said. "I'm some mysterious woman, overcome by the enthralling charms of an American leading man. It is so boring, I could write these scripts myself. I wish Mayer would give me something to sink my teeth into. I thought it was maybe my accent. But did you hear about this new theatre actress everyone's talking about? Ingrid Bergman? It's rumored she's being considered for another great script and she's Swedish. Why am I always the femme fatale when other Europeans are getting these great parts?"

George watched Gable being delivered a large Scotch.

"Why's Tracy so quiet?" he enquired, signaling for their own check.

"Oh, he's still smarting from having his nose put out of joint because of *I Take This Woman*. That was a nightmare to film and we had some real stand-up rows but most of it wasn't my fault. I had to double up with *Lady of the Tropics*, and I was tired, so let's say we had some artistic differences."

George nodded and they made their way back to the set.

"So, what do you think?" asked Hedy.

"About?"

"About what we talked about in the summer, about getting together regularly to develop one of these ideas."

George walked in a small circle, kicking at the ground, and she knew there had probably been some resistance from Boski.

"Look, it will be all above board, I'll even bring food, some dinner for you and your family. We can just toss around some ideas, and your wife is welcome to join us."

George looked relieved; that was obviously what had been bothering him.

"She would hate that, but I wouldn't," he stated, looking up with a half-crooked smile. But as he stamped out his cigarette, he nodded.

"Okay, let's do it, we can work in my studio."

To cement the deal, she held out her hand. "Inventing partners?"

He smiled, his eyes lighting up with the excitement. "Partners," he echoed back as he took her hand.

Chapter Twenty-Three

The first six weeks after she'd found out she was pregnant were the happiest of Judy's life. And even the grim progression of war and darkness befalling the country couldn't deter the giddy happiness that greeted her every morning as she woke up and remembered the baby growing inside her.

But it was nothing compared to Tom's joy. The careful, thrifty husband she'd known up to now had become a virtual boy with the announcement of her pregnancy. Becoming like some sort of benevolent Father Christmas figure, Tom appeared every night with something else for the baby, whom he liked to call "our little one."

He turned up one evening with a beautiful set of blue and pink booties. She looked at him with surprise. "I asked one of the secretaries at the lab to knit them for the baby," he said with great enthusiasm. "She was so thrilled. They all wanted to do something for him or her. And I wanted to get them for you as well." He picked them up between his thick sausage fingers and held one up by a little blue ribbon. "Now, can you imagine anything fitting into things as small as these?"

Judy shook her head with excited disbelief.

Tom was also taking extra care of Judy, insisting on her sitting through most of the lab experiments they were working on, keeping her away from any dangerous chemicals, encouraging her to take walks in the fresh air, and reading everything he could on nutrition for the growing baby and Judy's health. One evening he even arrived home with a secondhand car someone at work was selling cheaply.

"Well, we will be a proper family soon," he stated to justify his purchase. "When this war is over and petrol isn't rationed as it is now, we may want to take our little one into the country for a picnic," he informed her as Judy had stood there, open-mouthed.

But apart from the morning sickness, which was starting to abate, she was feeling amazing, which was why when she got to the end of her third month she was so surprised. It started one morning when she woke up with a sharp pain in her back. Putting it down to being uncomfortable in bed, she rubbed at the base of her spine as Tom went to the kitchen to get her a morning cup of tea.

Downstairs, it continued to niggle her as Judy started her morning routine, preparing Tom's breakfast, their sandwiches for work, and tidying the kitchen. But by the time they got to the lab that morning, her pains were becoming stronger. As the day wore on, they began to radiate around from her back, shifting to the base of her stomach. As she didn't want to alarm Tom, she tried to hide it from him as they rocked through her body. But when in mid-afternoon an incredibly sharp pain jolted her from her seat with a slight scream, he looked up in alarm from checking one of his drawings. He knew instantly.

"Judy!" he exclaimed, the fear and concern evident on his face.

Judy imagined her face was as ashen as his own. And then the pain came again, even stronger. It felt as if someone had just stabbed her with a knife, it was so intense.

Still wincing with the pain, she managed to splutter through gritted teeth and the breath she was holding, "The doctor said there could be some muscle stretching that goes on and the odd pain." And then she shrieked again and her legs almost buckled from under her as she clung to the office desk for support.

All around the room, everyone had stopped and was staring across at them both, alerted by her distress.

"That doesn't look like muscle stretching to me," stated Tom, helping her back down into a seat. When she screamed again, he responded decisively, "I have to get you to the doctor's. In fact, I'm going to take you straight to the hospital," he said, grabbing his jacket and hat and helping her up. Supporting her, Tom placed Judy carefully in their car, and she was grateful she wouldn't have to walk or take a bus now that the pains were coming every two or three minutes. They seemed to want to slice her stomach in half.

It felt as if the whole pit of her stomach was caught in a vice. She tried to breathe, becoming lightheaded as she held her breath with the pain. And she tried desperately not to scream out. She could see that her husband was already beside himself.

When they arrived at the hospital, Tom explained the situation to the nurse and they were taken straight in and examined. Tom was asked to wait outside. Judy knew he would be distressed and she desperately wanted to hold his hand, but it was customary for husbands to be excluded from medical procedures involving their pregnant wives.

The doctor quietly examined her methodically, nodding his head as she attempted to answer his questions in between gasps. Though he didn't say it, she could tell by his expression that he was concerned as she described the pains shooting through her body.

"And you say you estimate that you're nearly twelve weeks?" he said, looking down at her notes.

"Yes," she spluttered as she succumbed to another sharp pain.

"You need to go home and rest, Mrs. Jenkins. I'm going to talk to your husband and send you home with something to calm you. I want you to stay in bed for at least a week. Do you understand?"

She nodded as she tried desperately to fend off another pain.

"There's not much we can do at the moment. If we keep you here at the hospital, all we'll do is keep you in bed. You might as well go home where you'll feel more comfortable."

Again, she nodded.

He moved to the door and was about to say something more when the air-raid siren went off.

Unable to restrain himself, Tom just burst into the room.

The doctor spoke calmly to the pair of them, raising his voice to be heard above the screech of the siren. "We'll get Mrs. Jenkins down to the shelter. You can come with her."

Tom reached for his wife, his hot, clammy hand in hers, his face conveying absolute fear, though he tried to reassure Judy with his voice. "You're going to be all right, Judy, don't you worry, I'm going to take care of you, you're going to be…" His voice petered out as he tapped her hand to reassure her and swallowed down the emotion welling up inside him.

The hospital went into an organized but speedy retreat. Patients who could be were transported downstairs and into an underground shelter, while patients unable to be moved were being protected by pillows and extra blankets. As Tom helped Judy into the hallway, it was packed. Wheelchairs in motion, beds rolling down the corridor, nurses and doctors all moving at speed.

It was slow going, as Judy was now in terrible pain. They were halfway down the stairs before she informed him she couldn't go any further. Tom lifted her up into his arms and, pulling her in close to his barrel chest, he carried her down. As much as she was afraid, it felt comfortable to be in his arms with the smell of his aftershave, listening to the stilted breath rushing in and out of his lungs and the wild thudding of his beating heart.

Down in the hospital shelter, it was cramped. White brick walls and a tiled floor smelled medicinal and antiseptic. Locked cabinets, extra linen, bedding and blankets were opened as patients were offered ways to make themselves comfortable. Stacked along one wall, camp beds were lined up for emergencies. With nowhere really to sit, Tom insisted she took one of the wheelchairs also stored downstairs.

As the bombs started to drop all around them, the medical staff and the patients stared at the ceiling, which rocked and showered down dust and debris. Tom stood over Judy, using his body and his coat to shield her. Judy's eyes became heavy. The pain was wearing her down and she was having trouble staying conscious.

When a shower of cement dust came down upon them both, Tom carefully cleared the fragments from her hair and kissed her forehead. "We're going to be all right. Just you hold on there, Judy."

She nodded as she took and squeezed his hand.

All at once, there was another sensation, and Judy sat trying to understand what was happening. She could feel warm liquid running between her thighs and soaking the back of her skirt. New fear gripped her. Tears started to roll down her cheeks as she willed the baby to hold on.

She didn't want to tell Tom. She didn't want to face the reality of what it could mean. She waited until he went to get her some water. Then she tugged on the arm of one of the doctors, explaining her situation. He nodded and called over a nurse. The nurse took things straight in hand.

They moved quickly, unfolding one of the camp beds, laying her flat, and covering her with a sheet. As the doctor came to examine her, she could tell by his face what was happening. She was losing the baby.

When Tom arrived back with water, he was shocked to see what was going on. Grabbing his arm, she pulled him close to her. "Stay with me, Tom. Please don't let go of me. Hold me."

Tom put his arms around her. And she could feel his breath on her cheek coming fast and furiously as the nurses and doctors worked. By the time the all-clear was sounded four hours later, it was all over for Judy.

The bomb attack had not only robbed them of their peace of mind but also their child. Once the baby had been lost, the doctors wanted her to stay overnight, just for observation. They cleaned her up and took her up to the ward. Tom came to see her before they shooed him out for the night.

It was dark and gloomy in the hospital. The lighting was out because of the bomb attack. All she could see were the whites of his eyes in the moonlight streaming through the window. He looked absolutely devastated, as though someone had punched him in the stomach.

He reached forward and took her hand. "Judy, I'm so, so sorry."

"No, Tom, I'm sorry."

"You didn't do anything wrong," he said, and she could hear the quiver in his voice. She knew he was trying his best to stay strong. They sat there holding hands in silence for what felt like hours. Both deep in their personal grief, both unable to offer the other anything but the warmth of their companionship.

At 9 p.m., the matron came and told him that he needed to leave. Tom leaned in and kissed his wife goodbye.

"I will be back first thing tomorrow. You try and get some sleep."

She nodded, and as she watched him walk down the dark corridor, she felt so alone. Something she hadn't felt in three months. The reality hit her again; she'd lost her baby.

After Tom left, only then did she allow herself to cry. It had been too painful looking at her husband's face, and she didn't want him to feel worse, but once he was gone, she felt she could weep openly.

The kind nurse who came on duty at two stopped by to check on her.

"Can I get you anything?" she whispered into the darkness, only broken by emergency candlelight on the ward.

Judy shook her head, trying to hide the tears.

The nurse seemed to know anyway.

"I know it's hard," she said, "but I want to tell you something. I lost my first child too, at about this time, just before three months. And now I've got four children. Sometimes the first pregnancy is just our body practicing for the real thing. You'll get pregnant again soon, I promise you. And as painful as this is, the joy you will feel then will be what will outweigh all of it. You'll never forget this little one, but you will feel joy again, I can promise you that."

Judy nodded her head as the young woman checked her chart and tucked in her blankets.

"Now, you need to get a little bit of sleep," she said in a practical tone. "Your body's been through something very traumatic, and it needs all the rest it can get." The nurse gave her something to help her sleep, and before long, Judy's eyes became heavy.

She remained in the hospital for two days. And when Tom came to pick her up, she was looking forward to going home. But the emptiness in her heart and in her body was the worst pain she'd ever felt.

Entering the house, Tom had removed everything he'd bought for the baby, and the door to the little nursery they'd been decorating was now closed. For the next few days, Tom insisted she stay in bed and managed the best he could making eggs on toast and sandwiches to try and coax her to eat. But she was heartbroken and just couldn't manage anything. Slowly, she started to move back into the world again, immersing herself in her work to try and distract herself from her grief.

A month later, they were given the all-clear to start trying again, and Tom approached the subject for the first time, putting his arm around his wife when they were out on a walk. "It'll be all right next time, Judy, you wait and see."

Judy nodded reluctantly, but something had changed inside of her. Now all she felt was apprehension. She never wanted to go through this pain ever again.

January 10, 1941

Dear Hedy,

I don't know quite how to write this. I'm sorry it's been so long; I have the saddest of news to share with you and it is really hard to put into words, but you need to know. We have had the greatest tragedy; the much-wanted baby that I was pregnant with, I lost a couple of weeks ago. I can't even tell you the heartache that I've been through and how hard it has been on both Tom and me. I cried for days. And since then I have just felt numb. The hardest thing about this is the loss of the future and the joy to come. With the dark days of war all around us, this baby had been a tiny light of hope inside me, something Tom and I could look forward to, especially as our work has become even busier and the pressure intense.

The first couple of weeks, I wasn't sure how I was going to go on. But Tom was here. Though we seem to be grieving in different ways. He's quite shut down and thoughtful. And I just want to cry all the time. So many people say to me, "Oh, it's your first. Don't let it get you down." But it does get me down, Hedy. This baby was much wanted, and it feels like a huge disappointment. I can't even look in the nursery now. Tom has packed away the little cot and all the gifts. Thank you for the beautiful blanket you sent me. I folded it up and put it away with the other things. I know we'll probably try for another baby, but it's still so hard thinking about the loss of this lovely one.

This is going to be a short letter. I just wanted to let you know what was going on and that your Christmas parcel arrived. Thank you for the tinned butter and chocolate, a rare treat right now. You are so kind to send us gifts of some of the foods that we're missing. We can't thank you enough. And it's been the only cheerful light in this very dark time. Take care, and I hope you've all had a lovely Christmas.

Much love,
Judy

TELEGRAM

MY DEAR JUDY – (STOP) –
I AM SO SO SORRY FOR YOUR AND TOM'S LOSS
– (STOP) –
DON'T LISTEN TO PEOPLE WHO WANT TO
TRIVIALIZE THIS.
IT IS HEARTBREAKING – (STOP)
TAKE ALL THE TIME YOU NEED TO GRIEVE
– (STOP) –
SENDING YOU A HUGE HUG AND PLEASE LET
ME KNOW IF THERE IS ANYTHING I CAN DO TO
HELP – (STOP) –
MUCH LOVE HEDY XXX

HEDY LAMARR
10:03 AM

Chapter Twenty-Four

After that initial conversation, George and Hedy started to work together every evening and afternoon when they weren't on set. Sometimes, in between scenes they would sit, scribble through notepads, and get ideas. Hedy became obsessed, even calling George in the middle of the night when she would get an idea in her head. They worked on other inventions together, including a special type of anti-aircraft shell, all weapons to fight the enemy, but Hedy just couldn't move on from the frequency-hopping idea.

One day Hedy was over at his house when George suddenly had a flash of inspiration. He took her into his music room to show her his idea.

"Look at this piano," he said, getting excited.

Hedy sat down at it. It was a regular mahogany wood piano, but instead of a music stand, there was a roll of paper with a pattern of holes indented on it.

"Isn't this a player piano?" she remarked, trying to understand. "A piano that plays itself? What has this got to do with radio signals?"

"It could be adapted," he continued, unable to hide his enthusiasm.

He pulled out the roll of the piano paper for her to inspect.

"Look," he said, "each one of these indents here activates the note played by the piano. Couldn't we use something like this to create the signal that you've been talking about? In other words, if a roll of paper can activate piano keys, why can't it activate radio signals?"

Hedy started to see the idea. "We could have two piano rolls, synchronized together, one on the torpedo, one on the ship working the same, but hopping to the same signal each time on the same pattern of frequency. This is brilliant, George." Hedy jumped to her feet and paced the room.

"Let's see how we can do this," mused George, thinking out loud. "It could work on the same eighty eight encryption code that the pianos do and only the torpedo guidance system would know the song, or in this case the frequency it was hopping to."

She threw her arms around George and hugged him.

"This is brilliant, I know this can work."

The two of them started to work even harder on that one invention; they wanted something to show the Inventors Council and also had to polish their idea for the patent office, as they couldn't go forward until they had a patent.

After months of working together, one night, it was finished. It was 3 o'clock in the morning and Hedy put the finishing touches on the proposal. Putting down her pen, she stretched her neck. Looking at George across the room that was reeking with the stagnant smell of smoke and whiskey, she noticed he had fallen asleep.

She tapped him awake. "It's done, George," she informed him as she placed the proposal in front of him and, bleary-eyed, he focused on it and then beamed.

"I think the Inventors Council first, and see if they are interested in helping us."

Hedy agreed.

When they contacted them the next day, one particular inventor, Charles Kettering, agreed to see them. He was dazzled by the idea and connected them with a physicist in California, who was at Caltech and could design the electronics of their invention. They finally submitted it for a patent, and she received notification in the mail one morning.

Hedy was so excited, she drove herself to work not even waiting for her driver, and rushed over to the soundstage she knew George was working on. She caught up with him in the middle of the lot, just about to start work.

He looked taken back when she rushed up and hugged him, as all around him the other musicians he was with whistled their encouragement. Undeterred by the commotion she was causing, Hedy thrust the open letter into his hand.

He read it quickly.

It assured them that they could obtain and hold a certified copy of the file in the application of Hedy Kiesler-Markey and George Antheil, entitled Secret Communication System, and the patent would be active by April 21st. He picked her up in his arms and swung her around.

"This is it, Hedy, we're going to help win the war."

*

Once the patent was finalized, they presented their invention to the National Inventors Council, who were impressed, and they encouraged them to submit it to the Navy.

So, one morning they found themselves waiting outside a very official-looking Navy building to present their idea to a group that oversaw the development of new technology.

Hedy wore a navy suit, hat, and white blouse, wanting to look as professional as possible, and George, who normally wore an open shirt and sneakers, was wearing a tie and had even bought a new suit for the occasion. As they waited outside the office, watching people come and go, Hedy felt she was on a different planet. Here the world of the war was everywhere, and everyone and everything had a mechanical precision to it. A tight-lipped secretary with hair scraped into a high bun had told them to wait, either not knowing who they were or not caring and definitely not giving them any kind of star treatment.

A buzzer sounded on the secretary's desk. "You may go in, Mrs. Kiesler-Markey, Mr. Antheil. The commission will see you now."

Hedy got to her feet, and, grasping copies of their patent and invention, she and George made their way through the door.

Inside was a large oval table. Around it sat a group of official-looking Navy personnel. The room was sterile and quiet as they made their way into the center of it, nothing but the sound of Hedy's high-heeled leather shoes clipping on the highly polished floor to break the silence. She saw a couple of the men look her up and down with incredulity. She imagined that the two of them were an unusual sight within these walls, and tried not to feel intimidated.

If the commander at the head of the table was surprised to see what stood before him, he didn't let it show, just introduced the members in the room to them both in a cool and polite manner.

"Mrs. Kiesler-Markey, Mr. Antheil. You have been recommended to us from the National Inventors Council, whom we have great respect for, especially Mr. Kettering. Why don't you describe to us in your own words what you have invented and why you feel it may be of interest to the Navy."

Hedy cleared her throat and affixed her best smile that usually won over a room, but was greeted by the now familiar chill and stern expressions as George handed out diagrams of their invention for the group to study. They had decided ahead of time to have her present it, as they hoped her movie star appeal might help their cause. But now, as she reflected on the less than friendly reception they'd received, she wondered if that had been the right call.

She had barely started to explain the principles of their design when the commander at the top of the table, who had looked over their proposal briefly, threw it back down and addressed Hedy. "You are not American, Mrs. Kiesler-Markey?"

This was the first time since she'd arrived in the U.S. that she had felt the need to defend her loyalty. "I am not," she stated, feeling her cheeks redden slightly. "I am Austrian."

"When did you leave, before or after the annex with our enemy?"

"Well before, of course," she said, trying to keep the irritation from her tone. Why weren't they asking her about the design?

He paused, then nodded; but from that point on, she felt she was not only presenting the invention but defending her own patriotism.

"You got this idea from a piano," retorted another of the members as he peered at Antheil, unable to keep the cynicism from his tone.

George wasn't intimidated. "Yes, I am a musician as well as an inventor, and this is why we use the eighty eight encryption code here, similar to the number of piano keys on a keyboard."

After that comment, the room was deadly silent as the group continued to look at the paperwork in front of them. It could barely have been a few minutes but felt like hours as the two of them stood there waiting to be addressed again. Finally, it was the commander. "And you, Mrs. Kiesler-Markey, do you have any scientific credentials? Or are you a musician as well?"

Hedy swallowed. The last thing she wanted to do in this difficult room was utter her next sentence. "Not official credentials, no. I work in the film industry."

"The film industry?" he questioned. "There is a need of scientists in that industry?"

"Not exactly. I am an actress."

His eyes clouded over as he repeated her confession. "An actress."

George continued, obviously hoping it would help. "Mrs. Kiesler-Markey has just made a movie with Clark Gable and Jimmy Stewart. She works under the name of Miss Hedy Lamarr."

There was a collective drawing in of breath around the table as people realized who she was.

"My wife loves your movies," stated one of the men before he had time to catch himself and the commander took control again.

"But apart from playing a variety of parts on the cinema screen, you are an alien with no expertise in this area to vouch for your work here," he summed up with a sweep of his hand across the proposal.

Hedy swallowed down her frustration. And plastered on another smile. "That is correct," she stated, not understanding why this was suddenly about her and not the thousands of people being killed every day, not the poor, innocent children who had been killed by torpedoes from a German U-boat only months before. Why couldn't they let go of their prejudices to see what was right in front of them?

"I see," he responded coolly. "Well, we of course will give this the consideration it's due and we will send you a letter when we have reached a decision. Thank you for coming."

Hedy nodded, pushing down the tears that were threatening to well up. All that work they had done, and she was being judged on who she was and not on the design. Did they not know how important this was?

She and George made their way out into the office, where the same uptight secretary dismissed them with a bob of her head and continued typing at speed at her desk.

"Don't worry, Hedy," George reassured her in a whisper. "They have to be like that. This is the military. Give them time to look it over. They can't turn it down. It's brilliant."

She and George were halfway down the corridor outside the office when someone called her name.

Stopping, she turned to see one of the people from the meeting racing to catch up with them. Her heart quickened as she noticed he was smiling. They had done what George had said; they had looked it over already and were going to ask her to go back in so she could tell them more about the invention. As the naval officer reached them, she realized it was the one who had known who she was.

"Miss Lamarr," he repeated. "I wonder if I could have a moment of your time."

"Of course," she responded, expecting him to usher her back to the room. But instead he pulled out a piece of paper and a pen from his pocket.

"My wife would love an autograph. If it's not too much trouble."

Hedy felt her heart sink. "It would be my pleasure," she forced out, trying not to let her disappointment show as she signed it and he thanked her, shaking George's hand as he left.

She and George barely spoke on their way home. The disappointment was palpable in the car. He dropped Hedy at the farm, and as she got out, he patted her hand.

"They didn't say no, Hedy, and Kettering's name holds weight. Let's just see what happens, okay?"

She nodded, but as she walked back into her home she thought about Judy and the way she had talked about how she was treated too, never being taken seriously because she was a woman, even though she had the scientific credentials, and Hedy felt angry. Why was it not possible for people to see past the outward appearance and judge them solely on the merit of the work?

Chapter Twenty-Five

March 1941

One evening on their way back from work, Tom wanted to look in on a friend, so Judy made her way home alone. When she got to the front door, there was a note pinned to it from her neighbors, telling her to go around as soon as possible.

When Judy entered, she was surprised to see her mother sitting in her neighbor's kitchen. It was such a shock, it took a minute for Judy to register that this was possible. Her mother, who rarely ventured from Wales and had only ever visited Judy once at her house, when she and Tom had married, was there. Her face was stony and solemn, though, and a creeping fear started to drift up through Judy's body until it locked its hands around her throat, making her greeting tight and high-pitched.

"Ma, is everything all right?"

Her mother stood up and couldn't seem to look her daughter in the eye, but apparently not wanting to talk in front of the neighbor, she thanked her for her kindness and then moved to the front door. Bewildered, Judy followed her out to her own door. It felt as if the blood was draining out of her body with every step. Her knees felt weak, her stomach tight. Her hand shook as she put the key in the door.

Their footsteps echoed as they walked into the house, and how quiet the rooms seemed. Quieter than she'd ever remembered. To break the silence, she spoke.

"Do you want a cup of tea, Ma?"

Her mother nodded and seated herself down at Judy's kitchen table as Judy started to pour water into the kettle. Placing it on the stove, she turned to face her mother, and could tell her mother was trying as best as she could to summon up her bravery. She finally seemed to find the words.

"I wanted to tell you the news in person," she began, and the knot in Judy's stomach grew more prominent. Her throat tightened even more, and she thought she wouldn't be able to take in air. Quickly she sat down at the table, not sure if she was still able to stand with the feeling of weakness. Her mother tried to speak again, but tears welled up in her eyes, and she, too, seemed to have trouble speaking as she swallowed past her own lump in her throat.

Please, God, don't let it be Da, thought Judy over and over in her mind, *Please don't let it be Da*. She looked across, trying to read her mother's face. She'd never seen her mother so still. She and her father always joked about how she was like a butterfly because she moved all the time, flitting from place to place. This was not the woman that sat before her so stolidly, and it scared Judy more than the news that she was about to get. The stillness seemed to have a pain all of its own.

"Are you going to tell me why you've come, Ma?" she said, hearing the quiver in her voice. God, she wished Tom was here. Where was he? He needed to be sitting by her holding her hand to hear whatever this was. She imagined him sitting in someone's front room, laughing and joking, while here she was being dealt the hardest news. It had to be her father. There was no other reason for it.

Her mother finally spoke. "Judy, I know you have been dealing with a lot at the moment which is why I wanted to tell you face to face… The thing is, I've got some bad news." She spoke in Welsh, apparently unable to think of the English for it.

"It's Da, isn't?" said Judy, answering in English.

"It is. It's Da." Judy's mother seemed to go within herself, and as she tried desperately to get the words out, she pursed her lips, swallowing hard, but when her eyes flicked up, Judy covered her mouth with her hand. Was she going to be sick?

Her mother continued.

"As you know, your father was out fighting in Africa. I got a letter from him last week. On the whole, he's been out of a lot of the fray, which I've been so grateful for, but there was an attack this week. Many of the people in his battalion were killed or injured, and some were missing. Then I got this letter."

Her mother broke down then, unable to speak any more. She shook her head, reached into her hefty handbag, pulled out a crumpled letter, and slid it across the table. Judy opened the letter and tried to understand the words swimming in front of her eyes. She read it once. It didn't make any sense. She read it twice. She could just pick out the odd word, "missing," her father's full name, which she never heard him referred to by. A time, a date, a date stamp, all in official-looking type. But even though she read it and reread it, it didn't seem to make any sense to her.

Her mother seemed to understand. "He's missing in action, love. They're looking for him, but they haven't found him."

"It has to be a mistake," said Judy, placing the letter down on the table. "There's a mistake, Ma. They have to have made a mistake."

Judy's mother reached forward and took her hand, obviously in a different stage of acceptance to her daughter. "We can always hope that, but we have to face the truth, darling. We have to prepare ourselves." Judy grabbed her mother's hand, her eyes begging for more. "That's all I know, love. Everything I know is in that letter."

A key rattled in the front door and Tom made his way inside. He spotted Judy's mother straight away.

"Mrs. Morgan?" he said, the surprise evident in his tone. "What a lovely surprise to see you." And then he stopped speaking, registering both the women's faces. Judy imagined her own was as pale as her mother's.

"What is it?" asked Tom in a quiet, sober voice.

Judy's lip trembled as she forced out the words. "It's Da. He's missing in action." She passed the letter to Tom as if to confirm the news. Judy was saying the words, but she still wasn't believing them. Maybe Tom would help her believe it. "What are we going to do, Tom?" she pleaded, her voice tight with the restriction in her throat.

Tom read it carefully and then his eyes met her own. "It's all right, love. It's all right; we're going to get through this, together." He hadn't even taken off his coat and hat.

Suddenly the kettle sang out with a whistle, and Judy, wanting to be distracted, went to make the tea as Tom asked her mother more questions. As she placed the tea in the teapot and listened to them behind her, she stared out of the window, trying to make all the pieces of the information fit in some sort of pattern in her mind that made sense. Nothing made sense.

Why wasn't it sinking in? Everything was so unfair. She'd already been through so much lately. How was it possible that she would go through any more pain after the loss of her baby?

Her mother stayed the night, and they spent a sober, quiet time together. When she had finally got to sleep that night, Judy had tossed and turned, waking up every couple of hours, when the news would wash over her again, like a glass of ice water that hit her face and worked its way through her body until it found the knot in her stomach.

Her da was missing.

Judy took her mother to the train station the next morning; she'd asked her to stay with them, but her mother had shaken her head. "There's too much for me to do at home and you've got your own life here. We're going to hope for the best, aren't we, love."

Judy had nodded but not been persuaded. She kissed and hugged her mother, not wanting to let her go, holding on to her till the very last minute, until the final whistle blew. On the way to work, she was preoccupied. Clutching at every good memory she could summon up of her father. His laughter. The excitement in his eyes when she talked about her work, and his immense pride in her. So many things she hadn't had a chance to ask him yet, about his own childhood and his relatives, the things she'd heard in passing, but she'd never asked about in detail. Then she remembered a tiny scar on his chin. She'd always meant to ask him how he'd got that. Now she might never know. How could—in just a matter of weeks—her world seem so utterly empty? Suddenly there was a hollowness about everything. All that lay ahead seemed so bleak, sad and lonely.

*

When Judy lost her second baby, it was so different than the first. Gone was the trauma and shock of the air raid and grappling with the loss. She had got pregnant quickly and then been so preoccupied by the fact her father was missing. She had been scared from the beginning that there would be problems. So, she hadn't been surprised when the second baby slipped away on an unseasonably cold night in early April. They'd had a thick blanket of snow cover the ground the day before, and the only real thing Judy would remember about it was how beautiful the snowflakes were, falling outside of her bedroom window, in contrast to the pain she was going through. And Tom's face. His cold, stolid face, and his hand holding hers.

After losing the second baby, gone was the conversation between the two of them about "we'll try again, we'll do this another time."

When the doctor visited, he didn't say the things the nurse had said the first time around, which he had reinforced, about how often people lost their first babies. But with this second loss, his expression had changed to concern with the knowledge that this could be a pattern, indicative of a bigger problem. And even though Judy had been readier for this loss the second time around, she had not felt any less desperate.

If anything, she felt more desperate. Particularly when she looked into Tom's eyes. She couldn't help feeling that somehow, he blamed her for the loss. She was heartbroken, but so was he. She could cry. She could let it out. But Tom didn't seem to know how to do that. He would take himself off for long walks, and she'd see him wandering mindlessly around the garden with a spade in his hand, staring out across the Anderson shelter, not doing anything in particular.

It also seemed to have driven a wedge between the two of them. They were unable to process the grief together, because they did it in such separate ways. It was the unspoken emptiness between them. The empty chair at the table where a child should be sitting. The empty cot in the spare room. The world that would never be filled with two children's laughter.

When she recovered from that miscarriage, Judy went back to work. But a latent depression set in, not only with the ongoing war, which wasn't going well, but the loss of a future she had needed to help her get through this dark time in their country's history. Even though Judy and Tom were working hard, none of it seemed to mean anything to either of them right now. They worked politely by each other's side. And somehow, they'd forgotten how to laugh. It wasn't for want of trying to connect. But the grief was so immense it swallowed up the air between them.

Tom would sometimes bring her home little presents or flowers, but none of it seemed to have the same effect as it had had before the losses.

It was unsaid, but they didn't try for another baby after the second loss. It was as though they both feared the outcome. It was hard to grieve and think about new life at the same time. At the lab, Tom became more inward, more sullen while Judy worked non-stop, ploughing all of her sadness into her work and activity.

So, it was with great surprise that Judy found out she was pregnant for the third time toward the end of September. She couldn't even remember when it had happened. Then she recalled, Tom's birthday had been the month before. It had been the one and only time they had been intimate. Both trying to find the love that seemed to be lost between them. This time she didn't say anything to Tom. This time she went straight to her midwife.

The midwife tried to prepare her and told her not to get her hopes up, that a lot of people were suffering this kind of loss during such a traumatic time as the war. And after that serious visit, she couldn't bring herself to tell Tom. She was almost two and a half months pregnant before she found she was forced to.

He'd been talking about a work trip to London they would have to go on right about the time the baby was due. And as much as she wanted to go with him, it would be impossible if she had a baby or was still heavily pregnant.

They were on the river when she eventually plucked up the courage. They'd been trying to do things that brought them joy before their losses, and they were out boating. She, of course, was the one rowing, as he described the London visit and she suddenly knew she needed to tell him.

"Tom." He looked toward her and smiled. "I've something to tell you." He stared at her quizzically. "I'm expecting again."

Tom looked utterly shocked. He didn't speak at all, just sat there with his mouth open. Gone was the excitement and tears. Gone was the joy—only the fear of what that might mean if there was another loss.

He didn't speak again until they were settled on the bank, and he had laid out the blanket and sat next to her. "How do you feel?" he asked weakly. "Do you feel well?"

It was a cool response to new life, but she knew he was trying to find words that weren't congratulatory. Something that would appease the sadness between them.

"I feel well, but if my calculations are correct it's due on about the date of the London trip you were talking about," she said, unable to add anything further, and he nodded, taking her hand and squeezing it gently. Then they both just stared out across the water as she felt the chasm of grief once again stretch between them.

He didn't mention it again, just watched her carefully as one would an ill person, as if waiting for it all to go wrong.

The next time she went to see the doctor, he said he would like to speak to both her and Tom. Judy would soon be reaching that three-month mark, and the fear and trepidation of that date was a heavy weight between them. They went along to their appointment together and sat in front of the desk, as fearful as if they were seated before a headmaster.

The doctor, on the other hand, was more hopeful as time was going on. He talked about how each day, there was more chance of Judy keeping the baby. And he also felt there were lots of things they could do to make her chances better this time around.

"We'll do anything," said Tom. "Anything." And she could hear the desperation in her husband's voice.

"I think the best thing that could happen for Judy right now would be for her to have a little holiday." Tom sat back in his chair in surprise. "You've both been very busy at work, and this whole previous situation has been very hard on Judy, physically as well as mentally, not to mention the worry about her father. I think a change of scenery and some sea air perhaps is exactly what she needs right now to get her through the next few months. Is there somewhere you can go and stay for a few weeks? A parent or a friend?"

They both shook their heads, though Judy liked the idea.

They discussed it over dinner that night to see what they could arrange. She could go to Wales but her mother was away visiting a relative in Scotland for a few months to keep her own mind from the worry, and Judy didn't want to go to Wales on her own. Tom only had his aged uncle who lived in Hull. Not exactly the kind of person Judy would enjoy spending time with, so it seemed that the idea was impossible.

"We will keep thinking," said Tom optimistically. "Something will come up."

September 29, 1941

Dear Judy,

This is the third letter I've sent you, and still, I've not heard back. I'm beginning to get a little bit worried. At first, I just believed the post was going missing because of this blasted war, but it's not like you not to write back within a couple of weeks, even if there has been a missed letter.

I can't imagine how devastating it's been for you to lose another baby, so it just makes me worry all the more. Please write to me and tell me you're okay. My heart goes out to both you and Tom, but dear friend, there's always hope.

Even during this dark time for both you and the world, please, could you write back. My heart hurts for you. I wish you had a telephone. I'd call you. But in the meantime, I'll be thinking of you. A little gift is coming your way to cheer you up.

Take care.

Much love,
Hedy

Chapter Twenty-Six

Fall 1941

When Judy got the telephone call she'd been at her desk, and Tom working in the other lab; the secretary, Miss Stenner, had come to find her. "There's someone on the phone for you," she informed her.

Judy looked up from her experiment in surprise. They usually asked for Tom, and nobody she knew called her at the lab; most people didn't have a telephone.

Judy followed Miss Stenner to the secretary's office but as soon as she picked up the receiver, she knew.

"Hello, love," said a stilted voice, willowy and thready, just a mere echo of her mother's true character.

"Ma?" She heard the tightness in her own voice; it felt puny compared to the violent thrumming of her heart in her ears.

"I have some news," she continued, sounding so beaten down it was almost painful to listen to. Her mother paused then as if collecting herself, but Judy couldn't bring herself to say anything in the long silence; she just kept willing herself to breathe.

"It's your da. I got word today they found him."

For a fragment of a second, joy rushed into her heart; this was good news. Surely "found" meant he was alive. Why did her mother sound so sad? But her premature hopes were dashed with her mother's following words.

"He died, love."

Judy heard the words but couldn't comprehend them, couldn't digest them. It was as if they just hovered in front of her and taunted her, unable to filter into her consciousness. They echoed around her. *He died, love. He died, love. He died, love.* What did that mean?

All at once, realizing she was holding it, she hitched her breath, and it was as if she drew in the cold, hard reality with that desperate gasp. Then the pain came, stabbing at her heart as acute as a point of sharpened steel and making her whole body weak. She knew when her father had been marked as missing, there was a chance of this, and she had thought she had prepared herself for that outcome. But all her carefully constructed resilience was destroyed with those three words. Somewhere deep in the recesses of her heart, she'd hoped he'd been the one, the one they'd found alive. It just seemed impossible to her that her happy, larger-than-life father could be dead.

Judy was shaken from her contemplation by her mother's voice.

"They can't bring him home, love, they have to bury him with his comrades."

With those words her mother broke down. "We will have a service here, of course." Judy's body started to shake, and she tried to fix herself in the reality of her mother's words, find some sort of compass to anchor herself. As her mother continued to speak, she stared out of the window, trying desperately to fight the need to scream.

On the stone window sill, a calico cat trod lightly to a warm sunny corner. It curled up into a furry circle and licked at its paws. It was such an ordinary occurrence that she was struck by the comparison; how could the rest of life be continuing when her world had just collapsed from under her? She was free-falling into despair and sadness, and she didn't know how to stop herself.

Suddenly she felt an arm on her shoulder, and she almost jumped with the shock of touch. She looked up into the secretary's face, who must have sensed it, sensed the sadness that had descended on the room, sensed the bad news, something Judy imagined she was used to.

She was grateful for the reassuring hand as her father's smiling face danced in front of her, and she suddenly realized something. She'd only just figured it out; her dad had been her touchstone. He'd been the one person that had always encouraged her, apart from Tom. If it weren't for him, she would never have had the confidence to pursue her education, let alone go to Cambridge. She'd never have felt that she had any ability. He had been the one always pouring encouragement in her ear, even when her mother tried to dash those hopes, thinking that he was raising her for disappointment.

Familiar words once again echoed in her mind. "There's nothing wrong with raising a family and being a mother," her ma had argued. "Don't fill her mind with all those high notions. She'll think she can do it. She's a woman. We can't do things like that."

But her dad had only responded by winking at his daughter. "My Judy can do anything she wants to do," he'd said in his low rumbling voice. "She's always been special." All at once, she realized so much of what she was doing was for her dad. She wanted him to be proud. She wanted all the money that he'd invested in her education to be of value. How could he be gone before she'd finished what she'd set out to do for him?

She wasn't sure how long she sat there watching the cat on the sill, the weight of the secretary's hand resting gently on her shoulder. She wasn't even sure what her mother said to her for the rest of the call. The only thing she was now confident about was that her life was never, ever going to be the same again.

It wasn't until she heard the tone on the phone, one continuous note, that she realized that her mother had hung up, and carefully she placed the receiver down. She tried to get up, but it was as though her body was weighted with lead pinning her to the seat.

The secretary seemed to understand and gently squeezed her shoulder.

"Don't you rush, love. Take your time. I'll get you a cup of tea." She left the room, and Judy seemed to be moving as if underwater. The room swirling around her, everything out of sync.

Then all at once, she was holding something warm in her hand, and she stared down at this beautiful china cup with pink roses painted on the side. How could such beauty live alongside her darkness and pain?

She tried to sip the hot liquid, but her hand trembled so much she ended up just putting it back on its saucer and laying it down on the desk.

The next thing she remembered was Tom. Lifting her up from the chair and holding her in his arms. She allowed him to wrap his arms around her, just not sure what to do, where to go, hoping he would know. He didn't speak, just held her, and she drew from his strength. He walked her out and placed her in the car to drive her home. On the way, the silence was so deafening that Judy just felt she should say something. To at least try and believe what she had heard. "It's my da. They're going to have a service in Wales." Those were the only words she could manage.

Tom nodded his head somberly and squeezed her hand. Arriving home, he helped her out of the car and led her to the bedroom. She didn't even take her clothes off, just slipped her shoes off and tucked herself under the covers.

"Do you want me to stay with you, Judy?"

She shook her head. "There's no need, Tom. You should go back to work. I'm just going to sit quietly here and think about him, remember him, think of all the good times we had."

Tom smiled, ran his fingers through her hair, kissed her gently on the cheek, and he was gone. She lay there, staring at the ceiling.

"Da," she said into the silence, and then it was as if she felt the warmth of her father's presence for a second. As though he was right there with her, holding her hand, and she started to cry.

She heard his reassuring voice in her mind.

"Now, girl, none of this sadness; you have things to do."

As she sat there listening to his voice in her head, something snapped. Something happened to her that she had never experienced in her life before. She felt a growing rage that burned in her heart and churned her stomach like acid. And honestly, it felt good. She didn't want to feel all this pain any more. She wanted to do something and for the first time in her life she understood the need to kill. She understood what sent people to the edge where they felt vengeance was their only option.

The feeling shocked her, but it also felt powerful in a way that sadness and pain didn't. She had recently read a story about an airman who during the Battle of Britain had started out not wanting to kill people, but after his parents were killed in a raid he gone into the sky to seek vengeance on every mission. At the time she hadn't understood what could drive someone to do that, but now for the first time she had a taste of it and though it scared her a little it also emboldened her. Gritting her teeth together, she spat out these words into the empty room: "You're right, Da, I have things to do and I promise you I won't stop until this war is over. And I will do it for you."

*

The next few weeks for Judy were a mixture of familiar faces and unfamiliar feelings. She couldn't bring herself to share what she was going through with Tom. She couldn't put into words that she refused to be a victim any more and that the anger felt good. It actually made her feel alive.

She pushed it all down, swallowing down the acidic bile that rose up in her throat and occupied herself with the vehement conviction that she was going to put this right at any cost.

Though her father was to be buried overseas where he had been killed, the local church in the village they were from had a service so people could grieve. The whole day was like a blur for Judy. Even staring at her black clothes in the mirror, the day before his funeral, did not make anything feel real.

On her trip back to Wales on the train, Tom and Judy hardly spoke, both alone with their own thoughts. She had such a mixture of feelings going on, the pain, sadness but also now the anger that constantly simmered inside her. She wanted someone to pay for what had happened to her lovely father. With this inner turmoil it took all of her energy just to be able to concentrate from moment to moment. Staring out of the window, watching the countryside roll by and south-west England's pastures turning into the rocky hills and rugged terrain of Wales was all she could concentrate on. As she grew closer, the pain in her heart and the knot in her stomach grew more intense. Sensing her discomfort, Tom reached for her hand and gently squeezed it.

The funeral service had been beautiful and the chapel itself packed to bursting with lots of people from the village. She had stood at the front by her mother's side supporting her, with Tom next to her. Managing to hold it together until the minister had mentioned her father's love for his wife and his daughter. At that point, she'd wanted to roll down onto the floor, curl into a ball and just cry. She felt her body sag into Tom's, and he stiffened by her side to help hold her up.

When they'd walked out of the little gray stone chapel on the hillside, she'd looked out over the valley she'd grown up in. The sun had beamed, shafts of bright light broken and jagged through gray headstones, and as beautiful as it all was, Judy couldn't shake off the fury. She felt as if it was eating at her from the inside. All she wanted to do was scream, cry and throw something. But instead she politely greeted people, keeping it all buttoned down behind her dutiful daughter smile.

After the service and after the last person left from the wake at their home, Judy began to notice something strange. Everything seemed so familiar and yet she felt so detached. It was like a shadow of the home it had been. She had never noticed before how quiet and unassuming her mother was without him. His gregarious personality had brought out the best in all of them and without him in the rooms, the house echoed with the emptiness. Everywhere was wanting. The kitchen so still without his constant humming as he dried the dishes. The garden barren without him showing off his prize carrots. And it was almost painful to see the fireplace without her father stretched out in front of it. Even their old cat seemed to grieve his absence. It just walked into the room and stared at the empty chair for what seemed like an eternity before padding back out again without settling.

On the third day she finally felt she had the courage to face the most difficult room of all, her father's little office in the box room. The door had been closed since she had arrived but Judy knew it would haunt her if she didn't go in there. Tom had been out in the garden with her mother, where she had been asking some advice about one of her plants, when Judy got her chance. She wanted to do this alone; she didn't want to talk or feel the need to comfort anyone else's pain, she just wanted to absorb his presence. As she placed her hand on the doorknob she noticed her tremor and the weakness she felt. Hastily turning it to stop herself from backing out, she opened it quickly and closed it behind her, placing her back against the door for strength.

The first thing to hit her was the smell and instead of it making her sad, it actually made her smile. She closed her eyes and inhaled deeply the familiar scent that seemed to cling to the very walls. The smell of pipe tobacco and leather, with just the hint of his favorite peppermints that were always lurking in one of the drawers. As she drew in a deep breath she embraced the experience as if it was a soft blanket to comfort her. She wanted to keep her eyes closed, because in her mind's eye she could still imagine him here. Sitting in his office chair with the annoying squeak, poring over one of his ledgers, his pipe resting in an ashtray by his side, his tortoiseshell reading glasses perched on the edge of his nose. She wanted to stay like that forever, just embracing the shadow of his presence, because maybe, just maybe if she never opened her eyes she would never know he was gone.

Letting out a deep, slow breath, she spoke to him in a whisper as if he was sitting right there. "I'm pregnant, Da," she said to the empty room. "I'm having a baby, and there's just something about this one, a powerful feeling that this is a boy. I haven't even shared this with Tom. He wouldn't understand in the same way that you will. His scientific mind will want to work this out, whereas you taught me to also believe in more than what I could prove with a hypothesis. When he's born, Da, I've decided I'm going to call him Jonathan, after you. I just wanted to tell you." In her mind, she could see her father's face aglow with the joy of the statement, humbled by the recognition, and deeply in love with his daughter.

Her inner reflection was broken by her mother's voice in the garden. Judy couldn't hear her words but by her inflection it sounded as if she was coming to the end of her conversation with Tom and she didn't want to share this experience even with them. She opened her eyes and looked around. It was tidy. Tidier than she had ever seen it. He must have cleaned it before he'd left. She dragged her fingers along the leather books and ledgers on the bookshelf, bringing back a childhood memory of doing that. First on the bottom shelf when she had been young then the middle shelf as she was growing up and finally on the higher shelf once she was taller. That simple act connected her to the space in a way that automatically made her feel grounded. On a table to the side of the bookshelf were some pictures he had watercolored. They were not masterpieces by any means but each one displayed his own unique stick-figure style. Against the wall was his cabinet of medals from when he ran for the school, and propped up in the corner was his battered cricket bat. Judy smiled as she remembered hot summer days stretched out on her mother's knitted blankets surrounded by her aunties all drinking tea. Her father in his cricket whites and worn stripy black and white cap. His hands in the air as he shouted "Howzat" in his booming tones—the words any cricketer shouted toward the umpire when they had just bowled someone out. It was because she was making her way around the room so deliberately, she didn't see the most obvious thing in there. So, it surprised her when she got to his desk. On it was a very neatly wrapped package. She walked over to it, wondering what it could be and noticed it had already been opened but then folded back on itself. She peeled back a layer of the brown paper and stepped back, gasping with the shock. Being in this place with everything so familiar, she hadn't been ready for the uncomfortable intrusion of the unfamiliar, the strange, the unwelcome guest on his desk. She approached it again, warier now and uncovered the brown paper once again. Inside, folded into a perfect square was a clean, pressed army uniform. On the sleeve was his name: Sergeant Jonathan Morgan. She crushed the rough khaki-brown fabric between her fingers, unable to picture him in something so formal. But knowing he'd been the last one to wear this, she lifted it up to her nose, closed her eyes and inhaled. Instead of her father's familiar musky scent, the uniform smelled clinical, with a vague scent of antiseptic as if it had been washed at a hospital. Disappointed, she placed it out on the desk. Beneath it were some of his personal items. His pipe and half a packet of his favorite tobacco, his tweed washbag, a stack of letters, his watch, reading glasses and then she caught her breath; nestled at the bottom of the pile as if it had been waiting for her was his leather book. The one he kept all of his newspaper cuttings about her achievements in, and her heart ached. It was only at that moment that his death became real for her. Because she had never seen him without it.

Between these pages was the evidence of his love and devotion to her and she could barely stand to touch it. All at once there was a voice behind her. Her mother spoke in Welsh to her daughter. "You should have it, love; he would want you to have it." The tears streamed down Judy's face, as gently she picked it up and cradled it in her arms.

"Oh Da," she whispered out into the room, "why you?" and once again she felt the sting of the anger that was now her constant friend burning in her chest.

*

They'd stayed in Wales for a few more days, making endless cups of tea and consoling the steady stream of visitors that paid a call at her mother's house. Including each day her mother's three sisters, all so close in age it was impossible to make out who was the elder or younger. They appeared every morning and sat huddled around the kitchen table, all drinking tea and talking in Welsh, punctuating all their sentences in the same way. "I can't believe it," "So terrible," "An absolute tragedy."

By Sunday night, Judy was exhausted. She loved her mother but it was painful being in a house that was drenched with his missing presence, and she wasn't used to so many people coming and going. She missed the quiet of her home in Cambridge.

"If you need me to stay, Ma, I will be happy to be here with you," she informed her mother as they were washing up another batch of endless cups after hosting another group of mourners. Her father's life had touched every corner of their village and everyone wanted to share their memories.

"No, love," was her mother's gentle response. "Your father would never forgive me if I kept you here in Wales when you have important work to do. You have a world to change and a husband of your own. You get yourself back to Cambridge. I'll be fine. I have my sisters and the rest of the village too. We'll all take care of each other. Besides, you have that baby to think of." Judy drew in breath at the mention of her pregnancy. Automatically placing her hand on her stomach, she imagined her little boy in there growing, her little Jonathan.

She tried to labor the point of staying, but her mother was having none of it. Judy wondered if she needed her own private time to grieve, too. And so, bidding her goodbye, she left to go back to Cambridge a few days after the funeral. In her bag she packed his precious leather book without even opening it. She would need more strength than she had now to read his words.

As she made her way to the station, it was suddenly the hardest thing to leave Wales. Cambridge suddenly felt so foreign; all that was familiar was here in the valley with her mother, and family. But she knew the best way to honor her dad and though it took all of her strength to do, she climbed onto the train to leave them and her heart behind.

She had to remind herself: there was still a war on. She still had work to do, and she knew that Tom fared better when she was there. So, with a heavy heart, she left the hills that were so familiar to her and made her way back to Cambridge.

Just as they left the Valleys and the train picked up speed, dark looming clouds rolled forward to meet them, heavy with rain that descended on the train, buffeting the carriage. The ominous weather threatened to consume not only the whole landscape but also her heart, casting a shadow ahead of her that she wasn't sure she would be able to find her way through. She had such dark thoughts about everything. It was as if she was unable to tap into happiness even for the baby, because now everything was overshadowed by a new brimming rage.

TELEGRAM

DEAR HEDY – (STOP) –
WE GOT WORD MY DARLING FATHER HAS BEEN
KILLED IN BATTLE– (STOP) – SERVICE WAS

*YESTERDAY – (STOP) – WE ARE HEARTBROKEN
AND HEDY I AM FURIOUS AND DETERMINED
TO DO ANYTHING TO WIN THIS WAR.
JUDY – (STOP) –*

*MRS. JUDY JENKINS
12:21 PM*

TELEGRAM

DARLING – (STOP) –

*MY HEART IS BREAKING FOR YOU ALL OVER
AGAIN – (STOP) – SO SORRY TO HEAR THIS
SAD NEWS – (STOP) – SO MUCH LOVE TO YOU
AND TOM DURING THIS DIFFICULT TIME AND
YOUR ANGER IS JUSTIFIED PUT IT TO GOOD
USE – (STOP) – PLEASE LET ME KNOW IF THERE
IS ANYTHING I CAN DO – (STOP) –
MUCH LOVE ALWAYS HEDY – (STOP) –*

*HEDY LAMARR
3:31 PM*

Chapter Twenty-Seven

It was several months after she and George had visited the Navy when Hedy, wearing a high feathered headdress and a robe over her costume, pushed open her dressing room door and made her way inside. Tagging along behind her was the actor Jimmy Stewart. His hands were stuffed in his pockets, and his tall, lean frame looked elegant in a gray herringbone suit. As he stepped inside her room, he whistled.

"Well, this is some setup you've got here. I don't think I've ever seen a dressing room quite like this."

Hedy noticed he was peering down at her tables that she kept for inventing, stacked high with her test tubes, different science books, microscopes, and all her other scientific equipment.

Jimmy started walking around the table, inspecting things. "Are you working on some sort of cosmetics? Something has to keep you looking that beautiful," he joked with her. They had become firm friends on their first film, *Come Live with Me*, which had opened to much success, and they often joked about her screen appeal, as he stayed agog at his own. They had also both been cast in *Ziegfeld Girl*, which had released in the spring.

He lifted up a test tube and held it toward the window, observing a white powder inside.

"Don't touch that," said Hedy, in a mockingly dangerous tone.

Jimmy dropped it back down on the table. "Why? Is it going to explode?"

"No, but I don't have any more of it," she said, smiling.

He continued to survey the dressing room as she made her way farther into the room to get them both a drink. He was leaving soon. He'd joined up to fight the war, and she wanted to celebrate with him before he left.

"What about this?" he said, staring down at a picture painted on canvas on the floor, a pile of paint pots stacked up around it. "It's quite good," he said, admiring it from different angles. "Did you paint it?"

"I did," she said with a smile.

"Down here on the floor?"

"It's the most comfortable place to create. I used to give my teachers fits in Vienna. But that's how I like to work. I love to paint and I love to invent. That's what I do in between takes."

"Most women I know just file their nails."

"You'll find, Mr. Stewart, that I am not most women," she said, handing him a glass of champagne.

"I can vouch for that," he said, chuckling.

She held her glass in the air. "To my most favorite pilot-to-be. Please don't get your ass shot off."

Jimmy laughed as they clinked their glasses together. "A toast I could get *behind*," was his tongue-in-cheek response.

She smiled as they made their way outside again to sit under a palm tree next to her dressing room. Hedy had a short break from the set and even though it was a very warm day, in the shade of the tree a slight breeze cooled them as they sat drinking their champagne. She was glad to have some time with him before he left.

"You know, Stewart, you're very lucky," she said, eying him over the top of her glass.

"In what respect?"

"You get to go and fight and do something for your country. I wish I could do something, anything!"

"You made a stand, left Austria when Hitler wanted to annex it."

"It's not the same," she said, shaking her head. "You know, I told you about the invention that George Antheil and I came up with."

"Yeah, how's that going?" he asked, taking a sip of his drink.

"It's been months and we haven't heard anything. George was going to call them today to see if there were any updates. We have a contact over at the Inventors Council who might know something."

They continued their conversation, moving on to reminisce about the first movie they'd been in together, and when Hedy asked him if he would be leaving a girl behind when he left, he deflected her question, answering her with one of the lines from their movie, where his character insinuated he didn't need a wife.

Hedy jumped in with her own line, where she offered him a trade: she'd get a husband and he would get money. Hedy laughed. "I was saying it all wrong in the movie. What I should have said is, 'I'll keep the money, and you can keep the husband. They are nothing but trouble.'"

Jimmy chuckled, holding up his empty glass so she could top it up.

They were both on their third glass when someone came striding toward them. It was George Antheil. Hedy knocked back her drink and stood to greet him.

His face was set and didn't betray what he was feeling. She introduced him to Stewart, and they shook hands.

"So, you're the other half of the inventing partnership," Jimmy said. "It sounds like a mighty fine machine you've got there. And a mighty fine idea."

"I'm glad you think so," said George, thrusting his hand into his pocket. "I might need a glass of whatever you're drinking there."

Hedy's stomach started to tighten.

"They said no, didn't they?"

He began to pace, lighting himself a cigarette. "I just don't get it, Hedy. Everything about this technology is perfect. The council said so. Why wouldn't they take the technology and run with it? They couldn't get their head around the fact that they somehow thought we were going to put player pianos on submarines. I mean, are these people even qualified to run the war effort? The invention needs to be developed. We knew that. We told them that. We gave them all the details of the patent. And still, they told us to get lost. Apparently, a fancy, official version of that is on its way to us in the mail."

Hedy poured him a large glass of champagne as they sat down to commiserate with each other.

"Gee, that sucks," said Jimmy.

"I can't help thinking it's got something to do with the fact that I'm a Hollywood film actress," Hedy said. "And if I was a scientist, would it matter? Maybe so. Mind you, I have a friend who's a scientist, and she doesn't get the recognition she deserves either. It's clearly because we're women. They just seem to be less trusting and have less respect."

"I'm sure it has something to do with it," said Stewart. "I'm so sorry for the pair of you." He lifted his glass. "The Navy will never know what they're missing."

They all toasted one another, but Hedy was heartsick. She knew the power of the invention. She knew what it was capable of. Why were they turning down an opportunity like this? All she could think of was the children who had been killed on that ship. Who was now going to make it safe for people like that?

November 15, 1941

Dear Miss Lamarr,

I know this is slightly unorthodox, and I fear Judy would not be happy if she knew, but I wanted to write a letter to you, to thank you for your kindness and let you know that your letters have been arriving safely. But my wife is going through a very difficult time. She has become withdrawn after the loss of her father and also her health issues and I have great concerns for her, as she is still so unhappy. And now she is having another baby and I know she is constantly worried about it. She's read all of your letters, and I've seen her try to put pen to paper, but she doesn't seem to get past writing, "Dear Hedy." I find her half-written letters scattered around the house and often find her just staring out of the window. I know this is a huge request with your work, not to mention the war, but I think my wife needs you. So, I'm asking if there's any chance that you could come to England to see her. I have a little money saved to help with the expense and I know it would cheer her immensely. It might be the medicine that she needs right now. The doctor would like her to take a holiday but that seems to be impossible at the moment. So, I know a visit from you would be the next best thing.

If you do find yourself able to come, please could I ask that you don't mention this letter to Judy? I think she'd be furious to know I've written to you, but I had to reach out in case there was a chance.

Yours sincerely,
Thomas Jenkins

Chapter Twenty-Eight

It was as she was serving Tom his breakfast a couple of weeks later that Judy heard the letterbox rattle and a stack of letters fall onto the mat. She placed his egg and toast in front of him and went to retrieve the post. Shuffling through them, she stopped at one and just stared at it.

"Is there any butter, Judy?" Tom called out to her down the hall, but she hardly heard him as she was reading the back of the envelope and trying to decide what to do.

"Sorry?"

"Do we have any butter?" he repeated.

"No. Sorry, Tom, not today. The shortages seem to be getting worse."

"Oh," he said, sounding disappointed.

"My mother's damson jam is in the cupboard if you want it."

"Oh," he responded, sounding not very enthusiastic.

Slowly Judy came back into the kitchen and sat down at the table, opposite him.

"Anything more exciting than just the bills?"

Judy didn't respond right away because she was deep in thought. She only finally answered him once he asked her again.

"We have a letter from London," she finally said, distracted.

"London," he repeated with a quizzical look. "We don't know anyone in London, do we?"

"It's from Hedy."

"Oh," said Tom, and his cheeks flushed as he put down his knife and stared at the back of the envelope with as much intensity as she was paying it.

It wasn't that she didn't want to hear from her best friend; she had been meaning to write back to her for weeks now. But she had been caught in this fog of sadness and anger, this waiting and dreading; no matter how much she had wanted to share her feelings with her she had found it hard to put them into words. Judy slit open the flap of the envelope and pulled out the sheet of paper. She read it through quickly, and Tom sat intently in front of her, waiting for her to tell him what was in it. She stopped halfway down and placed it on the table. Getting up, she went to the kettle. She would need a cup of tea to make this decision.

Tom looked at her eagerly.

"She's back in England for a visit and wants to come to Cambridge."

"When?" asked Tom.

"She wonders if she could come to visit us this weekend."

Tom sat back on his chair and let out a breath, his face furrowed with concern. "That's good news, isn't it?"

Judy turned away, filling the teapot with the hot water.

"Yes, I think so," she murmured but knew her tone was unconvincing; she was in such a strange place in her life right now, with the loss of her dad and the babies.

"She said she would love to see me and also maybe talk more about her latest invention and wondered if it was possible to see the lab."

Tom shook his head. "No, they're never going to agree to that at the Cavendish. You know, security has really been tightening, and Finnegan, can you imagine what he would say about another woman coming to look around his laboratory?"

Judy started to warm to this new development and put the letter down on the table.

"Well, if she is coming, we should think about what to have for Sunday lunch. We should do something nice for her."

"Do we have to give her Sunday lunch?"

"Of course we do, Tom. Maybe we should eat out on Saturday. She doesn't say where she's staying. I suppose she could stay here."

Tom's eyes grew large. They hadn't been long in their little two-bedroom terrace, and there was still plenty of work to do on it. An older lady had owned it before them, and they were slowly updating everything in the house, though it was taking them a long time with their workload.

"In the little box room?" he enquired, now using that name instead of the nursery.

"I could make it pleasant. We have the new sheets that Ma gave me for Christmas, and I haven't put those on my bed yet. And I think I've got some curtains in the attic that might work."

"I'm sure she would find this way too humble for her. She'll probably want to stay in a swanky place."

"We'll prepare it just in case," said Judy, jumping to her feet, feeling more optimistic and starting to hum as she made her breakfast.

"I must say, that's a spot of encouraging news, isn't it? I think it is just what you need right now," said Tom, sounding enthusiastic. Then, sampling his toast with damson jam on it, he pulled a face. "These damsons could've done with staying on the tree just a bit longer, and without enough sugar because of all this rationing, they're very tart."

Judy laughed. "My mother's always way too eager to pick. She hates waiting. I will write a note straight back to Hedy telling her that we'll meet her from the train. We can pick her up."

Tom nodded. "I suppose that means I should do some cleaning," he said, looking around. Though Judy was very tidy and a good housekeeper, it was unsaid between them but Tom wouldn't let her clean anything because of the baby, and there were piles of things everywhere.

"Yes, it does, Tom." Though Tom didn't know what was waiting for him. Over the next three days, Judy had him doing all sorts of things: painting corners, rolling up mats, sweeping floors. He didn't mind, confessing he couldn't wait for the weekend to arrive.

*

They drove to the station midday on Saturday. Tom wore his church suit, and Judy had had her hair done at the hairdresser's that morning. It was a little shorter than she usually liked it, but it seemed to remove all the tight curls, leaving just a wave which gave her a pixie-ish look, Tom noted. They waited on the platform for the train to arrive as Tom paced up and down.

As people filed off the London train, it wasn't hard to see Hedy; not only was she in her usual American movie star clothes, but around her every head was turned. Men had stopped, standing with their mouths open as she walked down the platform.

On spotting her friends, Hedy held her arms out. "Judy, Tom," she cried out, greeting them with such enthusiasm.

Tom cleared his throat, and Judy noticed that his voice was a little high-pitched when he spoke. He coughed and said, "Mrs. Markey, it's so good to see you again." He quickly thrust out his hand as Hedy appeared to want to throw her arms around him to hug him. She shook his hand gracefully and then took hold of Judy and hugged her tightly.

"Hedy, please, Tom, call me Hedy and I certainly don't go by Markey any more. I'm so excited to be here in Cambridge and Judy, well—you are positively blooming."

Judy looked shocked as she hadn't told her friend about her third pregnancy.

"How did you know?" she asked. "Did a little bird tell you?"

Tom coughed awkwardly beside her.

With a swift sideward glance toward Tom, Hedy beamed. "I guessed; I follow the stars, you know, and I have always been a little psychic."

Judy shook her head with disbelief but didn't give it any more attention as she was so caught up in being with her friend again. "We're looking forward to showing you around," she said, diverting the subject from her pregnancy. It was still so hard to talk about it especially as she was hovering close to that dreaded three-month mark.

"Wonderful," enthused Hedy.

Hedy linked Judy's arm, and they started to walk off toward the station entrance.

She was telling Judy all about the trip from London and how she'd almost ended up on the wrong train. But all Judy could think about was the arm linked in hers. Hedy didn't seem even to notice that Judy was so dull; she was just so warm toward her all the time.

"I totally insist that I treat you both to dinner tonight."

Tom started to complain. "Oh no, we couldn't allow that…"

"I insist," said Hedy. "Otherwise I'll refuse to eat at all. Now, there must be some fabulous English pub or restaurant in Cambridge that you like to go to."

Judy and Tom exchanged a glance. They really didn't go out that much to eat. Judy liked to cook, and they were often very busy with their work.

"Well, I suppose there's The Eagle," said Tom, mentioning a pub in town.

Judy agreed, knowing the place he was talking about. A lot of the lab technicians talked about how nice it was to have their Sunday dinner there.

"Wonderful. Though first, before we paint the town red, if it's okay with you, I'd love to freshen up."

"Then, you must come to our house," responded Judy.

As they made their way from the station to the car, Judy found it very disconcerting that everywhere they walked, people stopped and stared at her friend. She'd always thought it would be amazing to be this beautiful. Now she thought it was just very invasive. Some people even recognized Hedy and asked her for her autograph. Hedy seemed to take it all in her stride; still, Judy felt sorry for her. When did she ever have time just to be a person?

Arriving at their humble terraced house, Tom started to make excuses for it and how they were still working on it.

"It's delightful," cooed Hedy as she walked inside. "You can't change a thing."

"Including the ancient wiring and the old rug here that's almost worn down to the floorboards?" retorted Tom.

"Especially the worn-down rug," Hedy said with a wink.

Judy showed her where the bathroom was, and she went upstairs to freshen up as Tom and Judy had a hurried conversation about asking her to stay with them. Tom was still concerned it wasn't good enough for the likes of a Hollywood film star, but now she was here, Judy just wanted to be close to her friend.

As Hedy came down, Judy asked her before Tom had a chance to avoid the subject, "Do you know where you'll be staying yet?"

"I haven't arranged anywhere. I just imagined there would be some sort of little hotel I could book here."

Judy gave Tom a look, and he cleared his throat. "We would be very honored if you would feel you could stay here with us."

Hedy stared at him, her eyes wide. "You would let me stay here?"

"Of course, though the room is very small and very humble."

"Why, that's just the loveliest invitation. I'd love to be here with you. Between you and me, it can be testing to be out in the world, particularly somewhere like a hotel. Porters so often make up stories. And I always feel like I'm on show and I have to be nice to everybody."

"Then I insist," said Tom, "and you won't have to be nice to us at all." Not meaning to be funny, he suddenly realized how that sounded and they all laughed.

Hedy couldn't hold back. She flung her arms around Tom's neck and hugged him. Judy thought he was going to faint on the spot and couldn't help but stifle a giggle. When Hedy stepped back from him, his face was flushed beetroot red, and he seemed to be bumbling even more than ever with his words.

"I'll show you the room," said Judy, taking her friend's arm and giving her husband a chance to recover from his embarrassment. She took her upstairs, and felt the tug she always did in there because of her loss. Pushing past her feelings, she walked into the tiny bedroom and opened a window for fresh air. Hedy sat down on the bed. All the baby things had been tucked away in a cupboard now and neither she nor Tom had had the heart to take them back out yet.

"It's so darling here. It reminds me of my grandmother's house in Austria. Your home has such a peaceful feeling about it."

Before dinner they took Hedy out and about in Cambridge, to do some shopping and to visit all the lovely places they knew, and she had a marvelous time. She didn't have to leave until Monday morning, so Judy was glad she had decided to save her from having everybody staring at her again by cooking Sunday dinner for them at home.

"I just have to go to the butcher's and see if I can get some meat for tomorrow."

There was a long line in the butcher's, and when she eventually reached the counter, while Tom and Hedy waited outside, she ended up having quite a tussle with the red-faced man behind the counter.

"We have to save it for the right kind of people: the elderly and children. I have to be very sparing, Mrs. Jenkins." He was about to fire off another rebuke when he noticed Hedy walking in the door, and his mouth dropped open as he gaped at her.

Hedy slipped to Judy's side, purring in her movie-style way, "Everything all right, Judy?"

"Miss Lamarr," he spluttered. "My wife is a big fan of your pictures."

"Nice to meet you," said Hedy, slipping into her public persona, dipping her chin and fixing him with her sparkling gaze through veiled lashes. She offered her hand across the counter. Wiping the blood off his own on his apron, he shook her hand so meekly, he hardly touched her.

"I can't believe you're in my shop!"

"I'm just a guest of Judy and Tom's." She smiled. "We are in here to buy meat, I believe, for dinner."

"The meat is for you?" said the butcher incredulously. "Let me see what I can get."

Next thing he'd disappeared out to the back of the shop, and suddenly a tiny mouse-like woman appeared and scurried to the counter.

"Miss Hedy Lamarr," she said with great excitement, "we have seen all your films. I didn't believe it. I thought my husband was pulling my leg. As I live and breathe, a real film star in our shop. Would you mind if you signed something for me?"

"Of course not," Hedy drew out evocatively, "I'd be delighted. I am looking forward to sampling your meat."

The scrawny woman ripped off a piece of butcher's paper, and Hedy wrote her name before the butcher came back and gave her a beautiful piece of beef for dinner. Judy shook her head in disbelief as he handed over the wrapped meat.

"I hope you enjoy it, Miss Lamarr," added the butcher.

"I'm sure I will," replied Hedy, curling her crimson lips into a smile and putting her sunglasses back on. They walked outside, and Judy started to chuckle.

"I can't believe you managed to get that out of him. He wasn't going to give me anything."

"Sometimes the attention helps," she said with a smile. "I could see you were having a problem."

*

They went out for dinner that night. As usual, groups of people stared at Hedy and asked for her autograph, but when they had time alone, they found themselves slipping into easy conversation because Hedy had an outstanding scientific mind. She kept up very readily with their conversations and went into great detail about her invention with George Antheil and how the U.S. Navy had turned them down.

"Honestly, they didn't even really look at it; I think it's because I'm a woman and work in the movies. It's as if in order to have a brain you have to have an array of qualifications and a pair of trousers."

Judy nodded. "I'm afraid you are preaching to the converted here and I supposedly *have* the qualifications. It so frustrating, isn't it. I have to have Tom present all my ideas."

"And I hate that she doesn't get the recognition," continued Tom.

Hedy looked pensive. "Do you think your lab here would be interested in developing the idea? I just know it could work and I'd hate for it just to sit on a shelf somewhere because of prejudice."

Tom caught Judy's eye as they both felt her pain.

"We could try," said Judy decisively.

Tom added quickly, "But please don't get your hopes up. What you saw in that U.S. Navy room is not the exception. Our manager is just that way too; he doesn't ever include her name on any of the scientific papers we have submitted. It's like he wants her to be invisible."

Judy grabbed her friend's hand. "I know this is optimistic, but the way I get through all the rejection is by believing that one day, if it's meant to be, my work will be recognized. Maybe not even in my lifetime. But one day someone might be reading about the things that you and I have created and then people will know and that's all that matters."

Hedy smiled reluctantly. "I hope to God I don't go down in history as just a skirt. I hope one day people will know I had a brain and was capable of so much more, if only I'd been given the chance."

Later, she challenged Tom to a game of chess, her favorite board game, and helped Judy make their cocoa. When they turned in for the night, Tom and Judy sat in their beds, whispering to one another.

"It's hard to believe she's a movie star. I mean, I know she's beautiful and everything, but she's so down to earth," remarked Tom.

Judy looked up from her book. "I think it's because she was raised in Europe. As much as she lives in Hollywood now, she's from Austria, and she told me she is Jewish. I think that would be a hard thing to admit in this climate. Fame doesn't change who you are inside."

Tom nodded thoughtfully.

Hedy slept for twelve hours that night, and the next morning when she got up for breakfast, she couldn't believe how long she'd been in bed.

"I sleep so well here," she said, running her hand through her curls. She wasn't wearing makeup that morning and had a freshness to her face and a natural beauty that reminded Judy of when she'd first met her friend.

After she'd had breakfast, Tom went outside to work in the garden, and Hedy stayed in the kitchen, helping with the dishes. When she'd finished, she lit a cigarette and looked toward the window.

"You're so fortunate, Judy, to have a man like Tom," she commented wistfully.

As she continued to dry a cup, Judy joined Hedy's side and looked out the window too. There was Tom, slightly overweight and awkward in his gardening trousers, an old shirt, hat, and the brown V-neck sweater she'd knitted him for Christmas last year. His face was bright red from trying to pull up a blackberry root. Judy thought about how strange that was. Here was a woman who could have anyone in the world, who spent her days kissing Clark Gable, and she envied Judy her life. It told her a lot about what was important and she loved her husband even more.

"He is a good man," agreed Judy, "but I won't lie to you, it's been hard, Hedy, with the loss of the babies. He has been very withdrawn and I think he blames me." Judy's voice cracked.

Hedy slipped her arm around her friend's shoulder.

"Nonsense. It's hard for men because they are conditioned to be the strong one. It's not the painful times that we go through, though, it's who is with us on the other side of them that matters; and I just know that Tom will always be there for you, Judy. I have never seen a man more in love."

"I wish I had the same confidence. I wonder if we can ever find what we once had on the other side of all this pain."

Judy paused for a moment, wondering if she could trust her friend with her innermost anguish. Then she remembered all Hedy had been through in her own personal life, beyond the glamor of her film-star existence.

"Hedy, have you ever…" she started falteringly and then tried to find the right words.

Her friend turned to her, her face registering concern as she tried to read Judy's expression.

Judy began again, "Have you ever felt such anger that you actually wanted to kill someone?"

Hedy chuckled, taking a deep drag of her cigarette as a wistful expression crossed her face. "Both of my ex-husbands. If I thought I could have got away with it I might have poisoned Fritz, he made me so mad the way he treated me, and when Gene broke my heart I had a few murderous thoughts along the way. Why? You're not thinking of doing Tom in, are you?"

Judy smiled. "No. It's just that since the death of my dad, so soon after losing the babies, I have really been battling some very dark thoughts, and I don't know what to do with them."

Hedy took her friend's hand and sat her down at the table. "Listen to me, Judy: we all have those thoughts, and it's only natural with all you've been through. The key is to find a way to get past them. You have this lovely new baby on the way. And just because you have had difficulty in earlier pregnancies doesn't mean this one isn't going to be born. You have to choose to think about better things, otherwise the bitterness and anger will consume you. I have seen it, especially in Hollywood, which can be a desperate place at times."

Judy nodded, understanding the logic of her friend's advice but at a loss about how to implement it. "The doctor wants me to go on a holiday to help me through this time. But that's impossible right now. Besides, there is nowhere for me to go."

Just then Tom came in from the garden and removed his boots.

"I'm ready for a cup of tea," he announced and Judy jumped up to put the kettle on. It was as they settled back down together that Hedy shared the secret she had been harboring.

"I haven't just come to England for a holiday. I also have an invitation. I know how hard the last year has been on you both, and I can't help but notice you have hardly mentioned this pregnancy since I arrived."

As if on cue, both Tom and Judy looked down at the floor and the sadness Judy had become familiar with descended on the room.

Hedy continued, "I have to assume it is because you are both so worried because of what happened in the past. So, I have an idea. Judy, I want you to take a month off and come back to California with me. It so lovely and warm and you can read on the beach and sleep till noon."

Judy flushed. "I couldn't possibly leave here, leave Tom, could I?"

"Of course you could go! Though we should check with the doctor first, Judy, just to make sure it is safe," her husband advised.

"It is probably safer than being in a country at war," responded Judy enthusiastically.

"You could sail over with me on the *Britannic*, it's wonderful," added Hedy. "Away from all this work and this war, then a lovely trip across the country on a train and then a couple of weeks with me at my farm. I think it is just what the doctor ordered."

"I would love to go, but could we afford anything so extravagant?"

"I have a little money saved," Tom intervened as Judy stared at him in bewilderment.

"I insist on helping with expenses," responded Hedy. "You can be my chaperone. It would help fend off all my adoring fans if I have company. So you see, you would be helping me out too. I have a gap coming up in my shooting schedule and we could spend time together in California. I have some film business I need to take care of in London next week, but then after that you can join me so we can start our trip."

Judy was completely swept up by the idea, although Tom was a little more concerned by all the traveling and being apart from her during her pregnancy. But before he had a chance to voice his fears, Hedy and Judy were already planning Judy's month-long holiday in the States. And though she felt a little nervous anticipation, Judy couldn't help but be excited as she stared out at the freezing rain falling outside her window.

Early on Monday morning, they took Hedy to the station.

"I cannot tell you how important this weekend was to me, and how much I needed it. Promise me we will always be the best of friends," implored Hedy with tears in her eyes.

She kissed them both on the cheek before she got on her train and Tom hardly even flinched. He was getting used to her demonstrative behavior.

As the train left the platform, Judy looked over at Tom, who had a bright red lipstick mark on his cheek. She smiled as they walked back to the car. She decided she wasn't going to tell him until they got home. She liked the way it looked.

Chapter Twenty-Nine

After Hedy left, Tom and Judy spoke extensively about how they would present Hedy's findings to Finnegan. "Her scientific knowledge is spot-on," reiterated Tom, studying the diagrams once again.

"It's an ingenious idea, and I can't see why it wouldn't work. But if we tell him who invented it, you know what will happen."

Tom nodded his head. "We have to present it in such a way that we get the least resistance possible."

"In other words, we do not have me present it," said Judy, reading his mind.

Tom looked up at her. "I wish I didn't have to say that, but I think that is best, Judy. Anything that comes out of your mouth will be automatically scrutinized just because of who you are. I wish you could present. She's your friend and anyway I feel as if you have more knowledge on this subject, but if we are to have a shot, if we're to have a chance of getting this into the right hands, then I think it has to be me."

Judy nodded. They decided that they would casually make Hedy's presentation at their next meeting with Finnegan, as once a week they met in his office to go through anything they were working on and receive any information they needed from the government. They were usually short meetings, Finnegan not being a man of many words. Tom had been presenting for them for a while now. However, he would always defer to Judy for anything that was her specific scientific strength in radio waves, giving her the respect that he always allowed her.

So, the next day, they made their way into the lab with Hedy's proposal, both of them watching the clock as it ticked from nine till ten, feeling like every minute was an hour. At ten to ten, they nodded at one another, collected up their file, and strode down to Finnegan's office. When they arrived at the door, his secretary alerted them to the fact that a major from the U.S. Air Force was here and was already in Finnegan's office. "He asked me to let you know to go straight in. There's information that may be of value to you too that the major has to share."

Judy gave Tom a sideward glance and swallowed down her apprehension as Tom knocked on the door.

In the office, Finnegan was already in a heated debate with the major about timings and procedures. They were all working under so much pressure, and time was of the essence during a war. "We're doing the best we can," said Finnegan in a stern tone, standing up and marching to his window.

Tom and Judy crept inside, feeling awkward with the tension in the room.

Finnegan gave Tom a sideward glance, frustration evident on his face.

"This is Mr. Jenkins, one of our lead scientists who worked on the project we're talking about. Mr. Jenkins, this is Major Thompson from the U.S. Air Force. He wants to see some early examples of the proximity fuse before they took on the project. The Americans have had some issues, and they were hoping you could help them out."

The major leaned forward and shook Tom's hand. Judy became wallpaper once again as the men all got into a lively debate about what was needed.

Finnegan swiveled on his heels. "Mr. Jenkins, would you be kind enough to take the major over to the lab and show him some of the findings you were telling me about last week?" Tom glanced at Judy as Finnegan added, "Mrs. Jenkins can update me on what's going on this week for once, can't you, Mrs. Jenkins?" He gave her a placating smile.

She pulled herself to her full height. She had wanted to present their weekly findings to Finnegan for a long time. Though without Tom, would it be right to present Hedy's invention alone? She decided this wasn't a good time.

The major seemed happy with that suggestion as Tom followed him out the door, giving one last reluctant look toward Judy as he went.

Finnegan strode to his desk and, with a considerable huff, blew out air and sat down, then pushed papers around it with annoyance. Without looking up, he bade Judy with a grunt and an outstretched hand to update him on their work from the last week. She was so flustered by the turn of events that, as she opened her work file, the proposed invention fell out upside down onto his desk in front of him. Before she could grab it, he was staring at it with a quizzical expression.

Snatching it up from his desk, he turned it around and scrutinized it.

"What's this?" he demanded, an accusatory look on his face.

She cleared her throat. "It's something that Tom and I wanted to discuss with you. An invention that we think could be very helpful to the Allies."

Finnegan spent time looking over it, reading the information. "Where did you get this from? I don't remember authorizing any invention of this type."

"A friend of ours." She corrected herself. "Another inventor."

"Here at the lab?"

"No, she's not from here."

"*She's* not from here?" he said, emphasizing the word *she*.

Judy wanted to kick herself. She'd intended not to mention the fact that Hedy was a woman yet. She'd hoped to win him over with the invention before she quietly explained where it had come from.

He sat back on his seat and stared at her. "Some friend of yours, is it, Mrs. Jenkins? From a knitting circle or a reading club? Think they can change the war by inventing something that'll win it?"

Judy bit her tongue. She was not going to respond to his patronizing attitude. He was already so angry with what had happened earlier that she knew he was being even more bombastic than usual. The invention was too important; she had to get it across. Taking a deep breath, she ignored his comment and quietly elaborated on Hedy's invention. She went on to talk about the patent and the fact that the Inventors Council in America had been enthusiastic about it.

"Well, if the Yanks are so interested, why are we even looking at it?"

How was she going to get around the fact that it had been turned down by the U.S. Navy?

"They have the money," continued Finnegan, "and the workforce. We come up with all the good ideas, and they take them off us. That's how it has been working so far. How does that work the other way around?"

"The U.S. Navy was interested," said Judy, hoping this wasn't too much of a stretch of the truth. "They were concerned about time for further development." She tried to tell him how the signal-hopping would work without talking about the piano keys, knowing that would be an instant shutdown. She could tell she wasn't winning him over.

"I'm sorry, Mrs. Jenkins, our hands are full with everything we have to do with the people we have in this country, without some crackpot American woman coming up with some idea that she wants us to pursue. We only have so much money from the government to get these things done. We don't have time to have a friend of yours having some crazy scheme developed. We're losing this war right now; we need you to be concentrating on things that matter, the things that this lab has been commissioned to do. Besides, what are her credentials? Where does she work?"

Judy wasn't sure how to answer this question without a bald-faced lie, so she thought maybe something else would appeal to him.

"She works in entertainment, and is very successful…" she said, adding quickly, "she has her own money to develop."

"Entertainment? What kind of entertainment?" he retorted with disgust.

This didn't seem to be helping. She tried her last-ditch attempt. "She is very successful in the film industry."

A muscle in his cheek twitched as he narrowed his eyes. "Film industry? I've never heard of her. Who is this Hedwig Kiesler-Markey?"

He still seemed set on his path but she also saw a glimmer of interest in his eyes. Maybe Hedy's star power would have some influence.

"She goes by the name Hedy Lamarr."

It was then that she lost him. He blew out air and pushed the file as far away as possible. "Hedy Lamarr! The film star!? Please, Mrs. Jenkins, spare me this ridiculousness. Stop wasting my time."

But something clicked in Judy and instead of cowering as she normally would have done, the anger she felt about the fact he would dismiss this just because of Hedy's background emboldened her. As much as she felt intimidated by his tone and his harsh way, she knew she had to stand up for herself and her friend.

"I don't think you should dismiss these things without looking at them. I think her invention is very feasible. I think you should at least present it." She knew this was really pushing his buttons, but he was already angry and this was too important to just let it go without a fight.

Finnegan's face reddened as he picked up the file and threw it across the desk toward her. "I don't have time for this, Mrs. Jenkins. I suggest you get back to work. It's what the government has paid for you to do. I can't have every crackpot scheme looked into. It costs time and money, and we don't have either of those at the moment. Show me your work presentation for this week, and then you can be on your way. I don't want to hear about this again. Do you understand me!?"

Judy felt her heart sink. She'd known it was going to be a long shot at any rate, and with her presenting, she knew it was the final nail in the coffin before she'd even started. She so wished Tom could've been by her side. She swallowed down her disappointment, picked up Hedy's proposal, put it back into the file, and mechanically started to talk through their week's work.

Finnegan sat staring at a spot above her head, not meeting her gaze as she filled him in with everything that they had done that week. Finishing her presentation, she placed the proposal for their week of work on his desk and bade him goodbye. She was on her way to the door when he called out to her. "Can I speak frankly to you?"

She turned around.

"I know that you think I am hard. But I treat you like I would a man because I think that's how it should be. Just because you're a woman, you won't get preferential treatment from me. And I will tell you why: this is not an easy job that I do. You have no idea the pressure that I'm under, and I need people that are up to the task. I don't need some soft-hearted woman breaking down and crying every five minutes if something goes wrong. This is why I treat you harshly, to toughen you up."

Judy strode toward him, and she didn't know what possessed her; she suddenly saw Hedy in her mind and the way she had seen her stand up for herself over injustice. She heard her father's words and thought of the babies that would never have life. And in the light of all of that, the words were out of her mouth before she could stop them. "Toughen me up? Without even knowing me, tender-hearted or otherwise, you have treated me this way from the very first day you met me, just because I *am* a woman. And I'll tell you something, Dr. Finnegan. I understand the pressure you're under. We are under the same pressure ourselves! But prejudice, in the form that I've seen from you day after day, can do nothing but halt scientific progression. I don't need you to treat me like a man or toughen me up. All I ask is you treat me with the respect that this lab coat affords me.

"Also," she continued, "I wanted to let you know I shall be requesting a month off to travel with Miss Lamarr."

Finnegan's jaw clenched and a nerve in his face twitched, apparently responding to her audacity. She knew he probably wanted to rebuke her for it, and tell her she couldn't go. But then he would have to admit he actually needed her here and that declaration was just beneath him.

She turned toward the door, the anger burning in her chest, knowing that she'd probably gone too far, but she couldn't take it any more. How many women had been held back and minimized because of this Victorian attitude that was so prevalent in the male-dominated workforce? Maybe he would sack her, but she didn't care. She didn't care about anything any more. She waited for his scathing reply, but it didn't come, and as she turned to close the door behind her, instead of anger she saw what she thought was admiration on Finnegan's face. But he quickly recovered enough to return a parting sarcastic remark.

"Tell Miss Lamarr my wife is a big fan, and once she stops playing war, an autograph would be nice."

Judy closed the door with a little surprise. His comment had been derogatory, but somehow, he seemed to have lost some of his steam.

Chapter Thirty

Hedy created all the plans for their trip and Judy spoke to her doctor, who put Tom's fears to rest and thought it was a wonderful idea. Judy would meet her in London and they would be heading off on the MV *Britannic* together. At work, Finnegan hadn't mentioned anything about her leaving. Since she had stood up to him about Hedy's invention, he had been very wary around her, as if he wasn't quite sure how to treat her any more.

Judy packed her suitcase and, along with her woolies, she slipped in summer clothing that she would need in the balmy temperatures of Los Angeles, and everything about that felt strange, surreal somehow. Closing the suitcase that creaked with its newness, having only been used twice before—once on her honeymoon and once to meet Hedy in London—she buckled the straps and looked out of the window. It had been raining for three days straight, and the damp and cold that permeated the very walls reflected the sadness of a country still at war. In many ways, she couldn't wait for a break. She also couldn't wait to get away from the pain that echoed around their home. The only thing that gave her pause for thought was that she desperately didn't want to leave Tom, and she didn't want to leave him when they were in such a strange place in their marriage.

When it was time to go, Tom insisted on carrying her suitcase downstairs for her, and she stood at the bottom of the stairs looking up at him.

"Do you think I'm doing the right thing?" she questioned.

"Of course I am a little concerned, but the doctor was very encouraging, so I do think this will be good for you, Judy," he said as he came and put an arm around her. "These last months have been very difficult for both of us. And I can't wait for you to get away and relax for a while. When you come back, hopefully we'll be able to look forward to better days."

He didn't say "the birth" or anything like that, but she knew that was what he meant.

He drove her to the train station that day and they stood waiting for the train together on the platform.

All around them, soldiers stood in uniform. Wives and mothers were sobbing, saying goodbye to their loved ones, and Judy couldn't help feeling guilty. Everybody else was having to deal with the war, and she was going to go off on holiday.

Then she thought of the little life growing inside her. She had to do everything to protect it this time around, and if a holiday was what she needed, that was what she was going to do. She had to admit she was looking forward to sleeping on the ship, walking on the beach, and enjoying more halcyon days.

When the train arrived, she turned to her husband and put her arms around him. They were normally too shy to show that kind of affection in public, but Tom didn't pull away as she buried her face into his tweed gray overcoat and gray woolen scarf she had knitted him and inhaled the familiar scent of Brylcreem. As she pulled away, she noticed the tears in his eyes as he let go of her.

Turning his head quickly, he coughed away his emotion, picked up her bag, and opened the door of the train for her. He found her a seat and made sure she was thoroughly settled on the train, sitting in her compartment, before he left.

Once the final whistle sounded, he stepped down onto the platform and stood in front of the window staring up at her, and all at once he looked so sad and alone. She wished more than anything that they didn't need to go through this. She would have done anything to change this sadness between them, that clung to them both like a shroud.

The train whistle sounded and Tom stood back as clouds of acrid smoke billowed into the air, marring her view of him, and as he disappeared in the murky bleakness, she almost wanted to jump off the train and into his arms. It hadn't occurred to her until now, but they hadn't been apart in years. They had traveled side by side since the first day she had met him, first as lab partners, then friends, and finally husband and wife. How would she cope without him for so long? It would be so strange to not have him by her side, encouraging her day by day. But as the smoke cleared and the cylinders started their slow shunt, she saw a deeply thoughtful expression cross his face and something struck her. Maybe this was what he needed to find himself again, too. Time to be alone, even cry if he needed to without the pressure of always being the strong one around her. Maybe a month apart would help him move through his own grief too, and she had to give that a chance to happen.

Pushing down her panic, she waved vigorously, and he returned it with a wave of his own. As the train started, he walked beside her carriage all the way down the platform, his eyes not leaving her own as he nodded his reassurance. As it started to pick up speed, Judy raced to the window and pulled it down, wanting to see her husband to the very last moment. When she looked back, she realized that he was the one solitary person on the platform watching it go, and even though she couldn't see his face from this distance, she knew his eyes were full of love—the love that she had seen in them for as long as she could remember—and suddenly she felt so fortunate. Even with all they had been through, they had always had each other and their love. She had never imagined that in her life she could have found someone who looked at her the way Tom did.

Chapter Thirty-One

When Judy arrived in New York City on the *Britannic*, she was overwhelmed with how huge America felt. It was a completely different world. Her small life in Cambridge, her familiar day-to-day with Tom, paled into insignificance with this country's grandeur.

Hedy had been right. This trip away had been perfect for her already, and she had enjoyed the sea voyage immensely. Even though there was tension on the boat as they traveled, especially as the Royal Navy's gunboats accompanied the ship for their protection. Because still, there was the reality that they were at war, and nothing was really safe. However, now she was in the U.S., she felt all the tension of her work at home melting away. Her day-to-day tussles with Finnegan, the fear of being bombed, and, once they finally got to L.A., the drizzle and cold of a November in England felt a world behind her.

She loved the trip down on the train through the States as well. Everything felt so vast and expansive. It was as though the sky itself was bigger. And in L.A., she saw palm trees for the first time. It felt so strange for her to shed off her winter woolens and put on a blouse when it was November.

"It's very pleasant this time of year," Hedy told her. "It almost feels like Vienna to me here right now. I'm not that keen on the summers here. It gets a bit too hot for me. My blood is European, you see." She laughed.

Her first days at Hedy's were incredible. She stayed with her at Hedgerow Farm, the home Hedy had bought in the Hollywood Hills, and even with all the glamor around her of Los Angeles, Judy loved Hedy's easygoing and comfortable home.

Hedy was on set for the last retakes of her new film, *Tortilla Flat*, which was due to wrap that week. And then she'd promised to spend a whole week with Judy. Judy loved waking up late, eating the breakfast that Hedy's housekeeper put out for them, wandering around the beautiful garden that Hedy managed herself, and writing endless letters to Tom. She understood now why the doctor had recommended her taking a holiday. And L.A., with the palm trees and the sunshine, was the perfect place for her to be. She had been so in awe of everything, she had practically missed the dreaded three-month mark of her pregnancy on the *Britannic*, and now she was already a couple weeks past that and all at once she started to have hope. Just a glimmer, but it was enough to drive away some of the darkness in her heart. The doctor had told her every week the baby would grow stronger and have a better chance of making it to term.

*

Judy had been at Hedy's for a little over a week when she had an unexpected visitor. She was just thinking of taking a swim in Hedy's pool when there was a knock at the door, and the housekeeper brought a very tall man with dark hair into the living room.

"Is she here?" he asked, looking directly at Judy. "Hedy, is she here?"

"She's on set," responded Judy, looking at her watch. "She should be here in the next hour. Can I help you at all?"

He thrust forward his hand.

"Howard Hughes."

"Howard Hughes, the inventor?" asked Judy, her eyes widening.

He smiled. "To some, yes. You must be Hedy's friend, the scientist from England. She told me about you."

"What gave me away?" asked Judy, feeling her cheeks redden.

"Well, the accent helped. And not many women get excited about inventors. I need to get hold of Hedy as soon as I can. Do you mind if I wait here for her until she gets back?"

Judy shook her head, putting off the idea of swimming, and felt that usual shyness she felt with strangers. What would she talk about with this man until Hedy arrived home?

But as it turned out, they had a lot to talk about. She shared a little of what she'd been doing in England. Nothing that was top secret, but a vague idea. And Hughes seemed to have some knowledge of what she'd been involved in.

"I know about the proximity fuse," he said. "I have friends who are working on that now. Ingenious. I'm trying to get some military contracts myself. It's partly why I want to see Hedy. I have an idea that I think she'll be excited about."

Just as he finished his second drink, brought to him by the housekeeper, Hedy breezed out onto the patio where they'd both been sitting.

"Howard, darling," she said. "I didn't expect you here today." She came over and air-kissed him on both cheeks while putting an order into her housekeeper for her own drink. "I see you've met Judy."

"Yes," he said, standing to his full height. "But, Hedy, I don't have a lot of time. I have an invitation for you."

"If it's a party, I can't make it right now. I have company, as you see. How's Katharine? Now she has decided to come back to film, is she back from her new set?" Hedy smiled.

"Not yet. Another two weeks. They're giving her so much trouble over this film. You know how that goes."

Hedy sighed as she took the glass from her housekeeper and sipped her own cocktail.

"Hedy, I have something you'll be interested in."

Hedy's face lit up with anticipation.

"I'm going to Hawaii this weekend to see about some military contracts. And a friend of mine is taking out the new flying boat that's been ordered by Honolulu. He needs a co-pilot and asked me if I wanted to come. I said yes. The plane will be empty, and he said if I wanted to bring any friends, I was welcome to do that. That's when I thought about you."

Hedy jumped to her feet. "I've wanted to go on the flying boat for months. You know that, Howard!"

"Didn't I tell you I'd try and fix it for you?" he encouraged. "But it's this weekend or nothing. It's a special contract just for this new plane."

Suddenly a cloud crossed Hedy's face. "But what about Judy? Would you like to come?"

Judy swallowed down her apprehension. "On a real airplane? I've never been on such a thing. Of course I would."

"This will be fabulous. Oh, and you'll love Hawaii. I've been before. Howard, can I bring Judy?"

"Bring whoever you like," he said, finishing off his next drink. "You need to be ready by this evening, though. We're flying out overnight, and we'll arrive tomorrow afternoon."

Judy couldn't believe it. What would Tom say when he heard she'd been on a real airplane?

Howard left, and they both started to pack. Judy wished they had a phone at home so she could let Tom know what was going on. There was one at the lab, but no one would be there at that time of day. It was two o'clock in the afternoon in L.A., so 10 p.m. in the U.K. She would have to write to him when she got to Honolulu.

That evening, they were ready to go and Howard picked them up in his own car and drove them all the way to the plane.

There it was, bobbing in the water and gleaming in the sun, a brand-new airboat. Emblazoned on the side in blue and white letters were the words *PanAm Honolulu Clipper*. It was three stories high and as long as a large luxury yacht, but with wings. They parked the car and made their way onto the jetty.

Inside, Judy was astounded to see it was more like a hotel than an airplane. Chairs were set out in comfortable lounges with a galley and dining room for food and curtained-off berths on the second level for sleeping.

"It's so comfortable," remarked Hedy.

"It's going to take us nineteen hours to get there," advised Howard, "but we do have the place to ourselves. Part of the reason I wanted to do this hop is I have in mind an idea to build my own flying boat to move troops and cargo faster."

The journey over was remarkable, the sight above the clouds was awe-inspiring, and Judy watched, fascinated, out the window, wishing more than anything that Tom could be by her side to see it. She sat glued to the view till it was dark and then went to bed in one of the little berths to write to Tom all about it. The next morning as they traveled, she enjoyed time with the pilots, who showed her how all their instrumentation worked.

It was at around 2 p.m. that she spotted the beautiful islands of Hawaii for the first time. Rising up to meet her out of the long stretch of blue water were tiny pinpricks of land with the whisper of a water spray breaking at the rocks that surrounded white sands and rows of palm trees. If she'd thought that L.A. had been gorgeous, she hadn't been ready for Hawaii.

Howard made a perfect landing on the water and then taxied the flying boat to the harbor. As they got off onto solid ground and stepped out into the hot sunshine and warm balmy breezes, Judy felt as if she needed to pinch herself. England and the war seemed such a long way away. On the harbor, Howard had arranged for women in Hawaiian outfits to greet them with flower garlands of fragrant plumeria, which they placed over their heads.

"I've booked you into a hotel in Waikiki, the Royal Hawaiian. It's full of servicemen to keep you company; it's beautiful down there," said Howard. "I'll be here for a couple of days talking to the military, and then I'm flying back on Tuesday. Will that work for you?"

"I had to twist Mayer's arm not to plow me straight back into another picture, but I managed to get the week off," Hedy said. "Tuesday will be fine."

It wasn't long before they arrived at the hotel, and Judy was in awe. They checked in, and she and Hedy spent the day sitting on the beach, enjoying the sun and talking. Judy was fascinated by the Hawaiian music, and that evening they even went to something called a "luau." She couldn't believe it was December. They'd only be there for a few days, but it was a chance of a lifetime for her.

That night, at the luau they enjoyed all the hotel festivities. Traditional Hawaiian female dancers performed in grass skirts to gentle guitar music and bare-chested men spun fire spears to a lively drumbeat. As she watched the performance she felt her whole body relax as the enchantment of the island intoxicated her with its magic. Judy felt stronger and healthier than she had in months. She hadn't realized how tense she'd been with the pressure at work and living in a country at war. In a private moment she sat back and placed both her hands on her stomach and connected with her baby for what really was the first time. "I can't wait to meet you, baby Jonathan," she whispered. "You keep growing and getting stronger and soon we will be a family. You have no idea how much you are wanted."

After they had feasted on a boar that had been roasted in a pit in the ground, they introduced themselves to a naval captain who was there with his wife, and struck up a conversation with them. Hedy asked if he had concerns about Japan being so close.

"Oh, it's not close at all," he responded. "And this time of year, no one travels the North Pacific. It's treacherous. Look. Look out there."

He pointed out across the water. Far off, they could see Ford Island, where the U.S. Navy was moored up for the weekend.

"There usually are only half as many ships. This weekend we are all there, ready to protect you," he said with pride. "We can fire back at anything if we need to, so you have nothing to worry about."

As they were departing, the captain turned to Hedy and looked slightly coy.

"I don't suppose you have a little time tomorrow to slip by and say hello to the boys on the *Honolulu*? It would really boost the morale and we don't get to see many movie stars out at sea."

Hedy beamed. "I would be delighted. Can I bring Judy?"

"Of course, you are both very welcome and we would love to give you a tour of the ship for your trouble."

His wife chirped in. "Why not invite them tomorrow morning, Howie? That way she could be a guest of honor at the Wives' Monthly Sunday Brunch Club."

"That's a great idea, are you up for that, Miss Lamarr? The Officers' Club is just down from the ship and some of the wives have joined us on this hop and will be getting together to talk and eat some amazing Hawaiian food. It would mean an early start, though."

"I'm used to it. I sometimes have to be in hair and makeup at five."

He chuckled. "So seven a.m. would be a lie-in for you, then."

She laughed too. "It'll be fine."

"Great. I'll send a car to pick you up at seven; that will give us plenty of time to tour the ship and then you and Mrs. Jenkins can join the wives right afterwards for something to eat."

Judy and Hedy went to bed that evening, unaware of what was about to happen. It was because they were so relaxed, having such a good time, that the next day—the day that Pearl Harbor was attacked—would live on in their memory for the rest of their lives.

Chapter Thirty-Two

December 7, 1941

Judy got up early the next day and met Hedy in the foyer, who looked every bit the movie star she was. She wore an ivory silk calf-length dress that rippled in a warm morning breeze, pearl earrings, and a triple-pearl bracelet. Around her neck was a long silk ivory scarf, and tucked behind her ear a fragrant plumeria plucked from the bouquet Howard had arranged to be delivered to their suite. With her coral-colored lipstick and nail varnish, she looked absolutely gorgeous.

At five to seven, a rather smart-looking sailor in a pressed white uniform arrived to drive them to the ship. There was a slight flush across his cheeks as he helped Hedy into the car, and she flashed him one of her dazzling smiles.

"Not too far to go," he stuttered to cover up his embarrassment, and Judy couldn't help thinking how he had probably never expected to be escorting movie stars when he'd enlisted to join the U.S. Navy.

On the way to the dock, he gave them a history of the ship and their time in Hawaii as he updated them on their last port of call. Judy looked out of the window. The golden sands of Waikiki Beach stretched out before her, its shore kissed by soft, rolling waves of emerald water that turned into silver shimmers under the morning light. Above her head, tall palm trees swayed elegantly in the sea breeze that drifted into the car, carrying with it the intoxicating scent of exotic flowers that peppered the landscape.

Judy realized she had never felt so at ease and happy.

She missed Tom, but being away with Hedy was so wonderful, like a dream come true. It was lovely to wake up and not have to worry about fighting with Finnegan, dealing with rationing, carrying a gas mask, or wondering if today was the day your office or home was going to be bombed. Living under a country at war had been such a considerable weight she been carrying, and she hadn't realized the extent of that until now.

Drawn from her thoughts, Judy realized the young man sitting in front of them was still talking. "... And there are nearly nine hundred people on the crew. Just built a few years ago in New York, it has completed a refit recently in the shipyard in Seattle, and we just sailed out of Long Beach before we arrived here."

The thirty-minute journey went fast, and it wasn't long before the *Honolulu* swam into view, a massive ship of gleaming gunmetal, studded and riveted, its parade of guns glinting in the sun.

He turned off the road and passed the Officers' Club. "This is where you'll be having breakfast, Miss Lamarr. The captain wanted me to get you safely onto the ship, and then you'll be down here about nine thirty for brunch. I know the women are going to love it," he added with a smile. "My wife is there helping and can't wait; it's already got around that you'll be the guest of honor."

"I'm looking forward to it," she drawled.

The car drew up in front of the ship, and it felt enormous. And as Judy and Hedy craned their necks to survey it all at the foot of the gangplank, people started to spot Hedy and shout out to her. Suddenly the deck was filled with crisp white uniforms and waving arms.

Shouts of "Over here, Miss Lamarr. Give me a wave!" were accompanied by wolf whistles and cheers. Hedy smiled and waved to them all before starting to board the ship.

"They have been prepared for you and told to behave themselves," their escort informed them. "But it's pretty exciting to see a real movie star."

"I'll be fine," said Hedy with a smile.

Judy felt a pang of regret. Tom would have loved seeing this battleship.

"Permission to come aboard," trilled Hedy as she stepped up onto the deck to shake the hand of the waiting Captain Dodd.

"Granted!" was his enthusiastic response as he shook both their hands.

"Can't tell you how much this means to us," he continued. "This is Commander Nockold. He's going to show you around. But, first, if it's okay with you, Miss Lamarr, some of the boys would love to meet you."

She nodded. "That will be fine."

They moved onto the deck and were instantly swarmed by a mass of beaming sailors, holding up bits of paper, pens and shouting to Hedy, who started to sign autographs. She took it all in her stride, obviously comfortable in this type of crowd, and Judy felt conspicuous as she hovered beside her. Occasionally, Hedy would plant a lipstick mark on a corner of paper or a letter from a sweetheart, and the whole group would cheer and jeer the receiver.

After twenty minutes or so, the commander came along, broke up the crowd of Hedy's admirers, and announced to the crew that Miss Lamarr would be touring the ship. Of course, there were exclamations of disappointment, but on the whole, everyone was in good spirits.

Hedy and Judy followed Commander Nockold across the main deck and up steep gray metals steps to the upper deck. On top was a panoramic view of the whole of the harbor, and in the distance, an outstanding view of one of the rugged black volcanos Hawaii was famous for. They strolled around the promenade as he explained how they'd been on maneuvers in the Pacific over the last few months and still hadn't seen battle up to this point. It was breezy on the top deck, and the sea-scented air tossed Judy's hair as she struggled to hear all he was saying in the wind.

All at once, an airplane swooped in low, across the top of the ship, and streaked across the sky with a roar, leaving a slick white trail behind it.

"Don't worry, Miss Lamarr, Mrs. Jenkins, just the Air Force showing off and trying to get a better look at a real-life movie star, no doubt. It's amazing how quickly word can travel."

However, his eyes registered concern when a second plane swooped in over their heads. The captain joined them from the bridge and also reassured them.

"Annoying, I know," he stated matter-of-factly, "and they are in a little low, but we don't have anything scheduled for today. They'll be out of your hair in a min—"

He was stopped mid-sentence when, behind them, a massive explosion ripped through the air. They all swung around in shock. Far off at the other side of the harbor, a plume of black smoke was climbing into the air. Captain Dodd turned to his Commander, "Don't tell me someone is fooling with using live ammunition. What the hell is going on over there? I don't have anything down for today, do you?"

"No maneuvers scheduled for today, sir."

"Go see what's going on."

The second officer nodded and disappeared.

"So sorry, Miss Lamarr, Mrs. Jenkins, I'm not quite sure what's happening over there. Maybe they've got an issue on the ship, and it is not—"

Before he could finish his sentence again, another massive explosion rocked the water. Further down the harbor, another plume of smoke mushroomed into the air. The captain's face contracted with genuine concern, and Judy had an awful feeling.

He excused himself before assuring them, "I'll send someone to get you safely off the ship until we can find out what is going on. It was lovely to meet you both."

He touched the brim of his cap and left Judy and Hedy watching the display in bewilderment.

All at once, a whole flight of planes roared in over their heads. Judy shielded her eyes to get a better view, and her blood turned to ice when she saw what she had feared, a red sun acutely visible on the side of the plane's fuselage.

Judy grabbed Hedy's arm. "Oh my God, Hedy, they're Japanese."

Hedy didn't seem to understand the implication until Judy turned and said, "They're attacking those ships over there."

It was as if the air froze between them. There was a second of silence as the reality sank in, then they were jolted from their petrification as sheer pandemonium broke out all over the ship.

Hedy and Judy raced to the handrail and looked down onto the lower deck. All across the ship, seamen were scrambling; they tore around the deck, issuing frantic orders and shouts of "Battle stations!", some even crashing into one another as they jumped to man assault guns and move the ship into attack mode. Another explosion rocked the harbor, and Judy grabbed Hedy's arm and pulled her toward the stairs. As they clambered down, Commander Nockold met them midway and led them down toward the cabins on the lower level. He pushed open a door, shouting, "Keep your heads down and take cover; stay away from the windows."

Inside, the cabin was cool and dark, and it took a second for Judy's eyes to adjust. A neatly made single bed and a picture of someone's sweetheart on a desk were a blur in her line of vision as they rushed to the far end of the room where the two of them cowered in the corner. She was shaking from head to foot, and she noticed Hedy's chin was quivering, either from the chill of the room or with fear. Then, another explosion ripped through the air, followed by another and another. The boat rocked with the disturbance and shouts escalated on the deck as a team of sailors rushed by the porthole carrying boxes labeled *live ammunition*.

Judy wrapped her arms around Hedy as her friend started to pray. All she could think of was protecting her baby, and what about Tom? What if she died here? She would never see him again, and the thought was just too painful to contemplate.

"It's going to be okay, Hedy. It's going to be okay," she repeated, trying to assure them both, though she didn't believe it herself, and neither did Hedy by the look on her face.

A massive jolt rocked the boat sideways, and they were both knocked off their feet onto all fours; Hedy screamed as all around them, things crashed to the ground. The ship rocked back on itself, and they were both knocked onto their backs and slid across the floor, crashing up against the bunk.

"Hedy!? Hedy!? Are you okay?" Judy screamed toward her friend as she reached forward to grab her arm, noticing that a sliver of glass must have nicked her leg, because small spots of red blood were marring the lovely fabric of her dress. Hedy's frantic eyes met her own as she dabbed at the wound with a handkerchief Judy produced, and all around the ship, the shouting intensified, now accompanied by swearing and cries of anguish.

"A torpedo must've hit us," hissed Judy. "Come on, Hedy, we've got to get off the ship," she continued, taking command.

Hedy cowered against the bunk and didn't move; she looked scared to death.

"Come on, Hedy, let's get out of here!"

When Hedy still didn't move, Judy grabbed her friend's hand and yanked her to her feet, and only then did Hedy seem to understand.

They tore out of the cabin and saw a fire was raging on the side of the ship where the hull had been breached. Thick black smoke billowed up, making it impossible to make out where they were. Its acrid fumes filled their lungs and stung their eyes. Disorientated people rushed past them, crashing into them without even stopping to apologize. Coughing, Judy pulled her friend toward the gangplank.

The sound of a plane engine screeched in low overhead, its view obscured by the smoke. It was terrifying to hear it but not be able to see it. Then, all at once, a rat-a-tat-tat, like hail on a tin roof, ripped through the air. The smoke cleared for a second, and Judy saw just in front of them a line of bullets had peppered the deck. In response, sailors had dived out of the way. Then, with a second of clarity, Judy got a glimpse of the gangplank about thirty feet away.

"This way," she shouted, keeping a firm hold of Hedy's hand as they were plunged back out into the billowing, searing smoke. Fixing in her mind's eye the place she had seen the gangplank, she rushed ahead. All at once, a sailor cried out in agony.

"Wait!" screamed Hedy urgently. "Look, somebody needs help."

On the deck to the side of them, they could see a man sprawled out, his face contorted in pain, blood oozing out of a wound on his leg, soaking his white trousers. Hedy shook off Judy and rushed over to him.

Judy joined her friend to pull the young man out of the line of fire and under cover. He was still screaming in agony. Hedy pulled her silk scarf from her neck and started to wrap his injured leg. As she did so, she spoke to him in soothing tones. "Don't worry, sailor; you're going to be okay."

He stopped screaming, either at the reassuring tone of her voice or maybe with the shock. She pulled the flower from her ear and placed it in his hand. He looked at it and gave her a half-smile before Judy rocked her back up to her feet.

They raced toward the gangplank one more time, the sound of planes soaring overhead. Then, directly in front of them, another ship exploded with a deafening boom, the concussion knocking them apart and Judy off her feet again. The heat of the fire rolled across the deck, forcing her to close her eyes. In the heat of the battle, Judy became disorientated, deafened by the bomb, and terrified by the fire. She lay on her back, not knowing what to do.

Then, all at once, through the billowing smoke, a hand reached out to her and took her own; it was Hedy.

"I'm here!" shouted Hedy. "Don't let go of my hand."

Judy grabbed her friend's hand so tightly she was afraid she might lose sensation as they continued to race toward the dock. She didn't know how but somehow, they managed to make it to the gangplank and scramble down it, fighting their way through throngs of sailors making their way up and down, trying to save the ship.

The heat, dust, and debris assaulted every sense, and the only secure thing was one another's hand until finally, they were on solid ground.

"The Officers' Club!" shouted Hedy above all the noise.

Judy nodded, coughing to try and clear her throat from the smoke, and rubbing cinders from her eyes as they raced toward the building about a hundred feet away. Another explosion rocked another ship further away as sailors were splayed into the air like a fountain and thrown overboard into the water.

"Don't look!" screamed Hedy. "Keep running." As they raced toward the building, another plane dive-bombed over the top of them, peppering the tarmac of the car park. Finally, in desperation, they dove into the cover of the Officers' Club, where waiting inside was a group of bewildered women who stood beside a beautiful banquet of fresh fruit and delicious-looking food. "What's going on?" asked one. "Is it a drill?"

"We're under attack!" shouted Judy. "We need to get to safety now!"

"I think there's a cellar," offered one woman, and they hurried with her toward some stairs. Then, another rat-a-tat-tat of machine-gun fire broke all the windows along one side of the club, and women screamed as they ran down toward the cellar. Then, once again, they plunged into the darkness. As Judy steadied herself, hot, acrid-tasting breath rushed in and out of her lungs, and the whole of her body shook violently with the adrenalin.

In the dark, they found chairs as, around them, women sobbed, knowing their husbands were all in the line of fire.

And then the pain started in Judy's stomach.

She knew what it was straight away, but she couldn't believe that she was going to go through this trauma one more time and so far from home. Bombs continued to rock the island above their heads and she closed her eyes and wished more than anything she was with Tom. To be in the midst of such a vicious bomb attack, so many thousands of miles from home, was just unfathomable.

She took a deep breath, knowing she would have to tell somebody.

As she grabbed Hedy's hand, her friend looked across at her, and she knew too. "The baby?"

Judy couldn't stop the fury she felt from rising up in her. Why her and why again? She had come halfway across the world to protect this baby and still the war had found her and she was livid.

Hedy jumped to her feet and rushed into the middle of the cellar. "I need a nurse over here straight away. Is anybody here? A nurse?" She was so decisive and forceful, people started running to help. Hedy explained that Judy was pregnant, and women from all around the shelter began to bring pillows and jackets and laid Judy down. The pains started as they had before, slicing her in two and reminding her once again of all the sadness and grieving that was ahead of her.

She didn't say very much this time; it took all of her strength to control her anger. She was furious, just knowing in her heart of hearts that this child, little Jonathan, would most probably have survived if they hadn't been in this attack. The pains continued throughout the whole bombing. Once the all-clear sounded, the women helped her out of the shelter. As they moved outside she noticed Hawaii was a mess. The beautiful tranquil beaches devasted, the beautiful palm trees that swayed in the breeze on the edge of the water, gone. One of the women drove her to a hospital, which was already overrun with casualties.

En route she could still smell the smoke mixed with the damp scent of vegetation burning. The raid had lasted just over an hour yet everywhere close to Ford Island was now ravaged, the beauty of her earlier morning experience destroyed by the horrors of war. In the hospital Judy was a low priority, but Hedy pushed her way in, talked to people, and made sure that Judy got seen.

They took her into a room that was dark and clammy and a sign on the wall saying, "Hawaii, paradise on earth," seemed only to mock her. Judy closed her eyes and thought about Tom. She didn't want to tell him about this again. She was devastated. All they had done to try to keep her pregnant had been in vain.

After a very short time, Hedy managed to talk a doctor into coming to see Judy; and after examining her and asking her some questions, he had that look, the one she'd seen on two doctors' faces before, and she knew she was losing the baby.

But this time, things were different. As she lay there in the bed, everything became so much worse, the pains of contractions ripping through her body so dramatically that she started to bleed profusely; and as minutes turned into hours she began to drift in and out of consciousness with the incredible pain and blood loss. The doctors and nurses worked furiously around her, trying to take care of her and Hedy never left her side. But the last thing she remembered that evening before she blacked out was Hedy standing over her, holding her hand and saying, "I'm here, Judy. And I'm not going to leave you."

The next time she was conscious, it was daytime. She could tell because the sun was streaming through the windows beneath the bamboo blinds. And it was quiet after the noise and activity of the attack and all the frantic energy in the aftermath. She could now hear birds singing. She could smell flowers and she noticed beside her bed, there was a massive bouquet of exotic tropical flowers. In the corner, she saw her friend seated, dozing. Even without makeup, and tousled from the bombing, Hedy still looked beautiful.

As she tried to assess her body, something felt different. She felt tight, somehow, and her stomach felt numb. Something simply didn't feel right. She started to cough and clear her lungs, and it woke Hedy, who came to sit by her bedside. "Good morning," she whispered. "How are you feeling?"

"I'm not sure," replied Judy. "I feel strange. What happened?"

Hedy stood up, avoiding the question. "Would you like something to drink? There's some water here."

"The last thing I remember, it was nighttime. What time is it now?"

Hedy poured the water and seemed to be pausing before she handed it to her friend. "You should just concentrate on getting well."

"I need to get hold of Tom."

"I've spoken to Tom," responded Hedy quietly.

"You've spoken to Tom? How did you manage that?"

"Believe me, it took some doing, but I managed it."

"Is he okay? Does he know about the baby?" she asked, not wanting to confirm her suspicions.

"I told him about the situation. You must drink your water."

"The attack was terrible. Are people all right after last night?"

Hedy swallowed down a lump in her throat. "The attack was three days ago. You've been asleep since then."

"Three days ago?"

"We nearly lost you, Judy. You lost a great amount of blood, but the doctors here saved you. They were amazing."

"What does this mean?" asked Judy, trying to understand it all. This was so different to the last miscarriages.

"The doctor said he'll come and see you as soon as you were awake, and explain everything. I'll go and see about that," said Hedy, scooping some of her dark hair over her ear and making her way out of the room.

A pleasant-faced Hawaiian doctor arrived and came to take hold of Judy's hands.

"Aloha, I'm glad to see that you're up."

"What happened, doctor? Please tell me."

The doctor took the seat that Hedy had just vacated and sat down. This had to be bad. Judy could tell by his face, and Hedy paced nervously behind him in the room.

"I'm afraid your baby is gone," he said quietly. Judy nodded. This was news she was used to hearing. "Has this happened to you before?" She nodded again as tears trickled down her cheeks. "I'm so sorry," he said, squeezing her hand again.

"Tom just says we can try again, but it doesn't get any easier, doctor."

The doctor sat back. She could tell there was something else. "I'm afraid, Mrs. Jenkins, that won't be possible."

"What won't be possible?"

"For you to try again. Your loss this time was too severe. In order to stem the bleeding, we had to give you a hysterectomy. That means that you won't be able to have any more children. I'm so sorry."

Judy couldn't quite understand what he was saying. She understood the words and the meaning, but it wasn't actually making sense. She couldn't figure out how to translate the information. Did he just say that she would never have a baby? He carried on talking to her about procedures, things that she would need to do, and Judy didn't hear any of it; she was utterly shocked.

"I will leave a list of everything you need to remember with your friend here." Hedy smiled and nodded, and the doctor exited the room.

Hedy came over, retook his place, sat next to her friend, and held her hand. "I'm so sorry, Judy. I really am sorry. I know how much you and Tom wanted this baby."

"Does Tom know?"

"He does. We had to talk to him to get permission to operate."

Judy didn't know what felt worse, the loss of her baby, or the pain of the fact she hadn't been with Tom when he'd been told this horrific news. She knew this would be devastating to her husband, to be so far away and have this happen to her.

"I need to talk to him."

"We will see what we can do. There are not many telephones here, and a lot of the services are down since the bombing. Also, Roosevelt announced this morning," said Hedy as she stood up, "America is now in the war."

"Thank God," said Judy, closing her eyes, resentment brimming up in her again. "It's about time. Imagine how much sooner it might have been over if they had joined us earlier. So many deaths might have been averted," she spat out with frustration.

Later that day, they managed to arrange a phone call with Tom, but she couldn't speak. It was so expensive and she felt so bad—Hedy was paying for it—but she just couldn't talk. Tom reassured her from over a distance, and Hedy ended up taking the phone from her eventually and explaining what was going on.

Tom understood, but just hearing his voice, just knowing the truth of this and being so far away… All she could think of was that if she was killed, she would never see her husband again. Hedy managed to pull some strings, and with the help of Howard, they managed to arrange passage for her from the island when other people were still waiting.

Once Judy was strong enough to walk, they traveled back with Howard on the flying boat, which fortunately had been parked in a different place on the island during the attack. This time the plane was full. People fleeing the destruction and military personnel going to report to superiors in the U.S. As they flew over the Pacific, Judy thought about the last time she'd been on this journey. About the excitement and the joy of being with her friend, and now here they were: nothing but loss, and the war she had been escaping had cursed her once again.

When they got back to Los Angeles, it was decided she would stay with Hedy, recovering. It was good to have a little more time, though America's fears were high, now they'd entered the war. But she needed a little bit of respite, a little bit of space before she made her way home and faced Tom.

Chapter Thirty-Three

December 15, 1941

Hedy stared down at the telephone receiver she'd just replaced, willing it to phone back with different news.

"There is a mistake," she mumbled. "It isn't true." She reached for her cigarettes and her hand was trembling so hard that she could barely keep it still to light the tip. The whole of her body felt constricted, as though an invisible force was wringing her out, twisting her stomach into tighter and tighter knots. Hedy gasped helplessly for breath, but no matter how she tried, she couldn't seem to take in air.

Throwing open the French doors, she staggered out onto the patio. It was then the reality of what she'd just heard seemed to hit her, and she started to cry—no, wail. She didn't know where the sound came from, somewhere in the pit of her stomach. It sounded like an animal in pain.

Hedy made it into one of the patio chairs, tears streaming down her face. She placed her hand to her throat and pulled out the silver heart necklace she always wore. Gripping it tightly, she whispered, "Please don't leave me, Stefan. Please, not you."

All at once, Judy was by her side. She was starting to heal and had been up walking around for the last few days. When she reached her friend, all Hedy could do was shake her head, and Judy understood. She put her arms around her friend and held her tightly.

"I'm so sorry, Hedy. So, you finally got through to someone who could tell you what was going on?"

Hedy nodded through her sobs as she wiped away tears with the back of her hand before she spoke. "He's in Japan. I can't believe he went to Japan."

Judy drew in breath, understanding the seriousness of that information.

"I finally got through to his editor from the international press, and the last message they got from him was that he had been ordered to go to an internment camp in Miyoshi along with all the other internationals."

Judy offered her a hankie, and Hedy blew her nose, before continuing.

"Stefan had been on assignment on the Chinese border and, Stefan being Stefan, had heard about all the ships disappearing from the Japanese harbor just before the attack. He slipped into the country to see if he could go undercover and carry the story. Why does he always have to be so brazen?" she demanded, folding and refolding the hankie in her hand with frustration. She swallowed back her stilted, rolling sobs and continued.

"He actually managed to make it to the coast before they found him and uncovered him for who he was. They had only just arrested him when the attack on Pearl Harbor happened. They let him phone his editor but since then, the editor has heard nothing from him. That was over a week ago." Her sobs escalated and her voice cracked. "He's the only friend who has known me since my childhood and has loved me regardless, the only man I can trust. And if this war takes him from me, I don't know how I'll go on."

Judy nodded, squeezing her friend's hand, listening intently to everything she was saying. And all at once Hedy watched her friend's face change from sympathy to fury. "I'm so angry at the toll this war is having. It is so wrong, so utterly, bloody wrong!" she said angrily.

And even in her blur of grief, Hedy was also concerned about the toll this war was having on her friend. The fury in Judy's eyes was terrifying.

Eventually, once Hedy had recovered her breath and had calmed down, Judy got up and made her a cup of tea and brought it out to her on the patio.

"What can I do?" Judy asked.

"Nothing," said Hedy, reaching over and taking hold of her friend's hand. "Just you being here is everything. Though I do have to be on set. What time is it?"

Judy looked at her watch. "Just after ten."

Struggling to her feet, Hedy ran her hand through her hair.

"I should have been there two hours ago. The director's going to be furious. Even with terrible news, time is money." She pulled in a full breath and looked down at her friend. "Judy, could I ask you a favor?"

"Anything."

"Would you come with me today? I just need to be able to look over and see a friendly face, somebody I know who cares about me, somebody who can just be the strength for me to get me through the shoot."

Judy nodded. "Of course I will."

They traveled in practical silence.

When she arrived at the movie lot, Judy appeared bewildered by all of the activity taking place and Hedy was reminded of her first day on the set of *Algiers*.

Hedy raced off into makeup, where a makeup artist tried to minimize the puffiness and redness of her eyes. Judy sat with her friend, handing her tissues as Hedy shared with her makeup artist what was going on. Fortunately, she only had a short set that day and apparently someone had told the director what was happening with Hedy, which diffused the tension there normally would be on set with an actress arriving that late.

In the afternoon they made their way home. In the car they sat in silence again as tears streamed down Hedy's face and Judy held her hand. Judy decided to cook dinner for them both. The housekeeper was given the night off and the nanny took James away on a long walk to give Hedy the privacy she needed to grieve in the open. After dinner the two friends sat quietly watching the sunset, both in their mutual pain.

Judy reached out. "It doesn't mean he won't come home to you. There's always a chance, Hedy."

"I know," she answered despondently. "I'm just heartbroken that he is in real danger." She sighed before continuing. "I don't know what I'd have done without you here during this time. There's no one here I can really look to or trust. I have no husband right now and my friends are all busy with their own movies. There are times that I've been very lonely here, Judy. Do you remember when we met all those years ago at the museum?"

Judy smiled. "It seems a long time ago now, doesn't it?"

"It does, but I knew then when I met you that there was something about you, something that I could trust, a person who could really see me for who I was. I haven't had many people like that in my life."

"Neither have I," said Judy. "Only Tom."

"You're lucky to have him."

"The loss of this baby will be such a blow to him. There's almost part of me that doesn't want to go home and face him. I feel like I've let him down," said Judy, her own voice starting to tremble.

Hedy put her arm around her. "How can you say that? It's not your fault what happened."

"I know, but I know how much he wants children."

"And so do you. There are other ways. You could adopt, like I did."

Hedy motioned toward James, who had returned from his walk and was playing in the corner of the room.

"He's so lovely, Hedy. You are so fortunate. And it's amazing how he looks a little bit like you, even though he is adopted.

Hedy quickly changed the subject. "So why not take the plunge?"

Judy shook her head. "I'm in so much pain, I can't even think about doing anything like that. I know it's possible, and children need a home, but there was just something about having Tom's baby. There was something about sharing that experience with him that meant so much to me. Maybe after this is all over, we'll think more about it. But right now, I can't think about anything but ending this evil war."

Hedy nodded. "At least you can do something of service. I have to smile and pretend to be stupid. I started in this business because I loved it, but now I feel so confused. It's nothing like what I expected it to be. So much is fake and insincere. I always thought it was just a stepping stone, a stepping stone to something greater. But now I just don't know. Stefan always said I could do anything I wanted to…"

She began to cry again. Judy drew close to her and put her arms around her friend. And they sat there, the two of them, sobbing in mutual solidarity. They were grateful for one another, thankful that they had each other during this hard time. And in some ways, Hedy never wanted Judy to leave, or she wished she could have gone back to England with her. Something was forged between them over those few weeks together, something profound. Something that could only happen in the mutual cavern of despair. They'd started the holiday as friends and by the end they'd become something deeper than family.

And when it was time to leave, Judy told Hedy that she was so conflicted. She missed Tom desperately, but she felt she would miss Hedy with the same intensity.

In response, Hedy hugged her friend tightly at the railway station before she left L.A. "Promise me we'll always be friends."

"Always," agreed Judy as fresh tears rolled down both of their cheeks.

Chapter Thirty-Four

January 1942

It was as the train pulled into Cambridge station that the moment she'd been dreading arrived. Most of the time in the last few weeks, she'd been able to tuck away her anger and pain behind a veneer of numb indifference. Tuck it somewhere deep in her heart, where her inner self was screaming in its grief. It had been easy with the strangers she had met on her trip. Hidden behind her limp smiles, behind her "thank you's" and "good mornings" on the ship and "what a tremendous view," in California.

Now she was going to be home—home with her husband and the reality of their loss. As the train pulled to a stop and settled back into its couplings with a gentle jolt, steam hissed up from the wheels and a billow of gray, dusty smoke obscured her view for a second. But when it cleared, she saw him through the window, looking desperately up and down the platform.

His face was ashen. In his look, concern. In his arms he held a bouquet of pink carnations, and her breath hitched as she was reminded of their first ever date. Such a time of innocence. Before wars and miscarriages. What if she just stayed on the train? What if she never got off? Just kept going until the pain disappeared? Her thoughts were interrupted by a conductor walking through the corridor.

"We're here at Cambridge. That's where you're going, right, love?"

She nodded and stood, and he helped her down with her suitcase. If he hadn't done that, maybe she would have stayed on the train. Quietly she moved through the carriageway and as she stepped down onto the platform, Tom spotted her.

He plastered a smile on his face. Almost a little unrealistic, as if he was overcompensating for the pain they were both feeling. He closed the gap between them carefully and they stood staring at each other, the hot, acrid smell of steam from the train still billowing between them. He was wearing his church suit, the brown tweed that he kept for special occasions, and there was the usual and familiar smell of Brylcreem.

"It's good to see you, Judy," he said, and the genuineness she could hear in his tone tugged at her heart. "These are for you," he added shyly, handing her the flowers.

She nodded, still unable to speak or articulate anything she was feeling. They didn't hug as they had done when she left. It was unsaid, but she sensed that Tom, not unlike herself, was afraid of the flow of emotions that would follow if they got too close.

"Let's get you home, love," he stated, picking up her suitcase and carefully guiding her toward the exit.

He opened the car door and, helping her in, he put her suitcase in the back. Coming around and sitting beside her, he tapped her hand gently, before starting the car and making their way home. Inside the vehicle, the loss was palpable. Not just of the baby, but their loss of dreams about their future. It was only then she realized how much of their conversation had been about their hoped-for family. She looked out the window at the familiar things they passed on the way home as Tom tried to fill the void with small talk.

"Mrs. Williams' son, Thomas, is home on leave," he said cheerfully, pointing toward one of the houses they passed.

Judy nodded absently.

"Mr. Roberts retired. You know, we said he might do that. His angina finally got the better of him, and he has decided to stay home and grow vegetables for the war instead. I wonder who'll have that office now," he mused, trying to sound mysterious.

He parked outside the house, and came around to help her out. As she moved toward the front door, she froze as her heart started to pound and her stomach churned. This house would never be filled with children. She'd always imagined it that way. Always imagined the door would open and that they would come teeming out, running, playing, calling out the word, "Mummy." Now there would only ever be just her and Tom.

Tom seemed to understand and went forward and opened the door for her. The smell of clean floors and fresh air greeted her. Tom had been busy preparing the house, as though some disinfectant and a little elbow grease would clean away all the pain. Finally, she walked into the hallway and looked around her, feeling a stranger in her own home.

"Do you need to lie down, love?" he asked her gently. "Or would you like a cup of tea?"

She ran her hand through her hair. "Tea would be lovely. Thank you, Tom."

He went into the kitchen, and she stood in the hallway. She felt suffocated by the pain; she needed to get away from Tom, needed to be alone.

She walked upstairs with the pretense of unpacking. But once she closed the bedroom door she just wandered to the window and looked out at the garden that would never have children playing in it.

As she opened her drawer to put her clothes away, something was sitting on the top: her dad's notebook, just where she'd left it. She took in a deep breath. And all at once, she wanted to hear his words. She wanted to feel his presence more than anything else.

Picking up the journal, she rubbed her fingers across the cover, feeling the warmth of the worn leather before opening it. Inside was crammed with neatly folded newspaper clippings, right back to before she even joined the Cavendish. Secondary school projects she'd scored highly in, grades she'd achieved in college, a photo of her leaving for university.

She reverently turned the pages until she came to his writing, his neat, tight little writing. She tried to figure out what he'd written, and noticed that he'd been copying out a word, a scientific word, that she knew he wouldn't have understood.

It was spelled out phonetically, as though he'd been trying to learn how to say it. And this brought tears to her eyes; he'd been working out how to say it so he could tell people about her and she was overcome by his devotion and sheer unwavering belief in her success.

She ran her fingers down the page, hoping to touch a little of his essence. And then, welling up in her heart, came the rage again. Starting in the pit of her stomach, it rose up until it took a stranglehold of her, cutting off her breath, pumping her blood so hard it was as if her heart wanted to pound out of her chest. She clenched her fists.

All at once, she snapped, picking up the thing closest to her. She turned and slammed it against the wall, and her grandmother's vase shattered into a dozen pieces just as Tom opened the door with a cup of tea. He stood there frozen in the doorframe, the shock and fear in his eyes.

She couldn't stand to look at him. Racing toward the door, she pushed past him without explaining anything and rushed out the house without even grabbing her coat.

She walked the streets for a few hours until she was freezing and knew Tom would be in bed. Creeping into the darkened bedroom, she closed the door and looked at her husband. His eyes were closed, but she could tell he wasn't sleeping. She sat on the edge of his bed. "Are you awake, Tom?"

She felt him draw in breath. "Tom, I'm so sorry. I don't know what came over me." Even in the darkness, she could just make out his head, nodding. "Do you hate me, Tom?"

It was then he reached forward and took her hand.

"I could never hate you." He whispered, sounding desperate, "I love you, Judy. I will always love you. I just hate this, this rage

I see or whatever this is. I don't know what to do. I don't know how to make this right."

She lay next to him, comforted by her back against his chest as she let him wrap his arms around her. And behind her, she could feel his shoulders moving; he was crying. He was really sobbing. And she felt hateful. She had done this to him. Her uncontrolled fury. She had thought she had kept it hidden, but he had known her, had seen it. She decided she would have to bury her anger and bury it deeper; it wasn't his fault and she couldn't hurt Tom like this again. Swallowing down her emotion, she bolted it behind a door to her heart: she would never let him see again how she really felt. She made a decision: not only would he never see her raw anguish, but she would never be open to the idea of having children again. Instead she was going to put all of her focus into her work.

*

The next day, she was up, dressed, and ready to go. Tom was already in the kitchen when she came down the stairs.

"Are you going to go to work today?" he enquired carefully. "I thought you'd maybe take a little bit of time for yourself."

"I need something to distract me, Tom," she answered, wringing her hands, as she circled the kitchen. "I want to get right back to work."

Though his expression seemed to suggest he didn't totally agree, he appeared not to want to contradict her, so he just nodded.

At the lab she threw herself into a new project, spurred on by her need to seek justice for her father's death. She was tasked with developing a method of confusing German radar. Her job was to research and test different reflective materials that would appear to be airplanes on the enemy radar screens. It was exactly the sort of work that Judy was good at. When Tom reminded her it was time to stop for lunch, she just shook her head.

"I think I'm going to work through on a couple more of these experiments," she said. "Why don't you go ahead and eat?"

He looked surprised. He'd even made sandwiches for her. It was a ritual for them. They stopped every lunchtime to eat together, often, if it was warm enough, in the little courtyard outside their office. But she just couldn't stand it. She couldn't stand being alone with him, a time they would once talk about the family they were planning. The pain was less evident if she kept working. If she focused on doing this for Da, if she just kept her head down, she would hopefully work her way through all the pain inside her.

Tom reluctantly went for lunch and returned later, and they continued to work till late in the afternoon. On the way out of the lab, she collected more files to take with her.

"I'm going to work on some of this at home," she informed him flatly.

Tom looked surprised. "Do you think that's a good idea, love?"

"There are things I want to finish," she responded abruptly, feeling irritated by his concern. Not meeting his gaze, she pushed back on his objections.

They made their way home, and she went straight to their writing desk in the front room, where she created a little area where she could think and be alone.

Tom came to enquire after about an hour, "Were you thinking about something for dinner, Judy?"

"I'm not hungry, Tom."

"I can make you something. What would you like?"

She just shook her head. "I'm fine, thank you."

"I don't really want to eat on my own," he responded forlornly. "Maybe I'll just have a cheese sandwich."

She nodded as he went back into the kitchen, and she continued with her work.

This became her ongoing way. She buried herself like this for weeks, getting up early, going to work, working through her lunch, working through the afternoons, and working through her evenings, as though somehow her hypotheses and tests would push all the anger away.

January 18, 1942

Dear Judy,

Thank you for your last letter with the kind words of concern about Stefan. We're still waiting to hear, and I'm beside myself. I have just received word from his editor that the Red Cross are in talks to get into the camps to check how the prisoners are doing. Let's hope I will finally get word. But I wanted to write to you because after you left, something struck me, and that is something I wanted to let you know. Judy, I've never had a friend like you before. Of course I had Stefan, but he's more like a brother. You and I—we think the same. And I'm so grateful for our friendship. You have no idea. It was just strengthened through such a dark time.

I don't think I'll ever get over the bombing of Pearl Harbor. That was one of the most traumatic things I've ever been through in my life. And then to have you lose the baby, I felt so guilty for bringing you here. Hoping that it would cheer you up, hoping that it would help. And instead, it caused the saddest outcome. I feel so terrible about that, Judy. But I also wanted to let you know that I'm here for you whenever you need me. Friendships like ours are few and far between. They come along once in a lifetime.

And I can't tell you how grateful I am that we met that one day in the Science Museum, now so many years ago. I know lots of people here in L.A., lots of people who are supposed to be my friends. And I have a few people I'm close to, but no one like you, no one that means as much to me. Please let me know if there's anything I can do to help you right now. I can't even imagine what you're going through. But I want you to know that you're not going through it alone. I'm always here on the other end of the telephone, and you can write to me whenever you want. And whenever possible, I always will come and visit, because true friends are hard to find. And I just feel so lucky and grateful to have found a friend like you.

Take care of yourself,
with much love always,
Hedy

P.S. To keep our minds off what is going on, here is a little riddle for you to work out.

Sisters four, dancing in turn. Two blessed on St. John's Feast, two locked in step as sylph and gnome. Who am I?

Chapter Thirty-Five

February 1942

Hedy woke up abruptly from a nightmare, gasping for breath; her heart was beating wildly, her hair stuck to the back of her neck, and a bead of perspiration was rolling down the side of her face. Sitting up, she tried to get her bearings.

She'd been dreaming about the bombing of Pearl Harbor again. She had the same dream over and over now. It always began with her smiling and signing autographs on the *Honolulu* and then the explosion. But unlike what really happened on that day, in her nightmare she had to fight her way through fire and smoke that burned her hands and face, and no matter how much she tried to get off the ship she was unable to find Judy or the gangplank. The worst part was that all around her the desperate screams and cries of the crew escalated until in terror she would jolt awake, covered in sweat. When she'd been in Europe, it had been nerve-wracking, especially the attack she had been caught in in London. But there had been a civility to the response from the British. They were prepared for the attack, and the British response was like a well-oiled machine, citizens responding calmly.

But in Hawaii, not only had the experience she and Judy had been through been horrific, there had been an overwhelming feeling of disbelief and vulnerability, as if no one could imagine that such a beautiful, tropical island would ever suffer such a deplorable act. There had been no warning. Though there had been preparations and concern, the Hawaiian Islands had just been taken by storm, and somehow it had intensified the severity of the experience.

In the bathroom, Hedy stared at herself in the mirror. She was exhausted. Her hair was wild and damp from the tossing and turning, and her eyes looked petrified. Reaching into her medicine cabinet, she took out the medication the doctor at the studio had just prescribed. The uppers and downers, as so many of her co-stars called them, were all that were keeping her going right now. Throwing back the little white pills that would give her the ability to face her day with a glass of water, she strolled out into her garden and waited for them to take effect. Even though it was February, it was still quite warm in L.A. And from her house in the stillness of early morning, she could hear the lap of the waves far off, and it calmed her. Since arriving home, the war had suddenly felt so real, and not only Hollywood but her whole world felt so fake. Until the Pearl Harbor attack, she had just been playing at being at war. And even though she had wanted to help with the war effort by inventing something, she had been so far removed from the realities of the horror of it since she had been living here in the U.S., and all that had now changed.

Before she had gone to Hawaii, and before the news of Stefan's imprisonment, all she'd been thinking about was the next picture and whether she could expect more money for it. And now, all she could think about was fighting for their freedom, and Hedy felt compelled to do something practical, anything she could. She was still an Austrian citizen and wanted to prove to the world how grateful she was for this new nation that had given her freedom.

Later that morning, on the set of her latest film, *Crossroads,* she heard a rumor from one of the other actresses that Mayer was looking for a group of actors to go on the road to raise money for war bonds. She was heartened; this was one way she could make a difference.

In between takes, she made her way over to his office. As she entered, he looked up from his desk. "If it isn't the most beautiful woman in the world," he announced, removing the cigar pressed between his lips.

Hedy smiled demurely, even though she hated the title. She informed him of her desire to go on the road with the group.

"I was going to come over and talk to you about that very thing this afternoon," Mayer responded. "We've got a whole crowd of people interested in going. Colman is in. And I think I can get Greer. And I was hoping that you would say yes as well. We want the country to invest about a billion dollars in one month, to help pay for the war, and you guys would be going from city to city on the train to raise that money."

She readily agreed to be signed up.

*

A month later, she found herself at the train station in L.A. on a special train to Washington, D.C. On the side of the carriage was emblazoned "**Buy War Bonds**."

The whole group of Hollywood's most famous actors and actresses stood on the platform at the back of the train and posed for photographs.

"How many more?" asked Irene Dunne, through a plastered-on smile and gritted teeth, her body shivering from the cool, drafty platform.

"They need all our beauty shots for the magazines, I hope they are getting my good side," stated Bob Hope. "I was in the makeup chair for two hours this morning just to look glamorous like you, Hedy," he continued to joke.

"Like I always say," responded Hedy through her own plastered smile, "any girl can be glamorous. All you have to do is stand still and look stupid."

The group tittered behind her.

They would be touring cities from coast to coast raising money for the war effort. As they stood and waved to the camera, they chatted nervously amongst themselves, having agreed to go to any city that would propose a million dollars.

As they rolled away from the station, Irene Dunne turned on her heel. "Good. That's over. Let's go and get a drink, and I need a cigarette."

They were a lively bunch as they made their way back into the club car.

"Well, here we go, folks," joked Bob Hope. "Maybe I can raise money by *not* singing."

"I don't mind singing," Bing Crosby responded.

"Well, there's a surprise," quipped back Hope.

Barbara Stanwyck ran her hand through her hair. "I'm just glad I can do something for this war, though I don't particularly like traveling on a train. I don't like the movement."

"That's nothing that a double Scotch can't cure, honey," Hope added as they settled at the tables.

"There's an awful lot of star power in this carriage," announced Cary Grant, beaming as he walked in and began to shake hands. "If this train leaves the tracks, that's Hollywood over. Mayer will be shuffling along the streets in his bathrobe."

"Well, we can't let flyboy Stewart win all the medals for the U.S., now, can we?" quipped Hope. "He needs to let some of us lowly comedians share in a little of the action happening in his trophy cabinet."

Hedy mused with fondness about her co-star on the films *Ziegfeld Girl* and *Come Live with Me*, the last that Jimmy had acted in before signing up to fly for the Allies, and she missed him.

Crosby started to sing a few lines from "The Star-Spangled Banner," and Hope harmonized.

"Not bad," joked Hope. "You keep singing with me and you could go places."

"All the way to the poorhouse, no doubt," quipped Crosby.

"Well, I would love to stay and chat," announced Dunne, finishing her drink and crushing out her cigarette, "but I do have to read lines and apparently that's what they pay me for." And off she went to find a quieter corner, shouting over her shoulder, "Save me a seat at dinner, folks."

"Have you got a load of the rest of these carriages?" stated Danny Kaye, striding enthusiastically into the club car. "There are two dance halls here and two pianos. We'll be able to rehearse as we go."

"I'll be sure to give those a miss," sneered Crosby. "Not sure I can sing, dance and rock at the same time."

"Can't do anything but improve my style," responded Hope optimistically.

"Style?" Crosby guffawed, lighting his pipe. "Is that something new we should all be aware of?"

Claudette Colbert entered the club car and, pulling off her hat, sat down next to Hope. "Here you are. I've been looking for you all. I thought I would be hoofing on my own in D.C."

"A nice little pony you would make too," stated Hope, kissing her hand comically. "Do you remember me, honey? I'm Bob Hope." He leered toward her with a beaming smile.

She pulled out a cigarette and narrowed her eyes. "I don't remember the name, but that wild-eyed stare is familiar," she quipped dryly as Crosby lit it for her.

The car rocked with laughter.

"That was good," stated Hope, wagging a finger at her. "I might have to work something like that into my act."

"An act?" added Crosby with an element of mock surprise. "That will be a nice change."

Hedy pulled her sweater around her shoulders, enjoying the camaraderie and quick wit between her fellow actors, though not always understanding all the jokes. She liked being in their company this way, as going from set to set she often felt relatively isolated and alone. They didn't really get to do this unless it was parties, and she wasn't a big fan of those.

Excusing herself from the group, she quickly set herself up in her own berth, to read over the script her agent had just given her before leaving L.A. She pulled out the screenplay and looked at the name of the film, *White Cargo.* As he'd thrust it into her hands, Hedy's agent had informed her that Mayer was eager to announce it as soon as possible as the next project Hedy would be starring in and she may be working with Walter Pidgeon, who was being considered for the role of her co-star.

As she read through the script she considered the journey ahead of her, which included a final stop in D.C., where they would be having tea with the First Lady. Hedy couldn't believe the amazing experiences she'd had since she'd arrived in the U.S. She'd never imagined when she boarded the *Normandie* that one day she would be taking tea with the president's wife.

When they pulled into the first station, they were overwhelmed by the welcome they received.

"Looks like the Hedy Lamarr Fan Club is here," joked Hope as the train ground to a stop. "And here I was hoping I would be the first to get my pin-up picture of Hedy signed." He flashed a smile at Hedy as she laughed.

As they descended onto the platform, well-wishers flocked to them waving U.S. flags, and a brass band played a lively patriotic number. They all mingled with the fans, signing autographs before a day packed full of activity and appearances.

What followed were days of the same, and the group became quite close by the end of the tour, raising millions of dollars in war bonds. For Hedy it was a way to distract her from her experience at Pearl Harbor, her worries about Judy and her gut-wrenching thoughts of Stefan so far away in a Japanese internment camp.

Chapter Thirty-Six

February 1942

Judy was up before dawn on the day of the first test for the latest invention she had been developing. She'd had a restless night and eventually got up about five thirty and made herself a cup of tea. A little later, she watched the sun coming up as she stood waiting in the kitchen for Tom to get up. When she heard the familiar creak of his bedsprings above her, she put the kettle back on for him. She listened with comfortable familiarity to his routine above her, the taps running in the bathroom, his cheerful hum of a George Formby song, his shuffled walk back to the bedroom to dress, and then finally his descent into the hallway.

She greeted him at the foot of the stairs.

"You're up early, love," he observed with surprise. "Did you sleep all right?"

"I haven't slept at all," said Judy as she strode back into the kitchen, her arms folded across her chest.

"Are you worried about the test today?"

"Aren't you?" she responded.

"It's not my project as much as it's yours. I just get to watch the genius in action." He kissed her on the cheek as he sat down in front of his breakfast bowl.

Judy fetched the newspaper and the post and brought it in to Tom as he sat sipping his coffee and looking at the headlines. As she nervously moved about the kitchen making his breakfast, he must have sensed something, because, placing the paper down, he said, "Come and sit down, love," standing up and ushering her to the table. "And have another cup of tea. You're a bundle of nerves. It's all going to be fine."

"But what if it's not, Tom? What if it all goes wrong and innocent men continue to be killed while we have to go back to the drawing board?"

"It won't," he assured her. "You have worked like mad over the last month, finishing this project way ahead of schedule. Now the next obvious step is testing."

She took a sip of the tea he'd poured her from the teapot and coaxed her to drink as she tried to relax. The project that she'd been in charge of, though unofficially because obviously Finnegan didn't like the idea of a woman being at the helm, was having its very first test today. She had been working on it before she had gone to America and it had consumed her.

The top-secret project known as Operation Window was a way to give the British an advantage. Judy had been working for months on different versions of the experiment, which involved dropping reflective strips from a British aircraft to confuse the Germans' radar signals. The reflective material, known as chaff, would send out false signals to make the Germans believe there were more planes in the sky than there were. Judy had gone over and over her figures, trying to make sure she hadn't made a mistake, but still she felt a great deal of pressure. Finnegan had been so reluctant to have her head up the project, and only if Tom supervised, that she knew if it abjectly failed, she might be washing test tubes and opening letters for the rest of the war.

Tom spread jam on a piece of toast and looked optimistically out the window. "At least we've got a nice dry day for it," he said. "And you've done a fine job on this, Judy. You can't second-guess yourself now."

She nodded. It had been six months before when they'd been visited by a top scientist who had first introduced them to the idea of confusing radar and the enemy. The British knew the frequencies that the Germans were using, and a lecturer at the Cavendish had gone into more detail about the idea of suspending wires from a balloon or a plane to confuse the radar signals.

This could be very helpful if the British wanted to create a diversion, sending the Luftwaffe in the wrong direction, and giving the Allies liberty to attack somewhere else.

Judy had taken what had been presented to her six months before and adapted it, thinking that maybe aluminum would be a light and cheap way to create the reflective surface that they needed. She and Tom had been looking at the different types of materials and wind buffering. Today was the first day that they would be officially testing it.

Tom finished his breakfast and placed sandwiches into a bag for Judy later, and they made their way to the lab to finish up their preliminary measures.

At ten o'clock sharp, Finnegan came into their laboratory with two of the top brass from the RAF. He automatically introduced Tom, overlooking Judy completely as per usual. Tom corrected the mistake. "And of course, you must meet my wife, Judy Jenkins, whose idea this was, and who has been leading the effort in this department." The officers greeted her politely but then continued to talk to Tom over her head, asking lots of different questions about how it all worked.

Tom, in turn, would turn to Judy and allow her to explain. It was very demoralizing for Judy, but she was so nervous about the test, she didn't even have the time to get angry.

After the introductions, she and Tom traveled out in the detector van with the radar placed on the top to the drop site. All their radar equipment was inside, and once the pilot had taken off, they would be able to monitor the responses from their own equipped van.

"It's exciting, isn't it, Judy?" Tom mused as they drove along. "As much as I hate this war, we're fortunate to live in an era where we can really see our inventions make their way all the way through to completion. And imagine what this will mean to the British if this works!"

She nodded, looking out at the countryside. They were out in rural Cambridgeshire, at a farm high on a hill where they would get a good signal and they could monitor the process.

Once they arrived at the destination, the RAF officers and Finnegan made their way outside to watch the planes drop, and Judy and Tom set up their equipment in the van and tested everything was working. Judy sat in front of her monitor with a headset on, checking that the radar was working correctly, and Tom sent a communication via a runner that they were ready for the test.

At precisely eleven o'clock, the plane was due to take off and make the chaff drop not far from them at about 11:10.

Judy started monitoring the signal. She held her breath as she watched the big hands of the dark clock on the wall in the van. Tom sat by her side, checking the rest of the instrumentation.

At 11:10, nothing appeared on the radar screen. At 11:11, still nothing seemed visible. By 11:12, she looked nervously over at Tom. He tapped her hand.

"Give it some time, love. They might've had problems on take-off. And it looks like it's a little bit windy as well."

All at once, as if on cue from Tom's reassurance, the screen filled up with a bright flashing white light. Exactly what they'd hoped for. Judy started monitoring the test. The chaff had been dropped from the plane and had reflected its signal, creating a distortion, a mirrored effect that made it appear there were many more planes in the air than just the one that was up there.

She looked over at Tom to see if he'd seen it as she had. And he was nodding and smiling.

"Congratulations, lead scientist Judy Jenkins," he said, putting his arm around her shoulder and squeezing her. "You did it!"

Judy felt lightheaded. She hadn't realized she'd been holding her breath. She knew Tom would probably get the praise for this, but she was glad she wouldn't be blamed for things going wrong.

After the first test, the plane went up two more times so Judy and Tom could monitor different strips of foil. The first that had been sent out were squares, and though it had been received well, there was the thought that other types of shapes or long strips of the aluminum would work better.

They went through the second test and recorded the results. And then the last test. It was unanimous between her and Tom. The long strips of the foil definitely worked the best. The effect lasted longer and gave a stronger result.

"Well," said Tom as they packed up their equipment, "they can't complain about that. We should get back to the lab and have some lunch. And then we have that meeting at three o'clock."

Judy sat in the van next to him on the way back and felt determined. Since she had lost her father and the last baby, this chaff project had become like the child she'd never had. It had driven her and she'd hoped more than anything that it would work. This was to be her only focus now, helping the war effort.

When they arrived back at the Cavendish, Judy joined Tom for the first time in over a month as they made their way outside onto the little area where they had their sandwiches and he handed one to his wife.

"Should have brought some champagne," he said, with a smile on his face.

She chuckled. They'd never drunk champagne in their lives. She imagined it was something that Hedy did regularly. But for her and Tom, he was more of a pale ale man, and she was happy with a gin and tonic.

Even though it was early in the year, as they sat there the sun came out to salute their victory, and it was absolutely glorious. As she started eating she realized she was starving, remembering she hadn't eaten breakfast. Judy demolished the potted meat sandwiches Tom had made for them both.

They met in Finnegan's office that afternoon, where the RAF observers were very animated about what they'd seen, and automatically started to compliment Tom.

"Judy did a great job," Tom insisted, "and the results we have are that the third test was definitely the superior of the three. Judy will fill you in on more of the details," he continued, as he swiveled toward his wife.

Everybody was staring at her; normally she would have been tongue-tied but then, remembering how she had stood up to Finnegan and the way it had seemed to make him gain more respect, she rolled back her shoulders, pushed down her nervousness and updated them all in a confident voice about the read-outs of all the tests they'd run. The RAF contingent listened politely and nodded their assurances. They stood up and shook hands with everybody, saying they were looking forward to presenting this to the RAF command and implementing it as soon as possible.

On the way out the door, the senior officer turned to Tom. "You have yourself a nice little wife there. You should take good care of her."

Tom gave him a tight smile, but Judy once again felt patronized. This was her project and he made it sound as if she had just baked a fine cake.

Finnegan, of course, reiterated the statement. "Well, it looks like you'll get to keep your job another day, Mrs. Jenkins," he said with grudging respect. "I won't have to send you off to the typing pool just yet."

She sucked in a breath to stop herself from saying something untoward as she followed Tom out of the door.

"Don't let them get you down, love," he whispered across to his wife as he grabbed her shoulder and gave her a hug. "You did a wonderful job, and the people that are important know that. There's a lot of big egos around here, and only one person without one, and that's you. The most important thing is you will save pilots' lives, that's the most important thing of all."

Chapter Thirty-Seven

Fall 1942

Once she'd finished her stint on the war bonds tour, Hedy was encouraged onto another project that Bette Davis was organizing. She had got together with some of the other Hollywood elites to create the Hollywood Canteen. The idea was to offer some free entertainment and a place to call home to servicemen while they were in L.A.

Hedy arrived the first night at the old converted theatre on Cahuenga Boulevard. The words "Hollywood Canteen" were emblazoned on a nondescript paneled building illuminated with bright Hollywood-style uplighting. Making her way inside, through the wolf-whistles from the swath of servicemen packing the door, she heard a friendly voice call out to her.

"Hey there, Hedy, glad you could join us. Bette's in the kitchen. She said to send you in when you arrived so she can show you around."

She acknowledged Dinah Shore, who, along with Deanna Durbin, was greeting GIs at the door.

The place was hopping, the air hot, sticky, and lively. Hedy found the kitchen and Bette Davis was organizing the serving and washing-up roster inside. She looked poised as she always did. Bette was in a neat black pencil skirt and white apron, her hair whisked up on the side, affixed by a black and white sequined flower for decoration. Seeing Hedy, she greeted her warmly.

"Hedy, darling, thank you for coming. It's been wild tonight. You couldn't have picked a better evening to come and help serve." She beckoned Hedy to follow. "Let me show you around."

She pushed the door back into the main room, where Xavier Cugat was leading the band in a lively samba. Most of the members were on their feet, swaying together to the toe-tapping rhythm, the echo of drums and maracas pulsating throughout the room. Bette and Hedy made their way carefully across the crowded dance floor as servicemen stopped to stare at Hedy or shake her hand.

"Mostly what we do is serve and entertain!" Bette shouted into Hedy's ear. "But I thought for today you could sign autographs, just to get you into the swing of things. Then later I might need you to help with the washing up."

"Anything but cooking," said Hedy with a sly smile. "If you want the GIs to come back, of course."

Bette nodded, laughing.

At the back of the room, an area was set up to sign autographs. Marlene Dietrich was already there, looking stunning in a floor-length black sequin dress, her white fur shoulder wrap decorated at the neck with a diamond brooch. She looked up at Hedy with her smoky eyes and dazzling smile. "Ahh, the cavalry has arrived, boys," she commented triumphantly. "Miss Hedy Lamarr is here." Then she added in German for Hedy's ears only, "Thank goodness, my hand is aching so much."

Hedy smiled and nodded, taking a pen and settling down to sign autographs so Marlene could take a break.

As the evening wore on, she soon got into the swing. Entertainers from all over the industry performed songs and comedy sets, interspersed with the band, whose lively music continued to pack the dance floor with sailors, soldiers, and airmen dancing with any girl that was available.

After that first night, Hedy started to work regularly in the Canteen. She would arrive there after a day on set, put on her waitress uniform, and serve the men. They were trying to raise more money for the war effort, and she even gave away kisses if somebody donated $2,000. It wasn't easy to keep smiling and performing after hours, but she got to meet some friendly people and she liked giving back to her new country.

Her life had become so busy since war had been declared in the U.S., but she still kept in touch with Judy. However, Judy had become more distant since her visit and the busyness of her own work, and Hedy was worried about her friend's preoccupation with making the Germans pay. It was all that she talked about in her letters, and it seemed so unhealthy. But Judy's letters were becoming few and far between again. Also, Hedy still hadn't heard from Stefan since war had been declared with Japan, and knowing he was incarcerated, she worried desperately about him every day.

She was finishing letters to each of them when she got a call from Bette one night. "I know it's short notice, Hedy, darling, but I have been let down by three actresses tonight and I desperately need help. Any chance you could just spare a couple of hours?"

Hedy glanced at herself in the mirror. Her hair needed washing and she was just getting over a cold, so her eyes were red and puffy. Her nose was still running.

She explained her situation to Bette, but she wouldn't take no for an answer. "Come in through the back door and I can at least put you to work in the kitchen. The washing up is piling up. I promise not to make you go out into the Canteen if you're not feeling your best."

Hedy sighed. She found it hard to say no to Bette and made her way over to the Canteen. It was as she was washing her second load of dirty dishes that Bette arrived in the kitchen.

"Good news!" she proclaimed. "I have managed to find you some help. John Loder, I believe you already know Miss Hedy Lamarr, the most beautiful woman in the world."

Hedy shook her head and balked. "Well, I might have been in some former life," she remarked sarcastically, raking her hands through her limp hair before looking up into the handsome face of her new kitchen partner.

"Good to see you again, Hedy, it's been a while. Hedy and I haven't seen one another since she was on the lot before *Algiers*."

Bette nodded. "Then you two old friends will have plenty to catch up on, no doubt."

John offered his hand, looking highly amused by the whole experience. Bette disappeared, leaving them to organize themselves.

Hedy felt her heart quicken. She and John had been rather more than friends when she had met him years before.

"How about I grab a tea towel and start drying?" he offered, breaking the awkward silence between them. Hedy nodded and showed him where they were kept. As he selected a tea towel, Hedy stole a surreptitious glance over at him. Wearing an expensive tweed jacket, he was as tall as she had remembered him, with his thick dark hair and warm brown eyes. He also had a very reassuring presence about him.

They fell into an easy working rhythm and once they had worked through the awkwardness of having at one time been lovers, though their affair had been brief, they settled quickly into easy conversation. He was under contract for Warner Bros. As they worked side by side, even up to her elbows in sudsy water, she felt the spark of a connection. As laughter drifted in the door from Red Skelton's antics on stage, she found herself very physically attracted to John Loder once again. As the evening drew to a close and they put away the last of the cups and plates, Deanna Durbin started to sing a sultry version of "Night and Day."

John offered her his hand. "May I?"

She looked confused. So, he took the initiative and, closing the gap between them, drew her close into his arms and started to sway with her to the music, the tea towel still in his hand.

Hedy chuckled. "You will probably catch my cold being this close."

"I don't care," he whispered back. "It will be worth it."

And it was as they danced in the midst of that kitchen to Deanna's beautiful voice that Hedy realized, even with all her adamant thoughts of never marrying again, that she might be in real trouble here.

Chapter Thirty-Eight

Summer 1943

Judy was making cocoa one night when they got the call. As the war had progressed, they had ordered a home telephone so they could be in touch with the lab in case of emergencies, but they rarely got calls this late. Tom went to answer it, and she listened, hovering by the kitchen door. She could tell it was something important because Tom used his official, polite voice.

"Yes, sir. We'll be there, sir. Thank you so much." He hung up as Judy finished pouring water into their cups of cocoa.

"What was all that about?" she asked as she approached him, offering him a cup.

"Get your coat on, Judy. We have to go."

"Go?" she echoed incredulously, looking down at the cocoa. "It's eight o'clock. Where are we going?"

"It's top secret," assured Tom with intensity.

"You can tell me. I promise not to tell any Germans." She smirked.

"It looks like tonight's the night."

She knew without any further explanation what Tom was talking about.

After over a year of work, they had been waiting weeks now for the first drop of their latest weapon. Bomber Command had informed them that when they were ready, they would let Tom and Judy come to the airbase so they could monitor the progress from there.

"The chaff?" she said, her eyebrows raised.

Tom broke out into a smile as he went into the hallway and got her coat out of the cupboard. "Time to see if that physics degree was worth it," he said with a smile as he helped his wife into her coat.

"You mean the one I earned, but they never gave me?" she leveled with him, a sarcastic edge to her tone as she placed their cups on the kitchen surface.

"Yes, that one." He smiled, opening the front door.

Soon they were on the road to the Bomber Command base, the address of which Tom had been given over the telephone.

They were quiet as they headed toward the sunset. It was summer, and it was quite warm, so Tom had the window open. The breeze rushed in and toyed with Judy's hair as she thought about the work that would happen tonight. It was one thing to be in the laboratory working and testing things; it was another to know that tonight, in another country, people's lives were going to be changed forever by what she had invented.

Tom barely spoke on the way there, and a couple of times, she had to remind him of his speed, as he tended to push the car faster with his mind on getting there.

When they finally arrived at their destination, it was dark. They pulled into the airbase, navigating by the headlights fitted with the special blinds to comply with the blackout. Showing their passes to the guard at the gate, they asked for the commander in charge of their project, and the officer pointed them in the right direction.

This was the first time that Judy had actually been inside a Bomber Command center and it was a hive of activity. People wearing headsets were monitoring planes on radar screens, and enormous maps covered all the wall space. A friendly WAAF greeted them, ushered them into the building, and introduced them to the commanding officers.

The spirit in the room was tense and excited as they anticipated the raid that was going on. The bomber commander took them to a map and showed them the route the planes with their chaff would be going.

"We're calling it Operation Gomorrah, and it's a huge raid over Hamburg."

Tom and Judy just nodded, engrossed in all the information.

"We won't know the full success of it until we start seeing the planes coming back, but we wanted you to be here to see how all your hard work turned out."

Judy was interested in following everything on the radar equipment and noticed the operator's surprise at her knowledge as she asked questions about frequency and codes. After the initial excitement of getting there and being introduced to the operation, what followed was a lot of waiting.

A kind WAAF brought her a cup of tea as the hours methodically ticked by on the large black-and-white-faced clock in the operations room, and as the evening wore on, people became more nervous, waiting to hear if the chaff's deployment had worked. Judy visualized the planes in the sky. The crew trained to operate Window, as the chaff drop was called, was being manned by 76 Squadron, and the commander had informed Judy that twenty-four planes had been briefed on how to drop the bundles of aluminum paper strips.

The job of 76 Squadron would be to take a diversionary path away from the British bombers to draw German firepower from the intended targets.

Tom and Judy had improved the chaff since the initial test, and the squadrons were now using a treated paper to minimize the weight and to maximize the time that the strips would remain in the air, prolonging the effect. The pilots would use flare shoots on the airplane to drop the chaff, using a stopwatch to time the drop in established intervals to give the most realistic impression of a plane being in the air.

As the night wore on, Bomber Command checked in with them periodically, informing them they anticipated that the raid would take place sometime after midnight and it would be five hours before they arrived back. As the first plane started to come home and check in with Bomber Command, they all stood around the map, counting the planes coming back from the bombing raids. Every time they counted another, both Judy and Tom felt a sense of excitement and Judy felt a twinge of perverse pleasure that somewhere out there Germans were paying for her father's death. When they were all back from that night raid, it was unbelievable. The operation had been a resounding success, with only twelve of the 791 bombers being lost on that first night and many of the German camps' radars being confused.

When the planes landed, the bomber commander shook Tom and Judy's hands warmly. "The war office thanks you for your hard work. Because of you, people's lives have been saved."

As she and Tom made their way home, exhausted, in the early morning light, she was surprised she didn't feel the relief she had expected. Her deep-seated anger hadn't seemed to abate with the success of the mission; if anything, she found the feeling had intensified, as if she wanted to do even more to avenge her father's death.

*

July 30, 1943

Dear Judy,

Just a quick note to let you know that we've just heard word about Stefan. At last, the Red Cross was allowed to go into the camps and check on the condition of the prisoners. I can't tell you what a mixed blessing this was. I had already started to hear rumors of atrocities in the camps holding service members, but the camp that Stefan is in for holding international citizens is maybe not so horrendous. However, the word is that disease is prevalent throughout these camps, and food is very scarce. They brought back photographs, and Judy, it was so sad to see how thin people looked. I tried to imagine Stefan, my dark-haired, handsome friend, emaciated and ill. The thoughts haunt me. Please keep me and him in your thoughts and prayers. I'm trying not to let my mind wander too far on this.

Much love,
Hedy

August 15, 1943

Dear Hedy,

Thank goodness you finally got word where your friend is. I know your prayers can help it. He is also in my thoughts, and let's hope this war is over soon so these wonderful men can come back to us. Don't give up the faith, Hedy. Be strong, and I know you'll see your friend again soon.

We just had a successful mission with one of our inventions. Another advancement to help the Allies. I have been spurred on by the success to do even more to end this horrendous war!

Here is the answer to your riddle. It took me a little longer than usual and I might never have got to it but for a conversation with a physicist with a passion for astronomy.

Uranus' moons—Ariel, Umbriel, Titania, and Oberon— are all named by John Herschel, the son of the man who discovered Uranus. He named them after characters from

English literature. Oberon and Titania are fairies from William Shakespeare's A Midsummer Night's Dream. *Umbriel, a gnome, and Ariel, a sylph, are both from Alexander Pope's "The Rape of the Lock."*

It took me a little while to get back to it, I've been rather busy with my work, but it was a fun distraction. Thank you.

Much love,
Judy

Chapter Thirty-Nine

A few weeks later, Finnegan came into the lab to inform Tom and Judy that, because of their outstanding work on Window, they'd been recommended for another project, working out in America. Judy smiled inwardly; she had been into Finnegan's office unbeknown to Tom and asked that he assign them to something bigger. She had continued to hound him regularly and instead of his usual put-downs of her he had appeared to diminish before her eyes. Now he was here with this offer. Proving the adage that the only way to defeat a bully was to stand up to him.

"Can't give you many details," he noted gruffly, "but they asked for you personally, Jenkins."

"And Judy?" enquired Tom.

"Yes, of course, and Judy," he said flatly, without giving her eye contact, almost as if he was a little intimidated by her. "You'll be briefed on it when you get there, but we need you to help us win the war. And now the Americans are in, at least there'll be money behind our projects."

They weren't given long to pack their house and get things ready. Fortunately, they managed to rent it out to a friend of theirs, though sadly because his own home had been destroyed in a bombing.

*

Within a few weeks they were on their way. This was the first time that Tom had ever been on a ship and he was in awe. He hardly wanted to sleep because he wanted to investigate everything, wanting to know how everything worked. To Judy's dismay, he would drag her around the decks at all times of the day and night, showing her different things he'd found with great enthusiasm, even getting a tour from the captain at one point.

They had been greeted from the ship in New York Harbor like English heroes by American government officials, American flags flying everywhere. Even a little band to greet them and other British diplomats arriving.

Hardly sleeping on the train from the East Coast, Tom made all sorts of friends on the trip down, utterly swept up by their American exuberance.

"It feels very different from all the worry and the dark, dank streets of England that we just left," he mused to Judy over breakfast on the train. "Quite an adventure really," he added with a grin.

"Well, to be fair, they haven't lived through a war for four years," responded Judy. "I'm a little worried I might miss my home and life."

As they descended from the train in California, the sun was hot and bright.

Tom particularly was overwhelmed by the heat, especially in his shirt and tie. Judy realized as soon as they had worked out how to get about she would need to get her husband some cooler clothes.

"We're sure grateful for your help," said the American who greeted them in San Francisco. He was a tall man with a head of bleached blond hair and a row of perfect white teeth who pumped Tom's hand enthusiastically. "I've sorted out your accommodation. I'll take you there now. We like to take good care of our guests," he said with a smile. "You have a lovely little house waiting for you, just outside Berkeley, close to where you will be working."

He placed Tom and Judy in the car, something called a Buick, which was huge and they sat hovering close together somewhere in the center looking around them in bewilderment. The driver was chatty all the way there, and Judy had to listen very carefully to understand him as his accent was very strong. He drove them to a gated community that he informed them had been selected for the visiting scientists in the area.

When the car drew to a stop outside their new home, Judy couldn't believe her eyes. The "lovely little house" was enormous. A vast blue ranch-style dwelling, spread across a lot that they could have got half of their street in back home. Tom looked at the driver in surprise.

"Will we be sharing this with somebody else?" he asked in disbelief.

"Oh no, sir. This is all yours. As I said, we like to take care of people over here." He helped them in with their bags and placed them inside the hall as Tom stood in the enormous open-plan living room, looking around.

"Good grief, Judy," he whispered as the driver was turning on their utilities, "if you need a grand piano, we've got room for it now."

"I don't play the piano," Judy hissed back, laughing and shaking her head.

"Have you ever seen anything so large in your life? I'm going to lose you in this place." He chuckled.

Judy felt overwhelmed and imagined she would be cleaning forever.

The driver excused himself and was gone, but let them know on the way out the door that their refrigerator and cupboards were already stocked for them and his wife had put a pot roast, whatever that was, in the oven to warm.

It turned out to be a joint of beef in a stew and they settled down to enjoy something they hadn't eaten for a long time because of the rationing, before going to bed early.

The next morning, the same beaming American arrived to pick them up at 7 a.m.

"We like to start early here," he informed them, in a somewhat chirpy manner that gave the impression that he'd already been awake for hours, himself.

Tom and Judy, who were not used to starting work before 9 a.m. and still recovering from the large meal, shuffled out to his car. As they drove through the Berkeley streets, Tom chatted about his desire to get a car as soon as possible as Judy attempted to come to terms with her new life. Everything about it seemed unreal. To have come from England to this strange new world seemed unbelievable. It was one thing to be here on holiday, another to move here and live.

Arriving at the University of California, Judy looked out on the sprawling campus of buildings.

"I'm going to drop you here at the main office," their driver informed them as he pulled the car to a stop. "You need to get badged up and get security clearance. You're working over in the Rad Lab."

Tom nodded, but Judy barely understood what he was saying. Though she guessed the Rad Lab was short for radiation laboratory.

They made their way inside the main building to a vast desk where numerous secretaries were already hard at work—the clatter of typewriters filling the air.

A beaming young lady under a low hanging banner that read "Welcome Desk" looked up to greet them. "Welcome to Berkeley. How may I help you?" she trilled in a perky, upbeat manner.

Judy couldn't help thinking back to the first time that she'd arrived at the Cavendish, and the way that she'd been greeted by Finnegan. Tom approached the counter.

"Mr. and Mrs. Jenkins. We've come here to work, from England."

The woman raised an eyebrow as Tom continued, "Something about the Rad Lab?"

Her face registered understanding.

"Scientists, I'm guessing," she said with a curl of her crimson lips. "Hey, Charlie," she shouted to a young man in an open-necked shirt with short-cropped hair and black round glasses, who was sitting across the room. "Will you take Mr. and Mrs. Jenkins over to the badge room? They are going to need clearance."

Charlie nodded, and, stashing a pencil behind his ear, he jogged over to greet them, beaming. Everyone was so cheerful, it was a little unnerving. "Follow me," he encouraged them.

Tom and Judy followed behind, trying to take it all in as he trotted across the campus, giving them a tour and a potted history of the university.

Arriving at what was apparently the badge room, Charlie hung over a desk chatting to one of the secretaries while another jolly woman led them into an inner office, where an official-looking man checked their passports and asked them numerous questions to vet them before creating identification cards for Tom and Judy to wear.

"Top clearance needed here. It's all quite hush-hush what's going on over at the Rad Lab," Charlie informed them, as they left the building. "I believe you guys are gonna be working on something top secret for the war, something no one's allowed to know about."

They followed their guide back across the campus, until they arrived at a building set apart and surrounded by the American military. At the entrance, Charlie bade them goodbye with a wave. "Make your way inside. Someone will greet you in there and look after you."

Tom nodded his thanks.

Walking to the main door, they showed their passes and, accompanied by a rather large Marine, were escorted inside to one of the main offices.

Knocking on the door, Tom and Judy entered and were surprised to see a familiar face.

Judy recognized him straight away. She had known him at university; he had come from Adelaide to work under Ernest Rutherford as well. Also, he'd been at the Cavendish for a short time.

Mark Oliphant had turned from the window he had been looking out of and broke into a wide smile when he saw them.

"Bless my soul," exclaimed Tom, "I didn't know we'd be meeting you here, Mark."

"I was the one who requested you," he said as he leaned forward to shake Tom's hand warmly, his Australian accent still strong. "I told Finnegan, send me the best. And if the Jenkinses are still there, I want them." He pumped Judy's hand too.

"The last we heard of you, you'd gone to the University of Birmingham," she added, bewildered.

"Yep. I was there for a while, but then they sent me out here. I've got a little project going on that we need you two for."

"So what exactly are you doing here at Berkeley?" asked Tom.

"Afraid I can't tell you all of it, Tom. Even I know very little. Things are kept very hush-hush, in case we get infiltrated by the enemy. Work packages are being separated out all over the country. I know that because I get to talk to so many different people and hear all the different accents. But it's something big; I know that. What we'd like you and Judy to do is work on isotope separation." This was a way to produce enriched uranium that made it a purer element. Mark continued, "That's what I've already been doing here. Also, I might need Judy's help with the ongoing development of nuclear fission. I know you scored high marks when you were at university." He grinned. "I think you actually beat me in most of my classes."

Judy smiled back. It was so refreshing to be with someone who seemed to appreciate her skills and didn't treat her like a second-class citizen.

He gave them a short tour of the lab they would be working in, and they were overwhelmed by the extent and size of it, the up-to-date equipment, and the relaxed and friendly manner of all the staff, which was so refreshing.

It was then Judy realized how much stress they'd been under back in England with the war. At least here, she'd get a chance to work without that constant pressure. Also, maybe with this fresh start, she and Tom would get an opportunity to put some of the anger and sadness of the last couple of years behind them. And there was one more reason she was glad to be in California. She had wired Hedy and now she would be able to spend much more time with her best friend.

Chapter Forty

Fall 1943

Judy sat at the restaurant table eating her dinner, and she could tell that her friend was nervous. Hedy had barely touched her food and was chain-smoking and talking rapidly. Even with the years in Hollywood, where her accent had become less pronounced, whenever she was nervous, she sounded much more Austrian. Judy had to listen carefully to understand what her friend was saying.

All at once, Hedy reached forward and took Judy's hand. "Do you think I'm doing the right thing getting married again? I'm hoping because John's European—did I mention he's British like you and Tom?—that it will be different this time. Also, he works in movies as an actor. Surely that will make a difference. I'd have preferred to wait a little bit longer, but he has a new movie coming up with Bette Davis, and he wants time to prepare. And, of course, we want to go on our honeymoon. He wants to take me to Big Bear. Don't you think that will be divine?"

Judy nodded, knowing it was a lake in the mountains.

Hedy sat back in her chair and let out a long, slow breath. "Oh gosh, I can't believe I'm getting married again, I'm so worried. I don't want to make another mistake. Can you believe this will be my third?"

"There's one thing you're not saying," said Judy, putting down her fork. "Do you love him? Do you love this man?"

Hedy's expression softened. "I do. But sometimes I think, Judy, maybe I fall in love too easily. I fall in love for both of us. Because all I want to be is loved. It's times like this I miss my darling Stefan. I know he couldn't love me physically how I'd want him to. But I always felt he loved me unconditionally."

Judy looked at her friend's beautiful face. Everybody in the world wanted to love her, but was it just her beauty that beguiled them? Did anyone want to love who she really was?

"I want love like you have with Tom, that kind of passionate love," Hedy continued.

Judy smiled to herself and thought of her sweet, awkward-looking husband. Passionate wouldn't have been her first choice of words to describe him. Kind, thoughtful, caring, maybe? How would he feel if he knew that Hedy Lamarr was making him out to be some sort of Valentino?

"Your life is different," reiterated Judy, shaking her head. "Your world moves so fast. It's very different from mine, so I think it's important that you take the time."

All at once, someone sauntered across to their table, a hand tucked in his pocket, a cigarette between his lips. It was George Antheil. "Well, if it isn't the beautiful Hedy, the bride-to-be. I thought you'd be home getting your beauty sleep."

"George, darling," she said, standing to her feet and kissing him on both cheeks. "Join us for a drink. This is Judy, I told you about her."

"Your fellow inventor," he said, his eyes lighting up and shaking her hand. "I would be delighted."

He pulled up a chair and sat on it backwards, his cigarette balanced in the corner of his mouth, blue smoke twirling up and creasing his eyes. "Are you two inventing something fabulous to put Hitler out of business?"

"We were talking about love."

"Ah," said George, leaning back. "The elusive love. Are you sure about that cad, John? Are you sure you can tame his wild ways?"

"Oh, you rogue," said Hedy, grabbing his hand. "He wants to settle down, the two of us both do."

"Are you sure John is the right person for you?" he continued. "Don't you want someone who's more intellectually stimulating?"

"I want someone who is faithful," responded Hedy sharply. "I want someone who will be there for me, not like my last husband, nor someone crazy like my first husband. I want somebody easygoing, and John… I love that he's so easygoing."

"Well, hopefully, you know what you're doing," he said. "May I kiss the bride for good luck?"

"You may," she said.

He leaned forward and kissed her on the lips. All at once, a flashbulb went off right behind them.

"Great. The press is here," he groaned. "God knows what Boski will say and what they'll say tomorrow on your wedding day. Sorry, darling." He got up, shook Judy's hand, and rushed away.

Hedy ran her fingers through her hair. "You don't think they'll make a thing about this, do you? The last thing I want is a big fuss tomorrow."

"I don't know," said Judy. "This is all new to me."

After they had dinner, they made their way back to the hotel, where Hedy would be having her wedding the next day, right there in the middle of the Bel-Air Hotel.

"I really should get some sleep," Hedy said to her friend, as she kissed her on both cheeks and made her way back to her room.

Judy also went back to her room on the other side of the hotel, walking past the main bar. She could see that John Loder, the groom-to-be, was already there, looking a little worse for wear, with a group of guys laughing and joking. She hoped he deserved her friend. More than anything, Hedy deserved love in her life.

On her way upstairs, she happened to notice the outside ceremony being set up. It was beautiful. In the middle of the palm court, white chairs and tables were being placed outside, and lilies were already being put out to decorate the place they would get married.

Judy couldn't wait to go to bed. She still didn't understand why Hedy had not had some sort of hen night with her movie friends, but had chosen to spend the time with Judy, instead. Sometimes she wondered if she was the only real friend Hedy had in her life, and it made her sad. For someone so popular to the world, she didn't seem to have many people close to her.

She arrived back at the room and put her key in the lock, and as she entered, Tom was already in bed reading his book. He placed his bookmark in it, took off his reading glasses, and smiled at his wife.

"Well, how was your night?" he asked. "Mine was a little unusual."

"Did you spend time with the groom?"

"For about an hour, before it all got a bit too much for me. He commandeered the bar, at one point taking over the piano and singing a raucous collection of songs, none of which I knew. There were lots of slick movie star types, and I wished we went to the movies so I'd know all the famous people I've been hobnobbing with. But on the whole, it was as crazy as what we've seen of this world so far. Sometimes I wonder how we got mixed up in all of this."

Judy shook her head. "Even though Hedy is a movie star, she's still a warm, kind person deep down. She's so intelligent, it scares me sometimes. I wonder if she hadn't been so beautiful, if she wouldn't have been able to pursue a different type of career."

Tom nodded as Judy went into the bathroom to get herself ready for bed. As she went to sleep that night, she thought about George Antheil's words, and she wondered about John. Was he the right man for Hedy? He seemed rather a cad, gallivanting around and getting drunk the night before their wedding.

*

The next day, Tom showed Judy the headlines as they were having their breakfast. The photograph with George was all over the front of the paper, Hedy's lips just leaving his, her looking into his eyes. Emblazoned over the top, a provocative headline about whether they were having a secret affair. This wasn't going to be good for Hedy.

She went up to find her friend in her room. Hedy was furious, pacing in front of her mirror, the newspaper in her hand. "Did you read this, Judy? Did you see what they said about me? I can't believe them, damn reporters and their gutter press."

Judy knew she needed to calm her friend down; she had such a fiery temper and she didn't want it to spoil Hedy's special day. She used her most soothing tone, the one she used to tame angry dogs and to reassure frightened children. "Surely John won't believe it."

Hedy pulled a cigarette from a packet and Judy noticed her friend's hand was shaking with rage as she lit it. "He won't even see me. It's bad luck to see the groom, remember? But I heard from one of my bridesmaids that he's really upset about it. He's already started drinking at ten this morning."

Judy didn't want to say what was in her mind: *I don't think he finished drinking from the night before.*

"I'm not even sure there should be a wedding today!"

Judy took hold of Hedy gently by the shoulders. "Listen to me, Hedy, you love this man and he loves you. You can't let other people get in the way of that. Tomorrow this will be old news, and you will be a happy bride off on your honeymoon. Why don't you think about that instead?"

Judy felt Hedy's shoulder relax in her grip. "You're right of course," her friend responded as tears of frustration glistened in her eyes. "I'm so glad you here; you are always the voice of reason for me."

As Hedy crushed the cigarette she had barely smoked into the ashtray, Judy continued to reassure her.

"It's going to be fine, Hedy," she said, coming up and holding her friend's hand. "You've just got to focus on getting married.

He'll realize what it's all about. You and George have been friends for years. Come on, you don't want to cry. You'll spoil your lovely makeup. And look at how beautiful you look." She turned her friend to look in the mirror. She looked absolutely stunning in a figure-hugging cream dress with Chantilly lace, a provocative slit up the back. Her hair was coiffed into a beautiful style, a stunning cream orchid pinned up on one side, and her makeup was flawless. "It's your wedding day. Enjoy it. Don't let something like a newspaper headline stop you from doing this, because for all that you know, you'll never even remember this moment. It's a stupid little thing. Just put your shoulders back and go down and get married."

When the time came, Judy went down ahead and slipped into the aisle beside Tom, who leaned over and whispered into her ear, "I think the groom is drunk."

"He must have read the newspaper," said Judy.

"Well, at least he's here; I was worried after last night," said Tom, looking down over his glasses as he read the order of service.

As they looked around the congregation, she actually recognized some of the movie stars. Cary Grant was there, Bette Davis, of course, everybody knew, and many other people she imagined were producers.

When the music started, the bride floated down the aisle, and she looked gorgeous. Hedy smiled broadly, playing the role of a bride, and sauntered toward the front without a hair out of place. They carried on with the service, and Judy wondered why she hadn't incorporated any of her Jewish roots. Then she wondered again if Hedy had told anybody else that she was Jewish apart from her. She seemed to be very circumspect about it. It was a strange time to be Jewish, even in Hollywood.

It was a beautiful wedding. White calla lilies scented the air, and when the groom kissed the bride, everything seemed to be forgiven. Tom and Judy followed the crowd to the wedding breakfast. The bride and groom were leaving quickly, as both John and Hedy had film contracts coming up.

As she and Tom stepped onto the dance floor, joining the bride and the groom after their first dance, he leaned in to talk to his wife. "Do you think they're going to make it if they're always filming in different places? He doesn't even work for the same studios as she does."

"We'd have been all right if we'd had to do that occasionally, wouldn't we? Although theirs is a strange life," Judy admitted. "But let's hope it works. They're in love. Love can always find a way."

But though she said these reassuring words to Tom, honestly, Judy just wasn't sure. Because she couldn't help feeling that if Hedy's heart was broken one more time, she might never recover.

Chapter Forty-One

John and Hedy finally got away on their honeymoon for a few days in the San Bernardino Mountains. They'd booked a little wood cabin close to Big Bear Lake, and Hedy looked forward to leaving behind the world of Hollywood, not to mention the ongoing war, where news only grew graver by the day.

As they drove higher and higher into the mountains, John whistled a happy tune as she rolled down the window and let the fresh air blow into the car. She shook out her dark curls and closed her eyes. She had changed into casual slacks and a cream blouse and had refused to wear makeup for the whole trip away. With the sun on her fresh, clean face and the smell of the pine trees, she could almost be back in Vienna. The mountains here weren't that much different than the ones she'd come from.

Hedy reached over and grabbed her groom's hand. "This is heavenly, darling," she purred. "The best time we could ever have, and the best honeymoon I could ever want. Thank you for arranging it."

He smiled his crooked smile and asked her for a cigarette. She pulled out her gold case, flicked it open, and pulled out cigarettes for them both. Lighting them, she passed one to him and then inhaled deeply the heady blue smoke. She already felt relaxed. The beauty and the stillness were working its charm on her, reminding her that deep in her heart, she was a simple girl. Hollywood was a rat race. Though she loved what she did, sometimes it just didn't feel real. Whereas this felt real, anything that reminded her of her past and took her back to her life before, in Austria.

They wound their way around the mountain until the road became barely wider than a goat trail, and John slowed down as they bumped along the unfamiliar path. Hedy stared at the little map and tried to guide him as best she could. They pulled into a driveway and, at the end of the dirt road, arrived in a clearing where a delightful log cabin greeted them, enveloped in morning sunshine. It had a cedar wraparound deck and a red-shingled roof where two windows blinked out, covered by a thin veil of moss. Two wooden snow skis had been nailed to the log walls as decoration, and in front of the door, a chainsaw carving of a bear, its paw extended in a wave, welcomed them.

John pulled the car to a stop, and they stepped outside. As he dealt with their luggage, Hedy strolled around to the back of the house, stood on the deck, and looked out at the incredible view of the lake. There was no one else for miles. The smell of juniper and pine trees scented the air as they reflected off the water, which was a deep azure blue, shimmering under the morning light. It was as still as a mill pond, the surf not even breaking around rocks on the water. But what she loved most was the silence. Hedy closed her eyes to drink it in. There was nothing but the sound of a lazy bee that bounced around the deck and a symphony of cicada chirrups drifting up from the woodlands.

She slipped her arms around her new husband, who appeared on the deck with their suitcases.

"I could get used to this," she crooned, pulling him in and kissing him passionately on the lips.

"I could get used to *that*," John remarked, the lilt of his British accent sounding sexy to Hedy.

They moved inside the humble cabin. Everything was rustic, but clean. A simple woven mat on the floor laid over bare planks and honey-colored logs stacked atop one another to create the walls. In the corner, a black cast-iron fire stove shone with polish and was already lit, adding warmth to the cool interior. As their eyes adjusted, Hedy noticed in the center of the room that a table was laid with a red-and-white checked tablecloth and a welcome note was placed against a vase of fresh wildflowers. Hedy read it out to John as he took their luggage into the tiny bedroom.

"It's from the wife of the man you rented it from," she called back to him. "She says there is butter and milk in the larder and a shop just down the road we can walk to for any other supplies."

John threw the suitcases onto the bed, and Hedy opened the window in the main room, which looked out onto the lake. John came and stood beside her, leaning on the frame, breathing in deeply the fresh scent of water mingled with the pine.

"Hard to believe we're still in California, isn't it?" he remarked.

"We should think of finding somewhere more rural to live when we return to Hollywood," she added. "Neither of us are party people and I love this."

"Anything you want," he whispered to her as he brushed her lips with another kiss.

As she stood next to her new husband, part of her just wanted to take him into the bedroom right away, but part of her didn't want to waste a minute.

She noticed there was a hammock out in the garden that she would take advantage of later and a little table for them to eat at outside. Heading into the kitchen, Hedy started unpacking the box of supplies John had brought in and carefully unwrapped a chicken she had brought with her. She wasn't the best cook but she wanted to eat simply for the whole five days, and at least attempt cooking every night for John. As she emptied the bags, her heart sank just a little to see the six bottles of Scotch John had brought with them. She knew he had another couple of bottles in the trunk of the car. She hid them at the back of the cupboard. Without the ongoing stress of their work, and if she kept him entertained enough, maybe he would forget about drinking while he was here.

John continued to amuse himself by pulling out and inspecting his fishing poles and checking his bait. Hedy was busy rearranging the kitchen when there was a knock at the door.

Pulling it open, John acknowledged their visitor, the owner, Mr. Bates. A stooped, older man with skin like elephant hide walked inside smiling at them both, and Hedy noticed one of his front teeth was missing.

"Welcome to Big Bear," he muttered as he shambled into the center of the room. Removing his worn hat, he placed it respectfully against his chest. "Hope you folks enjoy yourselves. Did you find the groceries in the larder?" Hedy nodded as he continued. "My wife made sure you were all stocked up. She said to remind you that there were spices and flour in the cupboards as well. If you're missing anything, there is Mrs. Burke's shop and we're just a mile down the road in a little wood cabin, with a green door. Anything else you folks need?"

"I would love to know how to work the stove," responded Hedy, staring at the simple, metal, wood-burning stove in the corner of the kitchen. "How do I know when it's at the right temperature? I'm hoping to cook a chicken for our dinner."

The man shuffled over to the stove and stared at it.

"Well," he said, scratching his head. "It's quite simple, really. You open the door. You light the wood. You'll wait for a bit. If you put your hand inside and it burns, then it's time to put your chicken in."

Hedy smirked at John, who just nodded. "I guess that a burned hand is about four hundred degrees, then?"

Their joke went over the head of the older man, who just nodded at John and then took him outside to show him where the canoe was and any of the other gear he might need while he was there fishing.

Hedy automatically started to move furniture around in the cabin. It was something she always did to settle herself and feel at home, even when she was staying overnight in a hotel. Once she had the cabin the way she liked it, she decided she would probably head off down the road to the little store.

"I hope you're not going to be too bored if I end up on the lake fishing," John said as she came to find him. The sleeves of his shirt were rolled up and a cigarette dangled from the corner of his mouth as he hooked one of his lines.

"Are you kidding?" she responded. "I love nature. I just want to lie under this tree here in that hammock and smell the flowers. All I need in my life is music and nature, and I'm a very happy woman."

"I hope that list includes me," responded John, with a smirk.

"And of course, you too, darling," she said, throwing her arms around his neck and kissing him again.

"Well, that worked," he stated, throwing down his rod. "Forget fishing."

"No, no, no," she said, pulling herself out of his arms. "I need to get something ready for dinner. You go down to the lake and check it out. I'm going to walk to Mrs. Burke's and get us all stocked up."

She slipped on her sandals and her sunglasses and moved with ease down the road. On the way, the sounds of nature echoed all around her. The smell and the quiet and the peace continued to smooth her feathers, bringing her heart into a place of calm, something she hadn't experienced for a long time.

"Just down the road" turned out to be about a mile and a half, but Hedy didn't care. She had a basket with her that she'd found in the cottage and was looking forward to puttering around a little store.

When she arrived, a hand-painted sign on the wall informed her she was at Mrs. Burke's Store, and the screen door, ancient with peeling, white paint, slapped shut behind her as she entered. A tiny bell heralded her arrival, and the smell of earthy root vegetables, ripe fruit, and apple pie greeted her. Inside, a plumpish lady with reddened cheeks and gray, wiry hair, wearing a flowery apron, was stacking shelves in the corner.

She nodded to Hedy and Hedy nodded back.

"Are you here on holiday?" the woman enquired, dusting off her hands and making her way back to the counter.

"Uh huh," said Hedy. "Just getting stocked up. We're staying at Bear Cottage, just down the road."

"Nice place," the older woman mused. "Very nice, the Bateses."

Hedy was noticing something straight away. People here didn't automatically recognize her; neither the cabin's owner nor this shopkeeper had. There was something about living in Hollywood where people expected to see movie stars, and so she got recognized all the time. Out here, without makeup, wearing her slacks and sunglasses, nobody seemed to know who she was, and she liked it that way.

She puttered around the store and bought some cornbread, some more fresh eggs, and a little local bacon, to cook for John's breakfast in the morning. She squeezed a fresh loaf of bread and it felt soft and was still warm; the shopkeeper assured her it had been baked that morning. She also threw in some homemade cookies, strawberry jam, and fresh vegetables she fished out of big wooden barrels in the corner. As she approached the counter, the older woman wasn't in a rush to serve. She folded her arms and leaned over her counter, telling Hedy all about the best places to visit on the lake, where to see the birds at this time of the year, and offered her a map of the area, which Hedy bought.

Walking back, the mile and a half felt a little longer, with the heat of the day starting to bear down on her and her heavy shopping basket. But she still felt joy. This was going to be better. Her marriage to John was going to be the right one. Finally, she was happy. She had what she had always wanted, a husband to love her just for who she was. When she arrived back at the cabin she chose to ignore the half-empty bottle of Scotch. He was tense; they both were. A few good months of marriage and she knew he would drink less, she was sure of it.

When Hedy looked back on her honeymoon in the years to come, part of her wished she and John had been able to stay in that little mountain oasis forever, because nothing could have prepared her for the heartache that lay ahead.

Chapter Forty-Two

June 1944

The Manhattan Project, as it was called, was now in full swing and Judy and Tom were settled in California. Over in Europe the Allies had just successfully invaded France during what was being called the D-Day landings. With great pride Judy and Tom were informed that Judy's invention, chaff, had been used during the invasion in Operation Taxable to create a phantom force of ships in the Dover Strait to deceive the enemy. Also, as London was again under attack by the Germans' new V-1 flying bombs, the proximity fuse they had developed was being used daily to shoot them down.

This bolstered their effort to continue to work in their top-secret environment on a device to detect radioactivity. Judy was also involved in producing enriched uranium as a new material. But even though they were given all the assistance they needed for the development of their experiments, neither they, nor any of their peers in the lab knew what the final use of it would be for.

The best part of being in California was that Judy and Hedy could get together more often, though. Judy would frequently travel down on the train Friday night to stay for the weekends, starting with a long-standing lunch date on Saturday mornings when Hedy wasn't filming. They would meet at a sweet little diner off Hollywood Boulevard, and Hedy would always wear sunglasses and a hat to make her way there so she wouldn't be recognized. Though, inevitably, one or two people would still find her, even in the seclusion of the booth at the back.

One particular Saturday, Judy could tell that something was on Hedy's mind. They met as usual and fell quickly into conversation, but she was aware there was an excitement about her friend. Judy was starting her tuna melt, and Hedy was toying with a salad when she put her knife and fork down.

"Judy, I have something to tell you." Judy looked up and smiled, and Hedy continued, "I'm going to have a baby, a brother or sister for James."

What Judy wanted to do was be happy for her friend, hug her, and congratulate her. What she found happening in her body was the opposite. Her stomach cramped. Her chest tightened. The breath caught in her throat, along with a lump that she forced down. She tried to anchor the back of her jaw to stop herself from releasing the brimming emotion making its way through her body. She forced a smile onto her face and hoped to goodness it wasn't a grimace.

"That's wonderful," she said, her voice tight and high-pitched. She tried to hide her evident emotion by grabbing her friend's hand and squeezing it tightly.

If Hedy noticed, she didn't say anything. Instead she went into a full-on list of all she was planning and what was going on. And Judy did everything to control how she was feeling. As she listened to her friend talk about her pregnancy that was just over three months along, she felt the pain come back like a sharp stab in her stomach that carved out her insides. Particularly when Hedy was blasé about continuing to work and not getting her sleep because she'd been out with her co-stars the night before. Judy wanted to shake her and tell her to lie down and not move.

When enough time had passed that she could excuse herself, Judy made her way to the bathroom as quickly as she could. She controlled her trembling chin as she pushed her way into a stall and sat down on the seat, putting her hand over her mouth to silence any sobs; she dry-heaved, the pain coming up from her stomach and rolling through her body, making her shoulders shake as she gasped for breath.

She didn't understand why she was having such a strange reaction. Other people in her life had become pregnant since she'd lost her own, but because of Hedy and how close their friendship was, this stung her somehow. She also found herself feeling jealous. She'd never been that kind of a person. She always thought everybody was entitled to whatever they had. But right now, more than anything, she wanted to hold a child in her arms. She wanted to be the one saying she was pregnant, and she wondered cruelly what kind of a life the child would have in Hollywood.

Judy could give it a better life.

She pushed away her thoughts. She had to pull herself together. This was her best friend; no matter what she was feeling, she had to find the joy and happiness that was right. Stepping out of the stall, Judy splashed her face with cold water. Combing her fingers through her hair, she made her way back to the booth. Hedy had finished her salad and was smoking a cigarette.

"You've hardly touched your lunch, Judy. Are you feeling okay?"

Judy lied, "I had a large breakfast, and I ordered way too much food. They do give us too much food in America, don't you think?"

Hedy nodded. "That's why I always order a salad," she said as she drew in blue smoke and let it twirl through her nostrils.

Somehow Judy managed to make it through the rest of lunch, and cried all the way home on the train. She wanted to get it out because the last thing she wanted to do was talk to Tom about this. Their mutual pain had been hard enough, and they'd just started to rebuild their relationship. The last thing she wanted to do was move them back into the pain and the loss. But he still noticed something later when he came to pick her up from the station.

"Your eyes look red, love. Are you okay?"

"Oh, I'm just tired," she said. "You and I have been working so hard."

Tom nodded but didn't look convinced.

*

Five months later the engraved announcement card came in the post with Judy's invitation to a celebration of Hedy's pregnancy. Judy's stomach tightened at the thought. She'd have to sit through two hours of people talking about babies, and as happy as she was for Hedy, it still felt raw for her.

She arrived at Hedgerow Farm the following weekend with a knitted matinee coat that she'd managed to buy in white. She'd been friends with Hedy for years now, but as close as they'd been, she'd never really been around Hedy's work friends, socially, the Hollywood stars. Inside, it was like entering into a different world. Everybody was glamorous and poised, wearing the latest fashion. Tom had talked her into getting a new dress for the occasion. She felt positively daring in a plunging neckline and a skirt almost to her knees. But inside this house, she looked positively dowdy next to everybody else. Everybody moved and glided around the room with such ease. Everybody spoke in a strange, forced way, as if they were all saying lines in a movie—lots of "Hello, darling," as they air-kissed one another and seemed to pretend to interact.

Hedy came to find her and threw her arms around her friend. "I'm so glad you could make it, Judy. It just wouldn't have been the same without you."

Judy smiled and looked around all these people that she was with. She'd never felt more out of place in her life.

They settled down around the pool to open gifts. And if she thought just being with these people was strange, when they started to converse with one another, it was definitely as though she was on a different planet. She began to lose count of how many times everyone had been married, and everybody's husband seemed to be sleeping with other women. The conversation was vapid and pretentious, and she started to squirm in her seat as Hedy opened gift after gift with people saying things like, "Just a little something I bought when I was in Tiffany's," or "I had the wool flown in from Scotland for that." The sensible matinee coat she'd bought at a department store felt ridiculous. But Hedy didn't let it show when she opened it, telling her friend how gorgeous it was.

Everybody drank way too much, and nobody seemed to eat anything. Judy tried to nibble on hors d'oeuvres and caviar, something she never imagined she would ever taste. Most of them were drinking champagne, but Judy had settled for an orange juice and she felt invisible. That was only confirmed for her when halfway through, one of the women came up and asked Judy to fetch her coat. She must have taken her for the housekeeper. Judy explained quietly that she was here as a guest, and after looking her up and down the woman plastered a smile on her face.

"Do forgive me," she purred, "I don't believe we've met before. Irene Dunne," she said, offering a thin white hand with polished red nails. Judy shook it.

By the end of the afternoon, Judy was drained. Her head spun with the conversation and the food and the drink. Even though she'd only had a little champagne to toast the baby, it had been a surreal experience for her.

She was exhausted by the time she got in a taxi on the way home from the train station, not wishing to disturb Tom's day. All the smiling and pretentiousness had worn her down. Judy made her way into the front room. Tom was sitting under a light reading the newspaper. Dear, sweet Tom. She suddenly felt so grateful for her husband. Going over to him, she approached him from behind and put her arms around his neck.

"Crikey!" he exclaimed in shock, not having seen her come in.

She giggled. "Tom, I'm so glad that you're my husband."

Tom chuckled as he folded his newspaper into his lap and removed his glasses. "I thought some handsome Hollywood star might've swept you off your feet, and here you are back to rough it with me."

"Tom, I am so glad. I am so happy for my dependable, trustworthy, faithful husband."

He quirked an eyebrow. "You make me sound like a sheepdog."

She started to chuckle in turn. "I've just seen the other side of life. And I can tell you, I'm glad we are who we are."

"Are you hungry?" he asked, getting up from his chair. "I could make you a cheese sandwich."

"Starving," she said. "I'm not even sure what I ate today."

Judy felt awkward as she sat down after her sandwich and looked out the window. She and Hedy were so different. Why did she even bother with her?

The telephone rang half an hour later, and when she picked it up, it was Hedy on the phone. "Judy, I just wanted to thank you so much for coming. It just wouldn't have been the same without having you there. Your matinee coat is so beautiful. I can't wait to see it on the baby. And I hope it wasn't too hard for you; there were so many people you didn't know."

Judy remembered what it had been like: all the women on the third and fourth husband slipping in and out of characters. Going from a femme fatale to a mysterious lover as they all chain-smoked.

"It was lovely," she lied. "Thank you so much for inviting me."

"I'm glad you enjoyed it. Now I can't wait. I was also hoping," Hedy continued, "I know this is early, but I was hoping that you and Tom could be godparents to the child."

Judy felt her chin start to quiver again and forced out the words, "That would be wonderful. I'll talk to Tom about it." And then she put down the phone and, rolling her shoulders back, she cleared her throat and went into the kitchen where Tom was buttering bread.

When she told him, she saw the pain cross his face only for a second before he smiled and said, "What a lovely thought. I would be honored."

Judy nodded and made her way upstairs. Once Tom had gone to sleep, she let the tears flow freely, the tears that she'd been holding back all day. Why was life so bloody unfair?

Chapter Forty-Three

May 8, 1945

Judy was at home nursing a head cold when Tom rushed through the door clutching a newspaper in his hand. She'd been lying on the sofa taking a nap when she heard the door rattle. As he dashed into the living room, she looked up in surprise. It was barely two o'clock in the afternoon. Why was Tom home so early from work? She could tell by the look on his face that something important had happened. Sitting up slowly in order not to provoke her headache, she tried to understand what was going on.

"It's over! In England, Judy, it's over!" Tom was shaking his head, and for a minute, she saw tears in the corners of his eyes.

He didn't seem to be able to say anything more and merely handed her the newspaper. In big, bold letters across the front were the words:

VICTORY IN EUROPE. HITLER SURRENDERS.

She couldn't believe it. She took a minute to digest what she was reading as Tom made his way across the room to put the radio on. President Truman was getting ready to address the nation, and a very excited reporter was talking about the different celebrations going on around the world.

Tom sat down on the sofa and grabbed her hand. He didn't even take off his coat and hat as they both sat and listened. The president came on the radio. It was his sixty-first birthday, and the United States flags were still at half-mast everywhere to mark the passing of President Truman's beloved predecessor, Franklin D. Roosevelt, a few weeks earlier.

The new president gave a very rousing speech, reminding them, "If I could give you a single watchword for the coming months, the word is work, work, and more work. We must work to finish the war. Our victory is only half over."

Tom reached and squeezed his wife's hand. They knew he was talking about the Japanese. And they both acknowledged the project they were working on. They'd discussed their suspicions that maybe the power of what they were working on could be used to threaten the Japanese into submission. She nodded her head.

After President Truman's speech was over, reporters started to talk about things that were happening all over the country and the world. Tom and Judy listened for hours, just sitting there drinking cups of tea and coffee and listening to everything being said, finding it hard to believe the war was finally over in their beloved home country.

The news reported on Churchill's speeches and the fact that King George VI wanted May 7th to be celebrated as VE Day, Victory in Europe. Eventually, he would compromise for his American allies and an official celebration would be declared on May 8th.

"We may allow ourselves a brief period of rejoicing," Churchill said, "but let us not forget for a moment the toil and effort that lies ahead. Japan, and all her treachery and greed, remains unsubdued. We must now devote all our strength and resources to completing our tasks, both at home and abroad. Advance, Britannia!"

Earlier in the afternoon at Buckingham Palace, King George VI, Queen Elizabeth, and Princesses Elizabeth—the future Queen Elizabeth II—and Margaret had been up on the balcony waving. There were also reports that Buckingham Palace was going to be lit by floodlights for the first time since 1939. A giant V of light was projected upon St. Paul's Cathedral, ending the darkness that had blackened London and the rest of Britain for nearly six years.

Just then, the telephone rang. Judy, almost completely forgetting about her headache, made her way to the phone and picked it up as she carried on listening to the radio.

It was Hedy. She was crying. "Judy, did you hear? Did you hear? We're free! Europe is free. We can now breathe a sigh of relief. I'm having a party this weekend; you can both stay if you want. I want you to come—you and Tom. And don't say you can't. I know you don't know anybody else over here. But we're Europeans; we must celebrate together. Come over and celebrate with me. I'm just having a few friends from work."

She made it sound like she had a regular job. Her few friends were probably going to be a list of celebrities that they only would have seen at the movie theaters.

"We'll be there," said Judy. Regardless, she wanted to be with her best friend.

On Friday, Tom got out his Sunday suit and whistled as he ironed his shirt. "I can't believe it, honey. I can't believe it. I'm so excited."

Taking a train to L.A., they took a taxi to Hedgerow Farm. They drove down the driveway, passing all the very expensive cars lined up on the way to the house. Going inside, the atmosphere was festive. Buntings was being flown of all different European colors, particularly Hedy's Austrian colors. And she'd already somehow managed to wrangle a band who were playing raucous war tunes and were in the midst of a rather jazzy version of "It's a Long Way to Tipperary."

Tom and Judy made their way into the front room where they were greeted by an already slightly drunk Hedy, who threw her arms around both of them.

"Isn't it wonderful!" she gushed.

She ushered them to the bar, where Clark Gable was pouring drinks. They tried not to draw attention to the fact they were both in awe as he asked them what they wanted.

"I'll have a sherry," said Judy.

"A sherry?" he said; the edge of his mouth twitched. "We've only got champagne on tap today. Champagne or hard liquor. Which will it be?"

"Well, I guess it'd be champagne, then," said Tom, answering for them both with great enthusiasm.

They took a glass each and made their way into the room. It was packed full of every type of creative-looking person, all speaking in excited tones.

She recognized a few, and the two of them hovered in a corner, Tom in his new lightweight church suit, the outfit that Judy had bought him since they had arrived. Still, they both felt inconspicuous as they always did.

All at once, Hedy tapped her glass and held it in the air.

"To victory!" she said. "And to my best friend Stefan coming home soon."

Judy knew he was still in the internment camp in Japan and she felt that now-familiar anger building in her. The righteous anger for this mad and awful war, which had sat just below her surface ever since her father's death. She also knew that was where the American government would be putting all their pressure now. Judy was determined to get the project to a place that would help pressure the Japanese. So why was she struck by a feeling of foreboding in her heart that she couldn't seem to shake?

*

When they returned to work on Monday, there was a lively energy in the lab. The victory in Europe had undoubtedly given them all a boost. Still, they were called into a meeting where they were informed that even though their European allies had managed to win their own victory, Japan was still a significant threat to the free world.

"I don't have to tell you," said their boss, "how important this project is. We'll continue to work toward a solution and only use what we are developing as a last resort, but we still need you to work even more diligently than you were before. The quicker we get a solution, the quicker we have our own victory. President Truman has already been in touch with our department, saying he wants us to up our production and work as many hours as we can to finalize what we need to do to get this project functional. So, I'm expecting all of you to do your part."

Tom and Judy went back to their lab and felt the intensity of what they were doing. The pressure was on now. All that was left between the world and peace was Japan. And all that was left between Hedy and her oldest friend being reunited was a victory there, but at what cost?

Chapter Forty-Four

July 10, 1945

They had been experiencing a heatwave their second summer in California when Tom and Judy were called into Mark's office early one morning. It wasn't unusual for them to have meetings with him, but they could both tell as soon as they entered the room that Mark had a restless energy about him, as, closing the door behind them, he encouraged them to sit at his desk.

"We need you both to get ready to leave," Mark stated, not beating about the bush. "You're going down to a test site to work on a secret operation connected to our project, Operation Trinity."

Tom looked at him in surprise and then at Judy.

"A test site, here?" he asked, knowing they didn't have many locally.

"You will fly down to New Mexico on a DC-3. We're going to be testing the gadget there."

Judy understood straight away "the gadget" was the code name for the thing they were all working on, and she felt a nagging concern about what they were all developing.

"New Mexico," said Tom, echoing his boss's words.

"It needs to be rather large for what we are anticipating. We'll need all your equipment and both you and Judy to be monitoring the radiation levels before and after the test."

Tom nodded. "You'll be going down this weekend, and that will give you time to set everything up down there before the test on Monday, July sixteenth."

Tom and Judy were on their way out the door when he said one last thing.

"I don't have to tell you both that this is secret, do I? I hope it goes without saying this is highly classified and you must not mention this to anyone. Please come to the office early; we're leaving at six in the morning. We'll drive you out to the airport and fly you down. You need to make sure your equipment's ready to go beforehand, and we'll get that packed up and sent off with you too."

Once they were alone, they discussed it between themselves. "The gadget is going to be used as a weapon, as I have feared, Tom, or why would we be going to a test site? I really want this war to be over; I don't want any more fighting. But I am scared, Tom, this could potentially be devasting, and not just to Japan."

Tom agreed. "It is concerning, I realize that, as radiation is such an unknown. I can only imagine what is possible."

The following Friday, they were both packed up and ready to go and made their way onto the DC-3. Tom, once again, was in his element. This was the first time he'd been in an airplane, though there was no luxury such as Judy had seen on the flying boat. This was purely military, and they were strapped into seats that lined the sides of the aircraft.

On board it was deafening, and it buzzed and vibrated as it flew. Arriving in New Mexico, they were met by a military escort who took them to the place they'd be staying, a base camp ten miles from the test site, in an area known as Jornada Del Muerto, which meant "the place of the dead" in Spanish.

If they had thought it had been hot in California, they weren't ready for the climate of New Mexico, which had an intense heat with a humidity that soaked their clothes in minutes.

On arriving at the test site, which was heavily guarded, Judy and Tom spent the day setting up and testing their equipment. As they spoke to the other personnel, their fears were realized. It became clear to them what they would be doing. On Monday they were going to test the world's first-ever atomic bomb.

They came to learn that many of the scientists there were having a bet, not believing that it was even going to work. Nothing like this had ever been tried before.

"What do you think, Tom?" asked Judy as they sat huddled under their damp, hot sheets in their military-style beds that evening. "Do you think it could destroy the world? Or do you think it won't work?"

"Between you and me, Judy, I'm not sure. It's just such an unknown."

On that Monday, they had to be up very early before dawn. The test was set for around 5:30 a.m. They were positioned in one of three concrete bunkers, nearly six miles from the actual site where the detonation was to take place.

The test they were doing with the gadget, nicknamed Fat Man because of the large round size of it, would be ignited, and their job was to monitor the amount of radiation it produced if it worked. Many other scientists and military observers were there to witness the phenomenon and reporters from the Manhattan Project to capture the event.

Everyone was mildly nervous that morning, Tom and Judy checking and re-checking their equipment as they waited for the countdown.

The time came and went, and they looked over at one another, believing that the experiment had failed, when all of a sudden, an enormous mushroom cloud of white light lit up the sky. It was so incredible, it took their breath away. Later they would find out that the explosion had covered an area of over three miles, with the ability to destroy everything in its path. It was so much more than they'd all expected.

Judy was horrified, suddenly realizing the power that something like this could unleash. All at once she knew the implication of what all this meant. She had been so caught up in her anger and desire to have people pay for her father's death that she had been driven to end the war at all costs. But had her thirst for blood blinded her to the obvious? That her name was one of the many on the side of that bomb? She had been prepared to aid in destroying an enemy nation without really weighing the consequences. Had it all gone too far? Was this what she had really wanted her legacy to be? She thought back to her naive dreams of becoming the next Marie Curie; they seemed ridiculous now. She could barely even remember that person. Who had she become?

She calmed her terrifying thoughts with logic. Surely it would only ever be used as a deterrent? They would surely let the Japanese know about this test and then it would be over. This kind of violent destruction would be devastating to any country.

That night they were shaken up. Judy couldn't sleep, and when they traveled back to California to update their boss on all their findings, she couldn't get the massive explosion of white light that had filled the sky and could cause so much destruction out of her mind.

She was so concerned about it that she decided she had to discuss it with Mark. She knew she had no real control over what the military did. But she wanted to make sure that Mark realized what was at stake. And she wasn't the only one who was concerned. One of the other top scientists on the project had started collecting names in order to send a letter to the president in Washington to plead with him to only use it as a last resort.

She went into Mark's office one morning after they arrived back in California to confront him on the issue. He was busy working. Since the test had been a success, all his energy had been focused on continuing their work and getting it to a point from which they could distribute the explosion if they needed it.

"Come in, Judy," he said, beckoning her in as she walked into the office. "How are you today?"

She smiled hesitantly. "I wanted to talk to you about... the gadget."

He nodded, and she could see the worry and the tiredness in his eyes. All of them were scientists. Here to try and make the world a better place. It was hard to put aside their personal feelings in view of all they were grappling with. The two of them had got into a lively conversation where she was outlining how she felt when Mark was called out of the office by a colleague.

"Excuse me for a minute, Judy," he said as he left the room, and she paced up and down while she waited, trying to work off all of her nervous energy.

As she passed his desk, she noticed a folder was sitting there, a folder she'd seen in his hands before now, but she'd often seen him lock away in a safe. But right now, it was on his desk.

Operation Trident Statistics was written on the front. She knew she shouldn't, and she'd probably be sacked if she was found out, but she stepped toward it and lifted the cover. On the first page was a breakdown, all the destruction a bomb like this could create if it were directed against a civilian population. Numbers were horrendous. The potential number of people killed by one explosion in a densely populated area was so frightening that Judy couldn't work her way down the rest of the statistics.

She closed the file and felt her chest tighten. Surely, they wouldn't use this. Surely, they would never use this bomb. When they'd called it the gadget, it had sounded quaint, almost fun-like. Now that she'd seen it in action, everything felt so much deadlier. Nuclear fission had been achieved and they had created the deadliest weapon known to man. Judy wasn't sure how she was going to live with herself if the bomb was ever dropped.

When Mark returned to the office, she spoke for a few more minutes but made an excuse. She needed to get away and think about what she'd seen.

When she got home, she discussed it with Tom. "Tom, I didn't become a scientist for this, and neither did you."

"But what can we do, Judy? We are just doing what they have asked us to, and we are in a war."

"Somehow, that doesn't make me feel any better," she said. As she turned over in bed, the numbers swam before her eyes as she went to sleep. Tens of thousands of people could be killed in a single blast, and she would go down in history as being a part of it.

Chapter Forty-Five

She saw it in Tom's eyes when he returned late from the lab one evening and sat down to eat dinner with her. And even though the meeting had been top secret, Judy knew that he would share with her what it had been about.

"They are going to use the bomb, aren't they?" she asked, just above a whisper. "And they're not just going to use it as a deterrent?"

Tom's eyes flashed up to meet hers. He didn't say anything, but she knew she was right.

She sat down on her chair, deflated. "How do you feel about that, Tom?"

"This is not my decision, love. People are weighing tough things at the moment. This war has taken its toll on everybody, and who knows how long it will continue if a deterrent like this isn't used? You weren't this upset about the Window Project."

"Window was completely different! That helped prevent deaths for the Allied bombers. No one was killed because of the Window Project."

"Except the people that were bombed by the bombers," whispered Tom flatly.

"They still would have died. The bombers still would have gone even if they hadn't had chaff. There's a big difference in my mind between helping save lives and creating something that will destroy them."

They finished their dinner in silence. She understood Tom felt the same way she did, but they were both in an impossible position.

Judy didn't sleep well that night and paced the bedroom, looking out on the dark streets. It wasn't just about the bomb, though. There was something that she feared on a much more personal level, deep in her gut. Something she'd been trying not to face.

And that was confirmed to her that weekend when she saw Hedy for their regular Saturday morning lunch. Judy arrived, her stomach in a knot, but Hedy was distracted when she got there, so she didn't seem to notice Judy's anguish. Hedy's immaculately coiffed hair wasn't cared for and looked as if it hadn't been washed. And when she removed her sunglasses, Judy could see that her friend's eyes were red and puffy. And though she wore makeup, her face looked pale, making her crimson lips look even redder in her waxen face. When the waitress came over, Hedy didn't order any food, but just a large pot of black coffee. Judy, not wanting much, ordered a small salad.

They had been making small talk for about ten minutes before Judy got the courage to ask her, "Is everything okay, Hedy? You don't seem quite yourself this morning."

The whole time they'd been together, Hedy had been glancing distractedly around the café, looking over Judy's shoulder, her mind somewhere else. She'd also been chain-smoking.

She took in a deep draw of her latest cigarette before she answered her friend, blowing out the blue smoke and staring at the table. She started to rearrange the salt and pepper as though she was trying to find the right words.

"It's my marriage," she finally said in a small voice. "We are having problems."

Judy felt her heart sink. "Oh, Hedy. I'm so sorry. Not again."

Hedy sat back in the booth and let out air. Judy could see her friend was fighting the tears. "Yes, it might be time soon to say goodbye to husband number three," she said with a sarcastic edge to her tone.

Judy found it hard to believe; this was the most beautiful woman in the world. And yet she could never seem to find someone to love her for who she was. She leaned forward and took hold of her friend's hand.

"I really am sorry, Hedy. Sorry you have to go through this again."

Her friend looked at her, tears brimming. "I thought having this new baby would help but now I'm thinking I made a mistake. Why can nobody love me? What is wrong with me?"

Judy had no answer for her. She just squeezed her hand. "At least you'll have the love of this little one and James. They love you."

Hedy balked. "Children who don't have a father, again. Children I may have to raise alone. It's not that I don't love them, but it's hard sometimes, Judy. I wish I could meet someone like Tom. A nice, dependable guy who loves me for who I am."

Judy felt her insides tighten with Hedy's light dismissal of her own children. "I would do anything to give Tom children," said Judy, uncharacteristically allowing the jealousy to slip out. Something she had carefully guarded through Hedy's pregnancy.

Hedy didn't miss it. "You have each other; you must be pleased about that. I would do anything to have a husband like Tom."

"And I would do anything to have your children, Hedy."

The atmosphere between them became cold and tense. They'd never spoken to each other like this before. There was bitterness underlying both of their voices.

A perky waitress broke the deadlock, offering to top up Hedy's coffee and wanting to know if Judy's lunch tasted fine. The women retreated to their corners, responding mechanically to their server. Judy had hoped this would be an easier conversation, because of what she had to ask now. But she had to know, even though it was awkward between them.

"Have you had any news from Stefan?"

"He's still in the camp in Japan," Hedy answered. "And I've heard nothing since the information from the Red Cross over a year ago."

That was precisely what Judy didn't want to hear. When she'd spoken to Tom that morning, he'd been sure Japan was the target the Allies would be bombing. They had to end the war at all costs, and Japan were the only real enemy left in it.

Hedy didn't realize the significance of what she'd said. So, crushing out her latest cigarette, she returned to what she thought would be a distraction. "What are you working on right now? Are you still involved with monitoring the radiation?"

"You know I can't really go into details," said Judy, hoping that would be the end of it. She needed some time before she answered any questions about her work.

"You've been able to control the levels, as you had talked about?"

"Yes, we think we have that under control now," responded Judy.

"You still don't know what you're working on?"

"We have an idea," Judy lied, taking a big bite and taking her time to chew.

Hedy's eyes widened. "And you're not going to share? We've been friends for years. You can tell me anything. I mean, if it's radiation, then it can be anything, right? It could even be a bomb."

Judy looked at her and was unable to control the redness growing in her cheeks.

Hedy moved to a whisper. "You're building a bomb. Why would you need a bomb now that the war is over in Europe?" She stopped in mid-sentence and sat back in her chair as it suddenly all clicked into place. "Unless, of course," she said, the pain and realization flashing across her eyes, "you're planning to drop it on Japan."

"I don't know anything for sure," garbled Judy, swallowing down hard. "I don't know what they plan to do with it."

"Oh God, my Stefan is there," said Hedy in a whimper, suddenly realizing what it all meant. "Oh my God, Judy. You can't let it happen," Hedy said, raising her voice to panic.

Judy suddenly wasn't hungry and pushed away the rest of her salad.

"Please, Hedy, keep your voice down," she hissed, "I shouldn't even be talking about this."

Hedy was furious. She leapt to her feet and started to pace the diner, drawing attention to herself as people began to murmur, recognizing her.

"I have to leave," said Hedy, "I cannot stay."

As Hedy leaned forward to retrieve her purse, Judy reached out and seized her friend's hand. "Please don't leave like this, Hedy. Don't leave upset like this. We need to talk about this."

"What is there to talk about? You want to take the last man on this planet who cares away from me. You and your scientific community. You and your happy marriage."

"It's my job, Hedy."

"Yes. A job, that's all. You have a choice in that, don't you? If you cared about me and Stefan, you'd have walked away from that job. You'd be sitting here now telling me that you'd done that. That you did it because we were friends. But instead, you showed me, just like everybody else has in my life, that you are only interested in yourself and your career, and in the process you've chosen to betray me. That you don't really care about me. You don't really care about what I need." She leaned forward and hissed to her friend, "You're going to kill people. Do you not even care about that?"

"Of course I care about that," said Judy. "I'm in turmoil."

"Don't lie to me, Judy. You have been out for blood since your father's death. I have seen it in you, the anger and the desire for vengeance. I'm sorry for your turmoil, but I'm finding it hard to feel sorry for you when my life looks a little crappier than yours right now."

Judy's resentment and anger brimmed. "You don't think my life has been hell? Why shouldn't someone pay for what I have lost?"

"Oh my God, Judy! You can't see it, can you, you can't see what you have become. I remember when we met you told me you wanted to be more like me. Be stronger. But look what your grief has done to you! I don't even recognize you. You're not killing the man who killed your father! You're killing Stefan. My Stefan." Hedy's voice started to break with the emotion. "This is more painful to me than the rejection of my three husbands. I thought you were different, I thought you really cared!"

Hedy threw the money onto the table for her coffee. Before Judy could say any more, she marched out of the door, leaving Judy at the table with her angry words ringing in her ears. There was nothing she could do. Her friend needed to calm down, but she felt such a devastating weight in the pit of her stomach and a loss she couldn't quite fathom. Hedy was right: since her father's death she had been on her own personal vendetta. To stop this war at all costs. But now she felt sick when she thought of the bomb they had built.

After the argument with Hedy, Judy knew she had to make a stand on behalf of her conscience. And because her friend needed to see that she cared about her opinion. Yes, maybe she would be throwing away a lucrative career. Perhaps she'd even be throwing away her chance to show all those men who had said that she wasn't a real scientist—including Finnegan—that they were wrong. But her friendship was more important to her.

As she left the diner that day she decided that, even though she knew Tom would protest, she was going to hand in her notice. It was too late for the work that she'd done, but at least this would make it clear how deeply she disagreed with what they were doing.

That night, when she told Tom, he did try to talk her out of it. "The work is done, love. What would be the point of handing your notice in now?"

"It would make Hedy know that I care about her. I'll be able to tell her that I did what she said and that she was right. It may give her a tiny bit of assurance that our relationship is true. She's been hurt by so many people. I don't want to be another person in her life who has deceived her."

Tom couldn't deter her, but as they made their way to work the next day, there was a lot of commotion. They hadn't had a chance to read the papers that morning because neither of them had slept very well, and neither of them had eaten breakfast. But when they arrived at the lab that day, they knew something big had happened.

They were called straight into a meeting, and they went in and sat down. The whole of the department was there. Mark stood in front of them all. "I'm sure you've all heard by now that we dropped a bomb on the city of Hiroshima in Japan this morning. This is the moment we have all worked for. I want to recognize every one of you scientists that have made this happen. It is because of you we have made the first step to end this war for the United States and the Allied forces."

Judy felt as though the room was spinning. Hedy would never believe her now if she said that she'd planned to hand her notice in. It was all too late. She was too late to make a stand. She was too late to do the right thing. Or show her friend how much she cared. And Stefan was probably dead, if not from the actual bombing then from any retaliation that may have followed, and Judy had had a part in that.

She reached out to take Tom's hand, her own trembling as she tried to steady herself, and she decided to make her way home. She told Tom to tell everybody that she wasn't well. What would be the point in handing her notice in now? Though she knew in her heart of hearts she couldn't continue to work on this project in any form.

Judy went straight home and tried to call her. Hedy snatched up the phone and Judy could tell she had been crying.

"Hedy... It's me."

On the other end, Hedy let out a whoosh of air. "You killed Stefan. You killed my dearest, beloved friend. And in all these months we have been meeting for lunch you never told me. You just sat there eating salad and making small talk while you planned his death. The least you could have done was tell me. Your bomb still would have been dropped but I would have known you really cared about me. Instead I am heartbroken."

Before Judy had a chance to respond, Hedy slammed down the phone.

Chapter Forty-Six

August 13, 1945

Hedy sat looking at the newspaper headlines. It'd been a long week since the first bomb, and now the second bomb had just been dropped and the tears rolled down her cheeks again as she read the news, sobbing with the shock just as she had every day of that week. The rest of the time when she wasn't working, she was calling anyone she could to try and locate Stefan. But from all accounts it was absolute devastation in Japan. And because of the high radiation levels there, the Red Cross couldn't even go in to check for survivors.

She still couldn't believe it. It was unfathomable what had happened. She stared at the newspaper and reread the front page:

The first ever atom bomb was dropped from a U.S. bomber at 9:15 a.m. on August 6th on the city of Hiroshima. Sixty percent of a city that had a population of over 300,000 was destroyed. The second bomb was dropped on the city of Nagasaki, destroying an estimated thirty percent of that city.

Hedy felt sick. Not just for the incredible loss of life, but also her thoughts remained with her friend. She had heard nothing since just after the Pearl Harbor attack nearly three years before. Whenever she thought about him now, it made her want to throw up.

Tucked in her heart until now she had always had this eternal hope. Her dear old friend had always been so lucky, his cunning charm managing to get him out of the worst of scrapes when they were growing up. Until the bomb she had imagined him running some sort of defiant stance in the camp, somehow twisting the guards around his little finger to get him the cigarettes and the reading materials he would need to survive. Maybe even a little romance while he was there. In her head she had romanticized it all in order to deal with the loss, but no matter how hard she tried, she couldn't manage to romanticize an atom bomb.

Of course, the U.S. government had justified it by referring to the fact the Japanese were defiant about never surrendering at any cost, demonstrating that it was a deep-rooted part of their culture to fight to the death and surrender was perceived as weakness. Apparently, even with that knowledge, America had hoped that one bomb would be enough, but instead of surrendering, the Japanese had dug their heels in even deeper, putting the Allies in an apparently impossible situation. In the newspaper it was reported that the government had tried to weigh the cost of more years at war. It was calculated that if they had just invaded Japan in the usual way, there was a chance that up to another million Allied troops would have been sacrificed. So, the government had apparently decided that another bomb was their only option. Still, it was gut-wrenching to come to terms with this incredible, sad turn of events.

Hedy looked up from the article and thought about Judy, the woman who had betrayed her. She knew on some level that her anger was misdirected, but she couldn't help feeling hurt again. How long had Judy known she was building a bomb? One that had probably just killed her best friend? She thought of all they had shared. She thought about Pearl Harbor and how close they had been then and how they had been there for one another in some of the most difficult times in both their lives. Had that not meant anything to Judy?

Hedy wanted more from a relationship now. She wanted to see people showing their care with action. Hedy understood dropping the bomb hadn't been Judy's decision. But how long had Judy lied to her? Laughed with her, eaten with her, shared with her, and all the time she must have known about the bomb she was building and its intended target. Hedy was fed up with people letting her down. Just another person in her life who robbed her of love, this time the most cherished and profound love of all: the love of her oldest, dearest friend.

On the second page of the newspaper, Hedy drew in a breath. Splashed across the top of the page was a photograph of all the scientists from the laboratory at Berkeley who had been working on the bomb. It stated the photo had been taken earlier that year, and there was Judy, smiling by Tom's side. The woman who had everything, while working every day to rob Hedy of the only man she'd ever loved. The pain and anger she felt was overwhelming and Hedy crumpled up the newspaper and threw it in the bin.

She had to learn to be independent now. There was no one going to take care of her but herself. No friends, no men, and no more husbands were going to be there for her. She had to figure out how to do life on her own, and that was the way it was going to be from now on. She would become completely independent and plough everything she had into her children and her work. It was all she had that she could count on.

August 13, 1945

Dear Hedy,

I'm writing to you again in the hope that you will read this. I can't tell you how sorry I am for everything that I said and everything that happened. We've been through so much together. I would hate if this thing stood in the way of our friendship. You have to believe it when I tell you we had suspected, but we had no way of knowing that bombs were going to be dropped on Japan.

The way the lab was set up at Berkeley was that none of us knew what each of the other scientists were working on.

They were afraid of it getting out to the enemy. Obviously, we're working with radiations and atoms; there was always a thought it could be a weapon. But never in my wildest dream could I have imagined what happened. You have to believe me, Hedy, and you have to forgive me. Please, please write back or answer the phone. Don't let this go, Hedy. This is the most important relationship in my life after Tom, and the last thing I want to do is lose you.

Love,
Judy

Chapter Forty-Seven

August 15, 1945

On VJ Day, Tom and Judy were invited to a massive party at the lab. Many dignitaries had been invited as well, and there were speeches and a lot of backslapping. But Judy just hovered in the corner, feeling isolated and alone. She couldn't enter into all the joy that everybody seemed to have as they skated over the fact thousands of civilians had been killed. She just knew that the devastation in Japan had to be terrible. And Hedy had made it abundantly clear she didn't want to see her ever again.

*

It was a few months after the end of the war in Japan that they were called back to the Cavendish Lab in England. They arrived home at their little house, and as they walked inside, Judy simply stood there and looked around her. The last time she'd been here, England had been at war. It was hard to imagine that there would be no more bombs, no more fear. And though she felt a great sense of relief, it was almost blotted out by her deep feelings of guilt and how she'd contributed to creating an invention that had caused so much death and destruction.

Tom seemed to have trouble with that as well, but he didn't let it show in the same way. As they started to settle back into their lives, Judy struggled to shake off her debilitating feelings of sadness and couldn't bring herself to go back to work at the Cavendish, feeling sick and fearful whenever she thought about what she had done.

Tom approached her tentatively one evening, trying to understand, reminding her she had just been doing her job.

She turned and looked her husband directly in the eye.

"You don't understand, Tom. It's not what I did; it's how I felt doing it. I *wanted* to kill people. Yes, on the surface I was being my professional, scientific self, detached and observant. But deep in my heart of hearts, I wanted people to die, and that scares me, Tom. It really scares me. And Hedy saw it. She was right, and she called me on it. She knew me well enough to see it. And only now, I see it too. I feel this overwhelming guilt. I don't know how to navigate because, in my blind-eyed need for revenge, I have just killed her best friend."

"Judy," he said, breathing out. "You make it sound as though you put a gun to his head. You were doing your job."

"Yes, doing the job. Just a job, nothing else. I could have walked away at any point, but the bitterness that ate away at me had its way, and now Stefan is dead."

Finally, after weeks of despair, she went to see her doctor. As much as she was glad not to feel the hunger for revenge that had consumed her since her father's death, it had empowered her and now it was gone, all that was left was her grief and sadness again. He explained to her a lot of people were feeling depressed after the war. Everyone had been holding on for so long, and now they had to rebuild. So many lives had been lost, so much destruction had been wrought, and Judy was merely another victim of that experience. He gave her some tablets to help her sleep, because she tended to walk around the house at night and was barely functioning during the day. She could tell Tom was worried about her. He would try to bring her little gifts or relay exciting breakthroughs he was having at the lab, but nothing stirred her. She just felt this huge black hole of pain.

She functioned like this for months when something happened that changed her. She had been gathering flowers from the garden and, as she started to arrange them, had knocked the vase onto the floor and it had smashed. Grabbing a sheet of newspaper to gather the shards, she noticed a headline that caught her attention. She hadn't read the papers since she'd returned to England. Even the good news was hard to take. She just wanted to live in her own world. But this headline was about the Polish refugees.

She scooped the glass into another sheet of paper and sat to read the article. They really needed help. And suddenly, Judy felt that she could do something. Would this be a way for her to somehow pay her penance? People needed homing and families needed to be reunited. This was what she was going to do, she decided. She didn't want to go inside another lab; she didn't want to think about physics for a very long time. She just wanted to help as many people as she could.

Responding to the address in the newspaper, three days later, she met with a lovely woman who put her in charge of working with relocation. Her job was to help find homes for the many people who had been displaced. And the first time she'd looked at the young children, clinging to their mothers and frightened, she knew she could finally be of some help. Her heart went out to the families, and she worked hard day and night to bring about the relocations.

It was while she was amidst the work that she realized she found great joy in helping the young children. Schools were badly oversubscribed because of bomb damage and shortage of teachers, and refugee children were seemingly of no importance. So sometimes she would set up small classes at the camps and she found she loved teaching the children. She would do fun experiments for them all, and would get so much joy out of watching them giggle and laugh. It took her back to why she'd fallen in love with science in the first place. And it made up her mind for her; she wanted to do more of this.

She approached Tom with her idea one evening after dinner. He was sitting in his armchair, doing the crossword. The wireless was on a low hum. And she was seated in the corner, pretending to read a book, when she placed it down on her lap.

"Tom?"

"Uh huh?" he said, not looking up from his crossword.

"How would you feel about me changing jobs?"

He stopped what he was doing, took off his glasses, and peered at his wife. Even though they didn't talk about it, he understood the pain she'd been through. He'd been through a version of it himself, though he still never talked about it.

"I think whatever makes you happy, Judy. What kind of job are you thinking of doing?"

"I was thinking of getting my teaching qualification so I can teach children."

She saw the fear pass across his face. "You think you'd be all right with children?"

She knew he was asking her about her loss, but she smiled. "It gives me so much joy being with the children at the refugee camp. I think I would like to do this very much."

"And I think you'll be a fine teacher," Tom encouraged.

Judy started then pursuing her teaching studies and in the meantime, she worked with the refugees.

Chapter Forty-Eight

January 1946

Hedy slammed her hand down on the desk and swiveled on her heels. Pulling a cigarette from her gold case, she flipped open the lighter and looked out of the window, her temper raging.

"What is going on?" she asked as she turned again. "Why are we having so much trouble in production?"

Her business partner shook his head. "I don't know, Hedy. I just don't get it. Distribution is normally so much easier than this. I hate to say it, but I think it might have something to do with the fact it's you who's producing."

Hedy looked shocked. "I thought my name would help."

"I think your name as an actress helps, but as a producer? You know what Hollywood's like. This is an old boys' club. Producers don't like the idea of a woman producing something and it becoming a success. They see you as the enemy. They're worried that you'll run them all out of town."

Hedy shook her head and her curls bobbed. "This is so ridiculous!"

Her partner shrugged his shoulders. "I know, Hedy. It's really unfair."

Her assistant knocked on the door. "They're waiting for you on set, Miss Lamarr. They want to re-film that last sequence."

"Yes, coming," she said. She looked at her partner, who just shrugged his shoulders as she grabbed hold of her script and made her way out of his office.

On her way back to the set, a runner came to stop her. "Miss Lamarr, somebody is waiting for you. I think it's a fan. He's a tall man with dark hair."

Hedy shook her head. "It's probably my husband again. I'm not speaking to him at the moment."

"He was most insistent."

"Yep, that'll be him," she stated and stormed toward the set. "Tell him I'm unavailable."

She filmed her sequence and had forgotten all about the earlier interaction until she walked back off the set. She was tired and just wanted to go home and take a bath when she saw a person loitering by the exit, smoking a cigarette. As she approached, she realized it wasn't John, so it had to be a fan. She sighed heavily, not wanting to pretend to be happy and smile and sign an autograph. She was still very grumpy about the fact she could not get the money to get this damn picture made.

As she approached the gate, the sun was shining and the light was behind him, so he was just a silhouette, but something made her stop as she looked at him again. There *was* something familiar about him. It was somebody she knew. He stood with a coat jacket draped over his arm, painfully thin, with hair as dark as her own.

"Oh my God," she cried, running up to him. "Oh my God! Stefan, is that you!?" She threw her arms around him and hugged him tightly. "Is it really you? I thought you were dead. I honestly thought you were dead."

"I almost was," he joked.

She drew his face to her so she could look at him closely. Fresh tears of relief flowed down her cheeks. "I can't believe I kept you waiting till the end of the scene."

"Ah, Earwig, you'll always keep me waiting," he stated, sounding tired.

"Never again," she said, covering his cheeks with kisses. "I will never keep you waiting ever again."

As he pulled away from her something snagged on his clothing and he reached forward and pulled out the heart necklace that she still wore all the time whenever she wasn't on set.

"You still have my heart," he whispered, turning it over in his hand.

"Always," she whispered back. And, closing her eyes, she rested her forehead on his, embracing this miracle.

She took him straight home, instructing her housekeeper to make a celebratory dinner.

She led him out onto the patio and couldn't seem to stop touching him to reassure herself this wasn't a dream.

He lit a cigarette and she noticed his hand had a slight tremor, and as she watched him she struggled to see the man she had known in this gaunt, introspective person. It was as if all the fight she'd once known had left him.

She approached the subject gingerly, sensing his vulnerability. "Where were you?"

He flinched with her question and, taking a deep drag of his cigarette, paused before he answered her. "In a place called hell, Hedy. I really don't want to talk about it. It was hard. Especially after the bombs…"

"How far away were you from them?"

"Far enough away not to die, but close enough to see the terrible atrocities they caused and experience the retaliation. I'm still having nightmares about it…" His voice petered out as his eyes glazed over.

Hedy's stomach churned. She couldn't stand what had happened to him and would spend the rest of her life helping him come to terms with the pain he had been through.

He quickly changed the subject.

"What about you?" he asked, trying to sound upbeat. "Are you still a big Hollywood movie star? We didn't get to see many films in the hellhole," he added, sarcastically.

"Oh, I'm doing okay," she said, poo-pooing away the question. "I've been trying to get a movie produced but I'm hitting roadblocks at every turn. I want to do more with my life. I want to do parts that are deep and meaningful, and if Mayer can't offer me a part in that kind of movie, I want to make them myself. But it would be easier to swim the Atlantic."

Suddenly her nanny arrived with the children, whom she was getting ready to go to bed.

"Who's this?" asked Stefan curiously, looking at the baby in the nanny's arms.

"That is my daughter," she said with pride. "These children are my life now."

She took the baby from the nanny and placed her in Stefan's arms, as the curly-haired bundle cooed and blew bubbles at him.

"Say hello to your uncle Stefan," Hedy trilled merrily.

Gentle tears slid down Stefan's cheeks as he stared at her in bewilderment.

"New life," he finally whispered, taking in all of his honorary niece's features as his voice croaked. "How wonderful."

Then he beamed, and as he caught Hedy's eye for a second, she saw a little of the old Stefan and her heart melted.

"What is her name?"

"Denise. I call her Deni. We just celebrated her first birthday."

He held her up in his arms until they were at eye level with one another, looking at her with such awe, before saying just above a whisper, "Hello, Deni. Do you want to hear a story?"

Denise was mesmerized by him, her eyes wide and expectant.

He pulled her into his lap and, cuddling her closely, he whispered into her ear.

"Once upon a time there was a beautiful princess called Deni-rina…"

Chapter Forty-Nine

December 1950

After the war, Judy continued to be busy as a teacher, as did Tom at the Cavendish Lab. Finnegan had moved on, after suffering a minor heart attack, but Judy had never wanted to go back. She would talk to Tom about his work, and he would sometimes ask her to return; he missed her in the lab. But she loved her new teaching position. She loved working with young minds and delighted in how much they loved what they were doing. It gave her optimism for the future and helped to pay the penance for all the children whom she had deprived of life in Japan. Though she still had nightmares about the bomb. She could not read anything about Hiroshima or Nagasaki. She often wondered about Hedy's best friend, but she had still not heard from her about him in all these years. Judy had hoped that after things had calmed down and the war had been over a while that somehow, they'd have found a way back to each other.

She still sent a letter occasionally with news of her life, explaining again what had happened that last day they had seen each other. How she had intended to hand in her notice, but the bomb had already been deployed. She wanted Hedy to know she'd heard her friend's words. But still nothing from Hedy. She found herself following her friend's life through the fan magazines, knowing they weren't reliable, but it was the only way she would know what was going on in Hedy's life, and she missed her terribly.

Judy still had trouble making friends easily. She didn't know why that was, but the point was something had just clicked with Hedy. Something on a much deeper level than just their love of science. They had both been women needing a voice, Hedy as an inventor and Judy as a scientist in a male-dominated world.

For Christmas that year, Tom suggested they go to the movies. They went so rarely that he thought it would be nice. Picture houses were offering so much. Rationing was still an issue, but less so, and they could get more things now. They made their way to the cinema, but when they saw what was showing, Judy's heart sank. Hedy Lamarr in *Samson and Delilah*. Tom looked across at her with concern.

"We could do something else, Judy. We don't have to see this film."

She shook her head. "I have to get over it, Tom. I just have to face facts that, for whatever reason, we're no longer friends." She sounded so brave on the way in, and Tom was still concerned, but the minute she saw Hedy on the screen, tears started to roll down her cheeks.

She was brilliant in her role. In some of the fan magazines, it was already being seen as the pinnacle of her career. She looked as beautiful as always, but there was also a self-assurance about her on the screen. As Delilah, she was powerful. It was no wonder Hedy had garnered so much attention for this movie.

Tom reached over and grabbed his wife's hand and squeezed it. "I miss her too," he said in the darkness, and Judy nodded, wishing there was some way she could put this right.

*

In 1952, she read about the two movies that Hedy had produced with vital female roles and how they had flopped because of a lack of money.

And then she read in the fan magazines that Hedy Lamarr was leaving Hollywood forever. Her heart hurt for her friend. She'd given so much of her life and time to her career, and all she'd wanted was to be treated as an equal. But she'd never been able to fight off the "most beautiful woman in the world" label. And no matter what she did, she was still always seen as just a face.

Judy wondered if her friend was still inventing and couldn't imagine that she wouldn't be. Sometimes, when she was doing something with her students, she would think of something, and she'd want to tell Hedy about it, maybe give her an idea for an invention, and then she'd feel that sinking feeling that they no longer had their relationship.

The most heartbreaking moment came for her in 1966, when she read in the paper that Hedy had been prosecuted for shoplifting. By this time, Tom had bought them a television set. It had even been on their news, as she was such a famous person. It was the first time Judy had seen her friend in twenty years, and she was still as beautiful as ever, proclaiming her innocence. Where was her friend? What was going on? Why was her life in such a terrible state?

She sat down in 1966 for the first time in fifteen years to write Hedy a letter, sending it via her agent.

She knew from the fan magazines that Hedy had become a recluse. She hadn't been seen in Hollywood for many years. But still maybe there was a chance.

May 8, 1966

Dear Hedy,

I know this letter may come as a surprise to you after so many years, but I had to reach out and tell you we saw you in Samson and Delilah *a few years ago. I know you always joked about us never going to the movies, but Tom wanted to go to the pictures at Christmas and it just so happened that your picture was playing. Hedy, you were magnificent.*

You came alive on that screen. Everything of the woman that I've known was there. I have to be honest. It was hard seeing you, and also comforting after so long. I think about you all the time, even after all these years. I always hope that one day, maybe you'll forgive me, and perhaps it's time now. I miss you, and so does Tom. Hedy, I miss my friend. Please write to me.

Much love,
Judy.

Chapter Fifty

Cambridge, 1990

Judy sat in the darkened bedroom watching her husband breathe. With each in-breath came the now-familiar rattle that reminded Judy that his lungs were filling up with fluid. The doctor had been back to visit him twice that day, and she could tell that they were just making Tom comfortable now. Maybe the doctor was coming just for Judy's sake. There were no more treatments, no more prescriptions, no more "We'll watch and see," only the nodding of his head as he listened to his patient's chest and the reluctant smile in Judy's direction, or the pat on her hand before he departed.

And now there was just the waiting. As much as the rattling breath was hard to listen to, it also reminded her that her husband was still alive. When he'd been diagnosed with pancreatic cancer, they had been shocked, but willing to try all the new treatments. Nothing had worked.

The radiation had weakened him, and Tom had lost thirty pounds. She looked at the skeletal body of her husband now, always joking with her that he needed to lose a little bit of weight. She realized with some irony that when he did, he didn't look like her Tom any more.

He started to cough, and she grabbed hold of the glass of water on his side table and lifted it to his dry lips. He seemed to have trouble even understanding what she was doing. Taking her finger, she dipped it in the glass and wiped his lips with it; he nodded, parting them so she could drop a few more drips into his throat.

He'd been going downhill like this for the last three days, sleeping longer and longer and awake for such short periods of time.

All at once he surprised her. His eyes sprang open, and he looked around the room as though he was looking for somebody or something.

She took hold of his hand, tightly. It was hot and clammy; he didn't have the strength to grab hers back. "Are you okay, Tom? Do you need anything?"

His eyes found hers, and there was that look, a look she had seen a thousand times, the look that told her that he loved her.

He shook his head, slowly opened his mouth, and croaked out a few words. She drew closer so she could hear him.

"I still can't believe…" She waited as he took another rattling breath. "… that you married me."

Tears welled up in her chest, but she swallowed them down in case he said anything else. She didn't want to miss one single word with misted eyes or not hear what he was communicating by giving into her own grief.

"Oh, Tom," she said, holding the back of his hand to her cheek. How could this man whom she had lived with for fifty years be leaving her? She just didn't know what she was going to do without him. He was speaking again, and she drew closer to him so that she could hear him.

"But I lied to you, Judy…" She furrowed her brows, trying to understand as his wheezing intensified. "When I met you at the lab for the first time. I pretended I didn't know who you were. But I did."

It must be the medication, she mused. She had never met Tom before that first day.

His eyes fluttered closed than sprang open again, as he continued in a rasp. "I knew you before, at university. I fell in love with you the first time I ever saw you walking alone across one of the courtyards, but I never dared to believe you could ever know me. I was so shy and you were so… beautiful."

Tears filled her eyes then. She had always wished she could have seen herself through her husband's eyes. Judy had always felt so dowdy, a mouse in a lab coat. But Tom had always seen her as so much more.

"I only dared to dream when the fates placed us together as lab partners that maybe one day you would grow to like me. But I never thought it was possible that someone like you could love someone like me."

Tears were streaming down her cheeks now, and, burrowing her face into his shoulder, she started to sob. Tenderly, and with great effort, he lifted his hand to stroke her hair, and for the first time in months, he was the strong one for her.

They fell asleep like that, and when she woke with a jolt an hour later, he was speaking again, as if he needed to get all these things off his mind before he slipped from this world.

"The babies," he said, rasping again.

Babies? Judy shook her head. What was he talking about now? Was he delirious? He had been delirious a couple of days before, but he seemed so lucid right now.

"The babies," he repeated and then indicated he needed a little more water. She brought the glass to his lips, and he swallowed some down. "The babies that you lost, Judy, our children."

Judy's breath caught in her throat. She put a hand to her mouth, so she didn't make any noise. "I'm so sorry," she whispered through her fingers, "Tom, I'm so sorry that I couldn't give you any children. Is that what you're saying?"

He shook his head and closed his eyes. As if it was taking all of him just to say these words. "No, no. You were always enough for me. Maybe I never told you that properly. But you were. I mean, when you got pregnant, I put aside some money in a savings account. I thought if... they wanted to go... to university or needed a down payment..." He spoke slowly, stringing the words out one by one.

She looked at him more intently then, trying to understand where this was going. He beckoned her closer again.

"I never closed the account. I don't know why; it just felt so final."

She nodded her head. She still had a beautiful blue matinee jacket that Hedy had given her she'd never been able to let go of, even though they'd let go of all other things that people had knitted for them. This one jacket was special.

"When I die, Judy, I want you to take the money from that account, and I want you to put it toward a flight."

Judy looked at him with surprise.

"I want you to go and find Hedy, I want you to put things right with Hedy," he added, his voice petering out, and then he started to cough again, lying back on the pillow. He gasped for two breaths. It'd obviously taken everything out of him, what he had to say.

She sat back on her seat with the realization of what he was trying to tell her. "Oh, Tom, you know that door is closed."

He shook his head. "There's always hope. You should at least try. I don't want you to be alone."

She started to weep again; she didn't want to be alone, either. She wept for the friend she no longer had, and she wept for the husband she was losing little by little every day.

He said nothing more that day. He closed his eyes and fell into a deep, restless sleep, leaving Judy with her raw pain and the anguish of his words. She'd watched him all night until the royal blue of the dawn crept below the curtains. He didn't wake up for the rest of the next day, but then that evening, his eyes opened again, for one last time.

She drew close to him and noticed his breath was slowing, the rasping was getting stronger. The doctor told her to call him day or night. He didn't say, "when Tom passes," but she knew that's what he meant.

"What is it, my love?" she said, getting close to him.

"I'm going to miss you," he rasped.

"I'm going to miss you too," she answered, drawing her face close to his.

"I will see our children soon, and I will say hello for you. I bet our daughter has your beautiful wavy hair."

She smiled wistfully, remembering how he always used to say that when she had been pregnant.

"Take care," he whispered, "and put it right with Hedy…"

Those were the last words he ever spoke.

He fell into a deep sleep then. His breath became slower and shallower. And she sat with him until he finally died. It was strange when it happened. She'd expected more emotion, but there was a stillness, a peace; he breathed in one last time, breathed out, and then never breathed again. He lay there so still on the bed. She looked at the clock. Three o'clock, the death hour, she thought. How ironic for Tom to be so punctual. He'd always been on time all through his life. She sat with him then for the rest of the night, just watching him, thinking of him, not wanting to be apart.

They buried him a week later, and many people they'd known through the years in the scientific community attended, all of them deeply saddened, respectful and kind. No one had a bad word to say about Tom. He was an upstanding, kind man. But for Judy, he was just Tom. Her best friend. Her everything. And she simply didn't know what she was going to do without him.

Judy had forgotten about the bank account. There had been so many other things to think about. But then she found his bank book a few weeks later when sorting through his papers and remembered. He wanted her to put it right with Hedy. It was Tom's last wish. She knew she would have to do something about it.

So, she sat down at her desk and wrote a letter. She wrote a letter to the one woman whom she could never forget, and to the one person, the one friend she'd loved. Could Hedy now forgive her after all these years for what had happened? She finished the letter and placed it in an envelope, and it took her another few weeks before she even posted it. She didn't know why. Maybe she was so fearful of the rejection. She knew that Hedy was still a recluse, withdrawing from everything.

She'd been tough to track down, but eventually, she'd found an address, a fan club that she hoped would pass the message along to her. She had marked it urgent.

March 8, 1990

Dear Hedy,

I will keep this short as I am not even sure you will read it, even though I wish you would with all my heart. My darling Tom passed away a week ago, and I am so lost without him. He was the kindest and gentlest of people, even if very much old-fashioned in the light of today's men. But he loved with his whole heart in his own way. I remember once you told me you wanted a husband as passionate as mine, and I remember thinking at the time that was never a way that I had ever seen him. But you know, Hedy, as the years have passed, I think there was some truth in those words. His passion wasn't outward or demonstrative, but it was deep and profound and non-wavering. A slow-burning kind of a passion that was with him till the day he died. When I met him, I was shy and awkward with no confidence but through years of Tom's love and seeing myself through his eyes, I began to believe in the person he saw in me. It is because of that love I reach out one more time. If Tom could have believed in the power of love and forgiveness to the very end, so can I.

Please forgive me.

Much love,
Judy xxx

Judy waited but never received a reply.

August 17th, 1998.
To Ms. Hedy Lamarr

You are cordially invited to the honorary degree
ceremony of Mrs. Judy Jenkins.

The event will take place on September 14th, 1998
at Cambridge University.

(Full address is enclosed.)

Please kindly confirm if you will be attending.

We look forward to seeing you at the ceremony.

Kind regards,
the Honorary Committee,
Cambridge University, England

Chapter Fifty-One

Florida, 1998

Hedy woke with a start and sat up. It was only 6 a.m., and she was already sweating. Her air conditioning must have failed again. With the early morning commotion, her dog Peppy eyed his mistress warily.

"It's okay, Peppy," she crooned, ruffling his fur. "I bet you're hotter than me in your fur coat."

She got out of bed and stretched. Walking to her patio doors, she opened them out onto the view of the lake. Her body was grateful for the warmth of the Florida temperatures that kept her moving, but there wasn't a day that went by where she didn't miss the Austria of her childhood.

She made her way into her kitchen, where she put on the coffee pot and found her cigarette packet on the side. She scanned for her address book to find the electrician she'd called before. She hummed to herself as the aroma of freshly brewed coffee filled the air.

Lighting her cigarette, she pulled the receiver from the wall in the kitchen and started to dial. People were beginning to get those mobile phones now. It made her chuckle to think that the technology that had enabled them had been based on her invention in the 1940s. And yet, she couldn't figure out how to use the damn things.

When the phone call clicked to voicemail, she left a short message, hung up, and sighed. She would call her son later and see if he could do anything about it. There used to be a time when it didn't matter who she called; they'd come over just to sit and stare at her. She thought wistfully, nobody wanted to stare at her now.

The best thing was to get out for a walk. There was a little bit of a breeze on Red Bug Lake, and hopefully it would cool her down. Going into the bathroom, she opened her cabinet and took out the tablets that she'd been reliant on now for so long: the uppers and the downers.

For some reason, they always made her think of Judy Garland. Judy had had a much harder time than she'd had, taken so young. But for Hedy, it was routine now.

When she'd started on them so many years ago, they'd been the only way she'd been able to sleep. And the only way she'd been able to wake up early enough to get on set. Even though her new doctor here in Florida had wanted her to stop taking them, she was too ornery and old now to do that. She was going to do whatever she wanted. She was damned fed up with men telling her what to do.

Getting dressed, she slipped on Peppy's leash and stepped out toward the park. Her mind drifted back, as it had for the last few days, ever since she'd received the invitation. Her stomach cramped as she thought of the war of the 1940s—so much sadness during that time.

For so many years, her friend Judy Jenkins had just been a part of all of that. Throughout her life, she'd met people who had gotten divorced and then never spoken to their closest friends again. That hadn't been Hedy's problem. After six husbands, she was used to it. She'd have ended up with no friends if she'd done that. But she understood the mentality of it.

Part of you wanted to move on into something new after a difficult time. The last thing you wanted was the disappointed expressions of your friends, with the word they didn't say—*why?*—blazing across their faces every time you saw them. There was part of her that felt like that about Judy; she didn't want to visit old wounds, visit any of that pain.

At least Judy was still alive. She was glad her former friend was at last getting the degree and perhaps the recognition she deserved.

Peppy began to bark. Turning the corner on the lake, Hedy saw why. Pulling tight the headscarf she always wore and keeping her sunglasses in place, she waved to Doris. Hedy hated being recognized now. But Peppy had a playmate in Doris's dog and they often met at the park.

Doris waved to her, and Hedy slipped Peppy off his leash. The Labradoodles greeted one another and started to gambol in the grass. Hedy moved to the bench where she usually sat, and Doris joined her, remarking about the heat as they watched the dogs frolicking together.

She liked Doris. She was a woman of very few words. And the words she did have were normally paying homage to her favorite game show or to recount her evening at bingo. Even after somebody had actually recognized Hedy in the park one day and had drawn attention to it to Doris, Doris hadn't seemed to know who Hedy was and had just blinked at Hedy in disbelief as she'd signed an autograph. Hedy liked it that way. This morning they were having one of their usual conversations—Doris's roll call of all the people who had died or become ill since the last time they had seen each other—when she said something that struck a chord.

Doris was talking about another woman she'd known who had just passed away.

"I've known her all my life," Doris was saying, shaking her head in disbelief. "She was a great beauty when she was young, you know. But men only seemed to want her for one thing. And she ended up dying alone and unloved. It's ironic really."

After she and Doris parted company, the dogs worn out and ready for their naps, she dwelled on those words as she made her way back to her house in her Florida suburb. She had always been an optimist and didn't like to remember things that made her sad. But in some ways her first husband's prophecy had been right.

She spent the remainder of her walk home reminding herself her children loved her, even if no man ever had in the end.

She went back into the house and looked at the invitation she'd propped up on her mantelpiece. England felt a thousand miles away, and a million years ago now, without adding the sting that she always had when she thought about Judy.

She should have contacted her after Stefan had come home, or at least after Tom had passed. She should have put it right, then. She'd been stubborn as a mule and somehow, life had come in and taken her away. She'd been busy with her children, her ever-long parade of husbands. There had never been the right time. Then, when there had been the right time, it felt too long, and deep down, she was afraid of rejection again.

So many people had rejected her. And yet the way she'd been hurt by Judy had been the worst pain she'd been through in her life.

Now, this invitation. She probably could have found Judy's number and called her, but something didn't feel right about that. After all their years of correspondence, she'd wanted to write back to her.

She'd sat down many times to pen that letter since the invitation had arrived. She sat down one more time at her writing desk and pulled out a sheet of clean, white paper. Putting her address at the top as she'd been taught to do at school, and the date, she started:

Dear Judy, Thank you for your invitation. I think it is wonderful that you are getting the recognition that you deserve. I'm unfortunately not well enough to travel, so I'll not be able to join you for the ceremony.

She stopped again, looking down at it, and then noticed the wastepaper bin beside her desk, full of similar letters. No matter how many times she wrote this, it just felt too formal and wrong. She wanted to convey something of her care, of her sadness, of the hole in her life that had been left without her friend all these years. But nothing of it seemed to translate through her pen.

She was pulled from her reverie by the telephone ringing. Going to the phone, she picked it up. It was the air conditioning guy, returning her call. She explained the situation. He said he would see what he could do and get back to her with a time he could come over in the next week.

As she stood talking to him, she stared at her letter in her hand and the words she'd just written. It was ridiculous. She was ridiculous. Maybe it was better not to say anything. Then perhaps Judy would think that the invitation had gotten lost in the post and she wouldn't have to open all these doors of the past.

Hanging up the phone, she crumpled the letter into a ball, threw it into the wastepaper basket, and lit herself a cigarette. It was better this way. Leave the past in the past.

Chapter Fifty-Two

Distracted by the silhouette of the woman in the doorway, Judy lost her place in her speech and struggled to find where she was. When she looked up again the door was closed. Had she imagined it? Had she wanted to see Hedy so badly she had projected the image of her friend there? As she continued to talk she scoured the room, looking for the figure she was sure had been there, but the woman was nowhere to be seen. She concluded her speech.

"My parting words to you are about conduct, not conclusions. Be passionate but not driven, have a desire to win, but not at all costs. If you lose sight of the very thing that you're fighting for, to change the world toward decency, peace, and the greater good, you may very well lose your soul in the process. This is a mistake I made and have paid for dearly all of my life.

"In these latter years, we have glamorized war, but there is nothing glamorous about it. It is a soul-searching, daily struggle for survival where you are forced to make decisions with no clear right or wrong. If you ever find yourself in a similar position, make those decisions with your heart, not out of vengeance. Life is precious, even if it is the life of your enemy.

"I was in Hawaii during the attack on Pearl Harbor. It was the most terrifying experience of my entire life. We felt the literal heat of battle as all around us, one after another, ships became metal infernos and it felt as if I was in a furnace. I was grateful to reach out and have a hand to take hold of mine and pull me through the smoke and fire to safety. The fact that hand was there when I most needed it was more important than every other success in my career, or anything else I have achieved in my life. These are things you should value, the things that cannot be explained by an equation. Not those things studied by the mind, but those things that can only be felt by the heart."

At the end of her speech, people were back on their feet, clapping, and she smiled and nodded, wondering how long it was polite for her to stay before she could go back to the comfort of her room. All at once she noticed something out of the corner of her eye, some movement. Right at the back of the auditorium, it was the woman she had seen in the doorway and she could see her clearly now in a dark hat and sunglasses. And even though the storm had blown over and the sun was shining, it was strange to see a woman dressed that way. Judy watched her get to her feet, nodding in Judy's direction, and drifting toward the end of the row.

Judy's heart started to pound as she watched her. She fixated on her as if there was no one else in the room. Maybe it was because she so wanted it to be her. As the woman moved to the back of the auditorium and opened the door, the light streamed in and highlighted her silhouette once again. And Judy knew who it was. She was older, the figure heavier, the hair now gray beneath the hat, but she still moved in the same way.

It was Hedy.

Judy's breath caught in her throat. Surely, she wouldn't leave before they could speak. Judy hurried to the edge of the stage and hobbled down the steps.

People rushed up to shake her hand and congratulate her, but Judy just stared at the open doors. The woman had gone again. All at once, her caregiver Karen was by her side.

"I need to go outside," Judy rasped breathlessly.

Karen, maybe thinking she was feeling faint, took hold of her arm and took charge. "Mrs. Jenkins needs to move on. Thank you for all of your support, but she does need to get home. It's been a very exciting morning for her."

Judy rolled her eyes at Karen's comment but was intent on a purpose. As she pushed through the crowd that continued to applaud and congratulate her, she fixed her eyes on the door.

Once she was outside, Judy scanned the area. The woman was there, dressed in black, standing underneath a tree, smoking a cigarette. Judy couldn't believe it was real. Karen was about to usher her toward the car they'd come in, but she shook her arm away from her caregiver.

"There's someone I need to speak to," she said sternly.

Karen was undeterred. "I think you should get home. You're exhausted."

"Please let me go," insisted Judy as she pulled her arm away from Karen and hobbled toward the woman under the tree.

All at once, Hedy turned. And there she was, her best friend, the woman she hadn't seen in over fifty years. Hedy pulled off her sunglasses, and there were those beautiful emerald-green eyes and that radiant smile. Tears began to stream down Judy's face. And Hedy, overwhelmed with her own emotion, was unable to speak.

Judy noticed with great sadness the years of plastic surgery that had taken a toll on her friend's face, mistakes that had been made that had left her a shadow of the beauty she had been. Judy thought how heartbreaking it was; the woman who'd never wanted to be judged for her beauty was so afraid to lose it.

Slowly closing the distance between them, Judy stretched her arms out to her friend and, pulling her close, held her tightly. Hedy sank into her shoulders, and the weight of the grief and sadness of all their years disappeared.

"I'm so glad you came," whispered Judy. "This wouldn't have been the same without you."

Hedy pulled away and stroked her friend's face. "I wasn't going to come. I wrote to you many times to tell you that, but then some words from a ghost in my past—words that were meant to curse me—actually had the opposite effect and changed my mind. I'm so proud of you, Judy; you stood by what you believed in. You deserve the recognition. You're an amazing scientist."

"Hedy, I'm so sorry. I'm so sorry about what happened between us."

Hedy shook her head and lifted her hand. "We all have so many things to be sorry about. I'm sorry too. But we are not going to mar this beautiful day with regrets. It's so lovely here," she remarked, looking around. "It's hardly changed since I visited you and Tom so long ago."

"You're not seeing the best bit," said Judy, now feeling buoyant. "Let me show you again. I want to walk you down to the Cam from here. This is where I was a student during my university life."

They began to stroll together down toward the water. All at once Karen came over to see if Judy was okay. She started to introduce her friend, and Hedy stopped her before Judy mentioned her famous surname.

"Kiesler," Hedy intervened. "Hedy Kiesler. Nice to meet you."

Karen didn't seem to notice the Hollywood movie star, the most beautiful woman in the world. She just saw an older woman similar to her own charge.

"We're going to take a walk down to the Cam," Judy informed her. "I'll find my own way back."

Karen looked beside herself. "What do you mean you'll find your own way back?"

"I can get a taxi. I'm perfectly competent. I'll see you back at the home later."

Karen looked surprised but, seeing Judy was adamant, nodded and went back to organize the rest of the ladies from the home as the two old friends walked toward the water.

Sun was now streaming down upon the earth, drying the earlier rain. The smell of wet leaves and grass filled Judy's nostrils as she walked along, feeling complete. This was the final thing she'd wanted. And when she got to the water, she had a crazy idea.

"Do you want to go out in a boat?" she said, suddenly not feeling old at all; the sight of Hedy made her feel young. "I can row you. I used to row for Cambridge."

Hedy looked at her with mischief in her eyes. "Will you sink me?" she asked, with a curl of her lip and still with that American accent with just a slight Austrian lilt.

"I promise," she said, "you'll be fine."

As they paid their money, the man joked about them being underage and looked a little horrified at them both getting into the boat together, but he pushed them out nevertheless. And Judy started to slowly row.

She couldn't believe how good it felt as Hedy lay back in the boat.

"I always feel relaxed on the water," said Judy. "There's something about it. Before he died, Tom and I would often come out on the Cam when we needed to escape, to get away from how we felt. It's how we broke the ice on our first date."

"I'm sorry about Tom," said Hedy. "He was a wonderful man."

Judy acknowledged that then asked the question that had weighed her down for so many years.

"Did you ever hear news from your friend Stefan?"

Hedy nodded. "He came back to us five months later. But he died of cancer a few years afterward. After he was released from his internment camp, being such an adamant pursuer of the truth, he went off to interview people who had survived the bomb without realizing the cost. The radiation was terrible."

Judy shook her head. "I'm so sorry."

"Oh, well. We are all without our men now."

"You never married again, I noticed?"

Hedy balked. "Why would I do that when I was so good at it? I think six times was enough, don't you?"

Judy started to laugh. "I always felt so sorry for you. You seemed to have everything but the love of a man."

"I just kept picking the wrong ones. Men that only saw my face. And now look at my face. Nobody wants me for that any more."

Judy shook her head. "I wish they could have seen your kind heart and your incredible intelligence."

Tears slipped down Hedy's cheeks. "That's why, Judy, we were such good friends. Apart from Stefan, you were the only real person in my life back then. The only person who saw past all that pretense. I'm so sorry I've not been in touch. My life has not turned out as I expected, and the last few years have been very difficult. I wanted you to know I got your letters, and thought that so much time had passed that it would be embarrassing to write back now. And I somehow convinced myself that you hated me. But when I got this last invitation, something happened. I remembered words my very first husband had said to me about never being loved by anyone. And as I dwelled on them something strange struck me. I was loved, not by a man, but by you. You loved me all this time and yet I had rejected it because of my own perverse ideas of the form that love should come in. And here I was rejecting love that was being offered to me all over again. I also realized that this might be our last chance to see each other."

They stopped the boat and hobbled out and sat on a bench, the wind playing with their white curls that drifted around their faces.

"I'm glad you came now because…" Judy paused, still finding it hard to say the words. "Well, there's something I should tell you. Which is that I'm dying too now, Hedy. I have cancer. It's only a matter of time."

Hedy caught her breath and reached forward and grabbed her friend's hand, the emotion catching in her throat. "I'm so sorry, I'm so sorry I didn't come before."

"You came now. That's all that matters." Judy suddenly remembered something. "I have some money Tom left me, and I was wondering, as it has been such a long time since I have been to America, maybe I should take a trip."

There were tears in Hedy's eyes as she spoke again. "Come and stay with me in Florida, Judy. I have my children, whom I adore, but no one in my life who remembers. Remembers who we were, especially during the war. You can stay as long as you like, forever if you want."

Forever? She didn't say "till the end of your life," but that was what she seemed to imply. Forever had become a lot shorter to Judy since her diagnosis.

Judy nodded and smiled and a long-forgotten peace returned to her heart. And she realized it wasn't just the happiness of being with her old friend, but of also being able to fulfill her dear and wonderful husband's dying wish.

She closed her eyes and listen to the sounds of nature around her. All at once a bird called out.

"Listen," said Judy, her eyes flashing open as she took Hedy's hand again. "It's a nightingale. Just like you."

"I thought they only sang at night," whispered Hedy.

"Only when they are lonely and don't have a mate," confirmed Judy. "When they're happy, they sing in the day, too."

"How ironic, that's just how I feel right now," said Hedy. "In this very moment I feel like singing because I feel so happy and loved."

Judy nodded and smiled. And on that riverbank in the warmth of the sun, two old ladies sat and felt complete, invisible to all the young university students, many of them women, as they rushed by them in a new world, on their way to make history of their own.

A Letter from Suzanne

I want to say a huge thank you for choosing to read *When the Nightingale Sings*. If you enjoyed it, and want to keep up to date with all my latest releases, just sign up at the following link. Your email address will never be shared and you can unsubscribe at any time.

www.bookouture.com/suzanne-kelman

The beginnings of this story started as so many of my other books have, in the middle of a previous novel. I had been doing a long, frustrated search for a quote about women during the war for the front of my book, *Under a Sky on Fire*, when I came across these words about a female scientist who made two very significant discoveries during World War Two. The quote begins with an assessment from a military intelligence expert, R.V. Jones:

"In my opinion, Joan Curran made an even greater contribution to victory, in 1945, than Sam [Curran]." And the article, in the *Smithsonian* magazine, continued, "Like many other female scientists who have faded unrecognizably into history, Curran and her work was discussed only by men and only in the context of that of her male counterparts. Her own words have never been published nor recorded in interviews, making her voice unavailable to a generation of female scientists who followed in her footsteps."

I remember being stopped in my tracks as I read these words. And with tears brimming in my eyes, I wondered how many other women in history had made significant scientific discoveries and never been recognized for their effort. It was then that I wondered if it was possible to tell a story that included turning the spotlight on Joan Curran's life and bringing a little recognition to her scientific achievements.

As I pondered a possible manuscript, I realized that even after comprehensive research for my past three WW2 books, I knew very little about any female scientists or inventors during the war years, although I was vaguely aware of Hedy Lamarr's signal-hopping story.

As I started researching both of these women's lives to see which one story I might want to tell, each had its drawbacks. Hedy Lamarr's story, which, of course, is well documented, wouldn't give me much leeway for fiction while at the same time Joan Curran's story was well-hidden.

So, it was with great excitement I found out that both women were in England in 1937, just before the war. And both women lived in California in the 1940s, and though I have no proof that they ever met, I have no evidence to the contrary, and I wondered if it was possible to honor both of their legacies through a story about friendship.

This did not come without its challenges, however; in order to create a fictional friendship, I would need significant leeway in Joan Curran's real-life story, and in order to keep the integrity of the real person, that would mean changing her name so as not to confuse the reader with the real Joan. I have to admit to really wrestling over this decision, as her invisibility was the very thing that had compelled me to write the book in the first place. But after many days of pacing my kitchen, I eventually concluded that it was the only way to be kind to the real person. So just to be clear, all of the scientific achievements of the fictional character Judy Jenkins are actually the achievements of the real-life scientist Joan Curran. However, many of the personal details of Joan's life are fictionalized for the story.

In Hedy Lamarr's story, all of her film career and the main events of her personal life are as true as I could find out through my research. However, her trips to England and her Pearl Harbor scenes were a work of fiction. I felt in order to deepen their bond of friendship, I needed to place them together in their own furnace. I also thought the bombing of Pearl Harbor was an important war story to tell. But to my knowledge, neither Hedy nor Joan were in Hawaii during the attack. The character of Stefan was fictionalized but was based loosely on the very close friendship Hedy had with costume designer Adrian Adolph Greenburg, who was openly gay, but for appearances' sake was married to Janet Gaynor. I felt that the character of Stefan was needed as a male cheerleader for Hedy and also to give her a real investment in the war. All of the celebrities in Hedy's story were real people. However, the conversations between them are fictionalized, such as at the Hollywood Canteen or aboard the war bond train. Lastly, in Hedy's story, some of the complications of her life I kept to a minimum. You may be surprised to know that baby James, referred to in my story, is the illegitimate child of Hedy Lamarr and John Loder, her third husband. For whatever reason, Hedy decided to keep the truth about her first child secret and then adopt him officially with her second husband, Gene Markey. But as Hedy chose not to reveal this during her lifetime, I only hinted at it in my story. There were many moments like this where I felt it was right to focus on her achievements and not on some of the intricacies of her relationships.

Her own children, in the documentary *Bombshell*, one of the many sources I researched for this book, reported that Hedy was very generous, a patriot with a strong work ethic, and I tried whenever possible to bring out the true Hedy in my story.

After writing this book, what became apparent to me is that it didn't matter if you were a well-known actress in Hollywood or a brilliant academic with an honors degree from Cambridge; if you were a woman scientist in the 1940s, you were patronized and invisible.

One last thing: if you are reading this on your mobile device, take a minute to thank Hedy Lamarr; it was actually her and George's signal-hopping invention that eventually became the foundation for cellular, Bluetooth and Wi-Fi innovation. The Navy sat on her design until the patent ran out before incorporating it into much of their military technology. Hedy wasn't even recognized for her scientific contributions until the 1990s. She died in 2000 with none of the money that she was entitled to, even though the market value of her invention today is estimated at 30 billion dollars.

My ultimate hope is that in telling these women's stories, their outstanding scientific achievements will never be forgotten and will go on to inspire the many female scientists who will walk in the power of their legacy.

I hope you loved *When the Nightingale Sings* and if you did I would be very grateful if you could write a review. It'd be great to hear what you think, and it makes such a difference helping new readers to discover one of my books for the first time.

I love hearing from my readers—you can get in touch on my Facebook page, through Twitter, Goodreads or my website.

Thanks,
Suzanne

 suzkelman

 @suzkelman

 www.suzannekelmanauthor.com

Acknowledgments

First, I want to thank my amazing publisher, Bookouture. I don't know how I got to be so lucky to be working with such a passionate and talented team, but I am eternally grateful for it every day. To my superb editor, Isobel Akenhead, thank you once again for your incredible work on this book. You are so good at taking it to the next level. Thank you for always guiding my stories from being a sweet little yarn to something compelling and heartbreaking. You are a master at what you do!

Also, to Jenny Geras, Peta Nightingale, Alexandra Holmes, Alba Proko, Alex Crow, Saidah Graham, Sally Partington, Becca Allen and the many others that shepherd my books. Thank you all for your skills, vision, and enthusiasm. To Kim Nash, Noelle Holten, and Sarah Hardy, the dream team who promote my work with such passion, you make me feel as if I'm the only author on the books and I appreciate every one of you.

In my own personal world, a huge thanks to my wonderful husband, Matthew Wilson; I can't believe this year we celebrate our thirtieth wedding anniversary when it feels as if we only got married last month. Thank you for all your work on this book. Your constant support and research skills were invaluable and saved me so much time and energy. Also, thank you for always being there for me, whether it is as co-pilots in a pandemic or creating stories of the heart. I only get more and more grateful for the depth of our love as the years go on. To my amazing son, Christopher, I still stand in awe at the wonderful young man you have become and still wonder how I got to be this lucky every day. I am so proud of you, son, and I can't imagine my life without your daily side-splitting humor and infinite kindness. I love you with all my heart.

As well as my own little family, I am so blessed to be cradled and loved by a family of the heart, honorary sisters, and a brother that forms the circle of love that is my world. Hands that reach out for me in the heat of battle. First, to my own "Hedy," my dearest friend Melinda Mack, who has always been there for me and has proved throughout this pandemic the depth and breadth of that friendship. Thank you for being there during the darkest times of the past year. For sharing food, sharing tears, sharing laughter, and sharing toilet paper; I couldn't have done it without you. Profound thanks to my brother of the heart, Eric Mulholland, who was the inspiration for the character of Stefan and who over the years has so often whispered into my own heart, "you are brave, you are safe, you are loved." I always feel so incredibly privileged to count you as a friend, and I can't tell you how glad I am that we decided to walk alongside one another on this journey of life together. To my other, wonderful sister of the heart, Shauna Buchet, I can't imagine this journey without you, you have always been such a bright spot in my life, and I can't wait until we are safely able to laugh, talk and share together again, one of my cherished friends for over twenty-five years. Also, to my number one cheerleader and best writing buddy, K.J. Waters, who has been holding my hand since we published our first books together. Thank you for all the laughs, all the support, and your infinite wisdom of this industry. Especially on the days when I doubted I could pull this off. I can't wait till we are celebrating our thirtieth book together.

I need to also thank Jake Watts, whose brilliant mind came up with the puzzles that ended some of Hedy and Judy's letters. Thank you so much, Jake; to someone who can barely spell "physics," you have no idea how valuable your input was.

And, a big thank you to my brother-in-law, Ian Causebrook, who helped me make sense of the world of Cambridge University. Thank you for your input, kind comments, and willingness to help; I so appreciate your time and enthusiasm.

Lastly, thank you to you, my reader; in writing this book, Judy taught and reminded me again how friendship and love are the most important gifts in life. And I owe my ongoing success to each one of you who buys and shares my books and your willingness to offer your own hands of friendship. I am always so touched by your reviews, stories, kind words, and lovely emails; it changes what I do from just being a career into an ongoing connection of the beauty of the human spirit, and I am so humbled and grateful.

Made in United States
Troutdale, OR
06/18/2024

20654915R00249